An Okaloosa Island Mystery

IN THE DARK, DEATH LURKS

An Okaloosa Island Mystery

IN THE DARK, DEATH LURKS

A Terrifying Storm is Coming

Okaloosa – Black Water
Oka (Black)
Lussa (Water)
(Choctaw)

GEORGE D KING

LitPrime Solutions
21250 Hawthorne Blvd
Suite 500, Torrance, CA 90503
www.litprime.com
Phone: 1-800-981-9893

Published by LitPrime Solutions   12/13/2022

ISBN: 979-8-88703-092-0(sc)
ISBN: 979-8-88703-093-7(hc)
ISBN: 979-8-88703-094-4(e)

Library of Congress Control Number: 2022920014

Contents

I loved this book-*In the Dark, Death Lurks*. It is a well written and a fitting conclusion to the Okaloosa Island Mysteries. All your questions will be answered by the novel's conclusion. Moreover, there are new characters that King deftly weaves into his ongoing story, but who have fascinating stories of their own. Miss Camelia and the three boys are realistically pictured and delightful. The tragedy of her lost husband will keep you wondering if she will ever find the truth about his disappearance. The terror and death of World War II and the Nazis lack of morality is the other engrossing plot which seems to abruptly end, but King ties it into a satisfying conclusion at the end of this page-turner as he skillfully brings the plots together. I love King's use of multiple points of view and new settings. Read it. You will not be disappointed!

—Patty Fleming, Retired Lead English Teacher,
Eldorado High School

Well, you've gone and done it! *In the Dark, Death Lurks* is great, one that I didn't want to put down. Good for you.
—Elizabeth Tilley, Retire School Administrator,
Albuquerque, New Mexico

Books to me are often like best friends. That's the way it was with *In the Dark, Death Lurks.* When young Zathan and his two buddies, Dylan and Little Mitch, visit his Great-Grandmother Miss Camelia Ledbetter in her story-filled back yard, they don't have cell phones or x-boxes, or even bicycles, but they hear all the memories and history of her over hundred-year life that she has lived on the little Chanticleer Lane in Fort Walton Beach. And when they venture forth on Okaloosa Island to visit the Prof, they are as little boys of long ago, using their cleverness to create their adventures innocent of the danger they will soon encounter. Their shenanigans take them on many adventures as they 'guard' the battlements of the La Mancha against their treacherous Cam but leading them toward an unlikely ambush. Miss Camelia hides as best she can the tragedy that has consumed her life for over eighty years as she sits in her rocking chair on Okaloosa Island where she has sworn to never go but has gone because of her love for the boys. We see through her mind as she talks to her God, how much she has endured. Her husband, Jere, left for the war, not returning, but had he died… This tragic love story will keep you turning pages and exclaiming 'No, that couldn't have just happened!' I am looking forward to the next book and hope it happens soon.

—Dr Isabelle Ragsdale, PHD. New Bern, North Carolina.

With the Most Love I have,
I dedicate this novel to the one who
took care of my siblings and me when
there was no one else to do it!

This novel replaces

Mud Puddles and Mockingbird Feathers

My other novels are

Death Doesn't Vacation on Okaloosa Island
Treachery on Okaloosa Island
Sweetest Revenge

The characters in my novel are totally fictional—made-up from my imagination. I have known so many people during my life: old people when I was young growing up in the Ozark Mountains of Missouri, thousands of students who were all different in unique ways, and scores of people I have known from many places where I have lived and traveled, but I certainly do not intend my fictional ones to represent any real people.

Much of the settings of the novel will be recognized by some readers, but many places have been altered and places have been added where they do not exist.

As far as I know, none of the happenings of this work of fiction has occurred on the Panhandle of Florida, in Brittany, France, or anywhere else for that matter.

Search the Internet for Guerande which is the setting for almost half of the novel. YouTube has several videos which show the area, especially the salt marshes and the old walled village which is still as it was in the thirteenth century. While you are searching, check on Brest and Saint Nazaire, home of the infamous U-Boats, both important in the novel.

Search the Internet for the Panhandle of Florida where you will find Fort Walton Beach and Okaloosa Island, which is a three-mile section of Santa Rosa Island, a barrier island stretching from Pensacola to Destin. The Sound is the 'river' of water dividing the Island from the Mainland. It empties into the Choctawhatchee Bay at Fort Walton Beach.

Author Notes

I invite you to this retelling of Miss Camelia Ledbetter's long life and the people and events that swirl around her and through her mind. I have learned so much more about her than I once knew and am hoping you accept what I have added to the tragedy of her life, and to the chaos of the many people around her, and their lives.

There are so many characters—enthusiastic extroverts who want to talk, so you might have trouble determining who the narrator is at times, but I have been kind and given you the setting and a hint after most chapter titles.

Meet Them Three—three quixotic little boys—who will swagger into their next quest as they defend the battlements of the La Mancha against their pretend foe—Cam. Their innocence and old-fashioned fun on their forays, as they mimic and kid their way through their day, will lead them to the disaster that looms over them.

Fly with Jere in the gunner turret of the giant B-17 as it crashes into the horrors of World War II. Forgive him, as he is as innocent as the salt the little village of Guerande sells, but some of the French are not innocent, and a Judas is among them.

Miss Camelia believes that the world is Better than Bad, but cannot be entirely Good, or there could be no Evil. Throughout her life of over a hundred years, she has delt with both sides, and her faith has kept her out of most mud puddles and cracks in the sidewalk on her way to God's house. Her favorite place, in one of her many rocking chairs beneath the ancient limbs of a Live Oak tree in her beloved back yard, is her only haven from the storms that fill her life…. It is sometimes near peacefulness…

"Theys tryin to tell me I have to quit walkin to church on Sundays! I been walkin that straight walk up to church for over seventy-five years. That's as long as the church's been up there because I was nearly fifty when they finally got it built. Jere did so much work on it before he left us. I do wish they would fix that one patch that is not paved and has no sidewalk. It's at the only bend in the street from my house to God's house. I always tell myself when I come to it, 'It's just like life, Camelia, just like life. You always come to a dirt patch and there's usually mud in it. Just like life.' Oh, there are cracks in that old sidewalk further on, and since I have to wear these high-top tied-up shoes, I have to wear a long skirt too…to hide these awful shoes. I wouldn't dare let nobody see them in church. So, when I come to one of them cracks in the sidewalk, I have to raise my skirt up to see it, and I say, 'Now, right leg don't you do what you did one day this last week, you just stay strong and don't wobble on that crack. And crack, don't you be no different than you was last Sunday cause I know how you feel and I don't need nothing new happening to me.' When I have to hold up my skirt to see my feet, that's so downright embarrassing. I always look around to see if anyone is watching."

—Camelia Ledbetter

The summer Great-Grandma Camelia Ledbetter was 102 years old, she had to break her declaration she would never cross the Sound and sit foot on Okaloosa Island because of her long terrifying fear of the place. We Three got into serious trouble one day on one of our forays against the battlements to the beach at the La Mancha, and she had to change her mind, which she almost never does.

Zathan Ledbetter

"And I have seen that drudgery and exertion is sometimes the result of resentment and conflict between a person and his neighbor. This is madness, meaningless, a blowing after the wind."

Ecclesiastes 4: 4

IN THE DARK.
DEATH LURKS

The moon hangs framed in the limbs of the Live Oak tree which are bare and look like medieval lances jabbing out in every direction. The storm clouds sail in across it, and the wind whispers his name chaotically in the Florida sky.

1

A Terrifying Storm is Coming

Chanticleer Lane – Fort Walton

The Moon hovers over her, a huge, big round lemonade-colored sphere with wrinkled skin and dark spots that look like the boogeyman to little boys sometimes. The storm clouds sail in across it and the wind whispers his name chaotically in the Florida sky. The moon hangs framed in the limbs of the Live Oak tree which are bare and look like medieval lances jabbing out in every direction.

Camelia Ledbetter squints as she suddenly opens her eyes and blinks rapidly, but then she shuts them as tight as she can. The juice slides out of one of the Moon's slices in big slow running drops and blurs as she blinks it. She wipes at her eyes with the back of her hand; it tastes like salt and is bitter, and she understands she is crying again.

Struggling to a straight-up position using both hands to push down on the arms of her rocking chair—as straight as her old body will allow—she knows it is awfully early in the morning.

Her current rooster is still asleep in the little fenced-in chicken coop with his ladies, content to rest, and not strut around announcing his presence with his loud crowing. She likes this one, but it will invariably end up like all the others Justin has brought home from the feed store over at Navarre.

But if his four ladies keep laying an egg a day, she will put up with his nonsense of chasing every little kid who comes into her back yard, and not throw him into a stewpot with a mess of dumplings.

Except them three…. Wonder why he avoids them three? Whether they arrive with loud shouts of what they aim to do that day, or if they sneak around the corner of the house to scare the be Jesus out of that silly rooster, he leaves them alone….

Disoriented, she glances around and finally realizes she is in her rocker in the crowded back yard of her little house on Chanticleer Lane. Justin placed the rocker under the Live Oak tree's largest limb, the one that hangs over the fence into his yard next door, the one that has big bundles of leaves that serve as a canopy over her rocker and is almost like the one Jere worked under, over in the other corner of the yard when he built the fort. *These old trees must be pert near older than me,* she thinks, and she laughs to herself. Like everything else on her little street, she loves the old things, but is concerned about their roots tearing up the foundation of her nearly as old house.

Once upon a time, she might catch a glimmer of the moon on the Sound, but all the construction and rearranging of the streets in her part of town has erased that picture for her. Now all she might get is the lonesome sounds of the barges as they growl and blast their horns as they inch their way around Egg Island. It is almost directly in line with her back fence, so on clear days, she catches a glimpse of the barges as their huge forms slip on down the Sound to go under Brooks Bridge, and on out into the great Choctawhatchee Bay.

She seldom raises her face to see above the barges and across the Sound for fear of seeing the barren dune tops of the Air Command on the other side, and to the left, the very top floors of the stark white buildings of the La Mancha that are capped with red bricklike mansard roofs. She remembers when the roofs were tiled with real Spanish bricks, but one of the big winds had destroyed most of those, years ago.

When she does look up across the Sound, her old frail body shudders with a long-learned fear of what happened nearly three hundred years ago, and of the mysterious violent deaths that have happened the last few years. As quick as she can, she gets up, and the screen door slams as she retreats through her kitchen door.

Justin bought that highfalutin thing for Zathan—a drone, he called it—and he drove all the way to Pensacola, launched the thing, and filmed all the way back to Fort Walton Beach.

When he brought the drone home, she scoffed at spending good money on such a silly thing, but when she saw the picture-show it was making as it came down Santa Rosa Island all the way over the Bay to the bridge at Destin, she changed her mind—which is a very difficult thing for Miss Camelia to admit.

She went over and sat in Justin and Claire's living room as all of them watched what she considered plumb nearly a miracle. *My my my…. I ain't never been past the ten miles west over to Navarre and the seven over east to Destin, in my whole life, and here I sit watchin way beyond there and feeling like I'm flying. Mose would be amazed if he had seen something like this in his lifetime.*

And the old folks, them that lived way back there before Zathan Bordelon ever came into Waltons Landing, way back there in 1737, would have jest fell over dead if they could've seen the Spanish comin this way from Pensacola.

My my my Zathan Bordelon, you sure don't know the mess you caused my family, but I always thought you were innocent, or I wouldn't have named my Great-Grandson, Zathan, after you. Oh yes, I named him… I caused his daddy Justin to think of your name, and sure enough, he and Claire called him Zathan.

The drone flew down the thirty some miles from Pensacola over what the Spanish had named, Santa Rosa Sound, until the almost glaring white buildings of the La Mancha appeared up ahead as it passed over the fence which divides the Eglin Air Command from Okaloosa Island, a three-mile strip the county officials persuaded President Truman to lease for ninety-nine years for just $5,000.

Then it veered out almost to the Gulf as it flew low over the big condo complexes.

I ain't never been over there, and I ain't goin neither. What happened long ago is enough for me. Even though they tell me the ground is almost all sand, there is too much mud over there for me to step around. Besides, that's where all them winds come from—them winds that wreck Fort Walton almost every time they happen.

"The Prof lives at the La Mancha, Great Grandma," Zathan said. "That's where the three of us visit and defend the place from Cam."

She had no idea who Cam is but knew the three boys always enjoyed their days of adventure at the Prof's.

I never dreamed that the part President Truman leased to the county would build up like it is. And I ain't goin over there to find out about it neither. My lands, Santa Rosa Blvd is mighty pretty, mowed nicer than the boys do for my own yard. It's four-lane and lined with palm trees. I see both sides of the Island as that drone thing zooms over the Blvd. I can almost see the Indian Mound on the left where the black water of the Sound shimmers—the Okaloosa water. The Mound where Jere and me courted.... Then it passes right under Brooks Bridge that's humped-up so barges and sailboats can get under it. It's over fifty years old, but it's the only way for 98 to go on toward Destin. In all my days, I would never believe it, if I weren't seeing it.

The drone flew on down Highway 98 that divides the Island which seems to brace itself between the Gulf of Mexico and its mighty power, and Choctawhatchee Bay that stretches out, way out on the left.

The Bay is shallow now because Hurricane Ivan filled it with sand blown from the 'Made-me-horn,' as high school teenagers had dubbed it—the highest sand dune on all the Gulf of Mexico from Florida all the way around past Texas. But Ivan took care of that as hundreds of tons of sand and debris were swept from the big dune— really named 'Matterhorn,'—and spread a good three to four hundred yards out into its water.

Even before that, the Bay was so shallow Mose use to walk out what seemed halfway across, fling out his net, draw the catcher string, and pull it all the way back to the shore to unload the flopping fish on the sand. I been thinking of Mose an awful lot...bet I see him soon.... As the drone flew over East Pass at Destin six miles away to the East, she laughed to herself again as she thought about that day three men had cut the East Pass from the Bay to the Gulf.

We had more rain that spring in '20 something than any I can ever remember, and of course, I was just a little girl and had to be told about this one later. Mose said it rained and rained, and the rivers flooded somethin awful and peoples' crops were ruined and the Bay swelled up and up till it got higher than the dirt road that is 98 now, and those folks over at Destin thought they was goin to be flooded, so three of them took picks and shovels and started gouging at the trickle of water that was all that run into the Gulf from the Bay at that time.

All of a sudden, there was a big whoosh, and the water of the Bay broke through and quick as can be, it broke a 600-yard-wide trench, and they had to run for their very lives. They wasn't real smart between the ears, I'm thinkin. My. my. my, they sure didn't appreciate what they were doin to things, turning the Bay from almost fresh water to saltwater, but I guess it turned out all right...

Jere was on her mind as he always was—living back there in the back where she couldn't lose him. She scoffed to herself and thought when was he not in her mind—not back in the back, but always in the front? His face was so clear, she felt like she could reach out and touch it, and the usual stab of pain hit her chest. *Lands, it's been over eighty years since he shipped out of Eglin for that never-to-return trip to somewhere in France. I can still feel his hands on my cheeks as he whispered, 'Milly, I'll be back before you know it.'*

My my my, I hardly lived while he was gone, and I still thought he was comin back. I'd wake up in the morning, if I had been to sleep at all, and the pillow would be wet, and I'd have to hang it on the line to dry that day. If it hadn't been for the two boys, I probably would have died when he didn't come back.

They never found him as the B-17 had crashed somewhere in France, so she never got to tell him goodbye and still ached to do so.

2

We Survived what Still might be the Worst of Times

Fort Walton—1930s. Camelia is still in her backyard

We withstood what would be known as The Great Depression as Fort Walton wasn't affected all that much, like the Ozarks and the Appalachians weren't, as we all had lived lives of want and hard work since the areas had become inhabited with European folks. The gardens in Fort Walton kept us fed and mine was the largest of them even in those days. The water of the Bay was full of all kinds of fish.

Mose had taken his big cotton net and whirled it out into an almost perfect circle many times as I watched, and he gathered in more fish than the whole town could eat at one time. *I got soaked that one time he let me throw the net—must have looked like a wet hen.*

He made it look so easy as the net swirled over his head in an almost perfect circle, and he turned it loose to spread out over the water catching it with the long strand he had woven into one edge. Then he pulled it tight like drawing a string on a potato sack. *I didn't turn it loose but just went in with it. Mose laughed for five minutes until he had tears in his eyes. He only stopped laughing because I was sulking and almost in tears myself.*

Grandma Pearl still had her Singer Sewing Machine and the Victrola which she wouldn't part with. I know that Mose and her sold a lot of stuff cause they wanted to help me so much.

I would take the boys down to Buck's store where the boat came twice a week now bringing supplies from Pensacola. It didn't bring flour every trip cause most of us ate cornbread anyway, but when it did, I wanted to be the first to pick out the sack—a twenty-five- pound cotton sack with a stamped pattern of some kind—which would become a dress if I accumulated three or four sacks over a spell of time, or a blouse for me if I just had one sack— or a shirt for one of the boys—after Grandma Pearl got finished with it on her Singer.

My grandpa Mose also stood guard over our little street, but I sat many nights in the corner of the back yard under this old Live Oak limb just like I am right now, but with my shotgun across my knees. It wasn't that my neighbors were dishonest, but many just didn't have anything to eat. And it wasn't that I didn't want to share. I just didn't want them in my yard and in my garden. *All they had to do was ask. I gave away many times what I really should have kept cause the boys always looked hungry.*

Jere had started working out at Valparaiso shortly after Mose had walked her up the steps of the Fort Walton School, for they had no church then. It was July and hot as blazes. They had cleared out the desks, and Grandma Pearl and some of the women had decorated the big room with all sorts of flowers and ribbons. Her Uncle Paul stood in front of them as they stood face to face saying their vows to each other. Jere took her to a little cabin his folks owned down on the Sound. She had never been so happy.

Some man had given the government over a thousand acres out there at Valparaiso, and it had been turned into the Valparaiso Ammunition and Gunnery Range. Jere joined the Army in 1939, after the Gunnery had been renamed, Eglin Army Airfield, and soon became the ace gunner at the Range.

Almost exactly nine months after the wedding, Albert was born. Jere was so proud of his little boy and me too. He would sit for hours, it seemed, and rock Albert and sing to him and tell him how when he was grown-up a little, and in school, that his daddy would be at everything he did. My my my, how that all vanished into the air….

Jere put Albert on a blanket while he built the 'fort.' An almost twin Live Oak to the one she is sitting under hugged the fence across on the other corner of the yard. One of the main limbs hung down so low the bundle of branches that had leaves on it nearly touched the ground. Jere worked underneath that canopy of leaves constructing the six-by-eight-foot platform on pilings that nearly touched the overhanging limb, and after he finished, its tin roof did rub a little on the limb above.

How many nights have I heard the scrape, scrape, scrape when first Albert and Dwayne used to play up there, and then Justin took it over and spent many nights sleeping up there…and now them three are always wanting to spend their nights up there….

Jere might have been the best gunner out at the Gunnery, but he wasn't so particular when building a fort in the back yard. He had made the platform too tall for four steps and not tall enough for five to lead up to the door. So, now four steps caused them three a lot of trouble, and one day last week Little Mitch fell into the rosemary bush when he tried to step high to the third step. He sulked, and the other two laughed at him, but soon they were all sitting together on the top step laughing and cutting up as they always do.

It has two windows where the lookout can tell if the place is being attacked, and that has happened over and over with every bunch of little boys who has ever used it.

Daniel Sheraton, Dylan's daddy, gave them wooden guns a couple of months ago, which they use to not only defend the fort, but to also attack it. I've noticed it's a lot harder to attack than defend, and Little Mitch always demands to be an attacker. My. my. my…. J C and Ester are goin to have their hands full with that little man— and J C is not even his real father.

She was pregnant with Dwayne, but Jere didn't know it, and Albert was almost two when Jere shipped out of Eglin headed to places, she had never heard of, where his job was to hang out of the gunner's turret on the bottom of a gigantic B-17. She had begged him to not go, but he brushed-off her objections.

Now you hush, Milly. I'll be right back before you know it, and I promise to bring you back something wonderful from France."

But that never happened....

Now, she sits in the dark almost every night, usually crying...but never knowing....

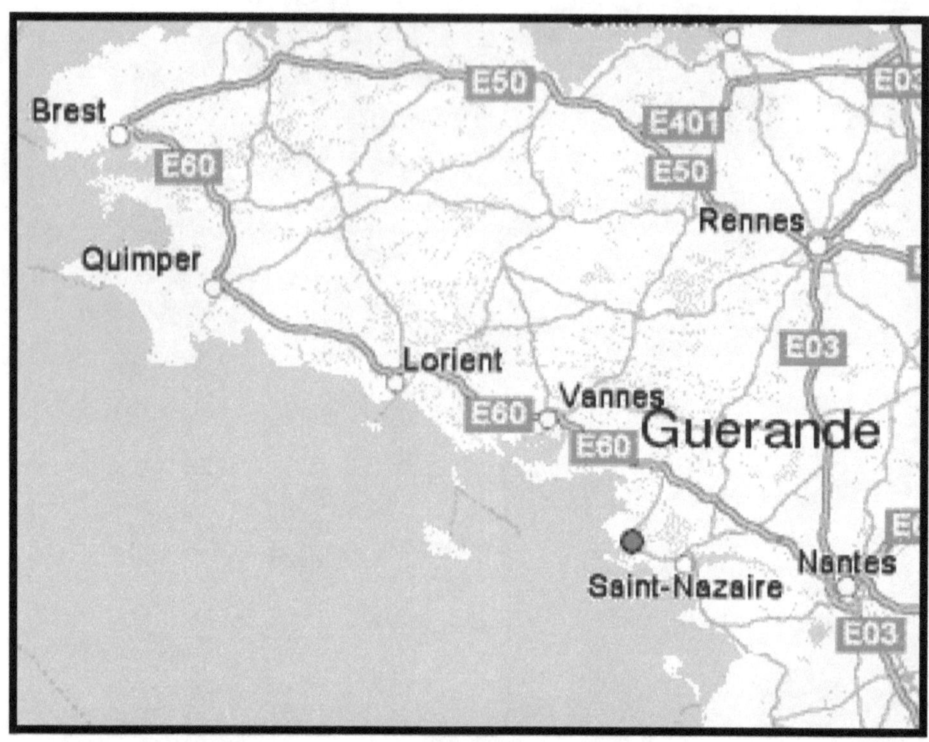

The Marsh Road stretches between Brest and Saint-Nazaire where the Nazis have sheds for their terrifying U-Boats. Guerande is caught in the middle with squads of Nazis passing by every day. Only Guerande's wonderful sea salt has saved it from attacks.

3

A Bash on the Head,
and then Chaos

Brittany, along Northwest Coast of France

The captain had complained louder than usual because of the heavy downpour and fog, that this was no day to fly low over the English Channel to drop bombs on cow pastures in Western France, but they had been ordered to do so.

One of the crew quipped that "We must have drawn the short straw because we're carrying the heavy load this morning."

The captain looked from one of them to another as he spoke, "We have been ordered to fly down to St. Nazaire and bomb the Hell out of the Nazi's U-Boat base and get back up here, if we can, or fly on down and land somewhere in Spain. The other B-17s will bomb lesser targets and turn out over the Atlantic and return here."

As the land crew was loading Jere's equipment into the glass bubble jutting out from the insides of the plane, one of them remarked, "How in Hell does he get into this thing? He's too tall. What do they do, fold his legs back under him? And God Almighty, his feet must be size fifteen!"

Jere walked up about that time and answered, "That's not the biggest thing I have to worry about."

The laughter that followed the remark was filled with "You got that right" and "Better use that tobacco can to sit on to protect that thing."

Another crew member, who had flown almost this same mission before, standing next to him said, "This has to be the biggest pile of manure ever thought up by our command. St. Nazaire is a fortification like only the Germans can build. Use to be a pretty seaport where the Loire River flows out into the Atlantic, but the Nazis went in there and with forced laborers from concentration camps as far away as Russia, they built fourteen sheds for their Wolfpack subs."

"We are crazy if we think we can do them any harm. Those concrete walls are too thick for anything we can dump on them. I hear that the roof is twenty-six feet deep, and we just don't have bombs big enough to crack that."

"It's like some hayseed pissing on a brush fire. I guess we might hit a sub as it was coming or going but doing damage to the pens is a lot of hooey. But that's what The Pug demands we do. You know he might have something about hitting a U Boat coming out in that big shallow bay."

Mose had given him a Prince Albert tobacco can a few days before he left Eglin, "You keep your valuables in this and when you close it, it'll float on water before it will get anything wet."

Jere had several little three-inch pictures he and Camelia had taken with the Brownie Box camera Grandma Pearl had given them when Albert was born, and one letter from Camelia that he had received, but not answered yet, folded neatly in the can.

One of the pictures was the three of them taken on a Sunday morning. Milly had her usual hat on with the camellias sticking all around, Albert was in his finest cute overalls, and Jere was standing tall with a proud look that Milly loved so much.

But the most important thing in the bright red can was his wedding ring that he had reluctantly taken off because he had lost so much weight in the last few weeks that it kept slipping off anyway, so the tobacco can had become particularly important to him.

Three of the land crew picked him up and held him as he entered the ball-turret feet first. His head and shoulders stuck out of the opening, and they had to push to close him in. One of them shook his head and whispered, "You're not catching me in one of these things." Usually, the gunners didn't get into their turrets until they were ready to drop their bombs, but this foray into France wouldn't last that long, so here he was stuffed into the glass bubble. He had no doubt that his buddies would have to pull him out when they returned for his legs would be asleep.

As the big plane roared down the runway, he could see the cracks in the concrete just a foot or so beneath the bubble. His butt was hanging mighty close to the runway, he feared, and this was always the time that sent a flash of fear through him, and he often wondered just why he had chosen to do this.

The mighty "Flying Fortress" struggled to get into the air as the fog seemed to be dragging it downward. Once it leveled off, it became the familiar safety the crew always felt—it was their home, their fort against all the barrages the Nazis could throw at them.

When they were boarding the ten of them always touched the curvy bottom of the almost too realistic nose art of a Vargas Girl, which adorned the fuselage of their plane for good luck.

Their flight from Molesworth took them south between Oxford and London. Jere thought he must be mistaken but he was certain he saw the dome of St. Paul's Cathedral as they flew parallel to the west of the city.

The Channel looked ominous this morning, but the fog was too heavy for him to see much. Occasionally, it would break-up in spots and Jere could see the dark, almost black, water just a few feet below. It was the color of the Sound at home but was rolling in waves more like the Gulf on the other side of Okaloosa Island, but it was still black in the early morning fog.

More clear patches opened in the fog as they crossed toward the west over the beach and were in French territory. The Nazis had taken this part of France when they captured the beaches of Normandy not far east of here.

He couldn't see any lights from the many villages he knew were below them and thought the Nazis had ordered a black-out that meant a firing squad for the whole village if it was disobeyed. He knew also that they were flying with no lights, but the sound of the plane was all a good gunner needed to send a barrage that would destroy them.

All was quiet except the engines, and his mind wandered to Camelia and Albert and the joy and happiness they had shared for nearly two years. He could see her face and smiled as he thought of her determination and strength. Albert's squeals of terror and anger came to his thoughts as he remembered Camelia rushing out to get him away from where the loud hammering was going on when he was building the fort for his little boy in the back yard.

Suddenly the roar of the mighty engines startled him out of his thoughts, and he felt they must be almost half-way to St. Nazaire by now. A battery east of them started shooting anti-aircraft barrages at them. He knew the shells would be exploding at predetermined altitudes—blasts of flying flak raining down upon them. The captain veered the plane to the right out toward the Atlantic. Jere felt the big B-17 shudder and felt his helplessness in his little glass bubble as the plane started to angle toward the ground. He saw, in a split second, that one wing was almost shot in two and fire was consuming that side of the plane, but he felt the plane struggle to go even further west to get to the coast.

He had his chute fastened on, ready to fall out. Suddenly, the latches above his head slid open, and his best buddy smiled down at him as he reached to pull Jere up into the plane, but there was another explosion as he was half-way out, and the turret went flying into the air. The blast ripped off his oxygen mask, and he gasped for breath as the below-zero air took his breath as he fell toward the ground.

As he thumped down onto a marshy area close to a fair-sized river, he was thankful for what was left of the fog. He watched with dread as he saw the plane plunge toward the Atlantic and hoped to see parachutes open as he watched. The big bomber hit the water out near the horizon and at the same time a tremendous explosion drowned the booming bombardments of the Nazis—the morning air was filled with the sounds and smells of war.

He sat down on the ground and hung his head down between his legs. He sat and shook back and forth, back and forth, for several seconds bent over with his hands over his eyes and struggling to get his wits about himself. What have I done to be in this Hell of a mess, he wondered? He was alone and unsure what to do, but then his training and his natural ability in the woods took hold of him.

Like they had practiced so many times in training, he freed himself and quickly dug a hole with his pointed shovel and buried the new light-weight nylon chute. A thought flashed through his mind that he ought to keep the chute for it was made of the new material, nylon, and it was light and would keep him dry and warm, but he quickly changed his mind for he knew it would identify him as a Yank, so he covered it with packed dirt which he covered with loose leaves.

Then he did something no American was supposed to do; he ripped his dog tags from his neck, stuffed them into his Prince Albert can and rammed it into the vee shaped joint where a limb came away from the trunk of a tree close by. He scooped up a handful of mud and leaves and hurriedly covered the can as best he could to cover its red color. He gashed the bark of the tree with an almost perfect chevron just like those he had cut into pine trees back in the groves at Fort Walton when they were sapping to make turpentine. He raked a handful of mud across the cut in the tree to camouflage it.

He heard a motor as a vehicle was coming toward him and he ran to the riverbank. Then he stopped and did the most extraordinary thing—an outlandish thing he would regret later. He stripped nude, bundled his uniform and skivvies together, and walked into the water. It took his breath away like the cold air had earlier. He stood up in the chest deep water and found he was in a slough where the water was calm and still. He struggled down to the bottom and maneuvered a large stone onto his bundle of clothing and the shovel.

He surfaced and swam as fast as he could out into the current of the river and headed downstream. The slow-moving water pushed him, and as his head surfaced on each stroke, he thought he heard the engines of the car getting closer and closer until he understood he was not hearing a motor, but a roaring sound.

He let out a surprised yelp as the river suddenly surged into a fast- moving current and he was tossed over the edge of a spillover. He struggled, flailing his arms and legs as he plunged over, and bashed his head on a thick wooden piling as he landed.

4

Wash Day

Fort Walton

Camelia pulled the heavy bucket of rainwater out of the cistern at the back of the house and carried it to the big black iron kettle that sat over the blazing fire she had built thirty minutes before. She had to make three trips with the bucket, lowering it into the cistern and straining to pull it back up as full of water as she could raise. A sharp pain shot through her right side every time she pulled the bucket to the surface, and she realized she was getting less and less water with each trip.

It was wash day, the hardest of her days each week. Albert was near the point where he would run and tell her when he had to pee or poop, but he still had accidents, so his diapers were a big part of wash day. She did them last, after washing her things, by swirling them around and around in the boiling water in the kettle.

The chaos she caused to make the water swirl around and around hypnotized her sometimes and then frightened her. She would always scoff at herself on those times, but also find herself trembling. *How am I supposed to make it with another baby coming…? How Lord?*

Mose gave her an old short-handled boat paddle she used to keep the clothes moving. The hard part was raising a dripping dress or pair of pants, she was notorious for wearing, out of the kettle. It took muscles she shouldn't have been using, for she was eight months pregnant with the new baby.

She hadn't heard from Jere for nearly a month, and he had said nothing about her expecting their second baby, so she thought *he doesn't know he's going to be a daddy again… he hasn't got my letters I wrote weeks ago… All he said was they were being sent on a really bad mission, but he was sure they could handle it for their American- made weapons were sure better than the those the Nazis had.*

She struggled to keep food for Albert and her and waited eagerly for the first of the month when she got a new ration book and could go down to Buck's store and get some of what she needed.

Albert always wanted a stick of candy or one of those pink pea- nut mounds that were nothing but sugar holding the peanuts together, and she was ashamed she couldn't always get him something. Sam Buck slipped him a piece of candy or an overripe piece of fruit sometimes, but she cried many nights when she was alone and thought if she couldn't take care of Albert the right way, what in the world was she going to do when the new baby came?

She had her garden in the backyard and was showing Albert what they could get from the ground. His favorite was a bright red radish, and she had caught him once with a freshly pulled one in his mouth—garden dirt and all. He didn't seem to mind the peppery flavor of the radish, and the rich garden soil didn't seem to bother him either. He always went straight to that part of the garden when he was back there.

Mose helped her a lot as she had trouble hoeing and getting down on her knees to pull weeds. *Thank you, God, for Mose… I don't know what I would do if he and Grandma Pearl weren't on my street…*

She had her things and the kitchen things washed, and they were hung neatly on the wire clothesline that ran along the side fence in the back yard. She carried the bucket of dirty diapers out to the big wash kettle and dumped them in. Grandma Pearl had given her a box of *Twenty Team Borax*, and she spooned out several spoonsful into the boiling water. She sat down in her rocker and waited for almost an hour before she decided the diapers were clean.

She started toward the kettle when she heard a racket in the front yard. She moved as fast as she could around the corner of the house to find Albert hitting at their present resident rooster. His chubby little hand could barely switch at the rooster with the tiny stick he held out toward the squawking angry bird that was closing in on him. She shooed the bird away with her left foot and told Albert to get into the house.

As he disappeared through the screen door, she felt a pain in her side and abruptly sat down on the top step. She sat rocking back and forth and gasping for breath. She saw Mose headed her way, but terror filled her eyes as she looked past Mose and saw what she knew was a government car that had turned into their lane, and that it had nowhere to go except to her.

Mose sat holding her close to him as the man in his crisp, clean uniform stepped out of the black sedan, took off his hat, and walked up her walk.

"Mrs. Ledbetter?"

She couldn't answer. She closed her eyes and hoped it all went away.

She yelled, "You lie! You lie! You're a liar! It's not true…not true… Lord, tell me it's not true…."

She heard Mose answer the man that yes, she was Mrs. Ledbetter.

She screamed and collapsed onto Mose. Little Albert appeared behind the screen door and was crying. She felt the darkness close in on her.

She awoke in her bed, and the midwife from over on Beal Street was sitting in a chair in her bedroom. She saw Mose standing in the living room door with his back to her holding Albert in his arms. She heard him say, "Your mommy is going to be okay. She just needs to rest awhile. You can go home with me for today."

He turned and saw she was awake, so he walked into her room and sat Albert on her bed. The little boy looked at his mom, started to throw himself toward her but stopped, looked up at his Great- Granddad Mose, and then reached out and clasped his mother's hand in his little fingers.

"Tell me Mose. Tell me…"

"He said the B-17 was shot down. He said that it crashed into the Atlantic off the coast near a Nazi submarine base. That's all he said."

Tears flowed down her cheeks, but she stopped when the tiny hand holding hers squeezed her finger.

She pulled Albert toward her, looked up at Mose, and then on up at the ceiling of the room, "Then he's safe, I know he is. He made it. I know it Mose, I know it."

Mose took Albert from her as the midwife was now holding her hand and trying to console her.

The walls of Guerande were built in the Thirteenth Century and not much has changed since then. They have never been breached, but the Nazis will try.

5

I Don't Remember

The River - Guerande France

"**M**erde alors, the unlucky guy has busted his head. Quick, help me drag him out onto the bank. We've got to get him into something to warm him up."

"He may not have drowned in the river, but we all might in this rain. When have you ever seen such rain, Henri? What is it, two days and nights?" the older of the two men said.

"There'll be no work in the salt pans, and worse yet, the water won't evaporate so we can rake-up the flakes of salt. He was an idiot for getting into the river this morning, but I'm guessing he didn't know anything about the big storms up around Brest that have caused our river to flood. Mon Dieu, he was lucky the first wave of debris didn't catch up with him and smash him while he was coming down. His good luck is that we were here to get him out,"

"Mon Dieu, why the hell did he take off his clothes. Those idiot Krauts were too busy trying to shoot down that plane—they might not have seen him. Yet, we don't even know he was on that plane, do we? He could be a spy for the Nazis, or just some shell-shocked lost soldier wandering around the countryside naked," Marcel said.

Marcel and Henri laughed at their joke. "We've got to get him to shelter. What about the Abbey and Father Jean? Or Mademoiselle Isabelle's house?"

The two Frenchmen had been in the car Jere had heard and had followed him until he flopped over the spillover at the mill.

Marcel and Henri had taken their turn staying with the village's herd of cattle, thirty Breton cows and nine calves, that was hidden in a century's old valley along the banks of the Vilaine River.

The river ran tumbling among cliffs west of their village and became a raging current when storms hit the area. Over the centuries, the river had cut into the fertile soil and gouged-out about a forty-acre valley.

When the Nazis invaded France, the people of Guerande had moved their prize Breton cattle into the valley. The narrow crack in the high cliffs was only wide enough for one cow to go through at a time, so it was very easy for one or two men to guard the entrance to Cachette, as they called the hide-out.

As they were tending to Jere, the two men talked together, and Marcel brought up the subject Henri had mentioned during their night tending the cattle.

"What did your boys do about the mussels?"

"They have spent the last three days pulling the rafts into a slough on one side of the river. Some of the lines the mussels are growing on were swept away, but most were saved. Our only hope is that the debris when it gets down this far won't tear away many more," Henri answered.

"That whole idea your youngest son had was very smart. Many along the Vilaine's estuary are thinking of trying to raise mussels."

"It's much work, and you can see what happens when the river floods."

"Yes but think about the feasts we have when the whole area gathers in the square on the happy days to eat all those mussels and that fresh bread."

They hadn't realized Jere was naked until they found him at the bottom of the spillover. Now, they knew they had better get him into a safe place, but more than that, get him revived.

"Mon Dieu, he's losing a lot of blood, and look at the knot that's swelling up on the side of his head," Henri said.

"Quick, stretch him out here on the grass. You have water in your thermos?" Marcel asked.

"Of course."

"Good mix some of it with a handful of salt and we will press it against his cut."

Henri rushed around and scooped a handful of salt from the bag stored on a tarp in the trunk of their old car. The salt was brilliant large crystals that had dried in the sun for hours.

He didn't need his thermos as he held out his hand piled high with salt. The rain could have quickly washed it away but he was fast to squeeze his palm together to make it into a lump—a poultice.

"Good, now pressed it against his head. Not too hard though for he may have a severe concussion."

Henri smoothed the salt on Jere's head and held it firmly in place.

Marcel took the scarf he usually wears around his neck and tied it around the wound, "We'll take him to my house and find some clothes for him and then decide".

"He's going to look strange in your clothes, Marcel, as old as you are," Henri laughed.

"He's too big to get into yours, you petit garcon," Marcel laughed right back.

Marcel, Isabelle DesMarais's uncle, and Henri, a tough little Frenchmen, have lived in the tiny village of Guerande, France their whole lives. Guerande is on the Atlantic Coast where the Vilaine River empties into the ocean.

The river is a wild free swift river until about three miles from the Atlantic, and as it runs into the flat coastal land, it slows until the Atlantic pushes it back at high tide pushing its estuary back four or five miles.

Guerande has been famous for centuries for the sea salt the inhabitants of the town sift from the lagoons-or pans, as they call them—they have created along the coast.

It sits on a wide flat plain so that from the ramparts of the little ancient village, one can see for miles around. Eons ago, the Atlantic had covered the area the land. The only elevation around is the Marsh Road that inhabitants have built up above the flat salt lagoons.

Looking down from the road, in most places, slopes are covered with thick marsh grass which is shoulder high to most men.

About two hours later, Marcel and Henri are half-way carrying the now conscious Jere through one of the four *portes* that are built into the thirty-foot ramparts around the old Medieval village, and as they pass through the thick wall, Jere gazes up in wonder.

A few people stand in their doorways and watch as the two men half-walked, half-carried Jere between them in the pelting downpour as they move toward Isabelle's house.

As they pass through the gated fence into her courtyard, Marcel mutters, "She's going to be unhappy that so many people saw him. We never know who have turned into Nazi conspirators. Too many people have seen the strangers who stay with Father Jean for a few days until they leave with you."

Isabelle opened her door, saw the three men standing in her courtyard and almost shouted, "Quick, get into the house. Get in out of the rain!"

Isabelle is the last of her family that has lived in Guerande. Her last name means 'of the marshes' and must have been given to her family, for they have worked the salt marshes for centuries.

She stood peering down at Jere as he sat on her sofa. "Qui es tu?" The slender attractive woman asked him.

Marcel and Henri stood guard ready to tackle this strange man they had brought from the river. He was now dressed much like they are—the garb of a French workman—non-descript so that anyone encountering him would not likely remember how he was dressed.

The man shrugged his shoulders and turned his hands up as if he didn't understand.

"I asked who you are?" She repeated.

Again, the man shrugged his shoulders, and winched in pain as he timidly touched the bandage around his head.

Marcel said, "He must be an imbecile. We don't know for certain where he came from. We first thought he was from that B-17 that was shot down by the Krauts, but what was he doing in the river naked? Americans and Brits don't do that. They're told to hang onto their dog tags no matter what."

"Maybe he is a Kraut trying to get us off balance sneaking around trying to find out what we are doing," Henri answered.

"Well, he's going to have a black eye and a sore head for weeks," Marcel said.

"No, I don't think he is a Nazi. He is too well-fed to be one of them nowadays. He's a flyboy for sure. Probably American because he doesn't carry himself like a bloody Brit," Isabelle said.

"What are we going to do with him?"

"Henri has a family, and he can't go there, so I suggest you take him to your house, Uncle, until we find out something about him."

Marcel objected, "Henri can take him on his next trip past St. Nazaire. It may be twelve miles of hell both ways, but we all know how important Henri's trips are. I hear they are building more sheds for U Boats.

He turned to Henri, "You ever hear anyone say how long it takes one of those U Boats to get to America?"

Henri shrugged his shoulders, "Some say two weeks and some say three. But how could I know?"

"Well, I sure as hell don't want to go on one of your trips down there, and I sure as hell don't want him in my house either. That's just all I need, some total stranger who may kill me in my sleep, or not know how to act when the Nazis come pounding on the door as they do about once a week. No, I don't want anything to do with it." "Then take him over to the salt marches and get rid of him,"

Isabelle commanded.

"You are being sarcastic, my little niece. You know we have to find out about him and help him if we can."

Isabelle stared at the man before her—a tall lanky man about her age who didn't seem to take much notice in what they were saying. He kept looking about her kitchen where they were now sitting around her table. She understood, got up, and carried the coffee and a croissant over to him. He grabbed it and started wolfing it down.

"No, wait, let me show you," she said as she stopped his hand on the way to his mouth. She took the croissant from him and dipped it into the coffee which was almost half-milk.

"There, that will taste so much better."

Jere smiled, and said his first word to them, "Thanks."

The three of them looked at each other and almost together let out breaths that they had all been holding since they had brought him to her house.

"Oh, so you can talk. Can you tell us who you are?" Henri asked.

Jere shook his head and said, "I don't know."

"Were you on the plane before it crashed into the ocean? How did you get into the river?"

"I don't know."

"Stop, we are getting nowhere. Let's get him to your house Uncle and get him some rest. We've got to look after that bump on his head. It's dangerous, and probably why he doesn't know anything about what we ask him.

We don't know what to call him, and we have to make-up a story to tell the people in town. We will call him Alain and tell every- body that he is your cousin who has escaped from somewhere close to Paris and has showed up here to hide.

"Ah, Alain, is it? We all know how you are with names.

Handsome, is he?"

Isabelle blushed, "So, Uncle, you have caught me. One would be blind to not see his good looks and those outrageous eyes—who- ever had eyes that color. Well, that's about as good as I can come up with— telling everyone he is your cousin, so do either of you have a better plan?"

All this time they had been talking to each other as if Jere—now Alain—was not in the room, but he had heard.

6

U Boat in Gulf

Camelia's back yard, 1941

It's got to be about time. I been sittin out here at least three hours. I wish I had brought the alarm clock, so I can be sure what time it is. The moon is so bright and big tonight that it's hard to tell if it's after midnight or nearly dawn. I feel in my bones that its early morning, though.

She heard two or three of the hens grumbling like something was disturbing their nests, and suddenly her rooster started squawking and she knew it was about to happen. She had sacrificed eggs the last two nights just to find out where that thieving snake would get out of the chicken pen when the rooster got after it.

Mose had wonder yesterday why she wanted her back-yard rocker moved over to where there was an open knot hole in the bot- tom board of the chicken pen.

I've got to be alert now, and I hope that thief has an egg halfway down its guzzle cause it'll sure as the world bite me if it doesn't.

The rooster got louder, and she saw the rat snake slip over the side of the chicken fence and hit the ground. The rooster was right behind it and charging at it with beak and claws. The snake headed straight for the hole as she had wished, and when about a foot of it was through the hole, she grabbed it.

The rooster was pecking at it fiercely, and the snake started twisting and turning and showing its underbelly.

It was quick and struck at her as she held it. She felt its teeth go nearly through both sides of her thumb, but she held on tight. She pulled, but it was stuck in the hole.

She could see through the fence and laughed aloud, "You're stuck in the fence, you egg thief. Got an egg halfway down your gizzard and it's caught you. Not so sly as you thought. You're still a snake, damned to crawl on your belly forever, and I've caught you."

"Milly, what is all the racket," Mose hollered as he came around the corner of her house, "You and that blamed rooster have waked up everybody on the street."

"It's that dang rat snake, but I've got him, or you have now. He's stuck because there's an egg in him and he can't get through the hole. You can break it and pull him on through. Put him in that cardboard box over there by the rosemary, and you can take him away in the morning."

"Did he bite you?"

"Two holes on both sides of this thumb," she said as she held up her left hand. "It's not a big deal, as I have some turpentine."

"I know they're not poisonous, but that will still get infected if you don't clean it out."

"Ain't no better than turpentine salve that the folks have been making for a lot longer than we've been alive. I was wondering what time it is," Milly said.

"It's almost two o'clock. I looked at the clock on the way out here. Now, let's all get back to bed."

"Will you carry that snake with you? And will you come over after the boys are awake, and walk with me down to Buck's? I need to git some things and you know the trouble I have trying to handle both the boys and git anything done."

"I need to go down there too; cause Grandma Pearl has quar- reled with me all week cause she wants some vanilla."

"Bet she's makin Dewayne his birthday cake. Hope it's not chocolate cause his diapers will be a mess to get clean.

They both laughed.

"Guess you heard what Jere's dad is doing?"

"Elmer doesn't come around like he did when Jere first left," she said. "Guess he didn't want to see me cryin like I was.… *like I still do.*… Guess he didn't want me to see him cryin inside like he is.…"

"Everybody's sayin he's lost his mind. And I don't blame him none either, but now he is really causin people to wonder. Guess you heard?"

"I ain't been nowhere for weeks, so how do you think I'd hear?"

"Well, he's over there on the Island. You know that tower that guy built over there a while back. He's climbed up to the top of what's left of it and is staying over there all the time. One of the girls is taking food and water to him, and he's sittin up there with his loaded shotgun across his lap and his binoculars up to his eyes scanning the Gulf for Nazi U Boats."

"What are you talkin about, Mose? I've been here at the house with the boys and not been anywhere to hear anything. You know I only talk with you and Grandma Pearl. What's a U Boat? What are they doin in the Gulf?"

"It's been in the news for weeks, but I know we haven't been reading the paper much at all since the boys came. I miss that Camelia.… But, anyhow, when I go down to Buck's store, it's all the talk. All the towns along the Gulf beaches are on black-out. Someone at Pensacola said they saw one of them come up out of the water and it scared the pee waddin out of them. Said the thing was at least two hundred feet long and as big around as a barge."

"Where they comin from? Why in the world would they be in our Gulf?"

"They're makin the trip clear across the Atlantic from the coast of northern France. They have U Boats in water sheds at several towns along France's coast, Sam Buck told me last time I was in the store— at Brest, Saint-Nazaire, and Lorient is what he said. Towns that are just words to me. I wouldn't have any idea where those places are."

Mose realized he had said 'France' and that Camelia was near tears.

"I'll stop talkin about it if you want me to?"

"No, Mose, I want to hear it. How do they make that long a trip? Jere said in the only letter I got from him that it took at least two weeks by a big ship to get across the Atlantic."

"They have other submarines that they meet somewhere in the middle of the ocean, and they refuel the U Boat, so it has enough fuel to get over here."

"They're comin over to shell Eglin?"

"No, they want to destroy all the oil rigs on the Gulf, so we won't have fuel to send for the war. They don't have guns on them that matter much, so they couldn't shoot Eglin from out in the Gulf. They have torpedoes that they launch out of tubes towards our boats and the oil rigs"

"Yes, I see now. Just another reason for me and the boys to not go over there to that Godforsakin place."

Forgive me God for doubtin you and your wisdom....

"Mose, I think I'll take the boys and go with you when you go down to Bucks this afternoon. I want to see the flour sacks and see if he has enough of the same pattern to make me a new dress. I only have two, and I do hate to wear the same one to church every Sunday." Mose laughed, "You're sounding more and more like Grandma Pearl. I'll be over just after we eat and take you and the boys with me."

Milly heard the snake hitting at the insides of the cardboard box and laughed, "Won't be stealing four or five eggs a week. You just don't know how much I need them."

Grandma Pearl decided she would make the trip with them, so the five of them set out along the narrow unpaved streets of Fort Walton.

Camelia hadn't been out of her yard, mainly the back yard, for months. She kept saying she saw things she had never seen before.

"Is that the Magnolia House? Is that where Al Capone and his bunch stayed?"

"No, they mainly stayed over at that place called the Shalimar Club where they played golf during the day and drank their hootch at night entertaining an ever changin bunch of women who was brought in almost every day in a string of fancy black cars. You wouldn't want anything to do with those gals," Grandma Pearl said.

Mose said, "Remember when Rusty Calhoun went roaring down the dirt road to his dad's place in his dad's almost new Studebaker? He and a bunch of his buddies had been driving around the Shalimar

Club hoping to see some gangsters, they said. And they were stopped by a big black car. A back window was rolled down, and a voice asked if they wanted to caddie that day. Of course, they said yes, and one of them said later, they made five dollars apiece. Good gosh, that was over a month's pay in them days…right in the middle of the Depression and all."

"They went back that night in Charlie Calhoun's Studebaker and found out that Capone and his cronies were over at Boggy Bayou where they went to target practice almost every night.

Of course, them boys had to see what was going on, and when they got over there, they heard fast gunfire and a lot of it.

After Rusty was killed by running his dad's Studebaker into the pilings at the end of their lane down to their house and being thrown out the front wind shield into the Sound where he was so drunk he didn't have his senses straight and he drown, one of his buddies said they were scared out of their wits by being threatened by one of Capone's men.

He said they were told to get their teenage asses out of there before they got hurt. He also said one of Capone's men gave them a bottle of whiskey, and that Rusty was gulping it when he let the other boys out at their houses.

Rusty's dad went after Capone one night after they drug Rusty's body out of the Sound. He had been drinking and walked into the Shalimar Club and approached Capone and threatened him. Some locals who knew Charlie Calhoun got him by the shoulders and walked him out of the place, or no tellin what might have happened."

"Mose let's talk about somethin else. Albert and Dewayne have big ears and will ask me a hundred times what you have been tellin."

"I'm sorry, Milly. I wasn't thinkin."

Grandma Pearl shook her head as if to say it wasn't the first time, and said, "Wonder if they might have some Cracker Jacks at Bucks." There was no shuttin up Albert and Dewayne the rest of the way down to the common meeting place and general store on the Sound.

Sam Buck met Mose at the door and asked, "Mose, will you stay out here and talk a minute?"

Camelia, Grandma Pearl, and the boys went on into the store, but Camelia looked long and hard at Sam Buck before she went in. *Wonderin just why I can't hear about Jere's dad…just like Mose?*

"Mose, he's left the wagon, with the oxen hitched up to it, sit- ting down at the end of the loading ramp twice this last two weeks. They just stand there and don't bother anybody, but if they did git loose and hurt someone, Elmer would be in a big mess."

"I'm not sure what I can do about it. You talked to Miss Bernice?" "She was down here at the store once during the time he's been on top of what's left of that tower over there, but she is besides her- self as to what to do."

"I don't know if I can talk sense into him or not. He's been torn up since Jere's been gone—just like Milly—but maybe worse. He did everything with Jere since he could walk. Everybody in town knew he treated Jere like a brother. He did an awful good job, and anybody ought to see how it's tearing him up. God, I don't know how I would be handlin it."

"He's gonna hurt himself, Mose."

"I guess you might be right, but I don't know if he will listen to me."

Later that afternoon just as the sun was setting, Mose told Camelia he was taking his john boat across the Sound to the Island to try to talk with Elmer.

"Here, take him some of Dewayne's cake that Grandma Pearl made this afternoon. Dewayne won't notice a piece has been cut out of it cause he'll be so happy to see the rest of it.

Mose wondered just what he would say to Elmer as he pulled on the long oars of his boat as it crossed the Sound, and how Elmer would act. They had been friends for years and had many memories they shared, not the least was Jere and Camelia.

He struggled to get across some high soft dunes that spread out between him and what was left of that tower. The high winds of sev- eral years ago had toppled it, and now it was just a pile of wreckage that no one had cleared off the beach.

He had always thought it looked just like a forest observation tower, and most people thought so too. It hadn't been very tall from the beginning—more of a look-out deck four or five stories above the sand. It was a popular place with the folks who came to visit, but some unnamed hurricane, or at least a straight wind, had destroyed it. Nobody had cleaned up the mess so now the concrete and rock center of the thing was still sticking thirty or forty feet in the air.

There had been a casino, a lounge which had a spectacular view of the Gulf, a boardwalk, of course, and a string of summer cabins which didn't have heat nor electricity. It was a popular place, though.

Mose saw that somehow Elmer had thrown a lasso around a railing that was still intact at the top, and he was now hold-up in what used to be the observation deck. He had nailed slats at places up the pile of debris so he could climb up there and see the Gulf all the way out to the horizon, so it appeared to Mose that Elmer was prepared to stay up there a long time.

"Elmer, you up there?" he hollered. "Elmer, Elmer Ledbetter, you up there?" he hollered again.

"Who's down there? Don't you try to git up here and bother me. I'll shoot straight down on you, and you'll wish you never came out here to bother me. I done told you last time you were out here to not come back and pester me."

"Whoa, Elmer, it's Mose. I ain't been out here at all. I just came out to visit with you and see if you are all right."

"Mose.... that you Mose? Well, that's mighty nice of you. Come on up and sit a spell with me."

"Elmer, I'm not about to climb those slats. I don't know how well they're nailed to them posts, and besides that, I'm too dang old to climb the thing. So are you…but, come on down and we'll talk down here? I brought you some birthday cake and some sweet tea that Grandma Pearl made."

All this time they had been shouting at each other as the waves from the Gulf had churned up and was drowning them out.

"I ain't comin down there, so you might as well git up the cour- age to climb up if you want to talk."

"Dang it, Elmer… I'm too dang old and clumsy to be doing this,"

Mose said as he put his foot on the first wooden two-by-four slat Elmer had nailed to one of the splintered pilings.

When he finally reached the top of the pile of shattered poles and chunks of concrete, after scaring himself several times on the way up, he peeked over the top making sure Elmer wasn't going to hit or shoot him. He was not afraid of Elmer, but after the things he had heard today and the things Elmer had hollered down at him, Mose was cautious.

"Elmer, what are you doing out here? Bernice and the girls need you at home, and we are all worried about some of the things you have been doing."

"Bernice can take care of herself and the girls. I aim to shoot that stinking sub out there and show them we know they're here. I shot my 30 30 two or three days ago when that thing popped up on the surface. I know its way out there, but I heard a ping, so I hit something."

"What if they come ashore? Yeah, yeah, I know they can't shoot anything but small arms back at you, and they can't launch a torpedo at you, but what if they come ashore."

"In what? They don't have a boat to land in."

"They could have a rubber inflatable one. They could slip up on you too. Why don't you come down and go home with me?"

Mose knew that the U-Boat had long gone on toward New Orleans or Texas where the oil rigs dotted the skyline, but he knew it would be useless to say that to Elmer. Mose knew too that it was not possible for Elmer to hit a submarine from where they were with a 30 30 rifle, but he didn't say anything.

"I'll shoot that rubber thing before they get to the first sandbar They'd never make it over them waves that pop over that."

"Even if they're still out there, they are way past the sandbar.

That thing would be way too big to get into the shallows up close to the beach. The gully between the beach and the first sandbar is barely deep enough for dolphin to swim. The fishing boats coming out of Destin can't get through it. And then after that first sandbar, the water is still shallow way out to the secondbar. No sub could even be in that water. They're way out there, but I bet they're long gone too. When did you see them last?"

Elmer took a bottle from under an old blanket he was on, unscrewed the cap, and offered it to Mose. It was more than half empty.

Mose shook his head no, and said, "What you doin drinking, Elmer? That's not goin to help things a bit."

"Hell, that must be the tenth bottle, and I've got a dozen more. Sam Buck didn't want to sell them to me, but I raised a racket with him, showed him my money for them, and he finally sold them to me. And then, the hypocrite started telling people I'm crazy, I heard."

"Sam's been your friend for almost since you've been alive. He wasn't bein a hypocrite. He's just worried about you… Just like the rest of us."

"Mose, you can't believe how much I'm hurtin. Why the hell did he go in the first place. We could've figured out some way that he didn't have to go. But no. He wanted to go…said it was his duty. Told Milly he would be right back and bring her and Albert somethin nice. Hell, Mose, he didn't even know about Dewayne. Mose, I'm havin a bad time…a bad time. I don't see much to change things neither.

They took him… killed him… and didn't even bring him home. Hell, Mose, I can't even fall down on my knees and pray at his grave." Elmer bent over and Mose realized he was uncontrollably crying. Elmer suddenly sat up and took swigs of whiskey fast, finally gagging on the stuff.

"Whoa…wait right there. Elmer, you've got Bernice and the girls and Milly and the boys. And friends like me and Grandma Pearl. And a whole town that respects you and knows how honest you are when it comes to dealing with you. And the people at church…"

"But you know dang well that nobody else in town, including you, has lost a son in this screwed up thing they're calling a war. Why would we ever git into it in the first place is beyond me. And it took my son, my only son…."

Elmer threw the bottle, he had been swigging out of, against a piece of concrete about ten feet away. The bottle smashed and shards flew in every direction.

A speck of blood appeared on his left cheek and started trick- ling down. He wiped his arm on his cheek, drew back his hand, and looked at the blood on it.

"Elmer, I know you're goin to tell me to go mind my own busi- ness for what I'm goin to say, but I'm goin to say it anyhow. Look what you just did. Yeah, I know it's just a scratch, but what if you got drunk out here and fell and broke a leg, or what if that bottle had really thrown big pieces back at you and cut your head or your throat. Why don't you just come on and go home with me. I've got my boat to get us across the Sound, and you can stay at my house tonight."

"Mose, I came out here to protect our little town. I saw that thing come up out of the water. It was well over two hundred feet long and dirty lookin. Real dirty…had seaweed stuck off it and dripping into the water. As it came up, fish and bottom feeders were sliding off the top and sides. The only thing I could make out was the number on it—U166. Good God Mose, how many of them do they have? How many are out here in our Gulf tryin to destroy our oil?"

"I don't know any more than you do. I do know that our boats are out here patrolling the Gulf and they'll drop depth-charges on them."

"Mose, it's so damn messed up. What a tempest in a wind- storm… worse than any hurricane. One side thinks it wears bigger pants than the other, so they begin the shoving. And the other side shoves back…. Back and forth, back and forth. With shoving and hitting and shooting and bombing and people running from one side, and then just turning and running into the other. It's worse than that, though, cause kids, little kids, are getting caught in its trap… robbed of their lives, not getting to be kids. Oh Hell Mose… I need to shut up.

But Mose, can you imagine being down on the bottom of the Gulf in that thing—that, U166, or any other number, and a depthcharge splits that thing in two? God what a way to die."

"I know Elmer…. And they're somebody's boys too. I mean…

Aw Hell, Elmer. Come on down with me and let's go home."

"Everybody's goin to laugh at me, and say how crazy I am."

"No, they're not. Everybody's talkin because they care about you. Come on, you can sleep in the barn with the oxen. You can scratch Minnie's ears and she'll love you for it. They won't laugh at you, and I'll tell everybody you're back and want to be left alone for a few days."

"Minnie's the only one left, Mose. I sold the wagon and the team to a guy over at Wright. I hadn't hooked them up to the wagon since… since…"

He grabbed a bottle and Mose thought he was going to drain it as he leaned way back. He couldn't drink it fast enough, so it started running down his neck and arms.

"Elmer, for God's sake. This isn't you. Come on, let's git outa this place. Elmer, for Bernice and the girls' sake. How in the world do you think she will make it by herself? Milly and the boys never would have made it without help.…"

"Now, don't you go tryin to belittle me and make me feel like I'm betrayin them. I'm out here trying to settle a little bit of what has happened to Jere."

"That sub is long gone from here. Why do you think they would hang around here? We don't have anything they want."

For the first time, Elmer blinked and shook his head, "You know, you're right Mose. It's long gone from our little backwoods. And Mose, I didn't really hit the thing. I just wanted to think I did."

"I know. Now, let's git down from this mess here and go home."

Elmer went home that night after Mose had rowed them across the Sound. Bernice, his wife, and his girls made a big fuss and told him how happy they were for him to be home.

They had homemade ice cream, fresh strawberries that were picked up at Baker yesterday, and some of Dewayne's birthday cake.

Elmer said he was going to spend the night with Minnie out in the barn by her stall.

During the night, he woke up from his restless sleep. He saw Jere in his mind in a thousand different times they had done things together.

The third time he woke up, he scraped his teeth along the barrel as he put his mouth over the end of his Smith & Wesson 38 Special and blew the back of his head off.

7

Pawpaw

Isn't Papa Elmer going to be here today?

Twenty-four hours later, Mose was headed toward Bucks Landing with Albert in the only luxury Mose probably bought just for himself.

"Why are we taking the Dodge?" Albert asked. "Usually, we just walk down there?"

"We may have to go someplace else after we leave Bucks," Mose answered.

"People always look at us when we're in the Dodge," Albert grinned big as he climbed up on the running board and into the seat.

Mose bought the 1938 Dodge Coupe in 1941. He always claims its Grandma Pearl's idea, but everybody who knows Mose, knows it's his pride and joy.

Troy Stone, at the bank, didn't raise an eyebrow when Mose went in to borrow $500.

"Is that all you need, Mose?"

"I have the rest saved up. It cost me $800, and I guess Grandma Pearl will be happy until she sees something else she wants.

Troy smiled and handed Mose the papers to sign as one of the clerks had brought them up to him.

They had promised Dewayne, they would bring him something

from the store, but he had cried long after they left Chanticleer Lane. In fact, he cried himself to sleep.

Suddenly, Albert shouted, "Stop, Grandpa Mose, stop!"

"What's the matter? You have to pee?"

Albert giggled, "No, I want to look at that tree we just past." "You want to what?"

"It's a paw-paw tree that papa Elmer always stops to look at."

"It's the wrong time of year, Albert. Those paw-paws have to turn yellow, and then the frost has to hit them real hard, and then they are sweet and make an awful good jam to put on toast in the morning."

"Papa Elmer and I picked some one day, and we ate three or four apiece. I sure do like them."

Elmer looked out his window as they slowly went down the hill toward Bucks. *How in this world am I gonna tell that little boy what has happened…?*

When Mose had parked the Dodge, Albert jumped out of his door and ran toward the store.

"Whoa, where you goin?" Mose hollered at him.

"I want to see if Papa Elmer is here," Albert shouted, "I want to scratch Winnie's ears like Mom always does."

Mose knew he was in trouble. How in the world was he sup- posed to tell four-year-old Albert that his grandpa Elmer would not be there today?

Albert ran to the boardwalk that goes clear across the front of Buck's and headed toward the corner where a shorter boardwalk runs down to the Sound.

Elmer always hitched Minnie to the railing, got out, and sat on a big rock where he waited for the pack boat from Pensacola. Some days he had a lot of merchandise to deliver to people around Fort Walton, as Walton's Landing was now officially called, and some days he just turned Minnie around and went back home for there was nothing to deliver.

Albert ran around the corner and came to an abrupt halt. Elmer's wagon and Minnie were not there.

"He's not here today, Mose. That's strange… He's always here. He says now that my dad is not here to meet the boat, he must. Wonder why he's not here?"

Sam Buck had walked out and was standing by Mose now, and he took ahold of Mose's arm and squeezed it. He looked at Mose and Mose looked back with a pleading look on his face.

Sam said, "Hey, Albert. Why don't you come on in the store? We'll check the mailbox to see if your mom has any mail, and then we just might find some treat of some kind for you and Dewayne."

Albert let out a whoop and ran toward Buck's front door. "Good God, Mose, how in the world you goin to explain this to him?"

"I don't know, Sam. I don't know. Camelia and I talked way into the night about what to do, and we don't know. And there's got to be a funeral too. How in the world do we explain that?"

"Dewayne is too little to understand, but Albert isn't. He still asks about Jere once in a while. And he was only a baby when Jere left. How do we tell him that Elmer is gone?"

Elmer has taken him on trips in the wagon when he delivered things, many times. Albert begs to go every time he sees Elmer.

A week later at the Methodist Church, Camelia walked Albert down the aisle. He climbed up the two steps, as she stayed down below, and laid a camellia from their backyard on Elmer's casket.

Bernice had made the decision that the casket would be closed because of the girls and little Albert and Dewayne.

Albert spoke softly because he was in church, "Is Papa Elmer going to be here today?"

8

Two Mud Puddles
to Get Around

Chanticleer Street in Fort Walton

Somehow, she made it through the years of snotty noses, scraped knees, and serious fights between the two of them. They were as different as fresh ham and smoked ham hocks.

Albert achieved everything a mother could desire for a son; except he married too young—just out of high school. They had a son, Justin, who still lives next door and who watches over her like a son. She thanks the good Lord for him every day.

Another pain went through her mind remembering the awful night Albert and his wife, Dawn, died. The policeman had come down the lane to her front porch and standing there holding his hat down in front of himself, told her about the accident out on 98.

They had put her to bed, and she stayed there for several days. *I know I shouldn't ask, Lord, but why? We just saw that wonderful movie, To Kill A Mockingbird, together last week and got to sit downstairs at the Palm... Didn't used to be that way even though everybody knows I'm Indian more than anything else... But we got used to sitting up there in the balcony in the back...folks is folks, no matter where they are. But when we sat downstairs last week, we was still with folks...just folks... and no one thought a thing about it. That's what I like about my town...*

everyone helps everyone else… no matter. And the world was good, as good as I've ever had it, and Albert was respected and so was Dawn. I don't understand, Lord…

Justin was just a kid, and naturally I took him in. He didn't marry til he was pert near forty, and his wife, Claire, is a lot younger than him.

And still another stab went through her—this time straight through her heart. Dwayne had started drinking while he was still in Fort Walton High School. She had caught him, and even turned him in to the police one night for coming home drunk.

She daubed her eyes with the tail of her apron as she knew tears were coming. Later, he and two of his buddies had robbed Drakes Drug store one afternoon but didn't make it two blocks before they were caught.

My, my my, he'd been goin in there since he was a baby. Didn't he know Mr. Drake would know him? And they got a total of $37. I sure failed, Lord….

He spent three years in Gulf Correctional Institution over off Interstate 10 west of Tallahassee, but when he was released, he was too ashamed to come home. Then he just disappeared. One time a few years later, she got a letter from a prison in Missouri that he had been released from there.

Since then, I haven't heard nothing from him. I cried for him for years; just as I cried for Albert; just as I cry for Jere every day.

She rocked two or three times, and words came whistling through her mind…*Love comes rushin faster than a hurricane and fills your heart forever, and the clouds roll in across the moon and it feels like rain…and sometimes it's salty like tears….* She jerked awake.

"What in the world are you doing out here, Great Grandma?" Justin asked as she finally understood he was the reason she had jerked awake in her usual place under the big old tree.

"Come on now in the house as there's a big storm coming. You can sit in the rocker in the front room and look out when it comes, or you can sit in the rocker out on the front porch, but I hope not, for it looks like lightning and thunderboomers," he said as he reached for her thin frail arm to help her up.

"I ain't got nobody to help me up when you or Zathan ain't over here, so jest you let me be. I'll get up when I'm ready. Zathan is too little to help much anyway."

She pulled herself up by pressing down on the wooden arms of the rocker, waved Justin away with one of her arms and a look that he knows better than touch her and straightened up to walk in the back door. He followed closely but kept his distance too.

"Great Grandma, why don't you move next door with us? Claire and Zathan are home all day, and they would git used to you being there too."

"Don't kid yourself. Claire is a good woman, but she don't want this old woman in her house all the time. And quit calling me, 'Great Grandma.' You know that I'm just your Grandma. Zathan is my great grandson, not you, his daddy."

She ended up in the rocker on the front porch as Justin went back through the fence gate to his house next door. Before long, the storm blew in and hovered over Fort Walton Beach like it does many times, especially in July, and the downpour began.

Thick streams ran off the tin roof and splattered on the flagstones at the edge of the porch. Justin had objected when she demanded the flagstones, saying grass would always be crowding them and they would be hard to keep. She had said, "Well, so long as them three behave, I'll have them cleaned. You should see them with scissors cutting round them rocks. They do scare me a little that they might cut themselves, but they haven't yet."

It sure was a gully washer. July has the big rainstorms usually, just like October brings them big winds. It's no secret really why the Panhandle gets hit by so many hurricanes, Camelia thought. There's a direct line when they come around the Keys way down there. You get in the way, and you get hit. That's always been what happens.

The rain didn't quit for over an hour when it suddenly left, like usually, and she saw the clouds head north up toward Georgia, like usually.

Big puddles of muddy water filled the indentions around the flagstone walk and water streamed down the street carving out trenches as it sloped downhill.

But the lane dried just as quickly as it got wet for it's nothing but sand under there.

That's why it's so easy for them to work in my garden…nothing but sand under there. Surely does grow things though.

My. my my them three would have had fun if they had been here today.… running around and squealing like banshees, but it wouldn't have been long enough, especially for one of them.

Zathan, Dylan, and Little Mitch are together way too much, Miss Camelia thinks. Their little boy antics are as preposterous as their intelligence whether in her back yard, or on their frequent forays when they visit the Prof at the La Mancha.

9

Them Three

Pulling Weeds, Little Mitch gets the broom....

She didn't sleep much that night, and what she did was filled with images of Mose, her own Grandpa, so she knew that sometime this day she would see more of him. As she opened her front door, she was not surprised to find Zathan sitting on the porch with his feet dangling over the edge.

"What you doin here this early? Bet you didn't come to hear that loud-mouth rooster of mine crow forty-three times, did you?"

"No ma'am, I'm waiting. It's Saturday, you know, and we're going to weed some in your back yard."

She looked down the street and saw J C Blevins's patrol car headed toward them. A prick of dread flashed through her mind for she knew that one day he would be coming to talk to her and Mylee about them helping that man they called Dolf Gaines recover from his injuries, but then, hadn't he gone off and went down with his boat?

But she knew J C wouldn't talk to her in front of the boys, so she smiled and waved as Little Mitch jumped out of the passenger side and ran up the flagstone walk. J C waved back and went back down the lane stopping to talk with Daniel Sheraton, in his Sunsetter Beach pickup, which was headed toward her house bringing Dylan, the last of the trio. Daniel's workplace, a warehouse where they keep the beach chairs, umbrellas, and a mess of other beach equipment, is just up the street past Hollywood Blvd close to her church.

Daniel and Lyn, Dylan's mom, had enrolled Dylan in a day care place a few blocks away, so needless to say, a few weeks after Dylan was there, Little Mitch was there also. They were inseparable, she knew. By coincidence, Justin and Claire had enrolled Zathan at the same place. Now, the three of them were together way too much, she thought.

Dylan jumped down from the running board of the pickup and hurried toward them. Daniel said through his opened window, "Miss Camelia, if they start driving you crazy, you have my number."

She smiled and waved, "I sure know what a kindergarten teacher puts up with, now!" He was laughing as he drove away.

She led the boys around the side of the house, and they followed single file like they were scouting out the area. Following one of the paths Justin had made through the many herbs, bushes, vegetables, and flowers back there, she made her way to the rocker under the Live Oak.

She glanced at the hole in the honeysuckle vines that almost covered the east fence; the hole she kept cut open so she could see the sun come up each morning. She had an almost identical hole cut into the big fat camellia bush on the other side of the yard where she enjoyed the sunsets almost every evening; even the flowers were dark orange to match the sunsets.

While she was looking, the mother mockingbird fluttered through the hole, flew to a branch in the Live Oak, and then dropped to the ground and began scratching in the loose soil in a patch of mint. Almost simultaneously, the papa mockingbird landed on the back fence with a bug of some kind in his beak, fluttered, and sailed up into the oak to feed their three hatchlings.

It's goin to be a great day, Lord.

The bees loved the honeysuckle—honeybees and bumblebees buzzed the vines all day here in the beginning of July. They loved, maybe even better, the patch of hollyhocks that filled one corner of the backyard.

My. my. my, how Albert and Dwayne and their friends had loved to catch bumblebees in the big petals of those hollyhocks—trap them inside and have some buzzing grenades to scare each other with.

They used to have 'wars' with those things, then throw them over the back fence and watch the angry bees emerge and fly in angry circles trying to find who had imprisoned them. She smiled as she recalled a few stings that needed baking soda poultices.

A green persimmon smacked onto the hard dirt of the chicken pen; she knew it would have been a bad one, for only the bad ones dropped while they were green. She wondered why?

She laughed aloud as one of her four hens pecked at it and then backed away.

Yep, sure is sour. Tastes more like vinegar than honey, don't it?

Just as she was getting ready to tell the boys where they could start pulling the weeds and grass out of one of the patches of herbs, Claire came around the side of the house with a tray with three bowls of puffed wheat and three juicy Georgia peaches. Camelia wished there were four bowls as she remembered that was her favorite cereal during the Depression.

"Good morning! You having a good day? Justin said you were up very late last night."

"Wasn't late, it was early."

They both laughed as they understood that she hadn't got to bed until early this morning.

"I brought these three hard-working young men some breakfast. I hope I didn't put too much sugar in the cereal, so they don't drive you silly."

Her own table, when she was a child, appeared in her mind, and she tasted the sweetness of the milk after all the puffed wheat had been scooped out. *Quit tippin the bowl so far or you'll spill it down your chin, Camelia.*

The boys beamed at the bowls—or maybe at being called young men—and flopped down on the grassy patch near her rocker. The noise they made reminded her of a bunch of piglets her father used to have just down the block from here when he had owned a few acres here in this part of Walton's Landing.

They reminded her more of the three tiny mockingbirds in that nest high up in the Live Oak—they always had their mouths open for food.

The peach pits and bits of pulp became missiles as they sailed over the chicken wire into the chicken pen.

Zathan just turned six-and-a-half and Dylan will be seven in September. Little Mitch is the oldest by a year as he was a toddler when Dylan was born that night, his daddy rescued those two young people from that tool shed way up there next to the National Forrest. But, like what we call him, he is the shortest of the three.

Sure is strange almost how different they are when they act just like one person when they are together—well, most of the time they act that way. Zathan is not the oldest, but he's usually the levelheaded one. It's the oldest one you have to watch out for, not that he's bad or anything, but just because he's filled with too much imagination and devilment....

They were standing in a row, with their fingers sticking through the holes in the chicken-wire fence, as the flock of hens grappled for the peach pits with little bits of flesh still on them, and sometimes mistaking the sour persimmon for a peach. They laughed and one of them said, "Just how dumb can a chicken be?"

As usual, the rooster had flown up to crow from top of one of the fence posts, and had jumped down into the back yard, so it was racing back and forth trying to find a place to get back into the pen, squawking madly all the time.

It's strange he never messes with these three, but he chases every other kid who comes back here.

"Now, it's time you earned your dollars. I'm not going to pay you, any of you," she said as she looked straight at Zathan, "unless you do a good job, listen to me, and don't pull up any of my herbs or anything else I want to keep. Do you hear?"

They stood as they often did, shoulder to shoulder, and nodded their heads up and down. "Pull the little, short blades of grass out of that patch right over there. Don't pull anything that has a thick stem." They invaded the patch, and she knew that she would lose something that mattered, but she didn't care very much. She went in the back door to fix their treat.

The weeding waned after less than an hour, and she knew they wouldn't last much longer, "You three can quit now. One of you get the broom, and you other two, pick up all the pullings you have and throw them over into the compost pile."

They all three ran for the back porch to get the broom until she stopped them, "Whoa there! Little Mitch git the broom, and Dylan and Zathan pick up what you can of the pullings."

They minded her, and as Little Mitch returned with the broom, he walked up and stood very straight in front of her.

"Miss Camelia, I jest got to git this off my mind. I jest ain't able to live with it."

"Are you trying to imitate me, young Mister? You quit talking like that or I'll tell your mom, Miss Ester, or spank you myself."

"Sometimes, you talk that way, Ma'am...."

"Maybe I do, but I'm a whole lot older than you and didn't have the schooling you're getting. Anyway, you just stop talking that way," she was careful the last sentence was standard.

"Anyway, I have to tell you that I hit that rooster of yours with the flat side of the broom one day when you were in the house, and I believe that's why he leaves Dylan and me alone. He never did bother Zathan...cause... because...Zathan is always here."

She laughed out loud, "My, my, my... So, that's why he doesn't bother you two. It's okay cause you didn't slow him down none. He still jumps the fence, pecks around in my beds, and thinks he rules the back yard."

Little Mitch heaved a sigh of relief and started sweeping the paths between the many beds.

"When you three are done out here, there's Kool-Aid and some pretty decent oatmeal cookies on the table in the kitchen. You bring them out here to eat, and you be careful getting them outside as I don't want you spillin them on my clean floor."

She heard Dylan whisper, "I hope its grape."

She also heard Little Mitch whisper, "It better be lime."

A few minutes later, three little boys were laughing and telling whoppers about how they were going to spend the dollar bills she had given them as the lemonade and cookies disappeared.

For centuries, Guerande has been famous for its sea salt. The paludiers rake the salt from the lagoons with their wooden rakes. It dries in the open air and they load it on their wagons to store in the salt house. Isabelle travels to many cities to sell their much wanted and much needed salt.

10

Blending In

Guerande France, a very cold winter

I feel it's unjust that anyone would be thrown into prison for nineteen years for stealing a loaf of bread to feed his family, but that is the fate of another Jean that Father Jean is reading to us in our classes. It's a long story and my favorite character is the little boy, Gavroche, who is brave and honest. We find out tomorrow what happens at the barricade they have built in the streets of Paris.

I have a bad feeling for them, but it's worse to hear Marcel and Henri say something about what they did as kids, and not have any remembrance from my childhood. It's like I'm in a void and everything's blacked-out.

Isabelle had persuaded Alain to sit in the classroom with the children of Guerande as they studied their English. Their priest, Father Jean, has lived in Guerande since he was the handsome young man the Church had sent them forty years ago.

Father Jean lives in the Abbey on the north side of the little town, and the vineyards he has planted stretch into the distance. He and his fellow Monks are proud of their wine crops. Isabelle once told Father Jean that his wine might become as famous as Guerande's salt. He had laughed his soft laugh and said he doubted it.

However, in the little building next to the Abbey where he teaches, he is strict with them, and several times had told Alain to pay attention and not gaze out into space if he ever wanted to learn about the wonderful world.

That's just what's wrong…. I get lost in thinking about nothing because I don't have nothing to hook onto.

"Father Jean, the story is good. It is fun. It is exciting. It is awful too—with the horrible conditions the poor people are suffering. But I don't know what being a boy is like. I don't remember any of that."

The priest crossed himself, "Yes, we know that Alain, and we are all trying to help you break out of whatever caused you to be as you are and start remembering."

"Merci."

Father Jean laughed, "Don't you mean 'Thank You?' You should not mix up the two."

"But I hear both of them every day and don't really understand either much of the time. It's just when things are calm, and I have time to think that I can understand. English is easier though."

In another room of the Abbey, three men sat all day long, it seemed, writing at their tablets.

"Perhaps you should be trying to read what Clarence is working on," Father Jean said, as he guided me toward the three men. "All of them are rewriting so that you and the other young people can read and perhaps understand the story."

"Clarence is working on one of the most famous stories we have in our little library. It is written by an incredibly famous Englishman, William Shakespeare. The story is called, *The Tempest*, and I think it will keep your interest because it is about a great storm that leaves the characters on a deserted island. The main character is a sorcerer who can cast spells. Maybe the most memorable character is a monstrous beast-like human, Caliban. I think the many spells and the acts of betrayal and villainy might keep your mind going. It's very difficult to read, but it is in English, and it might be easier than trying to read French right now.

"I believe that's what you had before you came to us. Keep on thinking and pay attention in case something jars your memory. Go sit on the rock on the hill overlooking the ocean, as that seems to calm you. But sitting with Mademoiselle Isabelle might get you thinking of something entirely different."

Alain smiled and said, "We must sit close Father because the winter is very cold this year, she tells me. Good-bye until tomorrow. And thank you."

As he walked through the narrow streets of the village, he saw that people were staring at him behind curtained windows or through the boards of their yard fences. Some out in the streets, going about their daily business bundled up in the heavy coats, turned to look after he had passed them. No one said anything to him even though he greeted several of them.

Marcel's house is outside the high ramparts of the old village. Those old solid rock walls must be thirty meters tall and thick enough to drive Isabelle's Renault along the top of them he thought.

He heard a bird in the tall marsh grass beside one of the salt pans. It was singing at the top of its lungs, and he was fascinated that it kept changing its song. A jolt went through his mind as, for a flash, he sensed he had heard this before.

"What is that bird by the salt flats that sings so many different sounds?" he asked as they were soon sitting at Marcel's little table eating crusty bread and some soft cheese.

"Mon Dieu, you will be saying 'pourquoi, pourquoi, pourquoi' just like those little kids you spend the day with! I don't know what kind of bird it is. I'm an old salt skimmer. We call them Monqueurs, and they come from the North once a year going South. Then, they come back from the South going North some months later, like most of them already have this year. They're only here for a few weeks. Nice to listen to though."

Marcel got up and put another stick in the wood stove in the corner of his kitchen.

"Most people who don't know answers, ask 'why,' so why shouldn't I?"

"I apologize to you, my new friend. It's just that things are in a hell of a mess, and now you appear out of nowhere and don't know anything that's going on. I do apologize."

"Thank you. That's what Father Jean says to say. And I do thank you, Marcel."

"Good. Now, tomorrow I'm going to see if you can drive a wagon with a couple of donkeys pulling it."

The next morning, they walked to the enclosure behind Marcel's house, and as Alain put his foot up on the bottom rail of the fence, a jenny walked over and stuck her head over the fence next to him.

"That's Agnus who likes to have her nose rubbed."

Alain started scratching her nose, and each time he hesitated, she nudged him to start again and wiggled her long ears. That flash of remembering something flashed through his head. A little foal trotted up from across the pen and started nursing.

"That's Mikey, or at least, that's what Henri calls him. We let him run loose alongside Agnus when we take them to the marshes to haul salt."

"And where is the other one?"

"You will have a time with him, I think. His name is Jacque, and he is one mean Jackass. I keep him away from the others most of the time. He spent the night in the barn."

"If he is so mean, why don't you just use another donkey with Agnus?"

"Because Jacque is the smartest of all of them. The mounds of dirt between the salt pans are very narrow, just wide enough for the wagon to go over them. Jacque keeps everything straight, and none of the others can do it like he can. I've had three fall into the lagoons. One nearly drowned."

"Well, let's see this monster. Maybe I'll just have to tame him."

Marcel laughed aloud, "If you do, everybody in town will hear of it. He's a bastard that bites and kicks."

We went toward the barn, and as Marcel opened the door, I heard a hoof slammed into the wall of the stall Jacque was in. I walked up to the gate at the front of his stall only to be suddenly encountered by Jacque's bare teeth biting at me. I grabbed one of his ears and reached around and started scratching vigorously behind his ear on that side.

He stopped just as fast as he had charged the gate and got the most contented look on his face. I turned his ear loose and stopped scratching. He nudged at me just as Agnus had done earlier.

"Well, I be damned." Marcel exclaimed.

Father Jean rode by on his bicycle as Marcel was talking. He turned the bicycle around in the Marsh Road and came back and stopped his bike by the rock fence which surrounds Marcel's stable. "My friend don't say the words that might condemn you later," he said. He pushed his bicycle away from the fence and went down the dusty road laughing his deep baritone laugh.

Marcel looked at me and smiled, "I've heard him say worse than that. It is good that Guerande has a strong happy priest in these times." We saw Henri walking down the road toward us with two men I had never seen before. They stopped at the fence, where the three of them lit cigarettes, and as Marcel and Henri were talking, Henri had a coughing fit. He looked at the cigarette in his hand and then at the two men who came with him, and they burst into laughter.

I noticed that Henri didn't introduce the two men to Marcel and thought maybe he knew them, and I had just missed seeing or hearing him greet them. After a few minutes, the three walked away, and I saw them head for the Abbey.

"Who were those men?"

"Oh, they are workers who will probably work the vineyards for a few weeks and then go on to someplace else," Marcel quickly said.

I gathered that he had not told me the truth, and it hurt that I was not trusted, but I also thought he had a good reason, or he wouldn't have lied to me.

"They had on clothes that fit worse than the ones you put me in the first day I arrived at Guerande," I said.

He looked at me like he understood I knew he had lied to me. I wonder what's going on with Henri and why he is gone for days at a time.

The next morning, Jacque wouldn't open his teeth when I tried to put the harness bit in his mouth. I was ready for him this time as I pulled a turnip from my pants pocket. He opened wide, and I put the bit in before he could take a bite of the turnip. He shook his head back and forth viciously and lunged toward me. I held out the turnip, and he chomped down on it. He was happy again.

"You've dealt with animals before, Alain. Do you remember? You know how to put the harness on and how to hitch them up to the wagon. Surely you have done it before?"

"It seems easy, but I did watch you and Henri the other day as you hitched them up."

Marcel looked at him and shook his head in wonder.

Henri walked up, "I'll need to use Trotter for a few days," he said to Marcel. "I wish I could still use Jacque, but he's too old and two stubborn lately."

"I'll have Trotter ready in the morning for you." Marcel answered.

Henri pulled a little package out of his pants, took out a Lucky Strike cigarette, stuck it between his lips and then offered one to me and one to Marcel. We both shook our heads that we didn't want one. But the package caught my eye.

"I don't think I have ever seen you with that kind of cigarette," I said.

He looked at me and shrugged his shoulders, "Oh, I got these yesterday from one of those men who came to work at the Abbey. They are strong, I tell you."

Why was everyone lying to me?

11

On the Death Train

Horror on the way to Paris

Isabelle knew she must deliver the protection money to General Oberg's mousy little pipsqueak of an aide on time, or she would be visited in Guerande by a loud contingent of Nazis. They had, before, loud and mean, strutting around to draw the attention of as many of the townsfolk as possible, clicking around in their bright shiny polished boots, parading her in front of them and destroying the silliest things that got in their way—like flowerpots and gardens. They had done it because the payment had been late.

She also knew they would not dare touch her as she traveled to and from Guerande on her way to Paris, or their SS boss General Oberg in Paris would line them up for discipline, maybe even death. She drove slowly along the Marsh Road headed southeast to Nantes where she would spend the night with her aunt, board the train the next morning, and arrive at the Nord Station in Paris the next day, that is, if everything went well. And she knew it would not, for it never did.

The roads would be clear if she didn't meet a troop of Nazis with tanks, horses, or whatever, but she was afraid of the French too because they would be saying, 'Who is this woman driving her Renault along the road by herself?"

Her little 1936 Monaquatre, Renault had been her pride when she had bought it, but now because of the war and its age, it was dented and scratched in many places. The salty air of Guerande caked on its fenders and tires which was her biggest concern, for she did not have the foresight to get better ones before it was impossible to get any.

The biggest amazement was the petrol; every time she parked it under the shed roof at her aunt's house and returned from the trip to Paris, the tank would be full of petrol.

The eighty kilometers from Guerande to Nantes seemed long today. She didn't have to go all the way to Nantes to get the train, but she did it to stay with her aunt who was full of news about what was happening at St. Nazaire and in Nantes.

The road closest to St. Nazaire was the most dangerous for the Nazis seemed to pretend that the local people did not know about the submarine sheds that were there and the new ones being built there. Those crazy Nazis had their heads up their butts, Isabelle thought. How could the hundreds of trucks and tractors, and the machinery not be seen by the local people? How could all those trains filled with workers not be noticed?

They guarded the road day and night and had checkpoints where identification was scrutinized, and she had heard of people being shot if there was any suspicion about their identity.

But it was a beautiful day really with fluffy clouds in the sky and beautiful fall colors painted the trees. She did notice that the fields were empty as there were no cattle, horses, or anything living. She knew that the livestock had all be eaten, stolen, or taken away by the Nazis. She was thankful to Father Jean that he had helped Guerande hide their Breton cattle in that hidden valley up on the Vilaine. She started to relax and think of better times when all she had to do was be concerned about her town. She knew they depended on her, but now there was Alain and what she did not know about him, and what she hoped for the two of them.

And then there was Henri who was obviously sick—but she had to depend on him and trust him on the so important trips he made South.

As her little Renault went around a corner, she was face-to-face with the business end of a Panzer tank. A squadron followed it, and behind them was a SS staff car with an officer who like all of them these days, looked like he was constipated.

Isabelle pulled the car to the bank as quickly as she could, but that was not quick enough for the cocky officer who flung his door open.

He was in full uniform including the outlandish riding crop that had become popular with junior officers of the SS.

"Chienne, Degagez la route. Maintenant."

"I am not a chienne, you bastard."

He lunged forward and raised his riding crop to strike her.

"Go ahead if you dare. General Oberg sera heureux d'avoir une conversation avec vous."

He stopped.

She laughed and stood tall in front of him, "Petit garcon, dagagez la route maintenant. Deplacez ces petits soldats sur le cote pour que je puisse passer."

He turned and ordered the troops to form single lines along the sides of the road.

Isabelle tooted the Renault's horn as she whizzed by them. She laughed aloud the next hundred yards and thought she just might like to have a good glass of Father Jean's delicious Cabernet Sauvignon which had won ribbons last season. She laughed a little as she thought Father Jean's wines might challenge Guerande's famous salt one day.

She told her aunt later what had happened on the road, and how she called the SS Lieutenant, a little boy, and had ordered him to get his troops out of her way.

Her aunt shook her head, "You are being too brave, niece. Sometime one of them will not back down from you and you will be hurt. So far, the Nazis have killed forty-eight people for the assassi- nation of that bastard Karl Hotz in front of our cathedral. Three men did it, and two of them are killed but the other one is on the run, and they are lining up citizens trying to scare someone into telling where the third one has gone. You need to watch your tongue around those barbarians."

"All I have to do is refer to General Oberg and they run like butter in the sun on the windowsill."

The next morning Isabelle boarded the train to the Nord Station in Paris.

The almost four-hour journey would shake Isabelle to her very roots and make her more determined than ever to get as many Yanks, Brits, and anyone else running from the Nazis, down into the Pyrenees Mountains in Spain where that young woman was becoming too well known for getting them to the Atlantic where they boarded boats to sail away to their freedom.

A thought ran through her mind that her own helping of so many was getting known. She had to warn Henri to be very careful.

When she entered the train coach, she saw she was the only woman and there were a few other Frenchmen. Several of the men had their heads down and covered with their coats as if they were asleep, and they might be, she thought. They were all sitting in the darkness of their own being. No one except the obvious Nazi troops were young. One of them turned and smiled at her in a way she didn't like, and she pressed her passport and what money she had tight under her armpit. She had them in a little leather pouch with its straps circling her neck. She felt safe about her bag the conductor had taken as she had traveled with his train many times, and she guessed he knew what was in the bag and who it was for. They know everything, she thought. Her aunt's words came back to her.

She quickly lowered her head and pretended she was going to sleep too.

Until the trains get within fifty or so kilometers from Paris, they travel on single tracks and one train must pull over at a side rail until the other train passes on down its way.

Twenty minutes north of Nantes her train was diverted onto one of those pull overs. The conductor came through the cars announcing they would be maybe a half hour waiting for a train going north, as they were, and so they had to wait.

She heard the train when it was still a long way off for its engines were not like the train she was on. They sounded powerful.

As it approached her train, it slowed considerably, and she notice the conductor was lowering all the windows that had been raised. He also pulled down all the blinds that now covered the windows. It was almost dark in the car with little patches of light where the blinds did not fully cover the windows.

A horrible putrid smell filled her nose as the other train started slowly passing by. It was unlike any smell she had ever known. ...Something was obviously dead, but she had never smelled this smell before. She had lived around farm animals all her life and had smelled dead horses and dead bloated cows in the fields, but nothing like this. She saw other passengers on her train hurriedly get their handkerchiefs or other cloths to cover their faces, and she was glad to find she had put her lavender scented scarf in her purse this morning.

She quickly held it to her nose and mouth and tried desperately to hold her breath.

The conductor came down the aisle, bent down and whispered, "Mademoiselle, quick! Come with me."

He grabbed her arm, pulled her from her seat, and rushed her back down the aisle in the direction he had come.

As he pulled her down the aisle, a blind on one window snapped up, and Isabelle saw the train on the track next to them. It had come to a full stop on the pull over, so her train could continue down the main track. It was only fifty or so feet from her window.

There was a lot of struggling to be the ones standing at the front of the other train and several Gestapo officers were ordering and shoving Nazis soldiers back as they protected their space where the wind made by the train blew the air back at them.

The conductor stopped at the end of the aisle, opened a door to a closet there, and shoved Isabelle in. He hurried away, and she saw him go through to the next car.

Someone had pulled the blind down again and for a second it covered the window, but suddenly it snapped up again and went flapping around and around the spindle that held it at the top.

Isabelle peeked through the door of the closet and screamed by what she saw.

They simply stood there not moving, not reacting to what was happening, like they were already dead. A cattle car full. Over a hundred of them. Skin and bone with ribs almost cutting through their sides. Sunken eyes that were vacant with nothing behind them. Like they were already dead.

Suddenly, several of the men on her train that she had thought just nondescript workers, had pulled guns from places where they had hidden them.

One had a Tommy-gun and the rat-tat-tat that it made was closely followed by the ping, ping, ping as bullets hit the engine next to them. She saw a Gestapo officer fall and get caught in the cow catcher in front of the engine.

In the chaos and fear, the man with the machine gun could not hold it steady and it whirled to his right, and the bullets hit the horror she saw through the chained slats of the first car.

As the bullets hit them, blood spurted from their frail emaciated bodies plugging the gravel below the putrid train with murky strings.

The frail men, or at least once they had been men for they were walking bones, scars, and sores now, began moving…crowding back into the dark corners of the cattle car they were crowded into.

From out of the darkness, they were huddled in, she saw eyes peering out. They were vacant, glazed over, and looking at nothing, she thought. She heard their weak cries and saw them stretching out boney arms clawing at the air through the slats of the car.

She knew she was going to be sick.

Other shabbily dressed men in the coach with her had drawn their knives and were slashing and stabbing the startled soldiers who were in the coach.

One of the older men yelled, "Viva la France! Death to the stinking Nazis and to Petain for being a traitor."

Their sudden ambush lasted but a few seconds before shots from the other train shattered the windows of the coach. Isabelle shrieked from the little closet and crumbled onto the floor.

She heard the doors at the rear of the coach pop open, and the room was filled with the rattling of Tommy gun fire and rifle shots.

It was over in a minute or two. The conductor pulled the door open as she was holding tightly to it.

Bodies were everywhere. Blood ran in the aisle. Four of the Underground men were still alive, and the conductor shouted to one of them that there was a hand car at the end of the pullover.

"Take the right track when you come to the division point, or you will be headed into danger down south toward St- Nazaire.

She stopped giving directions as she realized if they took the right track, it would lead them to Guerande.

The coach was a wreck with bullet shredded cushions and ripped backs on the seats. Most of the windows were shattered with some pieces of jagged glass hanging—dangling in the frames.

The acrid smell of gun powder mixed with the putrid smell of the train next to them.

Isabelle could clearly see the other train now. She gasped and whirled away from the sight as she vomited on the floor.

Making herself turn back, she saw the carnage of the last five minutes.

Movement started again. She saw bodies struggling to get out from under the dead ones. Arms began weakly flailing in the air as they clutched at nothing between the slats of the cattle car. She watched, horrified, as those eyes again gazed between the slats. Blood ran out beneath the doors and lower slats. It turned into dark black pools on the gravel below.

The conductor took her arm and led her out into the coach ahead of them.

"I'm so sorry Miss Isabelle," he said. "I am as sick as you…."

"Are you one of them?"

She saw that he plainly lied as he said, "No, no, I am but a friend of your aunt. She is very frightened you have to go to Paris so much to pay ransom for Guerande."

Isabelle relaxed a little thankful he didn't know about the other things she was doing, "Who are they?"

"They are partisans trying to bother the Nazis as much as they can. They have been on my train before."

"No, them?" as she forced herself to look at the other train.

"They cannot work any longer on the submarine installations down at St. Nazaire. They are prisoners of war; Yank or Brit crews shot down, or soldiers captured up a Brest or down at Nantes, and anyone else the Nazis decide to roundup and force into labor. They haul wheelbarrows of concrete until they are too weak.

The Nazis might feed them some bread and slop once a day. I hear though that food down there is running out. They take them outside of Saint Nazaire far enough so the local people can't see, load them onto what you saw on that other track, and I hear they tell them they are headed home."

Isabelle shuddered for she knew that Henri had to go by St. Nazaire on his trips south.

They heard the engines rev up as the train passed on by them and she said, "Where are they going?"

"Up to Pithiviers…that camp outside of Paris. The Nazis call that camp a transfer camp back to Germany or Austria, but those pitiful beings will be buried in a mass grave somewhere in the woods outside of Paris. It will be a respectful distance from the good people of Paris so they will never have to know or admit to it. After all, those poor devils are just prisoners, gypsies, and Jews."

Isabelle looked at him and shuddered as she realized his awful sarcasm.

12

Hatching Disaster, Maybe

We had about two months of calm when no Nazis came by our way. We heard reports that Brest, over two hundred kilometers north of us was being destroyed. The fighting there was reported to be hand-to-hand and street-by-street.

We worked hard getting the salt into cloth bags and into storage back of Father Jean's place.

The Nazis had always demanded part of the money Guerande had made from selling the salt, but now they demanded even a bigger share of the profits. Father Jean said he thought that indicated they were running low on money to carry out the war, or at least he prayed they were.

Isabelle was in Paris to try to sell our salt to the few restaurants that remained open. She was given the green light when she came to a check point for the Nazis command had passed the word along that she was a valuable asset. She had money, and they wanted it.

She also had the quarterly ransom of salt for the Nazis with her.

Marcel and I were sitting on the old rock wall that surrounds his stock yard as Henri appeared coming down the lane.

"He looks so tired and sick lately," Marcel said.

"He smokes too much."

Marcel looked at me as if I understood how smoking hurts you, and I realized he was thinking I had known about that in my other life.

"I'm going to need Trotter again tomorrow," Henri said as he climbed onto the wall. I wish to Hell I could use Jacque as he is so much smarter than Trotter, but that's not to be, because I can't.

"I've been thinking of letting Alain go with you on one of the trips so he can take over. You're getting older my little friend, and you don't look so good lately either."

"Hell no, I'm not taking him with me. He would stick out like a boulder on the beach, and besides, Isabelle would throw a fit if she found out."

"Yes, I know about Isabelle and what she might do to me if Alain did go with you, but I'm thinking about it anyway."

"Good luck keeping what hair you have left on your head if she does find out what you are thinking."

Marcel automatically reached up and rubbed the few frizzly hairs which remain on top of his head.

"Isabelle has gone to Paris with the salt to pay this month's protection from the Nazis. Let us all pray she doesn't meet up with the sick mess she did on that train the last time she went. I don't believe any of us know how brave that niece of mine is. She will be gone over two weeks as she is also going to try to sell our salt to the few remaining restaurants open there."

Alain sat and listened to them and wondered why they were so concerned about the trips Henri made down South. He knew that the men who suddenly appeared from the North were soldiers from somewhere who were escaping from the Nazis, but why were the trips so dangerous—more dangerous that living everyday dreading that a squadron of Nazis might appear at your front door?

"Well, make up your old mind if he's going or not because I leave in the morning. I know the trips are not safe, but the people involved along the way are comfortable with me. I don't need another stranger with me to explain. I'll already have two to talk about. Just remember, I don't want him to go, and I don't want to be responsible for him, and I believe Isabelle might just take what's left of your hair, if you do send him with me."

The three of them laughed, and Henri left the two of them on the rock fence and walked toward the Abbey.

The U Boat sheds at Saint-Nazaire where they are repaired. They swarm out of the shallow bay into the Atlantic to torpedo Allied ships. Jere and Elmer discover they go as far as the Gulf of Mexico to destroy the oil rigs.

13

Alain goes with Henri

A Sacrifice

Marcel and Alain talked until the sun went down behind them as they looked out at the Atlantic.

"I see why you two sit out here on this slab of granite so long into the night," Marcel laughed. "Sitting here with me is prob- ably not as much fun as sitting with her though," He laughed again.

"She is a fine woman, Marcel, and I am thinking I don't deserve to be with her. None of us know where I came from, what I was before, but I feel like I belong here now. I don't often think about what the other life might have been, and I don't think about leaving. I could go with Henri and get those men down into Spain, but when I got there, what would I say? They would ask where I came from, and I wouldn't know. I think you are stuck with me, my friend."

"We are all happy you are here, and you are my friend. Father Jean says you must have been a good man wherever you were, for you are now. I agree with him, and so does Isabelle."

"Yes, but you two agree with everything Father Jean says," Alain said.

They both laughed.

"Now, my friend, do you really want to make this trip with Henri, tomorrow?"

"We both know he is not going to be able to do it much longer, so yes, I will go. There will be many others who need us to help them escape into Spain. That young woman, what do they call her? The Nightingale? She must have a price on her head that's big, and she must be awful smart to stay one step ahead of the Nazis, but she just keeps helping service men who are trying to escape. So, yes. I will go."

We had been lucky all during the occupation. Father Jean had seen it all coming, and we had taken our herd of Breton cattle into a canyon off the Vilaine River that few people knew about. The canyon opens up into a valley which has never been grazed, so we were lucky to have pasture for a couple of the war years by rotating the herd into different sections. The only catch to the operation was that someone had to live over there, so it was really a herdsman's job. We had been lucky that everyone had kept their mouths shut that knew about the cattle.

Someone guarded them all the time, and we had to keep taking feed and hay to them beginning in the third year, but we enjoyed milk and butter, and sometimes, even ice cream. Marcel said once that we ought to be thankful that the Bretons are small cattle, for they didn't take too much feed.

Father Jean also kept the soil around the grape vines in the vineyard, back of the Abbey, planted with all kinds of vegetables, so we had almost as much food as we normally did. His vineyard of over twenty acres also provided what was becoming a prized wine, which everyone knows, is the Frenchman's water.

Just about all the three hundred families have kitchen-gardens, so no one was hungry, and it seems all of us work hard to help each other.

Our salt is the finest, and with Isabelle's management, we reduced the price to all our contacts. When word spread, we didn't have enough salt to furnish the new contacts. We had money which we didn't need for there were few places to spend it.

The best thing though is that the Nazis needed our salt, so they gave Isabelle leeway wherever she went. In the early months of the occupation, she made two trips to London, sold what salt she had with her, but found out important information about what the Brits were doing to invade us, and rid us of the 'nasty-heathens' as we called them behind their backs.

"This trip will be dangerous, and you must keep your wits about you with everyone you meet. It's less than twenty kilometers, but it is the strangers we don't know about who might betray us. Henri knows everyone who lives along the way by now, and they think he is taking salt to St. Nazaire. He gives those that live along the way their salt too, to keep them happy—but more to keep them quiet."

"I think we can take Jacque for he will mind me. What do you think?"

"Good luck with him minding you, but yes, I think you should take him. He is much faster and stronger than Trotter."

Henri did not seem his funny jokester self the next morning when he arrived at Marcel's house and found Alain waiting with Jacque ready for the trip.

"We're all going to be in big trouble when Isabelle returns and finds out you went with me," he complained. "I told you two yesterday that I didn't want Alain to go with me. It is a dangerous trip every time, and now I have to explain that Alain is not one of the ones to be sent to Spain but is to turn around and come back with me. I just hope this works."

"We are only doing it because you need rest, Henri. How many more servicemen we will have to make this trip, we have no idea, but we must prepare for them."

They traveled in almost silence for the first couple of kilometers with Henri saying nothing at all, and Alain urging Jacque on. The hardheaded mule wanted to stop at every sweet looking grass along the road.

"That stubborn kicker is going to get us in trouble," Henri growled. "Don't take it out on him, Henri. He's been couped up in Marcel's barn for weeks, and now he wants some fresh green grass."

"Green grass, my ass! He wants his own way about everything just like he always has."

He pulled his cigarette package out of his jacket pocket, tapped the bottom of it until a cigarette popped up above the others, and stuck it in his mouth. He turned and offered one to the two servicemen.

One eagerly agreed, and soon he and Henri were walking along like long lost friends.

"Where are you from?"

"I grew up outside of Mobile, Alabama—close to the Florida state line, played football in school, and ended up here in France fighting a war that makes no sense to me. How in the world are the Nazis going to get to Mobile Alabama?"

"They might if we don't stop them," Henri said.

"Nah, that's too far away. Someone would stop them before they got that far."

"I think you are being a dumb ass," Henri said. "that's what we are doing right now."

Alain, who was walking behind Henri and leading Jacque who was loaded down with provisions for the trip, looked at Henri. He knew Henri must be hurting and that his lungs must be about eaten away. He didn't know anything about cancer, but he knew enough to know Henri's days were numbered.

"We will travel down to Pornichet, across the countryside there and down to the ocean road to Saint-Marc and meet Claude who will ferry us across the bay to Saint Brevin les Pins across the bay from St. Nazaire. That's where we meet the contact that will take you two on down to Bordeaux where you will meet the man who takes you on down to Spain," Henri finally told us as we stopped in a wooded grove to eat a baguette and some cheese, we had with us.

"If any of us gets separated from our group, it would be wise to turn back to Guerande instead of trusting those down by St. Nazaire for most of them are so scared of the Nazis, they would turn their own brothers in.

They skirted the little town of Pornichet shortly after noon and started their walk down a trail that Alain saw was used a lot. They met a few farmers on their way to Pornichet with whatever produce they had, so were able to buy some apples and grapes.

When they got to the ocean road, they found it was not really the ocean ahead of them, but the Pays-de-la-Loire, or the mouth of the Loire River where it had created a bay that opened out into the Atlantic.

Henri led them along the busy road until he turned off toward the water. He said, "Watch carefully, and do just as I do."

They hadn't slowed down their walk, but suddenly Henri turned off, walked through a yard, and around a house, and into a shed in the back. The others were caught off guard, but awkwardly did as he did. "Leave that hardheaded beast in Claude's back yard and let's hope to hell, he doesn't start a racket."

"I'll take care of that," Alain said, as he pulled several apples out of the bundle on his back.

Jacque was content for several minutes.

They had been in the shed for almost an hour, and Alain was wondering why, but kept quiet about it for he didn't want Henri any more upset than he had been most of the day.

They all jumped involuntarily as the back door opened and a huge burly man came toward them. He was nearly seven feet tall Alain thought and heavy.

"I thought you said there would only be two this time," he growled at Henri.

"Just these two," Henri pointed to the servicemen, "this is Alain who lives at Guerande, and Marcel and he have decided I'm getting too old to make these trips, so he is going to take my place, I guess."

Claude looked closely at Alain, "He's too good-looking. He'll stick out like a sore thumb. Tell Marcel, he's got his head up his ass on this one."

Alain said, "I'll be able to blend in. Give me a chance."

Claude glared at him, but said, "Okay, you four, stay right here. We can't leave until it's getting dark. I'll get you some food, but it might not be much. Did you bring me some salt, Henri? We're out of salt, as well as almost everything else. You've got to be quiet. Get some sleep if you can because when you get to Bordeaux, you've got a long, hard trek through the Pyrenees. And, Henri, that crazy mule better not make a racket, or one of my fine neighbors might call a patrol to get him."

Alain did have a nap but was awakened about an hour later by the sound of motors that were getting louder and louder.

Claude came running into the shed, "Move those crates over there and get into that space back there. No one makes a sound, or we are all dead."

He went back out and ran to the gate by the road. A black sedan, followed by a Daimler-Benz off-road truck with eight or ten soldiers in it, were blocking the road. The sedan door flew open, the tail gate to the truck was lowered, and the street was filled with Nazis; the captain wore SS bars and swastikas flashed bright in the afternoon sun.

The captain stepped forward and stood as tall as he could in front of Claude, "Sie abschaum, wo sind die Manner berichted, hier ze sein?"

Alain could see the legs of all the men in the street and wanted desperately to laugh at the captain. He was a small man and looked even smaller on his tiptoes in front of the giant, Claude.

He stood as tall as he could in his crisp uniform with a crease in each pant leg that some fraulein probably had ironed, threatened if she didn't do a good job.

The only thing that messed-up his appearance, Alain noticed was a deep gash on the toe of one of his highly polished boots. The gash was raw and new, like it had only happened.

Henri whispered, "He just called Claude 'scum' and wants to know where we are."

Henri looked like he might cough, and a thought flashed through Alain's mind... *can I knock him out if he does start coughing?*

The Nazi captain spied Jacque standing in the backyard. Jacque was looking straight at him with his ears perked up, and he started stamping one of his front hoofs.

"What have we here?" the captain asked in excellent English. "Forget about some stray agitators. Someone will catch them before they get close to St. Nazaire. We will take this prized looking donkey with us. It will please the general."

Henri looked at Alain and a wide smile crossed his face as he whispered, "This will be fun."

Two hours went by. Alain could see Claude standing on his back steps agitated, he thought. Then he realized the sun was getting low in the west, and they had to be going.

Jacque broke the leg of the first man who approached him. His swift turn to show his rump, and the quick kick sent the man howling in pain back into the street. The others were wary now, but no one could get close to Jacque. He literally bit a chunk out of another's arm, and whirling in circles, he scared the others away.

The captain was furious, "Holt euch faule Esser hinein und peitscht seinen Nintern," he hollered at his men.

Henri whispered, "Called them lazy asses and ordered them to whip Jacque's butt."

Henri was on the verge of laughing, but Alain held his hand up warning him to be quiet.

Jacque turned his rump to the Nazis almost like he knew it was an insult.

One of the soldiers got a rope from the truck, and they soon had Jacque lassoed. Using all their strength, they pulled him to the ground, and soon he was hog-tied.

It took them another thirty minutes to get Jacque into the back of the truck as he struggled and bit at them.

They drove away after the captain warned Claude that he was being watched.

The sun was getting low, and by the time they got to the bay across from the U-Boat sheds, it was dark. The little motor on Claude's boat made way too much noise, Alain thought, but they finally arrived at Saint Brevin les Pins.

Claude said to the two service men, "Go straight down the street in front of you; just one house will have a light inside, and it will be hard to see from the street because it is almost blotted out behind the dark shade. Knock twice, wait a second, and knock twice again. A little old lady should answer the door and she will want you to get inside as quick as you can."

Alain said good-bye to the two and watched as they waded to shore.

It seemed the trip back across the bay was much longer than when they came across. Alain saw a beautiful lighthouse standing where the Loire River emptied into the Atlantic almost five kilometers away. He turned and saw the flat concrete heavy building that housed the

U-Boats. He counted fourteen slots. They looked like caves, totally in the dark, that monsters might emerge from at any second.

Claude cautioned them to keep low as the light from the lighthouse swung over them each time it made its circle.

Alain wondered why the Nazis would be so brave to leave the light beaming from it, and asked Claude.

"They are brave about it because of the disaster the Brits had a few months ago when they tried to ram the dock with the *HS Campbeltown*. The Nazis won that day, and those godforsaken commandos aboard were either killed or taken as prisoners. It was a total failure on the Brits part, and the Nazis still laugh about it, so they leave the lighthouse with its beam circling. It's more of a bragging than a beacon.

They reach Claude's house well after midnight, slept a few hours for they were exhausted from the row across the bay, but mostly from their frayed nerves, and started their walk back to Guerande.

The next morning, Marcel and Alain went out to Marcel's barn.

As they entered the front door, there was a loud 'whack' against the wall of a stall in the back.

Alain looked at Marcel.

Laughing, Marcel said, "He came walking home last night. You might want to stay away from him today because he is mad as a hornet."

Alain looked over the wall into the stall. Jacque looked straight at him, bared his teeth, and brayed loudly.

14

Late August 1943 – Guerande

Marcel's bravado wins

During a calm in the squalls of heavy rain that had slashed Guerande's stout walls all night, Henri, who was standing under the porch, smoking, outside the little café which was the usual gathering place for Marcel and his group, heard them coming when they were a quarter of a mile away from town. The Zundapp Cycles make a noise unlike any other—so he knew a squad of Nazis was coming at us. He hurried inside to warn the others.

They panted their way along the Marsh Road from the south; panting for that is way a Zundapp cylinder sounds—a panting like some fierce wild animal is inside the motor, and in the Nazis case, it was probably a Doberman that would rip your throat out in one lunge. One by one, they revved their motors spraying the gravel road until they reached the gates that stand open for people coming to our town.

"Alain, get yourself hid somewhere and be quiet. If they do find you, try to act like you are not all there." Marcel said.

"That won't be hard for him," Henri laughed.

"Just let me do the talking if they do find you," Marcel continued.

I disappeared into the tiny kitchen and slid a cabinet along the wall, so I could walk down the steps behind it into the cellar below. Someone slid the cabinet back into place, and all sorts of things started going through my mind. What if the bastards start shooting everyone just for the hell of it? What if they burn down this place? *Just be quiet and listen. Marcel is smart. He will fool those lousy Krauts.*

There were seven of them, six riding alone and a Captain riding in a Steib side car attached to the lead cycle. They made a great deal of noise entering Old Town through the Porte Saint-Michel, the main entrance through the ramparts, as they search their way up the narrow cobblestone street and saw the little café. Each driver revved his engine after all the cycles had come to a stop, surely to announce their presence.

The captain, who was at least ten years older than the others, made a big deal of waiting until his driver came around and opened the little open-air door of his side car. He looked foolish enough as it was, for he was under an umbrella, but still soaked in the heavy rain.

They stomped their heavy boots on the wooden porch and entered the tiny room where Marcel, Henri, and a few other villagers were now eating lunch.

When I stretched and stood as tall as I could, I could see the room they were in through a tiny space where a splinter of wood had been torn back. I guessed that they had used this room to hide someone before.

One of the young Germans who couldn't be more than twenty years old, announced, "Wir warden ihre Tische Brauchen." Marcel answered, "Pas parler allemand."

The captain laughed a loud false-sounding laugh, "Of course, nobody in this room speaks German. You are all a bunch of ignorant Frogs. Now, get your asses up and give us the tables, or maybe you would like to step outside with us."

Marcel and the others hurriedly stood and lined up along the wall of the room. Henri headed for the curtain that divided the room from the little kitchen behind it.

"Stop! Stop, I say," One of the young Germans shouted.

"I'm only going to get you some baguettes and civet de lapin," Henri answered.

The young German got in front of Henri, pulled the curtain aside with his revolver drawn, and looked through the curtain, "Mein Captain, there is no one back here except a fraulein who is cooking the rabbit."

Soon, a heavyset young woman came through the curtain from the kitchen carrying a heavy pot. Henri followed her carrying bowls and spoons. The woman sat the pot on a table, took off the lid, and started ladling out the rabbit stew.

Just then, we heard a tinkle of a bell as someone came in the back door to the kitchen. All the Germans were out of their chairs standing with their revolvers drawn as Isabelle parted the curtain and walked into the little dining room.

"Claudette—Oh, Mon Dieu," she exclaimed as she saw the Germans. The basket she was carrying flew out of her hands and fell to the floor. Two plump rabbits scampered across the floor.

The captain scooped up the one nearest him by its ears and laughed, "Ah, Mademoiselle here is your bunny!" he laughed as the rabbit was kicking wildly. "What are you doing here?"

Isabelle hesitated, looked at Marcel, and then at the captain, "I brought Claudette two of my rabbits to make stew."

The captain took two steps toward her, "Ah, someone as *delicta et beau* as you should not be out alone."

Henri thought Marcel was going to choke as he tried so hard to not laugh aloud.

"I live here, Monsieur, and I know how to get around my town," Isabelle answered the cocky captain.

"Ah, and she has some spunk! Now go away, you are bothering us as we eat our lunch. We must be on our way to Brest as quickly as possible."

Marcel noticed that the captain watched Isabelle through the curtained window of the little cafe as she walked down the street and through the open gateway to her house.

Henri kept bringing them bottles of wine which the captain first pooh poohed as being a little better than piss.

Henri glanced at Marcel, and it was his turn to choke back laughter because he knew Marcel was thinking the same that he was.

Finally, they all departed. Someone slid the cabinet away, and I walked up the steps out of the dark into the dining room. We watched through the windows as the water on the stones in the street whirled up from their cycle wheels.

Henri went out into the narrow street and watched as the cycles went out the Porte Saint Michel.

I took Marcel aside and told him what I had seen through the tiny crack in the basement door.

"Are you certain, Alain?"

"Yes, that Captain was wearing the same pair of boots as the captain that would certainly have shot all of us when I went on the trip with Henri. One of the toes of the boots has a ripped place that no amount of shining can cover. If Jacque hadn't raised a ruckus, we probably would have been found, and he would have shot us."

15

On the Route des Marais

Ambush

About an hour later, we heard one of the cycles coming back toward us.

"I knew it! I told you so. He's coming back to make out with Isabelle," Henri exclaimed.

"And we are ready for him," Marcel said quietly.

During the hour we had waited, we positioned ourselves behind some shrubs and in the chest-high thick grass that covers the bank below the road and above an old salt lagoon. All the paludiers had places they had pressed down in the tall grass so they could take naps, or breaks, from their strenuous work, so most of us crouched down in them.

The grass was wet and itched me as I tried to wipe the salt from my face and arms. It was futile and I knew I must be still and quiet.

Maybe the heaviest squall we have had all night suddenly lashed in from the Atlantic. It poured down so heavy that I could barely see the Marsh Road thirty or so feet above us.

I heard and then saw the lone cycle as its shining headlamp showed us where it was, Marcel stood up from his hiding place in the thick marsh grass.

"Why have you returned?" he demanded.

It startled the captain for a Frenchman had never dared to speak that way to him in the last four years, "Get your miserable ass out of my way," the captain growled as he got off his cycle and stood on the edge of the road above. He attempted to open the snap on the leather holster to draw his revolver.

Bursts of gunshots filled the air. The captain had one brief look of disbelief as blood shot out of his neck and seeped out, spreading splotches on his uniform in several places.

His body collapsed and fell face first into the old salt pan down below. His back stuck up above the salt-filled water and turned the water a sickening green from his blood.

We jumped from our hiding places, and Marcel took charge. "Henri and Alain push his cycle down into that salt pan into the deepest part. Lift his body up and fill his pockets and uniform with the biggest rocks you can find, and then hold him down until he sinks. You other two, clean up the road so nothing looks out of place. Hurry, for the others may have heard those shots and will be headed back this way. Hurry!"

We had barely finished as best we could when we heard the motors coming toward us again in the heavy downpour. This time, two of the cycles hung back from the other four—the one with the sidecar had a machine gun mounted on it now. They were not cautious as they approached our hiding place because they probably thought we were still back in the village.

The Marsh Road directly above us is the widest point as it goes over the salt lagoons. We had started construction on a deck where we could load salt onto the wagons and haul it back into the warehouse.

The first cycle slowed down and then stopped. The motor's panting put all of us on edge, and I felt one of us would give us away as the tension filled us. The other three caught up with it, and the five young Germans were talking among themselves. The machine gun was pointed straight ahead—not toward us at all.

Marcel yelled at the top of his lungs as he stood and started firing his gun, and we all stood at once and shot as many rounds as we could. We had caught them off-guard, and it was quickly over.

As Henri went up the bank toward the road, one of the young soldiers was crying in pain. I came up beside them and looked down to see a young kid who should have been back in his hometown going to school and wasting too much time with a pretty girl to have good grades.

He cried, "Please, please…. I am my mother's only son. Please let me live to go back to her. Oh, it is you…." Henri raised his revolver, pressed it against the soldier's head, pulled the trigger, and the young German's crying stop abruptly.

Red matter splattered on my pant leg and into the salt grass. I turned away and spit out my breakfast and an awful mouthful of sour tasting coffee.

Marcel once again took charge, "Get all of this into the pan with the captain. Sink everything as deep as you can. We must get salt from those piles that we raked up earlier this week.

Completely fill this pan. Let's just hope it's big and deep enough for all of them. Let's make it look like it is never used, and we are fixing it for a loading deck—just like we have planned. We must finish it today. I'll go to town and get some more help and tell Isabelle what has happened here. Others may be coming, and we must be ready."

A dozen of us worked most of the day carrying watery salt and filling the salt pan and then driving pilings deep into the clay bottom of it to hold the deck. By sunset, the deck was finished. If someone didn't know, it appeared the lagoon had always been full of old dirty salt and that the deck was old too as the wood we had used was old barn wood. The heavy rain pelted it so hard that everything looked smooth and undisturbed.

"I want to sit down on the rocks, if that's okay," I said. No one objected, so I walked the paths that are built to dam the water between several lagoons until at last I walked out onto the edge of the high mound where the Vilaine River slips out into the Atlantic.

I don't know how long I sat there staring out into the horizon. The moon was full as the storm had passed by, and it reflected down into the water way out there in the Atlantic. Closer into shore, waves crashed into the boulders several hundred yards south of me with a smash that should have irritated me, I guess, but it seemed to sooth my mind.

Something caused me to turn and look behind me back at the salt marshes, and I saw Isabelle headed toward me.

"Can I sit with you?"

"Of course."

"That was a horrible thing you had to do. War is never good, and we promised that the last one would be the last, but we were like cows going into the same stall when we let them into the shed to be milked. Hitler sold us a horrendous lie, but we saw how prosperous Germany was getting, and until he showed his real colors, we didn't do anything but 'chew our cuds.'"

"The part of me that I can't remember keeps me from knowing what you were just talking about."

"I know, and I don't know how to tell you all of it at one time.

It will just take time if that is your choice."

"I've told you I wouldn't know where to go. I have no place to go back to."

She inched closer to him on the slab of rock and slid her hand under his and squeezed it hard.

He leaned toward her and the clean smell of her stirred a new feeling in him.

"Alain, look at that moon out there. It is huge tonight and fills the Atlantic with its light as far as we can see. There is no storm out that far and the clouds just frame it calling it to our attention. I feel so terrible knowing that someone somewhere might be looking at it, guessing about what happened to you and not being able to do anything about it."

"The Atlantic looks calmer than it did a few minutes ago. How it shines in that patch of clear sky. Yes, it would be nice to know what all it can see, but I don't think I will ever know."

Isabelle looked up at him and saw his squared chin and those extraordinary dark eyes.

He sensed she was staring at him, and he turned to meet her stare.

Then he leaned down, raised her head a little higher, and smiled at the beautiful woman before him.

He pulled her closer and kissed her.

16

Mose

A Few Years ago, Today, and then a Long Time Ago

Mylee, who lives two houses down from Miss Camelia, had appeared one day after American troops started coming home from another war—a still stranger place in Camelia's mind, a place called Vietnam that was clear across the world from the war Jere had gone to. At first, Camelia disliked Mylee very much.

She disliked that house, for it was the only one on the street that wasn't hers. For some reason she could not remember, her father had sold it in the 1940's, and now it was a rental house that caused a thorn in her side.

Then one day, she opened her front door to find Mylee standing there with part of her daily catch from the Gulf. Mylee, in her polite diminutive way had said that Mister Dolph usually took part of her catch and paid her well for it, but she could not find him that day.

Camelia was always amazed that the little woman would get in that tiny John boat with its little-bitty motor, cross the black water of the Sound, climb over the perimeter stone wall that encloses the La Mancha—the wall Them Three call the ramparts around their battle-ground—and fish in the Gulf almost every day.

That day, Mylee's happy cheerful face beamed up at her, and forgiveness flooded through her heart. *Maybe, the Lord in Heaven has sent this woman to me to be my friend* in *place of my Jeremiah*. She seldom called him Jeremiah, for he didn't like to be called that.

She thought to herself that she wanted to meet the Prof some- time, maybe sit down with him and have some tea.

She sure wasn't goin over there—she never had in all her years— and she wouldn't in the few years she had left. She even cringed when Justin drove her over the humped-up Brooks Bridge on one of the few times she had gone into Destin. That trip had scared her, and besides now she couldn't say, almost in a prideful way, that she never had been further away from home than over at Navarre.

I would like to know how all those things are connected to each other. Mose always did say that my nosiness would get me in trouble someday.

Justin knows the Prof, he says. Said he had some dealings with him last year at the bank about a strange account that had a bunch of money added to it one day and that hadn't had any activity for a long time. Said he also had dealings with the Prof before about a much bigger account. Says the Prof is a good man and that I shouldn't worry about Zathan going over to his place on the island.

Mose zoomed back into her mind. Was he the reason Okaloosa Island scared her so.

She was in one of her usual places in her rocker on the front porch.

I'm not good for nothin it seems lately but sittin and watchin and dependin on others to help me do things I always done before. We sure is havin too much rain. Seems like ever July is the same.

This one is different though, cause there's wind and we never have wind in July. Lightnin and gully washers three days a week hap- pen in all the Julys I can remember, but not the winds....

Beating with a fierce staccato pounding that had no rhythm— the rain pounded her tin front porch roof. It wasn't a July rain that came suddenly, dropped a heavy downpour, and disappeared usually to the North, in ten minutes.

She had insisted the old roof be replaced sometime in the early 2000's because she loved the sound of the rain on the roof, but this rain hurt her ears.

She watched as the cracks around the flat stones of the walkway up to her house filled with dirty water, ran off the edge of her lawn, and soon filled the gully down her side of the lane. The real stream, she saw, was coming down the drain spouts. They were so full she was worried the gutters would soon be overflowing.

The stream broke out into the street down at the end of her lane, and she knew that the dirt patches on the way up to God's house would be muddy soon.

She pulled the tattered green blanket she allowed herself to use on the front porch, up over her head, and some of the sound was drowned out, but a flash of lightning and an immediate blast of thun- der were hardly over before the front screen door closed behind her. She shook a little and turned to see that one of the trees in her folk's old place down at the end of the lane had been split down the middle clear to the ground.

She almost fell into the front room's rocker and started rocking back and forth with a stern determination. Relax, she thought, or Dr. Arbogast will read you the riot act when you must see him in a few weeks.

She slowed down, and a few minutes later, her head slumped over on one shoulder.

"You shud know better young missy! You can't run with that stick and wheel on this rocky dirt road."

She looked up, and Mose was smiling down at her. He helped her to her feet, pulled his handkerchief out of the pocket of his bib overalls and wiped the dirt and few drops of blood off her skinned knee.

"Whoever flattened that tobacco can and nailed it to your stick didn't do a very good job. No wonder you can't guide your wheel. The can is all crooked."

She didn't have the heart to remind him that just two or three weeks ago, he had made it for her.

"Come on up here and we're goin to read the paper, and I'll tell you some more of the story."

She climbed up beside him on the ancient bench that covered one end of his porch and waited.

"Youse first."

"Which one of these papers do you want to start with?"

"The oldest."

Three papers laid on the end of the bench farthest from him. They had been brought down the Sound to Walton Camp by the mail and cargo boat that came twice a week from Pensacola. She looked at the dates, picked the oldest, got off the bench and sat in the only chair on Mose's porch that had a pillow, because she knew she would be there a while.

"I'm havin a hard time thinkin you can read, you and about ten other Waltons Landing kids. Who would ever believe that Methodist circuit Preacher came on the boat from Pensacola on his way to New Orleans, but broke his leg getting off the mail boat, and stopped here for the whole summer and gathered all you young'uns two days a week and taught you how to read and write, and do your numbers clear up to multiplying?"

Camelia smiled and stuck her bottom jaw up in the air a little like she always does when she is proud of something. *Now, that's somethin Jeremiah Ledbetter can't do cause he was too busy helping Elmer, his daddy, when Preacher Wilson was here. And besides that, I can read Grandma Pearl's Bible by myself. And Shakespeare. Now, that's somethin hard to read. The Bible is hard, but I hear so much of it each week that it's become easy, but Shakespeare…he just knows to dang many words. But I sure like his stories….*

"It's the Pensacola paper, and it's dated two weeks ago, April 4, 1931. It says a whole string of banks have closed their doors because of so many farmers not having any money to pay their loans.

"It also says that unemployment is above 16% for young men across the country."

"No wonder there are so many tramps knocking on doors for a little work or some food," Mose interrupted her. "I bet it gets a lot worse. If it don't rain across them prairies out West, we're goin to be in a real mess."

"Here's a little bit of news that you're not goin to like either."

"What's that?"

"We have a new National Anthem."

"Why won't I like it?"

"Cause you say it is so hard to sing."

"Well, what is it?

"*The Star Spangled Banner.*"

"Good Lord almighty, that's goin to cause some trouble, just you wait and see. It's so dang hard to sing."

"They're completin work on a new building in New York City that's supposed to be the tallest in the world, and they're callin it The Empire State Building.

This other little story says a loaf of bread is 8 cents. I don't guess we care about that cause we never buy bread anyway."

"Mrs. Eutsler loaned me another book last week. It's about a man who breaks a window and takes a loaf of bread. When they catch him, he has to spend nineteen years in prison bustin rocks. It takes place in France way across the ocean from us."

She heard the clanking of a bell and saw a cloud of dust coming down the road toward them, "Goin have to read later. Here comes Elmer Ledbetter hauling some logs over to Cracker's Neck to the sawmill. I'll have to pump some water for the oxen."

"You be careful she doesn't step on your toes. She's still wild, you know."

Elmer's lead ox, Minnie, was the youngest, and Camelia had petted her since she was a little calf. Minnie loved to get her head scratched after plunging her nose into the water trough and filling her stomach.

Camelia strained her eyes toward the wagon, shook her head in a huff, and started priming the pump with quick up-and-down strokes. The water started pouring out into the big wooden trough.

"I see Jeremiah is with him today. You jest be nice to him, you hear?"

"He thinks he's so dang smart being two years older than me. He's just fourteen but treats me like I'm a little kid."

"Boys are like that. Maybe, he's lookin at you different than he did before."

"Phooey! He's skinny, his nose is to dang stuck-up, and his feet are way too big."

"Youse noticed that? Youse noticed his eyes? They is the strangest blue I ever seen. Hazel, I guess you would call them."

Mose laughed, and she felt the blood run to her face. He noticed she kept looking up from the pump toward the wagon.

Have I seen those eyes…jest every time he races through my mind? How could anyone miss those eyes, those outrageous sap- phire eyes—nobody I ever saw had eyes like him…yes, Mose, they are sapphire…and every time he's around, I feel them lookin at me….

As the wagon rolled to a stop, Jeremiah had already jumped down and was carrying buckets of water to the two tail oxen. He'd hold one bucket and then the other under the noses of the two. She couldn't help seeing the muscles cording in his broad shoul- ders. *He's not so skinny anymore. He's getting so dad blame tall too.*

She walked away from the pump and stopped alongside Minnie waiting for her to raise her head out of the water. *She won't ram me on purpose, but I've got to be on the lookout cause she gits so excited when I scratch behind her eyes. Funny how her big floppy ears start waving back and forth when I do that.*

Minnie raised her head up and turned to look at Camelia. She felt the splashes of water streaming down from the big round nose hit her bare feet.

I can't look up to see if he is watching, but I know he is. Him walking around over there in his big old clodhoppers and me walking around barefooted like a little kid.

Minnie seemed to know not to swing her head back and forth as she once had, for Camelia had to dodge the wide sharp horns.

Out of the corner of her eye, she saw Jeremiah start to say some-thing as he stepped toward her a little bit when she reached out and started scratching between Minnie's eyes, but he closed his mouth and took the wooden buckets back to the trough to carry more water to the tail oxen.

Guess he never saw me do that before. Betcha, I'll show him a thing or two before we're through with each other.

She stepped away from Minnie, sat on the edge of the water trough, and swung her long legs around over the edge to wash the sticky sand from between her toes.

Why's he laughing at that? Didn't he ever wash his own big old feet? And why are his pa and Mose laughing?

Then she knew her skirt was well above her knees and that Jeremiah was trying his best to not look at her legs. Her face filled with blood as she swung back around, stood up, and hurried up the steps to the porch.

"Be sure and put the lid on tight when you finish." His pa was still laughing when Jeremiah sat the water buckets down, took a tin lard bucket full of sticky black axle grease, and headed toward one of the large back wheels. He took a brush and daubed the grease into all the creases around the axle. "You get sand in that bucket, and it won't be any good to keep that wheel from squeaking."

Mose and Elmer said some things to each other as the two young people tried their best to keep from looking at each other.

Elmer snapped his whip over the rump of the tail oxen after Jeremiah had swung his long legs up over the side of the wagon and landed on the hard wooden seat, and the wagon slowly moved on down the dirt trail toward Cracker's Neck over at Wright.

Camelia heard a tiny squeak in one of the back axles and smiled to herself.....*so the smarty pants did get some sand in the grease....*

It wasn't gone fifty feet till she raised her head from the newspaper she was now holding as she sat back on Mose's porch and looked straight at Jeremiah's back. She saw him take the floppy felt hat from his head, wipe his forehead on the sleeve of his heavy cotton shirt, and turn to look back at her.

Their eyes met—those piercing strange blue eyes didn't move—and held for several seconds until he suddenly turned back around, and she quickly looked down at the paper on her lap.

Mose was laughing, and she heard Jeremiah's pa laughing, and she was shocked when she heard him say, "You better watch out or you're going to get that big old tally Wacker of yourn in trouble."

She wasn't certain what that meant, but from the kind of laughs she heard, she knew it was a man thing. She cleared her throat and looked at Mose.

"As I said before they came by, there is a strange story in this paper. Up in Tennessee, they hung an elephant named Mary cause she had trampled her trainer. How do you hang an elephant?"

"Lawsie, I don't know, but hanging anything is awful."

"This little bit down in the corner says that strange kind of flu has killed more people than the Great War …the Spanish Flu…. Hope it stays away from our part of the world."

"We been mighty lucky so many times, like when those Grey Coats came down here in 1860 sumthin and sit up what they called Camp Walton to guard the Sound from the Yankees. Nothin hap- pened. They sat around a lot, drank too much stuff they stilled, and got several of our women in family ways."

"My, my, my, Scott Joplin died on April 1 almost fifteen years ago, and they're building a monument to him up in Charleston. I sure like his music. I heard some over at Grandma Pearl's house."

"It's your fault she bought that dang machine—what they call it? A Victrola? She just saw that picture in one of the papers you were readin to her, and you told her all about it. Took over two months to git it down here from somewhere up North, and cost too dang much good money, but she always was that way having to have the best and newest since we was first married."

"You know you like to hear it too."

Anyway, they had all gathered around and listened to every record she had, over and over again. She smiled cause she knew Mose had bought some of those records to surprise Grandma Pearl at special times.

"Alright, it's your turn. I want to hear you tell me again about when Zathan Bordelon rode out of the pine growth on that big Buckskin stallion of his."

"I allow I done told you twenty times."

"Yep, but you always add somethin to it. I want all I can, so I can remember it. So, jest tell it again."

Mose looked at her, shook his head, smiled a little smile, but started telling her again the story she always wanted to hear, "He appeared one day riding that big horse and leading a mule loaded down with everything he owned in the world. How he got all the way from New

Orleans across what was going to be the whole states of Mississippi and Alabama is a mystery to me. They was filled with Spanish at that time that didn't like the settlers in what was to be the United States, and really didn't like the French that they had fought with for control of New Orleans and the Gulf. And Zathan Bordelon was one-hundred percent French. How he got to New Orleans is still a mystery to me, but somehow, he had.

It was 1738 according to my own grandma who told me the stories. How he had run out of the little settlement, New Orleans, which was only a few years old, because he got word the Spanish were coming down the Mississippi to attack again.

"How did he tell anybody here? Who knew how to talk with him?"

"The Spanish had already been here before. They came several times and always with a priest who tried to get the natives to convert. The priests gave out silver crosses on leather thongs to hang around your neck, and the best lookin women got theirs with some bright stones on them—real jewels worth a lot of good money. And some of those women still understood Spanish, and so did Zathan."

"Then?"

"He had his guimbarde with him that the natives had never heard or seen before."

"His what?"

"Oh, so you are learnin somethin new this time. His juice-harp that the French called guimbarde. My great-great grandma Hattie's is still in there on that shelf above the kitchen table."

She hopped up and ran through the back door to return a minute later with the instrument, "Can you play it, Grandpa Mose?"

"Sure can, in fact anyone can." He laid down the heavy cotton seine net he was knittin to catch fish in the Bay. The net was already ten or eleven feet long and several feet tall and strung across the bench and the back of a rocker on his end of the porch.

"Here, you hold this circle part in the cup of one hand, hold it up against your mouth with your lips apart, and flick the twanger back and forth with your tongue. It gets wet and drippy, and that might be one reason we call it a juice-harp. Try it."

She did as he said, and soon she was making the twang-twang-twang sounds that rang across the porch. She giggled as it tickled her tongue every time, she flicked the thin little strip of metal that caused it to vibrate so much in her mouth.

"That's fun, but it all sounds the same to me. How do you make a tune?"

"It's the way you hold your tongue and your lips."

"If he played that thing when he took three or four months to come across from New Orleans, I don't see how he didn't get caught with all that racket. What happened next?"

"He like this place the natives called 'the peaceful shiny place,' so he built a hut out of branches and bark like the ones they lived in, out there closer to the Bay than theirs.

They were all sort of huddled around the Mound over there, but I guess he decided to stay a little away from them.

He wasn't here a week before he traded that mule with the chief for the almost twenty acres we live on now. How he kept it all those years is a mystery, and how we got to keep it during Reconstruction is a bigger mystery, but I guess it's because we are more French and Chatot Indian than anything else.

We're not Creek, not Choctaw, and sure not Seminole, but Chatot. Our people spoke a language that was different than all the others. They called themselves Yuchi or Chiesas and tried to get along with the others around them. Oh, they were fierce enough when they were invaded, but they normally lived in peace on the shores of the Bay."

"He explored the whole area because that's the way he was—he had to know where things were and what was around him—just like you do. He went out in one of the dugouts they had made from a single tree, probably a pine tree because the wood is light, and it has sap the water can't sink into. Somehow, the same young woman went with him—she had to have the chief's permission, so maybe it was all planned? Anyway, he became sweet on her, and they were married before he had been here a year. She was your great-great- great grandma, Hattie."

"He convinced the chief that the Spanish were on their way again, and that this time they were angry with all the settlers who had come into the place. He said that a band of Creeks were with the Spanish and were dealing hard with whoever they caught."

"So, for weeks they carried all the heavy stones they could find, filled three or four of their long dugouts with them and made many trips across the Sound with the dugouts filled so full they were ready to sink. He had ten or twelve pine stumps sharpened into pointed stakes—like pier posts, and on the last trip they loaded all their treasures into the boats and headed across the Sound to that island over there.

They had fresh-water pearls picked out of oysters for the last seventy-five to a hundred years—the big ones they hadn't traded off during that time. There was a large pile of fur-lined pouches full of them. One of the warriors brought out a bag of Spanish coins he had taken when he followed the clanking line of Spaniards when they left the last time. There were bags of carved oyster shell jewelry that the Yuchi are famous for. Not only that, but they also had all those Spanish silver crosses, some of them with valuable stones, that some silly priests gave a pretty woman for a short romp-in-the-hay."

The blood rushed to her face, and Mose apologized, "I forgit I'm not spose to talk to you about making babies and such…Anyway,
they loaded all those things into the dugouts and set out across the Sound to bury it over there. They were gone several days.

One of the scouts that stayed behind on this side saw a party of Creeks get into *Canal de Santa Rosa*, as the Spanish had named it, down toward Pensacola. They were still way up past where Navarre is today, and that gave our ancestors time to load up everybody and many belongings and get into other dugouts and head out across *Bahia de Santa Rosa*—the Bay—they got away without leaving a trail. They went way over to where Valparaiso is now and up into Hidden Cove. It's still called that today."

"Zathan and his band had been gone for three days, and heavy rains had battered the area for all that time. It was pouring down in sheets, blast after blast for days. It must have been in the fall, for as they were finally coming back across the Sound, tremendous winds had surprised them and now the winds howled around them. The Creeks appeared on the water from the west in their skiffs, and the fight was on.

But Mother Nature won. Much of the pine growth from the Island snapped off, and the trunks became jagged spears as they sailed through the air at our people and at the stinking Creeks. A pine dagger went all the way through one of the Creeks and into a Live Oak and crucified him. Dugouts became like little toys as they were thrown high into the air, and men in the act of killing one another were thrown even higher as they struggled to kill.

There was so much death that day, our ancestors and their fierce enemies alike. Men and boats were destroyed, and when it all ended, the Sound was a river of floating bodies, jagged scraps of ripped up pines, and broken dugouts bashing into one another.

Our people's rounded huts were blown into the forest, and when the winds passed, destruction and death filled the whole area.

Great Grandma Hattie and her people returned to a place that was unfamiliar to them as the Mound was the only thing left that they recognized. For weeks, they searched for bodies. They buried the Creeks just as they buried their own. They sang their prayers for their own and for the Creeks. They carefully took that one nailed to the Live Oak and buried him down by the Mound just like he was one of them.

Zathan Bordelon was never found. Grandma Hattie sat on top of the Mound for many days and nights facing the Island across the way until the chief ordered her to return to the hut that had been built for her. Your great grandma was born a few months later.

Hattie, Zathan's wife, just disappeared one-night cause some of the people were saying Zathan ran away with all their treasure."

"Wait, you never told me this before. Zathan Bordelon was never found? Did they go over to the Island and look for him?"

"Sure did, some of the warriors spent many nights over in that Gawd-awful place huddled around fires hoping to find him or his body. They never found him."

"And what about the treasure?"

"They never found that either. It's been many years, and we've had some awful hurricanes, so that stuff is long ago gone."

She sat a minute thinking, "You said, this juice harp was great-great-grandma Hattie's, right? What happened to Zathan's?"

"He wore it around his neck on a leather thong, so it was lost with him, I'm guessin."

"Oh, Mose… This is all new to me. I'm goin to think about it, and I'm goin walk down to Buck's to see if we have any mail, or some newer papers."

"You watch out for those dang new cars. What the heck is a Studebaker and an Oldsmobile? Might git hit if you don't watch out."

"Mose, you know there are only thirty-seven people in Camp Walton, so I don't think I'm going have trouble walkin where I want."

"Things are happenin too dang fast if you ask me. Here we are in a brand-new county—Okaloosa. What the hell does that mean, and why'd they name us that?"

She jerked awake like she had the other morning when Justin caught her in the back yard. She had a crick in her neck. *I must have been excited or something and strained it. I'll get up soon and make some sassafras tea from some of those roots we dug last spring. Maybe that will git my blood goin again.*

Mose and 1931 disappeared, but what he told her weighed heavy on her mind. She knew that today would be a time to mull it all over.

Many hurricanes hit Okaloosa Island over the years, and some of them had been disasters—like Ivan, and especially Opal. Then, there was that strange one in 1926 that just stopped over there on the Island and stalled around for several days until it petered out. That one had whirled around and around and when someone went over there after it was gone, they said nothing was the same as it was before. It has been too long and there has been too much happen over there.…

The Spanish came back again and brought the filthy Creeks with them and nearly destroyed my folks. All those colored folks came down trying to escape for their freedom. Then, the Yanks came but didn't find much they wanted, and didn't stay long. Those dang carpetbaggers that followed them found out soon enough they wasn't wanted. A lot sure has happened, and I'm still in the dark about so many things.

She slapped her right hand with her left, "Camelia Ledbetter, you're acting like you're still twelve, and not over a hundred, so stop it."

17

Remembering Wasted Time

'Monkey-Ward' House

I didn't see Jeremiah for a long time after that embarrassing day at the water trough, but I sure did think about him. I caught glimpses of him down at Buck's store where the Post Office is located. The mail boat comes twice a week, and I was always there by the middle of the afternoon to see it come in and then wait around until they had the mail sorted.

The mail boat also brings all the supplies on it for Camp Walton. Jeremiah would have his team of oxen, with the wagon attached, to haul things off to people who had bought freight. He would be way down at the end of the landing waiting patiently, it seemed, for someone to ask his help.

Minnie would be shakin her big wide head to get the gnats off, I guess.

Maybe he saw me, and maybe he didn't, but I sure knew he was down there. I overheard Mr. Buck laughing that I was showin off for somebody one day, and I was so embarrassed, I turned right around and went back home without ever askin for our mail.

It rained and rained and rained that Spring, so much that the Bay rose clear out of its banks, and the few people who had places down in Destin were scared they were goin to be wiped away. The marshes along the edges of the water all washed away causing us to be afraid the oyster beds would be swept away too, but they weren't.

The lot down at the end of the lane had been empty as long as I can remember until Daddy did the most outrageous thing our little town had heard of. Montgomery Ward was one of the biggest companies in the coun- try then, and, of course, everybody got the 'Monkey Ward' catalog.

They sold houses. I thought Daddy was joshing me when he first told me that, but he wasn't. When my Daddy first told my Mom about it, she laughed until tears filled her eyes. That just made him more determined, so he ordered a house. How in the world do you order a house? Even today, I can't imagine someone ordering a house from Amazon or anyone else. But he did—gave $810 for it. I still have the receipt. I remember the day it arrived on the ferry boat from Pensacola. Nearly all the people who lived in Camp Walton gathered down at Buck's store on the Sound to watch Elmer and Jere unload as much as they could into their wagon and head toward our little street. They had to make a bunch of trips.

I didn't go down there to see it unloaded but decided to hide in 'my tree' down on the vacant lot. That big old Live Oak must have been a hundred years old then, and everyone knows that the limbs on Live Oaks sometimes grow out almost horizontally above the ground.

My tree had a long limb that jutted out of the main trunk about ten or twelve feet above the ground, and there was a hollowed-out place where it came out from the trunk. I had found out several sum- mers before that I could shimmy up there and lay in that hollowed-out place and be hidden from everybody. It was my secret place.

When Jere and his dad arrived with wagon after wagon loads which were piled high with lumber and boxes that I would learn was all the parts needed to put together that house, I kept real quiet and watched them by peeking over the limb I was layin on.

He's gettin so big and strong, I thought. I scoffed at myself for thinkin about him that way cause I thought why in the world would he want anything to do with me?

He took great big strides as he passed back and forth under my tree carrying loads that had him almost bending over. When he went back for another load, he walked straight and tall almost with some pride. His dark black hair shone in the sun, and rivulets of sweat ran down his fresh-shaven suntanned cheeks.

But the thing that caused me to blush every time when he would be lookin up toward me were those bright, dark sapphire eyes.

No, what would that good lookin man want with me—a dark-skinned Indian girl? But don't sell yourself short, I told myself. He looks at you and you know it.

They worked almost all day, and I think my legs went to sleep from not moving. I needed to pee so bad but knew I wasn't about to climb down from my tree and let him know I'd been up there all day. I heard him tell Elmer that was the last load as he went past the tree toward where they had piled the lumber and boxes. I felt a big relief go through me, but as he came back toward the wagon, he stopped under the tree, pulled a bandana from his back pocket, and stood wiping the sweat from his face and neck.

Then he said, "Looks like someone has been polishing her toe-nails." He walked over, got up on the wagon, rattled the harness at the oxen, and Minnie led them away.

I thought I was gonna lay there and die. It was after dark when I did get down from there, make my way back down to my house, the one that's the rental house now.

They worked all summer putting the 'Monkey Ward' house together, and never once did I go down to see what they were doin. Mose wanted to know why, and I said I wasn't interested.

Then, one Sunday, he appeared in church. We met in Uncle Paul's barn then as we didn't have a true church house. We sat in rows, of many kinds of chairs, like we were in a church, and I had turned around to see who was present that day, and there he was sitting two rows behind me. I jerked myself around, grabbed the hymn book from my lap where I had put it, and started turning pages way too fast. Grandma Pearl shushed me, 'You're making a lot of racket.' Mose leaned up so he could look at me as Grandma Pearl was sitting between us and said, 'Don't do no good to look behind you cause you can't see past that row of big old hats right behind us.'

All the women wore hats those days, and it seemed each one was trying to outdo the next one. I was too young then, but now it seems I'm the only one in God's house with a hat on. Things change.

The next Sunday as we were walking over to Uncle Paul's, I kept saying, 'We're goin to be late.' We got there and went to our usual seats. A few minutes later, I turned in my seat only to hear Grandma Pearl whisper, 'Oh, he's here. He came in right after we did.' I opened my Bible and pretended to be reading as I heard her laughing into that handkerchief she always carried in her left hand. I almost got up and went home.

To make matters worse, Mose stepped over and started talkin with Jeremiah welcoming him to church after the service was over. He talked about everything in the world asking about people I had never heard of then, and all I could do was stand on one foot and then switched to the other. I thought Jeremiah was feeling the same as he kept fidgeting like I saw him do many times later on.

Things were busy for both of us, I guess, cause I didn't see him for months. But, one night, there was a knock on Grandma Pearl's door, and I went to open it. There he stood looking ever bit as good as I thought as I lay in my bed every night. He almost stuttered as he said, 'I was wondering if maybe you would like to go the pie social with me?'

I thought I was going to fall through the floor as I muttered, "I would like that."

"How am I goin to know which box is yours?" he asked me as I settled onto the wooden seat of his dad's wagon when he picked me up two nights later.

"Oh, I bet you will know, I said."

He shook the harness at the two horses, and they moved out toward Uncle Paul's barn.

He spent fifty-five cents on my pie-box. I was embarrassed about that cause no other box brought that much money into our 'church-building' fund. He didn't have any trouble knowing which my box was cause I put that big camellia on the top.

Seems like he was everywhere I was from then on. I would go to get the mail down on the dock at Buck's store, and he would be waiting for some freight or just sittin there watchin me walk down the ramp to the dock. Sometimes he waved a little wave at me, and sometimes I guess he was too busy and didn't see me.

Finally, Mose said one day that I ought to invite him to eat with us the next Sunday. I was horrified, but finally agreed. Grandma Pearl said I had to fix Sunday dinner too, so then I was really scared. Turns out, it was a set-up between the three of them, and Jere knew all along I was goin to ask him.

He ate more fried chicken, brown beans, corn on the cob, and cornbread than everyone else, and then put away the biggest helping of peach cobbler that I could get into his bowl.

He smiled after he was finished, and said, "That was a prime dinner, Miss Camelia."

I hurriedly cleared the dishes from the table without even saying a thank-you.

18

My Name is Ollie

Almost eight years ago in Launie Sanderson's strip joint.

The hard board of the bench behind the screen dug into his muscular thighs. His whole rear end felt like it was asleep.

He was tired of having to sit night after night behind the silly-looking oriental screen while Launie's girls enticed the johns to stuff money into their skimpy outfits.

The *ka-bang, ka-bang, ka-boom* of the drums grated in his head. He remembered another music, a music he loved, and it gradually took over his mind as he fell asleep…

"Spunk!"

"Spunk! You hear me? You get your sneakin skinny ass away from there. I can see you through that keyhole. I'm gonna pound you good! You hear me?"

He jumped back from the keyhole he was looking through and ran back down the hall as quick as his four-year-old legs would take him to his bed in the closet under a stairway. He had lived there all his life and didn't even know his real name.

It is a party! A party for me!!

"Blow!"

"It has five candles, Winnie! Am I five now?"

I'm not allowed to cry ever. My door is locked from the inside. I play with my toys the 'johns' bring me.

Winnie, you put thirteen candles on this time.

Winnie cleaned out the 'cribs' every day. She was really the only one who had paid any attention to him. She would shake her head and he could hear her mutter, "Honey, no kid should live in a place like this.

"Run, Spunk! Run!"

He ran down the street to the big park that has the arch that lights up at night. He marched in step with the bronze statues of figures that look a lot like Winnie's people.

Their solid forms look like they are twisting and turning to their music. He ran around the statues with the horns and tambourines and trombones and trumpets, and then ran around and around the whole procession pretending to be the leader jabbing a pretend cane up and down.

He mimicked the twisting and turning, and the cane kept time to the jazz that filled his memory.

He heard the music of that band swaying down the street to a funeral— the swaying of the leader with his fancy hat and the mourn- ful wail of the instruments.

He had the hat! He led the dirge as they marched along but above it all he heard the trumpet—Satchmo's trumpet.

He ran to the part of the park he liked best because that was where all the dancing and music was. He found the people he liked there; Winnie's people, and Creoles, and Cubans, and nearly whites like himself. Congo Square!

But I sit in my favorite place at the edge of the pond. I throw bread to the ducks. Pops Armstrong, the baddest dude of them all, stares at me blindly from his big statue.

Those kids are always passing by with their arms full of books.
"Why aren't you going to school? Mitch asked him.

"I'm not nobody. I got no name, and they don't even know I'm here."
"That isn't an excuse. You know how to read?"
"No, Suh."
"Well, I'm goin to teach you to read."

Mitch pulled out that old, tattered book that had a little boy, a little girl, and a little spotted dog on the front of it.

Who the hell was Mitch? What was he, an old white man, doing here in Satchmo's Park?

And then Spunk could read the words, "See Spot? See Spot run?"

He went anywhere he wanted now and knew everybody in the Old Storyville district. Not too many people called the area that anymore, but the old timers did, and they were the ones Spunk listened to. He found out if he went to the back door of almost any joint, bar, or café in the area he could get enough food to last the whole day.

The streetcar lurched around a corner, and he bounced in the seat as it rumbled over some ancient Live Oak roots. He rode all the way over to Prytania Street and saw a movie.

The Prytania Theater showed classic movies, had only one screen, and was the trickiest one to sneak into. But after his third or fourth trip over there, the old man at the door just waved him on inside.

The Green Arrow! He sat through it seven times, and when he left the theater, he would forever be known as Ollie, named by himself after Oliver Queen who played the Green Arrow.

Who is this Katrina bitch? Why was everybody talking about her? Somebody said she was out in the Gulf and headed toward the city. Gonna make a grand entrance, I guess. Highfalutin Diva!

He awoke in the movie theater as huge guns shot their Nazi shells out across the English Channel from a pretty little town called Calais trying to hit high cliffs, that looked like chalk to Ollie, at Dover twenty-six miles away. *The News Reel* had three U Boats riding high in the shallow water as they came out of their shed at St. Nazaire. They reminded Ollie of Vikings gliding down to slip into the Atlantic Ocean on their way to destroy whatever they met.

His seat shook, and he realized the old theater was shaking in another wind. He ran for the door.

The old man was not in the little lobby. Fact was, no one was in the theater except him. He grabbed a bag of popcorn as he ran through the front door. The howling wind grabbed it and the kernels looked like specks of fire as they shot through the air. By the time he was on the street, water was almost up to his ankles.

Trouble Ollie, trouble...

Gotta get to 10. Long ways to 10, but 10 will be high up off the ground.

He passed Lil Dizzy's.

"Lots of food in there. Just sittin there to be taken," somebody, running by him, yelled.

He whirled around and enter the front door—first time he ever did that.

He stuffed the backpack Mitch had given him, which he always wore cause it had all his possessions in it, with pork chops, cat- fish, collard greens cooked almost to mush, and dozens of pieces of Dizzy's famous fried chicken. Grease covered Dick and Jane, but he didn't see it. He grabbed a quart container of gumbo as he went out the door.

Running along Esplanade as fast as he could in the ankle-deep water, he reached a high place where there was no water on the street and as he turned a corner around a big building, he came face to face with them.

They must have been stranded on the high place for some time for they snarled, raised their heads in the air, bared their teeth. He didn't take time to count them, but the leader was a big dirty hound that snarled and howled in a higher pitch than the others. They charged at him as they smelled the food.

He hit the Pit Bull right between its eyes with the quart of gumbo. It burst open and the Pit Bull was not in the chase anymore. He ran back as fast as he could with the heavy load, and as he reached a fire escape ladder that had been pulled to the ground, he jumped up grabbing it with one arm while desperately holding on.

The High Yeller leaped at him at the same time and ripped a gash in his left calf. Ollie yelled in pain, felt a fear he had never known, and scrambled up until he was at the top of the six-story building.

He turned to look down, and past the snarling pack of dogs, he saw huge waves of water rolling down almost every street at him. He struggled, threw himself over the parapet that encircled the roof, and landed at Launie's feet.

"Ollie! Ollie, wake up! You're sleeping again."

He felt the sharp pain in his calf and jerked upright on the stool. Kitty, one of Launie's girls, kicked him again with her high wedged heels. She was standing there holding out a Styrofoam container from *Tides Inn*. Ollie smelled the fish.

When Katrina caused the move to Fort Walton Beach, Launie couldn't just leave Ollie behind. She had seen him in the streets of New Orleans before and knew who he was when he landed at her feet.

They had been on that building for three days and nights and the food in Ollie's backpack had been most of what the thirteen of them had to eat until the helicopter pilot had finally seen them.

Ollie's job is to act as a deterrent to any trouble which might happen inside the strip joint, the bouncer. He sits on the high stool behind a screen in a back corner of the big room and appears to be in some other world. But, if a customer becomes rowdy or too com- plaining about something, he feels Ollie's big hand on his shoulder as he is guided to the exit.

Several rowdy tough guys have challenged Ollie who is barely five-eight, but they find in a flash that he is strong as a young bull as they go flying out the front door. Launie has warned him several times that she doesn't want a ruckus that will get the police to come. When they can persuade him to come out from behind the screen, the girls take Coke cans to Ollie for him to smash. The customers get a kick out it too.

He doesn't play the game of smashing it against his head, even though that would not have hurt him, but he cups the can in his hand putting the bottom in his palm and wrapping his fingers around the top. He doesn't seem to exert any energy as the can flattens to a thin disk in his palm.

Hundreds of the flattened cans are tacked along the top of the mirror behind the bar. The customers always ask what they are, and then turn to gaze at the screen. Most nights Ollie never leaves his stool, and not too many locals have ever seen him.

The Dorm is a remarkable building behind the place where the girls dance—the place Launie has given the silly name 'The Gentlemen's Library'—as it has stood through at least three hurricanes.

Originally the whole plot of land that sticks out on a peninsula where the Sound empties into the Choctawhatchee Bay, had been a beautiful summer home that belonged to a large family from Atlanta. The kids had begged for a place to bring their pet rabbits with them, so a rabbit hutch had been constructed behind the big house. The doctor's wife spent money with abandon on all the projects she undertook, so the hutch was really a two-room building—one for the bucks and one for the does.

When Launie moved in, she built a bathroom adjacent to one of the rooms, and the little building became Ollie's home.

Ollie's one interest in life is to shoot his bow and arrows.

His Carbon Express Intercept crossbow which cost him over a $1000 is his prized possession. He found out one day it would shoot one of his steel-tipped arrows through the hull of an old, abandoned boat.

Even Ollie realizes he is obsessed with the Green Arrow. One night as he was watching his TV in his little room, he happened across the new Arrow series and now each Wednesday night he disappears for an hour. Everyone knows to not bother him.

He had begged and pleaded with Launie for days until she gave in and built an enclosure behind his little house. It looks like a base- ball bullpen from the outside except the walls are so high no one can see over them and the thuds of the arrows he shoots into the target sound like baseballs hitting a glove to anyone passing by.

Launie pays Ollie once a week in cash and he waits anxiously each week for his money so he can order more archery equipment on Amazon.

One of the girls, Ester, who Ollie talks with more than any other person takes his cash to Security Bank and deposits it for him.

He is astounded that he only has to put in some numbers and push enter, and then he marvels when a box arrives with his name on it. It is like something fell out of the sky to him. Launie might have shown more interest if she had known the arsenal Ollie is accumulating.

Launie thought from the beginning that Ollie was almost retarded and would be easy to control if she offered him the right things. She soon found out that Ollie really isn't retarded; he's just antisocial. He just wants to be alone. When he discovered her laptop, she was genuinely surprised how quickly he learned how to work it.

He spends hours now on his own computer in his little room admiring his one interest in life, Oliver Queen and his adventures.

The girls take care of Ollie like he is their protective brother. Since Launie believes none of the local folks know about Ollie, they bring all his food in for him. During the eight years Launie has been in Fort Walton, Ollie hasn't been out on the street.

At least that's what Launie believes, but she doesn't know his secret place down in the vacant space where no houses have been built along the Sound; a place left vacant so that storm waters have a ditch to drain into the Sound. Ollie slips out, usually in the nighttime after Launie's closes, and goes to his 'hideout,' a cave he has dug high on the bank of one of those channels.

19

Prospecting on the Beach

Launie Sanderson's first mistake—Retribution Ahead

Ollie was terrified more than he had ever been except when the Yeller dog had ripped his leg open as he hung from the fire escape trying to escape the water and chaos of Hurricane Katrina.

And now Launie had put him out near Angler's Pier east of the La Mancha, with a silly looking device which he certainly didn't know how to operate, but that she had told him to carry, just so and so, and to turn the red light on.

She bought him a hat with a green band which he was delighted with. She told him that he was to look for a package about the size of his shoe box and bring it right to her if he found it.

She warned him to keep moving the long handle of the device she had given him back and forth across the sand, but to watch all around him for the box. She told him under no circumstances was he to go beyond the red sign that he would see.

Ollie was scared, but no one seemed to pay attention to him. He had never been on this beach before.

He didn't want to get the sand between his toes. It felt nasty to him like chicken-shit he had stepped in once.

As he looked down the beach, he saw all kinds of people that he had never noticed before.

Up ahead was another man with a device like the one Launie had given him this morning. The man was moving it back and forth along the sand, so Ollie started copying him. When the two of them were side by side, the other man asked if he had found anything, and Ollie said no, but that he was looking for the box. The other man looked at him with a strange look.

He saw two small children who were filling plastic buckets with sand and carrying them to where they were building a castle. Ollie was intrigued and walked toward them. They stopped and stared at him and when he offered to carry sand for them, they agreed. About an hour later they had a large, but crude castle, built several feet from the shoreline.

The little boy took a bucket and ran to the water, brought it back and poured water in the moat they had created. Ollie was delighted. For the next half hour, he carried bucket after bucket of water for the moat. Grown-ups sitting in Cam's chairs, or lying on towels on the sand, became concerned that Ollie was getting too involved with the two children.

One lady asked, "Are you they're uncle?"

He shook his head back and forth several times, "No, I sure am not. I'm just looking for the box."

Then Ollie sat on the sand and created a huge arrow which looked distinctly like the ones he had in his arsenal. The father of the two children walked over and took them away.

He was disappointed and anger started building up inside him. He kicked the castle into a pile of sand, fell on his knees, and scoop big hands full of sand into the moat.

He destroyed all they had built except the arrow. Several people moved from the area where he was, and the father went to talk to Cam about the strange man who had just turned 'dangerous' he said.

Ollie knew enough to leave and started walking west again, saw the red sign, and was relieved that he could turn around and go back. He saw a brown box wrapped in burlap sticking up out of the sand just beyond the sign. He hesitated because he had been told to not go past the sign. But Ollie made a decision, stepped past the sign, pulled the box out of the sand and started walking back east.

Now everyone was staring at him. Cam started toward him, saw that Ollie was leaving and turned and walked away.

Ollie came to the ramp at the La Mancha's gazebo, hesitated, but then turned to walk up to the gazebo; his instinct told him it was the way out to Santa Rosa Blvd.

As he left the gazebo and was walking down the walk, a little dog stuck its head through the railing of one of the balconies on the third floor of the Dolphin Building and started barking furiously at Ollie.

He threw the metal detector down and ran for the parking lot as fast as he could. He was terrified and furious.

Launie had been driving up and down the Blvd for almost two hours wondering what had happened to Ollie when she saw him emerge from the lane at the entrance of La Mancha. She pulled up beside him and began to praise him when she saw he had the box.

Her need for the stuff in the box caused her to speed all the way down the Blvd and go through a yellow light at 98. She parked behind the Dorm and rushed inside with the box.

Ollie went to his rooms behind the Dorm, dressed in his full Green Arrow uniform, the plaid green shirt, and faded jeans, fitted the night-vision goggles around his neck, armed himself with as many quivers of arrows as he could, and started out down the Blvd. He had studied hard while they had just driven up it to remember where to go. The first shots he took were at the tires of the fire trucks at the station just across Highway 98. He beamed with glee as he saw three tires deflate to the ground.

He ran down the Blvd nearly getting hit by a pickup truck as he paid no attention to the traffic. He turned in anger and shot several arrows into the approaching traffic. A number of cars swerved into a low ditch by the road there, and two crashed into each other.

By this time Ollie was excited more than he could remember as he started running. He shot out all six windows at the Tom Thumb as he went by.

Then he stopped and decided he didn't want to play anymore. He headed north on one of the side streets and found his way back up behind *Tides Inn*, slipped across the 98, and disappeared down the drainage ditch to his hideout.

J C and the Okaloosa County deputies conducted a house-to- house search far into the night, but no one seemed to know who they were looking for. Scores of people described the spectacle from as many points of view, but none had seen where he had gone as they were all hiding. The descriptions varied from a young kid with a mask to a man with a crossbow.

20

I don't have the answers you seek. I'll be here though.

Confusion at Isabelle's breakfast table

We sat in Isabelle's kitchen around her table eating a breakfast of croissants, jam made of grapes from Father Jean's vineyard, and drinking what was supposed to be coffee. It was about as bad as could be.

Henri had returned from wherever he had gone, and I thought yesterday that those two men I saw him with by Marcel's fence were gone also.

"We got news the bastard has committed suicide with his woman in a bunker just outside Berlin, so maybe the nightmare is ending," Henri said with a sigh.

"What? You say Hitler is dead?" Marcel suddenly was awake and not staring at his coffee cup with dread.

"That's the news I heard when I delivered those two."

"Oh God, let it be so." Isabelle whispered.

Henri had pulled a package of cigarettes from his pants pocket and offered one to each of us as we sat there. He laid the package on the table, and I saw that the writing on it was strange to me—not English and not French that Father Jean was so patiently teaching me. I picked up the package and, as I did, I felt the eyes of the other three staring at me.

"I don't know what writing this is," I said as I looked at Henri. "That's Spanish," he said as he started one of his coughing fits.

I waited until he quit coughing and noticed the other two were looking at him with feelings I didn't understand and then asked, "Where in the world would you get Spanish cigarettes?"

Isabelle interrupted, "It's time we told you just what Henri does when he is gone so often. He takes Brits and Yanks and anyone else who is in trouble with the Nazis and leads them to Saint Nazaire and across the bay there and turns them over to some other brave men up from Spain, who leads them down across the Pyrenees to that young woman who takes them to the coast and freedom. Now that things seem to be winding down, we must be very careful...."

Marcel, Henri, and Alain glanced at each other, and Marcel shook his head a little and frowned. Alain realized he mustn't let Isabelle learn that he had gone with Henri that time.

She hesitated and almost choked over her next words. "Remember we saw those big planes this week when we were sitting on the rock overlooking the Atlantic? Those were Yankee planes flying down to Saint Nazaire to bomb the U Boat docks."

I looked at Marcel and Henri, but neither of them looked like they were going to interrupt her,

"Those were B-17s, Alain, B-17s," she repeated clearly to me. "Those are Yankee planes like the one that crashed the morning Marcel and Henri found you naked in the river. Did you not have any feelings when they flew over?"

"I knew what they were because you all have told me before. I thought they were going to bomb the Germans, but that's all."

Marcel said, "That's all? You didn't have one of those glimpses I see you do once in a while?"

"No. Why?"

Isabelle continued, "Because we know you had to have a life somewhere, and we don't know what to do about you. If you go with Henri on what may be his last trip, who do we give you to? The Brits? The Yanks? Or are you a lost Frenchmen who was running for your life from the Nazis when we found you."

"I just don't know. I've told you all so many times that I don't know. You two found me naked as a baby in that river, so how can I ever know what happened before? I have glimpses as Marcel says of things that poke my mind with something, but I don't know what."

Isabelle looked straight at me, "What do we do, Alain? What do you want us to do?"

"I don't know. Where would I go? I have been here for over three years, and I still don't know who I am. I don't want to go anywhere."

I felt Isabelle exhale and relax. I saw that Marcel had a look of agreement in his eyes. Henri looked at me and smiled at me, maybe for the first time since I've been here.

Marcel sat a long time at the table when the other three were gone. He thought Alain was innocent, or maybe ignorant was a better word, because he really didn't know anything but what had happened since they found him in the river.

Henri didn't care one way or the other as he had always kept his distance from Alain, but not more than he kept his distance from everyone except his family.

Marcel thought, "I really don't have any say in the matter even though Alain would agree with me if I did express my opinion, but I won't. I want him to stay, but I wonder what he's giving up staying here?"

His thoughts turned to Isabelle. He grinned as he thought about the many late evenings, he had seen her and Alain sitting on the big granite slab facing out to the Atlantic. His mind turned to other things they might have been doing, but so far there was no evidence of that. But he knew that Isabelle was keeping to herself about things like fingerprints and pictures and identification that would take Alain away from them. For now, he decided he would remain quiet also.

When I left Isabelle's house, I went to the Abbey to find Father Jean. The old priest was sitting at a potter's wheel holding the clay on the wheel with both hands as he molded the wet clay. He looked up from his wheel and said, "You want to try this?"

I shook my head and sat down in a chair across from him, "No, I want to talk with you and don't want to have to think about what my hands are doing."

"Bon, for now, but I want you to learn how to form the clay. What is it you want to talk about this time?"

"Isabelle, Marcel, and Henri all talked to me about going with Henri when he makes his next trip," Alain said.

He noticed that Father Jean did not flinch at all when he said Henri's next trip, so he thought Father Jean knew about taking the soldiers to Spain for their freedom. And hadn't the strangers always worked for Father Jean until they were not around anymore?

"And what do you want me to tell you?"

"I don't know. I'm mixed-up inside. What if I go with Henri and run into a terrible mess that I don't have answers for? What if I don't go and never find out that I am being looked-for by a family I have somewhere?"

"My friend, I don't have those answers for you. I don't believe anyone does. I believe you need to go out on that big rock and figure this out. You just might want to ask a Higher Source what to do."

"I have sat in your church now many times, and I don't know what I believe, for it is all new to me. How can a grown man become a baby in the mind and try to figure out what is best for him?"

"That's a start, my friend. I'll be here. But I don't have answers that you seek. I'll be here though."

"Merci…err, Thank you."

"You're welcome. And by the way, don't you think I better sprinkle about a gallon of Holy Water on the deck where the Nazis pissed before we have Holy Sacraments there again?"

They both laughed as Alain left.

21

Alain stares out at the Atlantic

On the slab of rock, he and Isabelle sit on so often

Alain walked down the sloping street toward the main portal of the old part of Guerande, past St. Albin, the huge Gothic cathedral. As he past he wondered how long ago so few people had spent so many years building the magnificent church, and more than that, how someone had kept them working on it—it had to have taken many, many years to complete.

His mind came back to where he was headed, past Marcel's house where he lived and to things, he could put an answer on, *Jacque always stood waiting at the barn door now and after about three weeks from the time he had kicked his stall before I scratched his ears, didn't give me any trouble when I hitched him and Agnus to the big, long wagon we hauled the salt in. He still nudged me for an ear scratch and stuck his nose down around my pants pocket hoping I had a treat for him. One morning, I was surprised when he happened to drop the turnip—we had lots of them, them and potatoes—I gave him. Mikey, the frisky little furry foal ran up and in one gulp, ate the turnip. Jacque raised his head, and I laughed as he looked straight at me with an expression on his face that said, "Dang, he's fast."*

When Isabelle had come home from her trip to Paris, She got physically sick as she told us what had happened on the death train. She ran into her bedroom, and we heard her throwing up in her night jar. She warned Henri that he must be very careful going around Saint-Nazaire as he made trips down South. If she only knew what happened on that trip, I made with him. I feel like I'm cheating on her about me going on that trip, and keeping it a secret

from her, and now the same as lying to her.

Marcel and his crew have done a clever thing at the salt lagoon where Jacque and Agnus pull the wagon up for them to load the rolled tarps that are filled with salt. The grasses grow tall and thick up by the road, and from the road down the slope, about all i can see is the tall grass. Sometime over the years, they have constructed a lean-to out of grasses and small branches of wood, down on the middle of the tall grasses. I could barely see it from the road unless I knew it was there. It has a canopy of grass as a roof and is long enough to pull the wagon into it, so the donkeys can be out of the hot sun during the day as we fill the wagon with the tarps of salt.

I reach the slab of granite where Isabelle and I spent many late afternoons on. I look back at the men, women, and some teenagers who were working at the salt pans.

In this late fall morning, I know the paludiers know this is one of the last workdays of the season. They are skimming the fleur de sel—the 'flower of salt'—the finest of our salt which forms a light fluff of crystals that resemble snowflakes on the surface of the water before the rest sinks to the bottom of the pans. They call them pans because the bottoms are clay and hold the water until it is released out the end.

The Nazis had come to Guerande and demanded a tax on all our salts that were delivered to many fine restaurants. The other salt that is raked up after the water evaporates is sold to the canneries around the area to salt fish.

I have sat many evenings listening to Father Jean or Marcel as I learned these things and other things like the names of the months, and I know it is nearly October.

As I pass the paludiers, several look at me as if to say, "Why are you not working at the salt pans?"

They have no idea that I hardly know where I am. Winter is coming, and the salt lagoons must be drained and cleaned so there was harder work ahead than the harvesting of the salt.

Suddenly, I hear several of those birds that mock lots of other birds, so

I know they are making their migration South. For a moment, I wonder why they attract me so much as others pay no attention to them.

Marcel had shown me his rake one day as I sat on the mound of earth that separated some lagoons. He was proud of it, for it had been his father's. It was all wood and had teeth of wood that caught the flakes of salt as he slowly pulled it toward him as it just touched the top of the water.

We had several tall mounds of salt ready to scoop into tarps to take to the warehouse, and after that we were to start draining the lagoons back into the sea.

The one lagoon we wouldn't be draining was the one we built the deck over—the one those Nazis are buried under. Father Jean had decided the deck would become a place of thanksgiving that we were still safe, and on Sundays he would come and serve Holy Communion to us after we had eaten our lunch there. He would break the long baguette loaves into large chunks, so we could dip them into bowls of Beaujolais, which was his favorite from his vineyard back of the Abbey, and then give thanks. I invariably thought of that young German who had died begging to get back home to his mother.

It was weeks after I was introduced to Jacque and Agnus and the salt business and Marcel had received word that the Nazis were getting their butts beat up at Brest and warned us all that there might be renegades trying to make it down to Saint Nazaire where the U Boats were dry-docked for repairs. Even though the Brits had bombed the Hell out of the facility there about three years ago, Saint Nazaire had not surrendered yet.

We were in more danger than we had been during the entire war because there were too many loose cannons wandering down the roads and doing whatever they wanted to do, so we never went anywhere now unless we carried our guns.

The salt workers are a motley crew of almost any villager from teenager to old grandparents. It is dirty work and back breaking, so the pace is slow and steady, and no one pushes anyone else to be quick about it. Nearly everybody has a place to rest, a hollow place surrounded with grasses that make-up the marshes.

I turned to see Marcel and Henri walking down the lane from

Guerande, and when they reached the marsh road, they walked down the slope toward the salt pans. Marcel greets several paludiers and I saw Henri walk on down the slope toward the lean-to that the mules

were under. H We heard them long before they were in sight, and by the time I saw the head of the column several hundred yards away as I peeked through the grass, all the workers were concealed in their rest places. Someone had dropped a rake as they had scurried to hide, and it caught my eye like a red flag. I wondered if some lousy Nazis would notice it or not.

When the first of the column of trucks, motorcycles with side cars, and men on horses got even with us, we were all silent. As if by some order, the Nazis piled out of the trucks and cycles and the three riders dismounted from their horses, and all walked to the edge of the road facing us, unbuttoned their pants and stood in a line several yards long pissing into the salt lagoons—there were thirty to forty of them, I guessed. By accident, some officers stood along the bank above the deck we had built—or maybe it was a bit of irony—and pissed down on those Nazis we buried down there.

Several of them buttoned-up their pants, and I saw some take little tin boxes from their pockets and little sheets of paper. I watched fascinated as I saw them empty their tobacco on the papers and lick one edge and roll them into cigarettes.

Soon, the smell of tobacco filled the air around me, and a thought flashed through my head that I had watched someone else do the same thing before.

And once again, I clearly heard one of those strange birds burst into song in a stand of tall grass.

The Nazis paid it no attention. It took several minutes for them to leave us, but just before the tail-end of the bedraggled army left, a group of loud-mouthed stragglers seem to be bragging about their good luck of going home. They looked to be among the youngest of the straggly group, and their high-spirited voices carried across the lagoons.

I had the feed pouches over Jacque's and Agnus's heads, and they were munching their noon grain, so they were silent. But sud- denly little Mikey stood up and starting bucking in the air as he does sometimes.

He ran out into the path that separates two of the lagoons and began scampering back and forth.

I watched in horror as two of the bastard Nazis raised their rifles and began shooting at Mikey. At first, they aimed low, and the dirt around his little legs popped up in dusty balls. But then, one of them shot him in a hind leg. He bawled in pain and started whirling around in one direction and then turning to go around the other way. He was confused and afraid and squealing. Another shot rang out. It hit his shoulder and bright red blood oozed out to string down his long hair. Another shot shattered the back of his head as he tumbled into the salty water.

I had been holding onto Agnus's and Jacque's harness for dear life and somehow had won the battle with them.

The son-of-a-bitchin Nazis sauntered on down the road. I heard them laughing and joking as they bragged about shooting a helpless little donkey.

My eyes had tears in them as I peered across the many acres of salt lagoons to Guerande in the distance. I didn't see anyone about, and realized they, too, were all hiding.

The bragging and showing-off must have spread through this dangerous bunch of thugs, for as they approached Guerande, two of the machine-guns were set-up and they started spraying bullets at the high ramparts that circle the old village. I saw chunks of stones flying off of one of the corner towers as it was exposed the most, and so easiest to aim at.

It was obvious to me that there was no discipline about this group; no strict officers we had seen before to demand attention and throw around their power.

I could hear the ripping of the bullets as they hit the century old wall, but like many before them, the over twelve-foot-thick wall took the barrage with very little damage. I guess they finally tired of that, for I saw them shut down their guns and pack them back up. They started on down the tree-lined lane out of town.

Suddenly two RAF Spitfires dropped out of the sky and roared over just thirty to forty feet above our heads. I caught sight of the bright red nose on the black one that had a wide-open mouth of shark teeth on its front and the yellow underbelly of the other one that had two bulls' eyes brazenly painted in bright red and blue.

They ripped down the road, side-by-side, and when they reached the tree-lined lane, all sixteen Browning machine guns they carried cut-up the ground and tree limbs with a spray of bullets.

They slaughtered most of the string of troops crowded into the closed-in space on their first pass. Three of the trucks exploded in balls of flames; a cycle rammed into a sturdy tree by the road and was hanging with its front wheel over a limb high above the rider's head who hung grotesquely from another limb.

One of the horsemen sat on his butt on the road and stared at where his hand had been. His horse was sprawled out flat on the bank next to the road kicking and trying to buck. Every time its feet kicked out; blood poured out of its neck where its head had been.

The screaming of grown men that sounded like children filled my ears, and the smell of blood and excrement burnt the inside of my nose. The Spitfires circled back with their guns firing so hard the wings were wobbling. We had dashed out of our hiding places and ran after the Spitfires as they first passed over us. Now, we had to dive for cover as they came back, but they were aces who quit firing as they passed over the last Nazis.

A few Nazis had escaped their fire and were running across the fields on both sides of the lane. We attacked those with our rifles, and soon none of them moved. Many were screaming their last breaths.

I walked up to one who sat hiding behind a tree, "You sniveling bastard. You kill that poor little donkey for no reason at all—just for fun. You are the kind of *baiser* who torments and laughs about it just because you have a gun. That's all you have, for you are no man— *petit penis with no testicles*. Well, you won't do it again...."

I raised my revolver and shot the ground in front of him. He cowered in fright as I shot another shot that landed squarely between his spread-out legs. "This one is for real, I said."

But before I could shoot, Marcel appeared over my shoulder, and pushed me aside. The double barrels of his twelve-gauge shotgun came into sight and went off near my ears with a shattering boom. Marcel had aimed for the man's groin and now he was screaming in pain as he clinched his stomach.

Marcel sat the gun down by a tree and grabbed a good-sized branch that had been blown off during the battle. He raised it above his head and slammed it down on the screaming Nazi. He hit the Nazi again, and again until we pulled him away. He looked down at me, "That was for Agnus and her little Mikey."

Isabelle was suddenly there, and she took my hand and held it between hers. After a minute, she looked up at me and a stern resolve filled her eyes, "What do we do with all this? We have to get busy and bury them and maybe take all their equipment to the deep gorge where the Vilaine cuts through the cliffs and the water is deep and sink all of it."

After the deafening roar from Marcel's shot-gun finally left my ears, and I could somewhat hear, I said, "It would be easier to cut deep holes in the old peat bog north of town and bury them and their equipment there. Can you imagine a thousand years from now when someone accidently digs them up?"

"Do you think we have time to get all that done before another displaced Nazi comes through here?"

"No one has that answer, but with you and Marcel leading the way, the whole village will get this done."

"Seems like you might be leading." She grinned her little twisted grin as she walked away.

That night, I spent hours digging a deep hole out past the salt marshes, and several men helped me bury Mikey.

A week later, we had cleaned the road so that no stranger could see any evidence of what happened there. We had many early October rains, and that helped wash away evidence as well.

Father Jean continued helping me with my English and kept teasing me about sitting with Isabelle on the big granite slab that's on top of the hill past the marsh grasses that overlook the Atlantic.

And that evening as the Atlantic was pounding at the bottom of the cliff under our hill, Isabelle and I sat on the slab of rock, and I proposed to her.

22

July 1945, "Until Death"

Saint-Aubin Cathedral – Guerande

The estuary of the Vilaine River is about five kilometers long before the river's lazy water empties into the Atlantic. It has tumbled through boulders which dump it into high roaring waterfalls, or along gravel filled bottoms which become trickling falls down rocky grassy slopes. The cliffs along it banks are scarred with ancient cuttings. It rages along during storms and slows to a gleaming mirror at other times. Since the land around its banks is only a few meters above sea level as it approaches Guerande, the river moves slowly until it meets the tide zone where it slips out into the Atlantic. During the ages, it has cut into the plain that surrounds Guerande, so close by the salt lagoons, high hills overlook the ocean.

Henri's sons seed the water with spat from mussels and farm the harvest when they are large enough to eat which takes almost two years.

Henri and Inez had five strong boys; the oldest is a grown man with children of his own. In the early 1930's, their youngest son read where in Southeast Asia, mussel farming had been going on for years. He persuaded his brothers to quit working in the salt lagoons and become mussel farmers.

They spend time in the shallow water of the estuary attaching spat, the tiny seedlings of the mussels, to lines of strong ropes that hang from rafts, which are six meters wide, that float about two kilometers along the estuary.

The tides do the rest as the plankton comes and goes and feeds the mussels until they grow big enough to harvest

At harvest time, Isabelle has agreed to tell her salt customers about the mussels, so Henri's sons have a thriving business.

Until the invasion by the Nazis, Guerande had a celebration each year. The five sons pulled the ropes up out of the water. Mussels had attached to them in a mass several meters around, and it is easy to pick the largest one from the mass. The ropes are dropped back into the water after new spat is tied on, and a new harvest is underway.

The storm that had caused the river to rage toward the Atlantic that Alain had barely escaped when he first came down that river and bashed his head on the piling, had done some damage to the mussels but the boys had pulled most of the rafts into a slough that was backed-up out of the current.

The entire village would feast today on the mussels, vegetables from their gardens, and wine from Father Jean's vineyard.

Butter and wine and garlic filled the air for blocks around St. Albin as the village prepared for the important occasion.

Isabelle DesMarais, their acknowledge and respected leader, was getting married.

Father Jean looked completely out of place to me as he stood in front of the huge crowd of people gathering in the massive nave of the great cathedral, for he was dressed in a new brown habit. Two altar boys dressed in everyday clothes assisted him, one waving the incense globe, and the other opening the various homilies to the correct one and removing it when Father Jean was finished with that reading.

The years were taking a toll on him as I saw the strained look in his face and realized that his body was bent over, something I had not noticed before.

The doors of Saint-Aubin were all flung open, perhaps for the first time since almost five years ago when the Nazis had come to our town. There had been no pews in the cathedral as I had learned they had been removed and hidden in some ancient buildings at the Abbey, so the Nazis couldn't sit in the cathedral, but now they had been brought back.

Family after family arrived, and soon many were standing behind Father Jean as they tried to crowd in. I couldn't believe that every woman carried a bouquet of flowers from her garden or from the countryside around us. I was amazed too that each woman had a veil over her head—many of them elaborate and fancy.

Where had all these people come from, I wondered?

Isabelle walked down the long center aisle and every bouquet in the huge nave was raised as high as her waist as she passed. Then, I appreciated how important this woman was to Guerande. She was the last of her family that had lived here for generations. She had pro- tected many who were here as the Nazis had threatened the town. She had used her money and influence to protect their salt fields. Now, they were showing their respect and gratitude to her.

What am I getting into?

I was unfamiliar with the ceremony, but I remembered Father Jean had told me that during the Middle Ages, few worshipers understood the priest who was required to deliver the Mass in Latin while most of the people listening only understood English, French, or German—or their own native language.

There would be no Mass today during our wedding, for Catholicism is still strange to me. But today I will get a new last name, for I haven't had one since I have been here.

Isabelle coaxed me over and over about the vows as we had sat in our favorite place. I told her that it was simple that I only have to listen and say, 'I do.'

She stood by me now, and I was shaking with an uncontrollable emotion as I glanced at her. She was dressed in a beautiful silk gown that reached down to her ankles. Her grandmother had worn it for her wedding. She wore a little veil that brushed her shoulders. I have never seen anyone as beautiful in my life. How lucky I am that she accepted my proposal?

I have spent so much time with Father Jean during the last five years learning how to spin the potter's wheel, learning English and French with him and at the Abbey's school where young people learned both French and English and have for hundreds of years, for Brittany is so close to England.

I had heard him say maybe a thousand times that I needed to be careful when Isabelle and I were on the big granite slab that hangs almost over the edge of the cliff above the Atlantic, and now I turned red I'm sure, for I finally understood what he meant.

Five years is a long time for someone my age but not very long at all for someone who has no past.

Father Jean's voice interrupted my thoughts, and I heard his words, "And do you Isabelle DesMarais take Alain DesMarais as your lawful wedded husband, to have and to hold, and to be together in sickness and want, but also in plenty?"

I waited and heard her almost whisper, "I do."

"Do you Alain DesMarais take this woman, Isabelle DesMarais, to be your lawful wedded wife, to have and to hold, and to be together in bad times and also in plenty until death doth part you from her?"

"I do with all my heart."

"The two of you may kiss each other if you want," Father Jean said, as the large crowd burst into applause and laughter.

I thought, this is the only time today that he sounded like the man who had helped me so much since I was pulled out of the river and plopped down into his village. His voice hadn't had the jovial spirit we all knew until just now as he caused the crowd to laugh.

I looked closely at him and saw suddenly that the war, and his responsibility for his flock here in Guerande had taken much out of him.

We were the last to leave the church as Father Jean insisted.

We were met by cheers and laughter and shouts of good-will.

I was surprised that each man held up a bottle of what I would find out was his best wine.

Tables looked like they were bending in the middle as I saw they were all filled with dishes brought by from miles around.

Several small fires had been built along one side of the park and large pots of water simmered over each. Huge scoops of butter, cups of diced garlic, and bunches of thyme and crushed rosemary were dumped into them. Next, tubs of mussels were dumped on top, bottles of wine were poured over them, and the pots were covered. The whole area was filled with the aroma of the feast. The pots were opened and put on the long tables. What water that was left in the bottom of the pots had turned into a delicious broth,

We spent much of the afternoon scooping one mussel out of another using the shells as tongs and treasuring the tasty, salty morsel. Crunchy French bread pieces were dipped again and again in the broth.

Isabelle said, "They just needed a reason to do this…"

"No, they are doing it for you," I smiled at her.

23

The Heart of the Matter

Alain stands on the ramparts at Guerande

Rainstorms mixed with sleet and snow had fallen on Scotland the entire month of November, and by December those storms had inundated northern England, but the temperature changed in January because of a warming in the Atlantic.

London was usually swallowed in fog which pleased Winston Churchill and his assembled crew in the War Room deep below London. The Pug, as he was called by his admirers and his protesters alike, seemed to not care at all what people thought of him. He went about winning a war that would save his country, and perhaps the whole earth from the brutal Nazis and their insane leaders.

It seldom snowed in Guerande, and it never had ice that stuck on the ground or trees, but this winter was different. Unusual winds blew over the North Atlantic and fierce storms filled the North Sea. The English Channel acted like a funnel for those storms as they had to swirl through the narrow channel to reach the Atlantic. The islands in the Channel had to be evacuated because of high water and the storm surges.

A huge nor'easter swirled out of the Bay of Biscay hitting Guerande head on.

But nothing on the coast of Brittany compared to the horrific conditions on the Eastern front of the war. Siberia was an ice cap and soldiers froze to death as they were standing. No one should have been out in it, but those in charge of the war didn't seem to care.

It was the coldest morning that Guerande had all winter when Henri told me he had to make a trip south. "This may be the last trip if all the news we are hearing is true," he said to me as we stood on top the wall that surrounds the old village of Guerande. You should hope so, because you might have to make a trip with me if it isn't," he smiled strangely at me.

We stood looking over the edge of the parapet down into the side of the old wall that had an ancient natural spring which filled with water causing what the old timers would call a moat.

"Looks like there's a skim of ice on that water," Henri said.

"I think you are right, but the wind will keep it from forming solid."

He turned and left me as he walked down the top of the wall to a flight of steps that would take him to the ground.

I saw a puff of smoke float up from the stairway, and knew he was down there smoking. The puff of smoke was followed with his coughing fit.

I wondered just how much he was hurting and how weak he had become.

I looked out past where the new part of Guerande had spread past the old ramparts and saw what we had been seeing nearly every day for two weeks—an almost endless straggling line of people.

There were a few old slow-moving vehicles slowly inching their way along amongst the people, but none seemed to be passing the ragtag line.

I wondered where they were headed and what would they do when they could not walk another step, or when they ran out of petrol. Then I realized, they did not know either.

For weeks, the Yanks had been landing troops at Brest which was, before the Nazi invasion, the French Fleet harbor.

It had an even larger line of sheds for U Boats than Saint-Nazaire twelve miles south of us, but we had not been concerned about that as we had to get our surviving soldiers and airmen down into Spain. I was shivering as I stood on top of the old rampart. I laughed at myself and thought my.. my.. my, Father Jean, what a good job you have done with me. I must know why and how things happen, and I don't have any history to connect it with.

Like these walls I'm on. They are thick enough that Isabelle could drive her Renault down the top of them. Did so many soldiers have to be up here sometime long ago when they were defending our village? We are only around 600 now, and I'm thinking we couldn't defend the whole place.

Wonder what happened? Father Jean would know, I bet. I remember him praying that there will never be a murder in our church again—that the Nazis will never do what happened so long ago in St Aubin.

I sensed how cold I was getting and wondered for a second if one of Henri's many cigarettes would warm me up like he says they do for him.

And just how did they ever get the stones to build these thirty-foot-tall walls, I thought as I looked out an arrow slit? I rubbed my fingers along the outline of the slit and thought who a long time ago was responsible for the perfectly formed slot in the wall?

It had been here for hundreds of years which said a lot for the man, or men, who cut it out of the cliffs. Marcel had told me when I had asked him, that those cliffs along the Vilaine still had ancient scars where the rock had been cut out.

How did they ever do that more than seven hundred years ago? We have two corner towers in the ramparts which are being prepared as stone had been shot out of them by that marauding band of Nazis. One of the towers has taken a lot of damage and the stones are crumbling on one side of it.

I frequently laugh at the gargoyles which protect those towers from evil—they had failed—or had they? No one has breached the walls…yet.

It was as if they took just as much pride in this wall as they did in the wonderful Gothic windows and decorations in St. Aubin.

And there's another outrageous accomplishment to think about. How and when and who decided to build our monstrous cathedral—in our little village?

There are no rocks around Guerande as it sits on the wide open plain and the river bluff of the Vilaine are far away. Maybe they lifted them up from the beach, but Mon Dieu, those boulders are straight down thirty to forty feet below our hill.

I smiled as I thought, I just thought in French.

We had celebrated with several cases of Father Jean's best wines when the Brits and Yanks came across the Channel in an armada so strange looking and so frail looking too. They had gained a foothold at Normandy with such horrific losses that Father Jean prayed for over an hour one morning during holy service.

We had only heard tales and rumors about the daring landing, but we were so very thankful. It was the beginning of the end of the horror we had lived through the last four years.

Now, the Yank's 18th Infantry Regiment had been fighting the Nazis, street by street up in Brest. We were told by the people on the road that the once beautiful city was a ghost town inhabited by pockets of Nazis who didn't realize the town had been lost to them, and by terrified citizens who gradually picked-up what few belongings they had left and became pitiful strings of people walking the roads in almost any direction.

We would watch as a group approached the salt marshes from our concealed places wondering if it was a marauding bunch of Nazis like we had routed before—the one who had slaughtered Little Mikey or was this group the old men and women holding desperately to the hand of a child and carrying another on one hip.

Their eyes were blank like nothing was left between them and their brains. Their shoulders slumped nearly to their waists, and they turned frequently looking behind them like they were being chased.

"But why are they going South?" I asked.

"They don't know where they are going," Marcel had said, "but you are right. If they go South, they will meet Hell when they get to St. Nazaire where the heathen Nazis are fighting to hold onto their U Boat sheds there."

We fed as many as we could. But they just kept coming. We finally posted the roads entering Guerande with signs that we had no food.

I was walking the next morning on top of the wall with its high parapet protecting me from the cold wind, and from my high vantage point, I saw a woman with two little boys in tow coming towards the salt marshes.

One of them might have been five and the other one was smaller. Their shabby coats looked very thin to me, and I saw that a sole had torn loose on one of the older one's shoe and was flopping with each step he took.

She stopped and read the sign. Even from where I was, I saw her shake, turn, and hit the oldest one knocking him to the ground. She threatened the little one shaking her fist at him.

The oldest one pushed himself across the frozen ground away from her, but she turned and left them there in the road.

Remy and Eli, two little refugees escaping from Brest with their mother, but on their way to equally dangerous Saint-Nazaire are deserted at the Marsh Road gate at Guerande.

24

Remy and Eli

I rushed to the steps going down from the rampart nearly falling I was running so fast.

I ran down the stone street of the old village, through Porte Saint-Michel, across the almost half mile to the Marsh Road gate.

As I arrived, I saw several people stopped huddling around the two kids. They fell back when I approached, and maybe it was because I was so much better fed than the lot of them or that I told them I was from here at Guerande, or maybe it was the shot gun I always carry now slung over my shoulder by a strap. They struggled to get out of my way, fear peering out of those almost vacant eyes, and then started on down the road.

I squatted down by the two kids and said, "Can you tell me your names?"

The oldest one said, "I'm Remy and that is Eli. He doesn't talk. Will you go get our Mommy for us?"

Looking down the road, I was looking at the backs of that straggling bunch, and i could not see anyone who looked like the woman I had seen from the rampart.

I felt a lump in my throat as I said, "Why don't you come with me now, and we will look for her when you have had something to eat."

"We don't have food." He said in a matter-of-fact way as he had probably heard his mother say many times.

I reached into my jacket pocket and pulled out the crust of bread I always carry for Jacque.

He eyed it hungerly and said, "But, isn't that yours?"

I reached it out to him, and he snatched it from my hand. He stopped and tore it into two pieces and handed what looked like the larger one to his little brother.

I thought, Dear God, what have we done? Then I said, "Mon, Dieu…. Slow down, you will choke yourselves."

I was talking to the wind for the crust was soon gone.

Just what is a crust of bread worth, Father Jean? ran through my mind….

Come on, we will go to my house where I can get you two something to eat.

If someone from the village was watching us as we headed toward home, I'm sure some of them were thinking, "What the hell are you doing, Alain. We can't take in people."

If someone from the road was watching our backs as we headed toward Guerande, I'm sure some of them were begging, "Oh, if that were me…."

Isabelle wasn't too happy until I told her what I had seen and then her big heart just about burst open. I saw tears welling up in her eyes, and I wipe my own eyes on my sleeve.

"We're going to get a big kettle of water boiling and you two are going to have a wonderful bath while I fix you something to eat," she said.

"We can wait, ma'am."

She looked at me and had to turn her head. There was a knock at the door.

I opened it, and Inez, Henri's wife, stood there holding an arm full of clothing.

"I saw you coming across from the marshes and figured there were no little boys at this house, so I gathered up these things that I've held onto for some reason since my boys were little. I hope they fit."

"We'll make them fit," Isabelle laughed as she went to Inez and hugged her tight.

Soon the washtub that hangs on the back fence was on the kitchen floor. Isabelle poured boiling water she had heated on the kitchen stove into the tub as I went to the cistern back of the house and carried in buckets of cold water so the boys wouldn't be burned.

Remy turned his head to one side, looked at Isabelle, and said, "That still looks hot."

"Here, dip your hand into it and see," she said.

Very carefully he did and soon he was stirring the water around and around with his little hand creating a swirling whirlpool.

Suddenly he was shouting, almost screaming, as loud as he could as he started hitting the water with the flat of his palm. He was shaking uncontrollably, "We haven't had a bath in a long, long time. There was no spare water where we were—only the yells of men shooting at each other," he hollered as his voice pitched higher and higher. "And the screams of little kids…and the shooting of guns…and our Papa going out into it." He almost fell as tears were in his eyes as he stumbled over to Eli and gathered him into his little arms.

Isabelle drew them to her and held them against her apron. They struggled against her pull for a few seconds, but then collapsed against her hugging her tightly. She looked at me with tears streaming down her cheeks.

They stood still and silent as she quickly took off their ragged clothes. Soon, they stood as naked as they were born, and they were a sorry sight. Remy, a slender lanky five-year-old looked like he might weigh no more than twenty to twenty-five pounds, and every rib on his sides was sticking out.

Eli suddenly said, "One, two, three, four, five," as he counted his own ribs.

Remy shouted, "Eli, you talked! You talked!"

Isabelle looked at me and I said, "Remy told me up at the road that Eli doesn't talk. Right, Remy?"

"He has not talked for months." He pulled his little brother to him and held his head with his hands on both cheeks.

"Okay, you two. Time for the tub," Isabelle almost whispered as she saw how Remy was loving his little brother.

She took a bottle of lilac scent from off a shelf and started to pour some in the tub.

"Madam, that's for girls," Remy almost pleaded.

We both laughed. She put the bottle away, "Are boys all alike all over the world?"

They were squirming by the time I got finished scrubbing them.

Thank God they had no cuts or wounds, but when I was drying Remy, I saw a bruise developing, obviously from his mother hitting him, and I guessed he would have a blister from where his shoe sole had been flopping up and down and rubbing his heel.

Neither of them had socks.

Eli was almost asleep, but when the smells of the vegetable soup filled the air, both of them were wide awake and without being asked, were sitting at the kitchen table.

Two cups of wonderful soup with crusts of buttered bread disappeared in a flash. Remy sat staring at the pot of soup, turned away, and gave out what sounded like a sigh.

Isabelle got his message as she spooned more soup in each of their cups, "You must eat slowly as we don't want to make your tummies hurt, so this is all you can have tonight."

"We haven't tasted butter for over a year, Madam Isabelle, and that soup is the very best!" Remy stated in his almost adult fashion I would learn to love. Eli shook his head in agreement.

They were both so tired, as were Isabelle and I, so we went to bed early.

As I was pulling the cover up to his chin, Remy said, "Mommy was so happy to see the sign that said you wanted two little boys at this village. She said we were to stay by the post until someone came for us, and that she was going on to find a place. That's when I cried and then Eli cried. That's when she hit me, but not all that hard. She loves me."

"Remy, how do you know English so well?" I choked out, so I would not cry before him.

"Papa was from Warsaw where he taught English to Polish kids in the Ghetto where we lived. He said when things looked bad, that's what he said, we would go to Paris. Things were worse there soon also, so we made it down to Brest. That was a big mistake according to Mommy.

Papa went out the door that awful night with the scary shouts filling the street, and the beams of lights from their torches bouncing around from side to side and did not come back. We heard a gunshot.

That's when Eli quit talking, started wetting the bed, and screaming in the night."

"I'm sorry Remy. We'll have to help Eli all we can."

"I heard Papa shouting for them to stop. Then I heard the gun.

After that, Mommy cried for days, sometimes forgetting to feed us what little we had in the house. And then the men started coming to our house, and after they left Mommy had new food—a bag of potatoes or turnips, or a broken loaf of bread, and maybe a scrap of meat. But she wasn't happy, so we decided to leave there.

We just headed this way, and one of the cars stopped for us. A man was in the car, and he brought us to just the other side of your river. He stopped and Mommy and him went away for a while. When they got back, he shoved us out of the car.

It's a long way past the river when you are three and scared your Mommy will leave you again."

I thought, it's a long way when you are five and your scared and your shoe is falling apart. "You are safe now, both of you. Can you go to sleep? Eli is starting to snore, I think."

He laughed a genuine little boy laugh that I would grow to know so well.

"I must say my prayer. Papa would be so sad if I didn't." He folded his hands and what he said surprised me.

"May it be Your will, Adonai, My God and God of my father… to lay me down…in peace…and, and then to raise me…up…in peace. And… please…please smile down on little Noemie this night."

"Good night, Mr. Alain."

"I liked your prayer, Remy. Can you tell me who is Noemie?"

"She was just too little, Mommy said. She was just too little." "Who was she though?"

"She was our sister. She was older than Eli, but she was too weak and little. Mommy says she is asleep under a rose bush in a big yard in Brest. She will be a pretty pink rose next year.

25

The End of the War, 1945

Celebration and Reckoning in the streets of Guerande

"Put exactly twenty-seven piles and make sure you leave space between the piles on the bed of the wagon, so we can easily count them," Father Jean said to me.

"What in the world are you up to?" I asked.

"Oh, you'll find out soon enough and I want it to be a surprise to you like I hope it is to everyone else."

The war is over. The Nazis surrendered and signed a military surrender on May 7 at Reims and a day later a formal surrender at Berlin. The rest of 1945 will surely be better than the first months. The news that the war is over spread like a slow fire across France, and we were among the last to know about it.

Is it possible that I have been here over five years?

To the north at Brest there was awful destruction—it had been flattened to a pile of rubble and many people had been captured or killed in street-to-street battles.

I so happy that Remy and Eli escaped from that terror. I have decided they mother was a very brave and loving woman. She was brave, or scared might be the best word, to set out on the road with them. I even forgive her lie about what out sign said. Remy has begged me several times to try to find her, but I tell him there are just to many people who are disappearing and never be heard of again. He seems to accept that now.

But, Guerande had been spared from the horrors that so many people had suffered. We had those two incidents, and every time I'm working the salt pans and must get on the deck, I think about that Nazi Captain and his motorcycle troops buried down below me. Ironically, they will be preserved for years in all that salt.

And I shudder at the other blood-soaked fight out south on the road, when those thugs were leaving town after killing Mikey and shooting at the battlements of our old village. They were slaughtered by the Spitfires and the villagers, and none of us seemed to think about what we were doing as we were in the middle of doing it. I dreamed about that one Marcel shot with his twelve-gauge shotgun for many nights. I can't say enough about how insane war really is.

I hitched two donkeys to the salt wagon and headed toward the lagoons. I remember the first time I made this trip. Marcel was still alive, and I had those two donkeys, Jacque and Agnes, and little Mikey. Marcel warned me about Jacque's temper, but it didn't take me long to get the best of him.

Those strange birds that mimic other birds are in the tall grass next to the lagoons as they are headed north on their migration.

I fill the two tarps I have in the wagon with the best salt I can take off the top of a big mound near where the skimmers have been working. I didn't ask Father Jean how big the twenty-seven piles of salt should be, but two tarps full should be enough.

I stop the wagon and get down and leave the harness hanging to the ground which I know will keep the donkeys from going any- where. I walk up the hill of the flat plain where the salt flats are, toward the hill overlooking the Atlantic and can hear the waves thumping against the rocks below. I wonder what's on the other side of that huge ocean in front of me.

The whole village was a flurry of activity as we prepared for the celebration. I saw Isabelle three or four times from a distance as she hurried from one place to another as she went about planning things. She was in charge. Something inside me stirred as I realized how attractive that woman is; the woman who will be mother of our baby, and already is mother of Remy and Eli.

Father Jean showed me where he wanted the wagon parked outside the main entrance to St Aubin, "Make the piles of salt tall enough that the tops can be seen from way over there," he said as he pointed to the other side of the square, "I want everyone to know what they are for and how many there are of them."

I was still puzzled, but I had learned over the last years to trust this intelligent man with my life, and I also had grown to admire him very much, so I did as he said.

"That looks fine to me," he said as he passed by again fifteen minutes later. "Unhitch the donkeys and take them back to your place as I don't want them causing a ruckus."

As I led the two donkeys back to what was our house since it was bigger than Isabelle's old house, as Marcel had passed away during the winter, I met her coming toward me. "I am taking the best tablecloths and some dishes to use."

I laughed to myself wondering why she would be telling me that news, "I bet we never see a bigger celebration than the one we are having today," I said.

"Yes, and I want you near me the whole day," she laughed as she walked away.

I looked after her and smiled, "That won't be difficult for me."

The square in front of our big Gothic cathedral was filled with tables full of food and hundreds of folks that I now recognize. Father Jean moved from table to table blessing the food but mostly saying greetings to his people.

Finally, he stepped up on the little platform someone had put next to the wagon where the piles of salt were. I had taken the side boards off the wagon, so now it was a flat-bed, and we could plainly see the piles of salt.

"In the Holy Scriptures," he said as he crossed himself, "Jesus said to some ordinary people just like us, that they were the salt of the Earth, and that's why He chose them, and I am saying to you who are gathered here today that you, too, are the salt of the earth. There are very few of your families who do not work most days of the year down in the salt lagoons sifting up that very thing that is so common, but so necessary to all of us."

"We have piles of that salt up here in front of us signifying not only our livelihood, but the very lives we tried to save. There are twenty-seven piles of it, if Alain can count, that represent the twenty- seven service men from at least three countries we tried to save during this awful war."

There was laughter through the crowd as he made the joke about me.

He went on, "Jesus also said in that same conversation that some of the salt might lose its savor and be of no account to those who were around it. Sadly, we are in the same situation for one among us has wasted our efforts and destroyed others."

He was looking straight at Henri who had stood up and appeared to be leaving.

"We trusted you with the lives of those men. Trusted you to deliver them down to that brave young woman who took so many soldiers across the Pyrenees into Spain and saved them.

But you were a Judas to us. You took them down just past St. Nazaire and turned them over to the Nazis. I shudder when I think what they faced when they knocked on that door twice and it was opened.

He crossed himself.

I learned yesterday when that brave woman sent word asking why we hadn't sent her any men. Now, I'm asking you?"

Henri ran away from the table, rushed across the square, and bolted up the steps toward the top of the wall. I was fast behind him and was catching up when I sensed that most of the people in the square were trying to follow us.

They cleared the way for Father Jean and soon he was at my side as we stood in front of Henri.

Henri pulled his revolver from inside his jacket and pointed it at me, and in the middle of coughing seizures, said, "Stop or I will end your life here too."

"Why, Henri, why?"

"Go to Hell, I'm dying of cancer and my family will not have to worry about money and living after I'm gone."

"What about the twenty-seven families you destroyed?" Father Jean asked.

"I don't give a damn about them. I don't know any of them."

"How can you live with this? How can you ever face the people of Guerande again? We will never blame your family for any of this as I suspect that even Inez, your wife, and those five fine sons of yours, know nothing about it, but how do you expect us to forgive you?"

"You won't have too," Henri said as he ran over to the corner tower that had been damaged by the Nazis machine-gun fire, stepped over the parapet, and grabbed hold of a gargoyle on the tower. The grotesque figure which had horns and a snarling face, cracked loose from the tower and Henri and it fell into the water thirty feet below.

We were shocked—not moving for a minute, but then as we rushed up and looked over the edge, we saw his body spread out face up. Red ran down his neck and onto his shoulder and was turning the water a strange red color. He had landed squarely on the ancient gargoyle that had fallen with him. Its evil looking snarl glared back at us, and its long, twisted horns were sticking through his neck.

I turned to Father Jean who was making the sign of the Cross.

Isabelle had disappeared, and someone told me she went into the church.

I rushed inside and found her sitting in a pew crying. I sat beside her, put my arm behind her and hugged her close to me.

She looked at me and I saw her cheeks were streaked with tears,

"Oh, Alain, what if some of those men on that horrible train were the very ones, we sent with Henri down to Saint Nazaire.

I turned my head as I could not bear to look at her. I squeezed her close to me as she sobbed uncontrollably on my shoulder.

Guerande was in shock. The people at the celebration we had been having in the square just silently started drifting away.

Our little village would not be the same for weeks as almost everyone had known Henri and could not understand why he had betrayed those soldiers.

It was almost a month later when Inez brought Father Jean several cans of our best salt that she had taken off the shelves in their cellar.

"I do not know when these came into our house as I had never seen them until last night," she said. "I know they are not full of salt though for some of them feel like they are empty, and some are way too heavy for our salt.

"Here, we will open them together. No, wait, let us get Isabelle to be here when we do it."

"And Alain…."

"And Alain."

A few minutes later the four of us were in the Abbey's little cellar room that Father Jean uses as his office. He took one of the cans, and using an old-fashioned turn type can opener, he opened the first can.

"Saint Pere," he said, and crossed himself, "It is full of German deutschmarks. They won't be worth anything." He looked at Inez and quietly said, "Henri thought the Nazis were going to win.

26

Our Own Reign of Terror

Isabelle is filled with terror again…

In many ways, the months after the war were more dangerous to us at Guerande than when we feared a rogue band of Nazis would come pounding on our doors demanding anything they wanted that day, or that one of the many planes that flew over would make a mistake and fire on us or drop a bomb on us.

France was in chaos; some had helped the Nazis believing they would end up the victors as Henri had, and some had reverted to bands of renegades who struck fast and deadly at anything the Nazis had controlled.

Now, those bands roamed the countryside making decisions on the spur of the moment and condemning anyone they believed were guilty.

It was the 'guilty' that I caught myself agonizing about.

I wondered what had happened to that conductor on the train that probably saved my life. What was he guilty of?

I wondered about Claude who had helped Henri save so many servicemen. What was Claude guilty of?

'Guilty' was a terrifying word, no matter which way, or side, you were on.

A truck went lumbering down the Marsh Road yesterday. It was going slowly, not much faster than a person could walk.

The flatbed behind the cab was crowded with women whose heads had been shaved. They were 'guilty' of selling their bodies to the Nazis.

No one seemed to wonder why? Were they greedy who just wanted the money? Were they power hungry whores who enjoyed the fear in the eyes of many when they were escorting a SS Major to a restaurant?

Or were they mothers who sold their bodies because they were trying to keep their children alive?

Was Remy's and Eli's mother one of those? Did she make the five-day march from Brest because she was trying to escape the stigma that was attached to her, or the life Remy had hinted at when he said there lots of men around after his dad was shot. Alain has decided she was a brave and honest woman caught in the horror we had been living through. He has even forgiven her lie to the boys.?

Remy and Eli are doing fine. Jacque has become their hero. Remy stood amazed when he first heard that Jacque had made the almost twenty-kilometer trip home by himself.

"Amazing!" He drew the word out in a whispered about that morning Jacque had showed up back at his barn demanding food and water and giving the closed stall door a swift kick.

Father Jean has accepted Remy and Eli in his school with the rest of Guerande's children. He was uncertain at first. He visited Alain and me one evening.

"The Pope is having a hard time with this question," he said. "The ancient teaching, still believed today by too many, is that the Jews killed Christ."

He crossed himself.

"Any intelligent person can see the leaders of the Jews at that time were afraid to lose their 'trough.' I nearly said pig trough, but that would have been crude. But too many still blame the Jews. Our horrible example is the Nazis.

All I know is that we have two struggling little boys who need to learn to read and write. Ironically, they will learn many stories, and lessons about their forefathers as I use the Bible for so many lessons. They are welcome at the school as any of our other kids."

Alain stood up from the kitchen chair and walked to Father Jean and leaned over and kissed the top of his forehead, "Thank you for that. They will become your best students, for both of them are very smart."

Some in town disagreed, and some disagreed violently for my fence was painted during the night with the familiar Star of David and the word 'Jude.'

Alain claimed that my hard head kept me from being afraid, but he was wrong for inside I was terrified for the boys…and for us.

Alain teases me about the many books I have in the house. I have always loved to read, and it is clear to me that we are living through a time just like after the Monarchy fell.

Alain says we forget that after the heroic struggle of those schoolboys in Hugo's wonderful book against the unfair laws of the Monarchy, there was a reign of terror because those that won, couldn't agree on how their new life should be, with those that disagreed.

Thank God the guillotine is gone, but now it so easy for anyone to have a gun, and in their minds turn them against their fellow countrymen.

We are envied by those around us because we, especially Father Jean, had had the wisdom to prepare us for what he believed was going to happen. He had been right, and we suffered less because of that, but those around us couldn't, or wouldn't, blame themselves for not seeing, or not believing those that forewarned about Hitler and his plans.

It was like they were standing in a wind that was blowing in their faces, but the wind went on both sides of their heads just whispering in their ears, and they never felt it—and certainly never listened to it. And so, we are living in this spasm of distrust and envy—this chaos of death and fear. A horrible, weird wind is blowing across France.

The propped up Etat Francais that the Nazis had put in power— The Vichy—is the best example. The two leaders, Petain and Laval, are suddenly treated different; probably because of their reputations before the Nazis crossed our borders. Laval will face the firing squad this week, but Petain, who was condemned to the same fate, will be turned loose, rumor has it, to go abroad to live a long life.

The next day, Isabelle looked from her kitchen window and over the parapet of the east wall, the sun broke through some morning clouds with streaks that spread out like an open fan.

As she watched, the sun peaked over the wall and flooded her kitchen. She shivered in the emotion of it. The baby squirmed inside her now large stomach. She hummed herself through the morning with tunes she remembered from her childhood.

She greeted the boys when Brother Lawrence, one of the Monks from the school, brought them home from Father Jean's classroom at the Abbey.

"Father Jean says that Eli is the one to watch," Brother Lawrence said as he was about to leave.

The two of them were standing at the garden fence while the boys were in her kitchen smacking and laughing as they hurriedly ate their peanut butter and jelly sandwiches.

The peanut butter was a new thing in their lives since the Americans had shipped so much of it to France and other countries. It was loved by the boys almost as much as a seldom seen Hershey chocolate bar. They knew the story of the American pilot who was dropping Hershey bars from his plane and were thrilled one day as bars fell in the village and they were lucky to each get one.

She didn't like either of those things as much as the French treats, she had grown up with, but the boys had never known them.

Maybe someday they will...Maybe someday when all this is behind us.

The next day, there was a knock on her door. Alain was busy at the salt pans, and as she answered it, she felt a dread. She let out her breath, and almost reached out to hug Father Jean.

"Father, you seldom come to visit when school is happening." "Yes, but I must tell you right away what we have learned this morning. The school is fine with the monks I left to lead it.

As you know, we have many people moving back and forth on the roads and we are helping as many as we can with what food and clothing we can spare.

This morning one of our vineyard workers returned from down by Saint Nazaire where the needs of the people are the worse than anywhere else close by. He said it is almost a ghost town, and that the sheds for the U-Boats look like haunting caves from the bay. They stand empty, as the Nazis took all the subs out into the Atlantic and sank them.

But, as usual, I got off why I came to see you. We should sit down for it will be a shock to you. The baby may be disturbed very much."

They sat at her table with cups of coffee and some peanut butter cookies she had made for the boys this morning.

"Claude is dead," Father Jean said without anything leading up to the announcement.

She instantly realized the danger to Guerande and maybe other villages who had sent servicemen to him to be helped in their escape from the Nazis.

"What happened?"

"They found his boat smashed into splinters on the bank of the bay, and when they went to his house, they found him hanging in a tree in the back yard."

"Oh, Mon Dieu!"

"It is hard to imagine how many of them fought and struggled with that stout burly man. The fight had to be long and loud, and his neighbors had to hear it, and yet they did nothing, it seems, to help him. It may not cause us any trouble. I mean, we have lost a good friend who helped us to try to save so many that were in great danger. But Saint Nazaire was always a stronghold of people who believed the Nazis would win, so it is still full of sympathizers. Maybe they don't know what villages Claude was helping. Maybe they will never look this far from there."

"And maybe they will, Father Jean."

Isabelle wished she could reach out and touch Alain's hand. He was always calm and quick to come up with a plan when they seemed to be in trouble.

We put several men on top of the wall during the coming weeks. They sat, built their fires to have hot coffee, drank too much wine, and reminisced about times they remembered. They sat with their shot guns or rifles across their laps or stood them against the parapet nearby.

I wonder how long we will be doing this. Is this the life so many had died for? Is this any way to live?

And I realized I, too, was making futile thoughts; thoughts that I could not act on. Thoughts that blew away the next morning when the sun came up over the marshes and the paludiers went to the salt pans to rake up the salt of the sea.

27

Okaloosa Island

Prof at the La Mancha

I thought the other day, I've lived at the La Mancha for over seven years now—seems like home. It's so unlike Albuquerque where I lived over thirty years teaching high-school seniors. I've become entangled with the happenings and intrigues of Okaloosa Island.

Because I worked for the *NorthWest Daily* writing the happenings at Lounie Sanderson's murder trial and before that, the mystery of the bodies on the beach at the La Mancha, I now have free reign of the archives for the paper. I spent most of this morning searching for the time when our island became Okaloosa Island.

The paper used to be called *Playground News,* and the headline in the July 13, 1950, read *"Island Tract Turned Over to Okaloosa – Formal Transfer Completed With $4,000 Payment."*

I stopped, on the way back, at my favorite fast-food chicken place on Eglin Parkway, got my usual ten-piece order with no breast, a large red beans and rice, four of their delicious biscuits, and a large, mashed potato that is smothered in the most outrageous gravy. I have food for the week, but I've got to stop stopping there so much.

I drove down to Highway 98, turned left, and stayed in the outside lane as I drove slowly over Brooks Bridge, for at the end of the bridge at the bottom of the hill, I needed to turn right onto Okaloosa Island. Santa Rosa Blvd runs down the middle of the Island that's barely over a half-mile wide at its widest point. Palm trees have been planted down the median, and the grass is manicured as neat as any well-kept lawn. On the north side, many single homes line streets that run down to the Sound, and circle back around to the Blvd. A few businesses and some older apartments dot the Sound toward the east end.

On the south side of the Blvd, condo complexes that bring in millions of dollars a season stand side-by-side down the three miles. There are public parking areas that split up the condos and this summer it seems the county has a lot of money, for four of those areas are getting new facilities and new parking lots. Big sturdy gazebos with bathrooms are rising out of the sand and add that to the thousands of visitors we have this summer; Santa Rosa Blvd is a mess.

But, the biggest construction, or should I say demolition, that affects the La Mancha is what is happening over the fence from us in the Air Command. The Blvd ends abruptly even with the northwest corner of the La Mancha's property; a barricade eliminates the right lane, and traffic is controlled into the Air Command in a single line.

Don Herd who has live here over thirty years, once said the La Mancha looked like a war zone after Hurricane Opal hit. The huge waves and fierce winds had destroyed the growth of pines that stood across the fence from the La Mancha and had thrown it all into the Sound where it bashed up against the shore on the other side and into the streets of Fort Walton Beach. Somehow, the old woven fence had withstood Opal even though it was ripped in jagged shreds in places, and even more peculiar, the mighty force of the storm swirled around that corner of the La Mancha's property leaving a big mound untouched but had gouged out a large hollow in the Air Command. When it was all over, they had poured a concrete slab that was about a foot thick and as big as a basketball court and built the guard shack on it.

Now, for some reason, Jack hammers have been pounding the concrete for about a week now, but it looks like only a small area has been broken up, for we have had five or six straight days of heavy rains.

I walk Skipper down to the corner of the La Mancha's property almost every afternoon and usually look down at what's happening over there. The La Mancha's perimeter fence sits up a lot higher than the guard house now because of Opal. That mound of earth sticks out above the entrance to the Air Command. A huge old oleander bush that Craig and his crew have cut many times fills the corner.

No telling how many years it has clung to the sandy soil.

Thankfully, the jackhammering stops at five o'clock, but when the weather allows, the days have been very loud, and many of the La Mancha guests have not been happy.

I hadn't been home fifteen minutes until there was a knock on my door. I opened it to face my good friend, J C Blevins. I swung the door open wide and asked him in.

"Why do I have the pleasure of your company?" I said in an exaggerated way. "I didn't tell Little Mitch to do whatever he might claim I did, if that's why you are here."

We both laughed for we have lived through many of Little Mitch's tall tales and schemes.

"No, he's probably off telling some startled lady that he is honored to meet her and will help her walk her dogs if she wants."

"I've heard that from my balcony many times when he meets Sally Smyth as she is walking Sam II and Missy."

"No, I just wanted to sit on your balcony a while and have a beer if you have any."

"You know I do because you left them in my fridge the last time you were here."

J C was still grinning as he brought back a bottle of Stella and climbed into one of the tall chairs on my balcony.

"I see you have your four ounces of red wine. Don't you ever drink more than that?"

"Only when I had a hundred pages to grade, or a Florida State Trooper who asks too many questions of an old man... Now, what's on your mind, today?"

"You laugh at me, and I will get my feelings hurt...and go home,"

"When have I ever laughed at you?"

"I know... I can't tell you how good it was to be able to come up here, even when you were not at home, and sit on your balcony to try to figure out things."

"I know...."

"I remember the first time I saw her. It was just a couple of days after Launie took Ollie down the Sound and shot him. All Launie's girls were loading their things into two taxis and headed to the air- port. They pulled off on Memorial Drive and drove into Memorial Cemetery where Ollie is buried."

"You never told me this part before."

"Yeah, I know. I stayed back a good distance because I was afraid, they would see my patrol car, and that would have ruined everything. They were too busy to notice me. They were all doing something strange as far as I was concerned. They were all putting something on Ollie's grave—something that caught the sun occasionally, so that it glittered. Then two of them took her arms and helped her get back into the taxi. She looked like she was crying her heart out."

"Of course, you know who that was now."

"Of course, I sleep with her every night."

The Prof looked over at J C, Little Mitch's adoptive dad, a straightforward good guy who smiled a lot and was happy go lucky until he had this murder trial thrown at him.

He knew that J C had come within a phone call to Porter of resigning and had been so stressed that Little Mitch had mentioned it one day.

J C grew up in Destin which is the biggest tourist destination in the area and had been on the force for seven years when the first body washed up in front of the La Mancha. Until that time, he spent most days parking beside busy Highway 98 so he could slow down or stop speeders. He was only responsible for Okaloosa County as three or four million tourists come into the County each year to vacation with their families on the beautiful white sands next to the emerald Gulf or come in the winter months to escape the cold from up in New England and even Canada. He had become a trooper just out of the two years of college he spent at *Northwest Florida* up at Niceville.

He was smart enough to patrol around and then sit quietly in his patrol car secluded from sight near Launie's place, and he had recorded many license plates which were regular customers even though they were from out of state.

"Well, I'm in trouble enough at home with all the time I spend in the Prosecutor's office trying to figure this whole mess out, so I better be going."

He appeared back in the balcony door in a second, and said, "By the way, what is this scrap of the *NorthWest Daily* on your table?"

"It's about a lady I'd like to meet, and somehow, I bet we do before this is over. I hear she is one smart lady."

NorthWest Daily

From: *Who We Should Know*

Judge Bonita Boyd

She came into the world in 1939 in a traditional Hogan built by her grandmother's family in the depths of Canyon de Chelly, by a fast-running creek, near the Four Corners area of Arizona.

Her grandmother was chosen to name her and the first word out of the old woman's wrinkled sun bronzed mouth was 'Bonita.' The old woman was wise, for she was a terribly beautiful baby.

She arrived in this world just as the sun peeked over the top of Eastern Holy Mountain, so holding her in one arm and gathering a handful of maize in the other, her mother had stood in the doorway, scattered the maize on the ground, and held Bonita up toward the bright sun; her eyes glistened, but she did not blink.

Her father had performed the 'Blessing Way' that night as all the family sat on the dirt floor of the Hogan and sang the blessing. Later, she learned all the words as did her brothers and sisters:

'This home, my home, shall be surrounded with sa'ah naaghei bikk'eh hazhoo. May I live in this home happily and peacefully and with respect. May my house be in harmony: From my head, may I be happy, to my feet, may I be happy, all around me, may I be happy. May my fire be well made and happy. May the sun my mother's ancestor, be happy from this gift. May I be happy as I walk around my house. May this road of light, my mother's ancestor, be happy.'

She had learned it well for it was not her house that she thought about when she sang the blessing, but herself, and she had accomplished nearly all the happy blessings.

She graduated from Arizona State and was persuaded to enter the Miss Navajo Nation Pageant which she did thinking she could use the money if she won any. She did, as she won the pageant and immediately entered law school at the University of New Mexico Law School where she quickly became a favorite among her fellow students because of her quiet humor, good manners, and helpful attitude.

She chose to move to Florida to become an advocate for the Seminoles as they struggled to hold on to their traditions and land with the ever-increasing intrusions around them. She defended them well and gained recognition by the Governor who appointed her to the State Court of Appeals, and ten years later, she was the Senior judge of that court.

She outlived her husband of many years, Charles Boyd, who was also a lawyer and judge. Their six children blessed her with many grandchildren.

When she retired in 2011, she moved into a little bungalow which faces east on the Sound in Mary Ester, a few miles west of Fort Walton Beach. She lives there with her Australia Sheep dog, Coxy

28

What a Change from a Foul Villain to What appeared in Court

Prof writes Launie Sanderson's trial for NorthWest Daily

I don't remember seeing Launie Sanderson but two times, and what walked into the courtroom that first morning was not what I remember seeing.

I have the habit of walking up Santa Rosa Blvd to the 'Thumb,' as all of Daniel Sheraton's boys call the quick stop store, about a mile from the entrance to the La Mancha. I remember that morning almost two years ago like it was yesterday.

I was within a hundred yards of so from my goal of getting a raspberry fruit pop at the store when I saw this bizarre figure approaching me. She was wearing high heels, as high as I have ever seen, with voluminous pants that clutched in at her thick thighs, and a flimsy blouse that strained to cover her massive bosom. Her face caused me to think of a clown as she had thick make-up in various shades plastered from neckline to hair high on her forehead.

I thought of my favorite actress of all time—Bette Davis. I regret that I thought of her when she portrayed an ugly old maid who was living in guilt because she had been lied to about hurting her sister when they both had been upcoming figures in vaudeville. I suppose this all came to mind because Launie had escaped reality with drugs, and Davis's character had escaped reality by living in the past, as her prize possession was her Baby Jane doll.

But it was Davis's hideous face coated almost white with a painted-on beauty mark that I remember most. And here coming toward me in real life was that apparition walking down the running path. I almost turned and went back home because I didn't want to pass her on the path, but then she stopped and looked at the upper floor of one of the tallest condo complexes on the Island, and then she turned and walked back the way she had come.

Her wobbling rear end must have been as wide across as 'two axe handles' as my granddad used to say, and her butt halves were like two pigs fighting each other in a sack.

She had a hard time getting in what I later learned was her new dark green Caddy. The engine roared as she made a U turn, and the tires squealed as she sped down the Blvd.

I had no idea then, but it was Launie Sanderson who I almost had to meet there on the walk.

I did see her again one day shortly before we all had read about Ollie's death in the *NorthWest Daily*. I was in Tides Inn which is the wonderful seafood restaurant at the end of the Blvd at Highway 98. I eat my lunch there often and was late that day. At about three o'clock I guess, as I was finishing an oyster Po' Boy, she walked in.

All the usual noise and banter from the friendly waitresses stopped, and for a moment there was almost silence in the place.

Launie stood there with a blouse which was stained all the way down her fat sides from sweat coming from her arm pits. Her face was covered with the same stinking sweat, so she grabbed a big hand full of napkins from the pile on the bar and started mopping her face. She caused the make-up to smear in several places as I heard her order crab claws to go.

As she stood there waiting for her order, Celeste, one of Tides Inn's friendliest waitresses brought her a tall glass of water. I saw Launie's face as she turned toward Celeste and realized that Launie was so high on drugs that she probably didn't know where she was.

Celeste also brought Launie her crab claws.

I saw her pull a bill from the fat wallet she took from the bag she was carrying, put it on the counter, and start for the door. We all watched as she first bumped a table, let out a string of cuss words, and then had a lot of trouble getting the front door open.

We could see through the front window as her new bright green Caddy squealed out of the parking lot and into the traffic. It raced across Highway 98 and around the corner toward her place.

"Do you believe that? She almost caused a wreck out there too. My Gosh, she's left a $50 bill! Glad I was persuaded to wait on her."

Launie is a loud-mouthed painted frowning woman most of the time. It would be hard to put an age on her, as her hair changes colors at her whims, and her face reminds me of a painted Japanese geisha. She must be in her fifties, but she has started to sag in the wrong places. Her face looks like she was burned badly sometime which may be why she conceals it with so much make-up. Her massive breasts are supported with a bra I've seen advertised on TV as able to support the biggest. I know that because of the tops she wears— those that have thin straps. I've never seen her in a top which doesn't emphasize their size.

The sign outside the *Launie's Gentlemen's Library* has a picture of her taken years ago. Even then she was 'full-figured' as the ads say, but she was not heavy. Now, she wears loose fitting skirts or pants, and her thighs look like they are fighting a battle with each other. I don't imagine she exercises much and probably sits around a lot. She reminds me of that Disney villain from that movie about the little mermaid.

Launie chain smokes Winston Lites so her nails are stained with nicotine. A manicurist visits her once a week to apply new fake nails which are nearly always painted with miniature beach scenes.

She's nearly six feet tall and I'm guessing at one time back before she let herself go, she was the main attraction at a strip joint like the one she now owns.

After all the 'wasted' time as far as I was concerned, the trial would become a reality this morning in Judge Jeffery Bickel's courtroom.

The woman who was escorted into the courtroom this morning

was totally different. Mr. Schaberg, her lawyer, had done a good job getting Launie ready for the trial. She was dressed in a plain blue skirt and a frilly blouse which still struggled to cover her huge breasts, but it wasn't vulgar by any means. Her face had extraordinarily little make-up on it, and my eyes were drawn to several scars on her face that appeared to be caused by being burned. Her nose was still swollen and a little bent to one side. Her cheeks were more pronounced now that she had lost so much weight.

She caught me staring at her and turned to look at me with eyes that were clear and had emotion in them. I saw her hands and the long fake nails which were stained with tobacco, that I remember from that time at the High Tide, were gone and her own nails were short and had what looked like clear polish on them. She really looked like a conservative middle-aged housewife.

"That sure doesn't look like the creepy thing I've seen out on the walking trail." Dolf leaned over and whispered to me.

"Careful, or you're going to have Bickel on your case again," I answered him.,

I'm not to sure how Dolf Gaines, my friend from the La Mancha gets to be in the courtroom, but he told me last night that he would be sitting with me, so we might as well ride together.

We had all heard about Launie hitting the guard and shuffling frantically down the hall of the third floor of the jail screaming that they have killed me and thinking she would go through the big window at the end and land in the Sound, but instead had landed on the hard dirt below.

We kept track of her stay in the hospital with broken ribs, broken nose, and concussions. Her stay there had undoubtedly postponed the trial—postponed it for the first time.

The same guard Launie had overpowered, a short woman probably close to thirty years old, was with J C Blevins as they walked Launie into the courtroom, and she now stood behind Launie at the defense table.

I remembered that poster which was plastered about town when Launie first opened her place. It showed her standing in a provocative pose beckoning you to come visit her. Part of that attractiveness had returned now—the hideous clown was gone.

I realized it was her eyes that I remember from that poster. Now they were sharp, attacking, and continually searching the faces of the jury and the people in the courtroom. I got the feeling she was looking for a particular person, but that may just be my imagination.

I would kick myself for the rest of the trial because when I look at Launie, I hear lines from that song from back in the 1980's about Bette Davis eyes. She had once been a truly remarkable and uniquely attractive woman staring with those eyes, but Launie's stare even now could transfix you.

"She'll unease you" and "she'll lay you on her throne" and "she'll make a pro blush" and "she'll throw you like a dice" with her "precocious "eyes…

29

Ester Haynes

Three months later in Bickel's Courtroom

JC Blevins stood ten feet behind the Defense table, just far enough that if someone lunged at him, he would have time to evade them. He felt his state issued revolver on his belt.

The two lawyers were at Judge Bickel's bench discussing some- thing in low voices that he could not hear. He was getting tired of this trial, just like the Prof had told him he was. He liked the Prof who he had met last summer when all that trouble broke loose out at the La Mancha.

He wondered why he stuck with this job with its dangers and long hours. It sure wasn't because of the money—about the only lower paid professional were those poor dedicated teachers who put up with today's teenagers.

Blevins is a tall stout young man about thirty-five years old with an easy smile and happy disposition.

When Ollie was killed in the middle of the Sound which is State Property, Blevins suddenly found himself in charge of the investigation. Sometimes he regretted the responsibility of overseeing this horrific case which had gained so much publicity. He knew things about Launie Sanderson that had nothing to do with the murder of Ollie, but which Judge Bickel was determined to keep out of this trial. He had put the cuffs on Launie that night he and others had raced through Fort Walton Beach on a tip from that young couple who saw the murder, as she walked up the gravel path from the little dock where she had tied-up that huge yacht of hers.

The next morning, he saw two cabs pull up and the drivers started loading many pieces of luggage, so much that some of it had to be tied to the racks on the tops. He saw both cabs fill up with Launie's girls and as he followed them, they turned onto Memorial Drive until they reached the entrance to Memorial Cemetery where they turned in. He pulled in behind them and went across the way quite a distance where he took as many pictures as he could with the long lens of his camera. He was afraid they would notice him, but they were too engrossed in what they were doing.

He saw them surround the fresh covered grave and one-by-one lay something by the tombstone. Helping one of them, they got back into the cabs and headed for the Destin-Fort Walton Beach Airport at Valparaiso.

He followed and parked his car and went into the airport after waiting long enough, he thought, for them to get their tickets and go to their departure gate. He was just in time to hear an agent at the United Counter exclaim to another agent, "Did you see that? They all paid their tickets to Memphis with $50 bills. I have a whole drawer full of $50 bills!"

Blevins had learned all he needed to know.

Even though they had the eyewitnesses to the murder, District Attorney Curtis Porter wanted more evidence about what hap- pened at Launie's place the days before the murder. Blevins and Porter talked for hours about what to do, and it was decided that he would go to Memphis to try and locate one or more of the women.

Memphis is the biggest metropolitan area on the Mississippi River and is sprawled out on hundreds of acres as the land around the city is very flat.

Blevins slogged through the mud of West Memphis, Arkansas more times than he could remember. He heard the Blues so much he developed a keen hatred for it. He spent over three months 'living' on Beale Street at nights and traveling many of the shabby streets where there were 'houses' on every block and girls on every corner, but he had no luck finding any of Launie's girls, and he returned to Fort Walton Beach to an unhappy Porter.

A few weeks afterwards he was driving down Memorial Drive and as he passed the cemetery, he remembered the women had laid something around the tombstone and he was curious. He slowly drove his trooper's car into the drive and stopped a few yards from where he thought the grave was. He got out and started walking to it and then saw one of the young women sitting on a bench over at the side of one of the paths. He recognized her immediately for they were all clear in his mind from looking for them and showing their pictures so many times.

She saw him and jumped up to leave but as she hurriedly pushed the baby stroller away, he was close behind her, "Wait! I don't mean to arrest you or anything because I have no idea if you have done something wrong."

She turned to him as he saw she was carrying a grocery sack full of something. "I didn't mean to stay so long," she said.

He saw that her face was stained with tears. "How long have you been back in town?"

"How do you know who I am?" she said quietly.

"I watched when you and the others were here that day when you were going to the airport. I watched all of you put something around his tombstone."

She pushed the stroller back to the bench and sat down and he saw she was weeping uncontrollably now. "Here is what we put on his grave," she said as she dumped the flatten beer cans on the ground. They were not just flattened but crush from end-to-end in little flat medallions. "He did all of these. They used to hang at Launie's place. I just wanted them. I have left them there at his grave for weeks since I came back, but I want them now for his son."

"Miss, my name is J C Blevins. I am working on trying to get Ollie some kind of justice. It's obvious to me that you cared a great deal for him. Will you help me to see that the person who killed him pays for it?"

"Oh, yes. Yes. Mr. Blevins, my name is Ester Haynes. I didn't know what to do and am not brave enough to do away with her by myself, but I will help if I can. I was scared to come to the police."

J C sat down beside her, "How long have you been back in Fort Walton Beach and what are you doing to keep you and the baby fed?" "I was in Memphis about two weeks before he was born," she pulled a cover back from the baby's face and ran her hand gently over the top of his head as he was sound asleep. "I couldn't stand being there away from him," she said as she looked over at Ollie's grave, "and I had to bring the baby to show him....

I didn't know anyone here in town but one of the waitresses at the Tides Inn had been nice to me, so I called her one night and she met me at the bus station when we got here. She knew this nice lady, Mrs. Kirk, over on Pleasant Street who had a back apartment for rent."

"What do you plan to do?"

"Well, I have to live somewhere and there wasn't anything for me up in Tennessee. I don't have any family that I know about so this was the logical place. I got a job at a grocery store over on Mary Ester Cutoff. It's close enough for me to ride the bus and living on Pleasant Street is close enough for me to push the stroller here to the cemetery."

"How old is the baby?"

"He's old enough to be getting into everything that interests him. He likes to crawl around here on the grass, and he likes to play with the medallions. He looks just like his daddy. His name is Mitch."

"Miss Haynes if you help me and Prosecuting Attorney Curtis Porter at Launie Sanderson's trial it will be an awfully hard and very long time for you. We are dealing with a ruthless and stubborn defense that will drag you through everything they can think of. But if we have you to tell us first-hand what was going on at her place and what was happening with Ollie, we could very well convict her of Ollie's death as premeditated murder."

"Mr. Blevins, I was one of the girls who worked at her place and did things I am ashamed about. Oh, I didn't do anything unlawful and not anything immoral, but I used my body too convince lots of those men to spend their money at that place. Maybe no one will believe me if I tell what happened there."

"Let's leave that for Mr. Porter to decide. Will you meet with him?"

"Yes… if I can clean-up what I have heard since about how crazy Ollie acted, I must."

"Good. Do you have a phone?"

"Yes, I must afford a phone because I need to keep in touch with Mrs. Kirk when I'm at work or someplace else. I was really lucky to find her for if she loves him like she loves her grandkids, Mitch is in good hands. I don't think it will be long before he starts calling her Grams like they do. The arrangement has work out so well. She takes care of Mitch during the day and makes some money and I have the opportunity to work."

"Good, I'll call you later this afternoon. In the meantime, watch out for yourself and Mitch. I don't want some people in this town to know you are back. Don't be afraid but don't go to any of the old places that you use to go to."

And now he looked across the courtroom and saw her sitting straight with her arms crossed across her chest like she was trying to be alone and not seen. He must be staring at her for he realized she was looking back at him. Their eyes met and he smiled at her and thought he saw a timid little smile back.

Suddenly he felt responsible for this woman who he had come to know in the last few months. She is a good mother and from the reports at the grocery store she is a hard worker.

A thought whizzed through his mind that he hadn't considered before; she was very attractive and very interesting. Blevins blushed. He looked around to see if anyone was watching him.

He forced his mind back to what was happening in the court room. Prosecutor Porter was questioning Ester.

"We were on top of that building peering over the edge looking at the filthy water rushing toward us for Katrina had busted through the levees, and… and… he came around a corner from Esplanade Street with a pack of dogs chasing him."

She started shaking again, and Porter got her a glass of water. "Can you go on, Miss Haynes?"

"I'm sorry… Yes. Just as he jumped for the fire escape, one of the dogs lunged toward him jumping up and it bit down on his calf tearing a big gash in it. It's a big, jagged scar that I've seen many times since. That's why he was so terrified of dogs. That's why he went on that rampage down Santa Rosa Blvd… last summer." She paused and quickly looked around to see if anyone had caught her mistake.

She hurried on, "He kicked the High Yeller one still biting down on his calf with his other foot and broke loose from it. He climbed on up and we pulled him as he got close enough, and he tumbled over the parapet right… right in front of Launie's feet.

He had a big bag of food he had taken from *Lil Dizzy's* and that food was about all we had for three days until a helicopter saw us and got us down from there."

"Weren't you all afraid that Ollie's injured leg would get infected?"

"One of the girls, Kitty, had thought to bring the medicine case with her as we ran away from the water. It had penicillin in it, and we gave Ollie shots in his thigh."

"Miss Haynes, I would ask you why you all had penicillin at the place where you all worked, but I better not."

Bickel smiled.

"And then what happened?"

"We were at the Super Dome for several days until Launie rented two U-Carrie vehicles that hauled all of us and we took off for somewhere. We ended up in the parking lot at Walmart here in Fort Walton Beach.

Launie had just as much money it seemed as she use to have in New Orleans—a lot of money—and took care of us until she bought that place down on the Sound and named it *Launie's Gentlemen's Library*."

Ester glanced at Launie who was glaring at her as laughter burst out in the courtroom. Judge Bickel pounded his gavel on the block on his desk and warned the whole courtroom that he would clear the whole room if there wasn't order immediately.

"So that's how you came to be on Okaloosa Island?"

"Yes… We were here until…" She finally broke down and could or would not say another word.

"Can you just answer Yes or No, Miss Haynes?"

She shook her head affirmatively.

"You were here until after Ollie's death and funeral?"

She shook her head up and down with little jerks, whispered "Yes," and collapsed onto the floor.

J C Blevins was the first one to reach her. He lifted her up and laid her on the defense table.

Judge Bickel recessed court until the following day

Before court began the next day, Judge Bickel came into the court room and stood in front of the room announcing, "Ladies and gentlemen in this room, I want you to very carefully listen to what I am about to say. There will be no more talking, responding out loud, or disruption in this courtroom. I will empty all people, including future witnesses until they are called, and we will have a little private trial. Does anyone need this repeated?"

He slowly looked around the room, and his eyes stopped on Dolf who was in his usual seat next to the Prof.

J C looked across the room to make certain Katrina Hart was at her post. She was standing against the wall with her legs apart in a combat stance, it seemed to him.

His hand involuntarily went to the handle of his revolver that hung on his belt. It forced him to grin at himself. He knew he was doing that a lot recently.

The courtroom was, if you will use your imagination, a 'Southern Courtroom' straight out of many movies made in the South.

Judge Bickel sat on a dais which was a good two feet above the floor—Prosecutor Curtis Porter and Schaberg had to stretch their legs to put their arms up on the railing that ran along in front of his desk, when they were having a conference.

One side of the room was nothing but windows, big windows. that opened wide to let in air for there was no air conditioning. Old fashioned 'church' fans swept back and forth in the hands of most in the room, and their sound lulled some to fall asleep. We had a new modern jail close by, but the old courthouse had never been remodeled.

The back doors were double doors which swung open from both sides. They had big vertical metal handles on the outside.

The door behind Judge Bickel opened out onto the back parking lot so he could enter court without anyone engaging him.

"Okay, then, let's resume, Mr. Porter."

Curtis Porter asked for Ester to return to the witness chair.

J C watched her as she walked up to the witness box, stepped up the three steps, and sat down in the chair. She was probably in her middle thirties but looked quite a bit younger. Her figure would make most women jealous, and J C could see that her legs were her best asset. They were muscular and firm from dancing so much, he guessed.

He caught himself staring at them, and jerked his head up, looked around the courtroom to see if he had been caught, lowered his head and grinned.

For an instant, another pair of legs like hers flashed through his mind but he couldn't place where he had seen them.

The other striking thing that made her face appealing were her eyes; they were wide apart and always looked straight at whoever was talking to her, except when she lowered her head to compose herself.

Again, J C looked around to see if anyone was watching him. He glanced at Launie Sanderson, and she was looking straight at him with a smirk on her mouth. He quickly walked toward the back of the room and stood at the back doors.

"Miss Haynes, yesterday you were telling us about how you just arrived at Fort Walton Beach and that Launie Sanderson had bought the property out at the east end of Santa Rosa Blvd and opened *Launie's Gentlemen's Library…*"

Laughter erupted in the room and Bickel pounded his gavel. "I have warned you and I will empty this room on the next disruption." "Miss Haynes, I apologize for the people in the room and ask you to go on with telling us about the job you had with Miss Sanderson." Schaberg was on his feet, "That's already been answered, Your Honor…"

"Overruled, I'll take care of what we hear in this court, Mr. Schaberg."

Schaberg looked startled and turn to look at Porter who also was looking at Judge Bickel with a questioning look. The whole courtroom was silent, and everyone was looking around wondering what has just happened.

"Continue Mr. Porter."

"Okay, now Miss Haynes… What did the girls do at Miss Sanderson's place?"

She hesitated, "About the same as we had done in New Orleans except toward the end…."

"What do you mean 'toward the end?"

"Well, Launie seemed to lose interest in what we were doing." She looked toward Launie and was met with a stare so steely that she quickly turned back to Porter. "There were lots of days we didn't see or hear from her. She was out on that big boat, the *Lollipop*.

There were snickers of derision. Bickel who had been looking down at some paper jerked up his head and the courtroom became quiet.

"Kitty, the oldest of us and probably the most outgoing, almost ran the place until she just disappeared one night. And then Chuck disappeared too."

"Chuck disappeared?"

"Yes, they had a big fight… Him and Launie… And then he was just not there anymore."

"How do you know about the fight?"

"Some of us heard Launie cussing and screaming that night. One of the girls knocked on her door and when she didn't open it, one of us did. We all gathered around the doorway and some of us went inside where she was sitting on the floor surrounded by broken glasses and a spilled bottle of something. The table was overturned and looked like it had been slammed against the wall.

Her face was all swelled up and turning purple. She was going to have a black eye and did for many days. After that she wore so much eye make-up that you couldn't see her eyes, just the sockets."

"And Chuck was not there?"

"I never saw him again after that."

"Miss Haynes, you've mentioned Chuck twice. Who was he and what did he do for Launie?"

"He used her yacht a lot. And we found out after he left that he really was her own son. I can't imagine how they could've sat there on the floor of her room hitting each other until she was black and blue in the face."

Schaberg bounced out of his chair, "Objection! How does the witness know it was Chuck who hit Launie Sanderson?"

Ester didn't hesitate, "They were the only ones in the room that night. I was there and know that."

Schaberg scoffed and sat down.

Bickel smiled, "Go ahead, Miss Haynes."

Ester looked at Porter, and he shook his head, and asked, "And then the same happened with the girl you call Kitty?"

"No, I mean yes, she was gone all of a sudden, but she and Launie didn't have a fight because Launie was very upset and called her a bunch of names because she… …Kitty just disappeared. But Kitty was gone a long time before Launie and Chuck had the fight and he left."

Launie Sanderson looked like she would come out of her seat and spat out, "You ungrateful bitch. You will pay for what you say." Schaberg grabbed Launie's arm, but Porter was fit to be tied,

"Your Honor, I call for a mistrial!"

"Oh, come on Mr. Porter, you know very well that is not going to happen, not in my lifetime."

Bickel turned to Schaberg, "Mr. Schaberg, if you cannot con- trol your client, I will her gagged and put her back there in that wooden cage so we cannot hear anything else she might say to disrupt these proceedings. Continue, Mr. Porter."

Porter looked in Schaberg's direction and I thought I saw a slight smile as he rubbed his hand across his chin. "Miss Haynes, I had just asked you when the woman known as 'Kitty' had disappeared before we were interrupted."

"Early in the summer, I think…June or early July. Some weird guy was coming in regularly and asking only for her. After she did her routine right in front of him, they would sit, and he would drink, and she would keep the drinks coming. I saw her leave with him one night."

That pair of legs J C had thought about a few minutes before suddenly were attached to that first body on the beach last year and he almost caused a disruption in the court as he thought he knew who it was.

He must have made a sound because Judge Bickel said, "Sergeant Blevins, do you have something to say?"

"I apologize, Your Honor. My mind was working out loud." The whole room burst into laughter.

Bickel was livid and pounded his gavel until J C thought he would break it.

"I will empty this room on the next disturbance," Bickel shouted.

Many in the room looked from one to the other seeming to think this was a strange way for a judge to act.

Bickel didn't lower his voice as he said, "Mr. Porter continue." Porter cleared his throat, "Now, Miss Haynes, you said Miss Sanderson was not paying much attention to you girls?"

"Just before the end…"

"The end?"

"Before Ollie's death," Ester was crying again "before his murder." She sat and sobbed uncontrollably for a few minutes until Porter started again.

"Miss Haynes, I am almost finished asking you questions. Will you try to answer just a few more? … Now we know you and Ollie were spending quite a bit of time together, and that people could see that you were going to have a baby. Had you and Ollie talked about any plans?"

"That was all ruined, of course when he…" It seemed like minutes as she struggled to get the words out, "Yes. We were going to just disappear like Chuck and Kitty had. We were going to go two nights after…" The next came out of her like a scream, "…two nights after Launie Sanderson took him out and shot him in the back of his head!" The room was in an uproar again at hearing those words. Bickel was pounding his gavel furiously and everyone was talking amongst themselves.

Ester Haynes' face suddenly went blank. She was crying hysterically and saying, "That's when my world ended. That's when I lost him. Oh God that I could have died with him…no, no I was going to have Little Mitch…I had to live."

She disappeared back into her thoughts, thoughts of that day when she and the other girls stood around Ollie's new dug grave, and they all laid the beer can medallions around the stone they had bought for him. How someone had given her a stack of money and she had bought her ticket to Memphis. How Memphis had been a hell for her as she had Little Mitch in a dump of a motel with two of the other girls helping her with the birth. How she had finally said good-bye to the others and returned to Fort Walton Beach. How Fort Walton Beach had been little better than Memphis except she had a job, little Mitch, and a place to sit close to where Ollie lay.

And then another time came to mind; they were like little chil- dren as they dug into the bank of one of the drain-off spaces that are along Santa Rosa Blvd to drain rainwater down into the Sound. She had been amazed at the trove of things Ollie had hidden there.

He said, "My hero had a special cave for his equipment, so I had to find a place also. It took a long time to build my cave because it kept falling in so I put all these rocks in here. I kept thinking that the utility men would find it and destroy all my things, or that some kids would find it and tell their folks."

They had taken all his bows and arrows and the many articles that might belong to the Green Arrow of Ollie's imagination back to Ollie's room. It had taken them two nights to finish the mission as he called it and they had laughed like high school kids pulling a prank as they smuggled in his treasures.

He had marveled when the baby had kicked him one night as they snuggled together and had laid his head on her stomach as the baby continued to kick. He had talked to the baby and called him Mitch and promised to make a good life for him. She had stopped him in midsentence when she had asked, "What if it is a girl?" He hadn't even flinched as he replied, "Then she will be beautiful like her mother, and I will dance with her when she is homecoming queen, and I will chase no-account boys away. They had laughed for minutes. But a homecoming queen can't have parents who aren't married to each other, so let's figure out how to get married," he had said. She had sobbed on his chest for five minutes or so before she said, "Maybe we'd better wait until we leave here because Launie might try to stop us."

"No, I'm going to find out tomorrow how to get a license, and we're going to do it, that is, if you will marry me?"

Then she had laughed and laughed, and he thought at first, she was laughing at him but when she made it clear that he was silly for that for she would be the happiest woman if they were married, then he had laughed too.

The next morning, they had gone to the courthouse and and were told they would have to wait three days after their blood test came back to get a license; Ollie was furious and as they went back to the Dorm on the city bus, he had blurted out, "What if we don't live that long?"

Ester slid out of the chair and landed in the floor. Schaberg was shouting that her last statement should be stricken. Judge Bickel was pounding his gavel with sharp fast bangs.

J C Blevins rushed forward to tend to Ester Haynes.

Launie Sanderson sat with a wide smile, but her smile turned to a vulgar snarl as she looked squarely at Ester.

Bickel recess the court, again

30

It's Over

No Silencer this time....

The next day Judge Bickel reconvened court.

Schaberg requested a meeting at his bench with Porter and Bickel allowed it.

"Your Honor, my client is not getting a fair trial. How in the world do you or anyone else expect this jury to be able to remember what has happened in the courtroom with the numerous recesses we have had? Besides that, they have been secluded in some motel or resort somewhere and have been away from their families, work, and friends, whatever. Therefore, the Defense is asking for a mistrial in this case. I have prepared the papers and will file them with you this afternoon."

Porter interjected, "Your Honor, part of the Prosecution's stand on this matter agrees with Mr. Schaberg but I would remind the court that it is not the Prosecution's fault that these proceedings have been going on so long."

"Bull Shit, sir. You have dallied around with witnesses like Ester Haynes which really had no bearing on the murder trial. You lost your two eyewitnesses to what you are claiming was murder. So, how can you say that the Prosecution is not responsible?" Bickel spat out. "I would remind the Judge that many of the recesses were call by himself. I would remind him also that he could not control the crowded courtroom and that he took personal time to be away from the trial."

"Mr. Porter, you are close to being held in contempt."

"I respectfully ask that we try to proceed, and I will start my summation if that is your ruling."

"Agreed. Mr. Schaberg, will you agree to going right to the summation?'

Schaberg looked like he had won the lottery as he answered, "Gladly, Your Honor."

Judge Bickel could not believe that Porter had just conceded, or almost conceded, the case. It was eleven o'clock and he decided that court would resume after lunch.

"Ladies and Gentlemen of the Jury, we have decided to resume the trial right after lunch today. Court is now once again in recess until after lunch."

There were groans from all corners of the courtroom and I saw some looks of total disbelief on the faces of several jurors, but as Bickel left the courtroom the jury was also dismissed so Katrina Hart could take them to lunch.

I wondered what Dolf would be saying to me, but I haven't seen him for several days. No one at the La Mancha has seen him either.

I saw J C rush through the back door of the courtroom and go quickly to Mr. Porter's table. He leaned in and Porter looked shocked and then he smiled. Now all he had to do is get out of what he had agreed about summary statements for Blevins had Sam Ripley and Alice Pearl in a cell upstairs in the jail.

Forty-five minutes later when court was called to order, Porter and Schaberg stood before Judge Bickel's bench.

"Your Honor, I would like to amend what I agreed about this morning. I would like to call two eyewitnesses to the stand." He had broken the rules of a meeting at the bench for he said the last part loud enough for the whole courtroom to hear it.

Schaberg looked like he had been shot as he almost stuttered, "Your Honor, I strongly object. Mr. Porter agreed this morning that we would start our summations and I have worked through lunch making ready to present mine."

Bickel did something that Porter would never forget until he realized what Bickel said was just for show, "Mr. Schaberg, the public and Okaloosa County would never again agree with anything I did. I would be the laughingstock of the whole county. My courtroom would never again be the place where the important trials of the day would be held. So, I am letting Mr. Porter proceed."

Schaberg look at Bickel like he had just signed both their death certificates; he looked sick, extremely sick, as he had turned very pale. He requested a very short recess so he could go to the restroom.

Bickel allowed it.

"Ladies and Gentlemen of the Jury and members of the court, we will recess for ten minutes for Mr. Schaberg to go to the restroom."

There were groans first and then fits of laughter.

Blevins was talking with Porter and then he walked out the back door of the courtroom on his way upstairs to get Sam Ripley and Alice Pearl and escort them down to the court.

Schaberg leaned in and obviously told Launie that the two witnesses were upstairs and that they would be testifying. He walked quickly to the rear door of the courtroom and left.

Launie was stunned. Her face was filled with rage as she jumped to her feet cussing, held the edge of the table, but looked like she was headed straight for Judge Bickel.

Katrina Hart stepped in front of her, raised her gun and shot Launie right between the eyes, "It's over you ungrateful ass."

A faint look of disbelieve cross Launie's face as blood gushed from the little hole in her forehead. As she crumbled to the floor her body lodged against the Defense table; she slid down one of the legs of the table and landed sitting upright blankly staring out at the courtroom.

The courtroom was in total silence until the shock of what had just happened enveloped them for this time Katrina Hart's revolver did not have a silencer on it and the loud explosion had startled all of us. The gruesome figure of Launie sitting there with that vacant stare of death caused the people in the room to almost stampede to the back door.

Above it all I heard Ester Haynes scream, "It's done, Ollie, it's done."

The jury started as a group toward the backroom where they always entered but saw that Katrina blocked it, so they turned as a group, and headed for the back door where they crushed up against all the other people trying to get out. There was pandemonium as everyone in the courtroom tried to exit there.

Katrina shouted above the roar, "Either stop or be shot. I will start killing the ones closest to me and continue as long as I have ammunition." People stopped where they were.

During all the confusion she had made her way up to Judge Bickel's chair, she walked around behind him, encircled his neck with her arm, held the gun to his temple and ordered him to stand. She hollered, "I have Judge Bickel and will shoot him as easily as I have Launie if anyone tries to stop us from leaving." She pulled Bickel through the door behind his bench and locked it from the out- side as they left.

Porter sat at his table in shock.

The killing of Launie Sanderson and the confusion after the shot took only a few minutes, but Schaberg had been very busy as it was happening. He had run from the courthouse down to the Sound where the *Lollipop* had been anchored since Launie's arrest. He started the big powerful engines and had it ready to leave.

I was near a window where I could see out toward behind the courthouse. I saw Katrina Hart and Judge Bickel hop into the golf cart that was waiting there. They sped down the sidewalk and jumped aboard the *Lollipop*. Schaberg pulled the big yacht away from the dock and headed out into the Sound.

Schaberg steered the big blue and white yacht carefully down the Sound keeping it in the deep water the barges used. He kept glancing back toward the County Jail expecting water patrol boats to come speeding out from the dock underneath the building, but he didn't see any and he knew he couldn't go any faster.

He was unfamiliar with the *Lollipop* and didn't know where the barge channel was so he had to watch for the buoys and so they were going down the Sound very slowly.

The calculating little lawyer started thinking to himself, "Is this really going to work? Are we going to pull this off?" The answer was no, of course, he realized because even if they got all the way back to Miami someone would be coming after them.

He knew also that since they had messed up things so much that Katrina's dad would get rid of them anyway. He wondered what her dad would do to Judge Bickel. Would Bickel's wife, Diana, be able to talk her dad out of killing him for the sake of their seven kids—his grandkids?

And then, Schaberg decided he just didn't care. He was never going to go back to Miami. He was going to get off this boat some- where between here and there and disappear for good.

Katrina Hart walked up just then and stood beside him. As he turned toward her, she said, "Schaberg you played your part. You did a great job of being the idiot you are in the courtroom, but we don't have any more use for you."

She held the gun in her hand up to his forehead and shot him. She had no concern that anyone had heard it. She turned to Judge Bickel and said, "Well, I have no more use for this," as she threw the gun over into the black water of the Sound, "And we'll dispose of this when we get out into the Gulf down past Destin," as she stepped over Schaberg's body and reached for the steering wheel.

Bickel smiled at her and walked to her and wrapped his arms around her as she faced away from him cupping her breasts in his hands, "We made a good pair in that court, didn't we? Let's see if we can continue this. Let's not go to Miami. Let's just go off and get lost somewhere."

She looked up at him and smiled, "I thought you wouldn't ask me." They both laughed and he leaned to kiss her neck.

Either Dolf Gaines had told the man who came up from Miami yesterday the wrong setting for the explosion after the big yacht had gone so far, or the man had made a mistake.

The explosion rocked the Sound from the jail to Brooks Bridge. The Narrows shook with the reverberations for several minutes. Bits of the *Lollipop* blew so high that they fell on the roadway that goes across the bridge. The big tanks Launie had installed in the yacht so it could travel a long distance had been full when the man had attached the timing devise to the engine of the *Lollipop*.

"Damn it to hell," Dolf Gaines cussed, from his hiding place on the Island bank of the Sound, as he saw the flying debris of the *Lollipop* as it careened about the two shores of the Sound smashing into windows that shattered into sailing missiles, "that wasn't sup- posed to happen until it was past the bridge and way out into the Bay." He heard the crash of cars smashing into each other and into buildings along Main Street.

He imagined bits of Judge Bickel splatting down into the dark water of the Sound to become catfish food. He laughed aloud.

31

Following Orders

When the Kingpin pulls the strings, the puppet responds.

"I have her."

"What do you mean, you have her?"

"She's unconscious in the back of my Jeep." "How in the world? Is she still alive? What happened?"

"Schaberg had tipped me that he was terrified of her and that there was no telling what she was about to do. He said they had a plan that if she had to take out Launie in the courtroom, he would have the *Lollipop* ready, and they would come down the Sound to the Bay and on down to Destin and out into the Gulf. They thought it would work, and they could outrun anything, because Launie had souped-up the yacht so much.

"What were you supposed to do?"

"That was unclear and as it turned out, I didn't have to worry about it. I rented the most powerful wave runner that place down at the Harbor Village in Destin had and tied it up at Launie's old dock. With all the construction going on there, no one asked me any questions. I could see all the way down the Sound to the new jail from there, and you better believe I almost poop my pants when the *Lollipop* exploded."

"I bet you did. It shook all of us here also."

"I was circling around the spot where it exploded while pieces of it were still sailing through the air, and just as I was getting ready to call the hunt off, I saw her floating thirty feet or more in front of where it happened.

She must have been blown out like getting shot out of a cannon. I got in the water and threw her up on the seat of the wave runner, got on behind her, and took her back down to Launie's old dock not too far away and I carried her to my jeep."

"How is she?"

"She's been unconscious since I found her. Her right leg is obviously broken, and I think her left hand is too as it is all swollen. She has several cuts on her face and chest, and her face is burnt a lot. I made sure she is unarmed. I got the bleeding stopped by wrapping my shirt and underwear around her that I had in my Jeep.

"Good. Get her over to Bickel's place. You know the code the gate?"

"Yes."

"I'll send you the code to open the garage door. The panel is on the door and the garage should be empty as Bickel's car is still at the courthouse.

Once you get inside, take her into the library and slide out the volume of his law books that does not have a number on it, and then the bookcases will open.

"You're bull-shitten me, right?"

"No, I am not and now, listen to me. I've hidden in that room several times during the trial when he brought her there and found out a lot of things. I was just lucky they didn't decide to go into that room, or they would have gotten rid of me.

"Get her into that room, tie her up on the daybed with the plas- tic ties I have left there, and get out of there. Be sure to slide the law book back so it's even with the others. I'll get over there as soon as I can."

"You going to call her father?"

"Yes, just like we've been instructed to do. He'll send a doctor up as soon as I tell him. I don't think he will come up himself, but I'm sure all hell is going to break loose.

Now, you hurry up, get everything done like I told you, and get back to the beach before someone complains to Daniel Sheraton."

She deleted the call from her phone and placed another call to

Miami, "It's over. She's alive. Hurt a lot with broken bones and burns. Need a doctor."

No one on the other end said a word, but that was as it was planned.

Lori Cherry slumped back into her office chair, took a deep breath, and decided to go out and walk around the La Mancha property.

32

A Wood Clamp Will Work

It is over, Katrina Hart

She sat in the ornate chair she pulled in from the living room, sipped her bottle of flavored water, and waited.

Craig, the Manager of Grounds and Maintenance at the La Mancha, had taken two days off to go to Panama City for some reason, which gave her the opportunity to go through his maintenance room back of the Rental Office.

She went out the back door of her office, down the hall past the sauna room where Dolf Gaines had visited every afternoon, and out the back door. She looked around to see if any of Craig's crew were around, entered the storage room, and started exploring.

Some of this stuff must have been here for forty years, she thought. Hanging on one wall was a clamp like one she had seen before, a wooden clamp, used for laminating strips of wood together to make a cutting board or something, and she was sure Craig would never miss it.

As she left the room, she saw a box of latex gloves the cleaning women use when they do dirty work. She helped herself to a couple of pairs.

Now, she sat in the fancy chair wearing the gloves.

"What are you doing here?" Katrina Hart mumbled through bleary eyes.

"It's my sister's house too, you know," Lori Cherry answered. "How did you know about this room?"

"Oh, I've spent hours in this room listening to you and that cheating Bickel carrying on. You two thought you were so smart, but you were a couple of novice idiots. Everyone knew what you were doing. Diana found out about it, and we started planning what to do with the two of you.

"How did Diana find out about it?"

"I told her, of course. She's my real sister, you know. She's not some scum who lived next door to us just because we all had the same father.

Do you think she was going to let you and that no count hus- band of hers get away with all your afternoon romps here on the daybed where you are now?

Even that blowhard, Dolf Gaines, knew why court was recessed so many times. Our father will decide what to do as he always does."

"Yes, and he'll take care of me now too. I always was the favorite," Katrina said with a look of disdain. "He'll get me out of here and back down to Miami."

"You may be right. I'm waiting for him to tell me what to do." Katrina laughed a weak little laugh, "He won't let you hurt me.

I'm his favorite little girl."

"You're a dangerous bitch. We had everything figured out, and after Launie's trial, we would have carried on what we were doing, and nobody would have known about it. But, no, you idiot, you had to shoot my sister right there in front of a full courtroom. You're crazy and dangerous. Why did you kill Schaberg? Oh, yes, I read when they recovered what was left of his body, there was a bullet in his forehead. Your trademark you are so proud of."

"He knew too much."

"And now maybe someone else does too…You."

"You just wait and see. My father will call me back to Miami and you can just go to hell."

"Well, say whatever you want. You don't have much time left to shoot off your big mouth. You are wrong for your father, my father, told me last night he didn't want to see you again. He said to take care of things, and that is what I plan to do. You shot my sister Launie, right between the eyes, and that's my plan for you, deary.

"You don't even have a gun, and besides we both know you never shot guns when the rest of us did."

"Yes, I have the gun. I have one just like the one you use on Launie," Lori said as she pulled it from the folds in the cushion of the chair she sat on, "See, just like yours."

"You don't have guts enough to shoot me. You always were a wimp. That's why father put you in the rental office away from any dealing with moving the stuff."

"Oh, maybe so, but I have hatred that will cause me to do it. I'm smarter than the lot of you, and you've always known that. You see, I'm prepared to do to you what you did to the others. That bottle of water I gave you about fifteen minutes ago is about to do its work. When you wake up, you will see if I have hatred enough."

A few minutes later, Katrina's head kept bobbin up and down until she finally passed out.

Lori Cherry is the oldest of the girls that grew up next door to each other in Miami. She has grown to hate the man she has to call 'father' because of the *no me importa un bledo* attitude he has toward the two women he calls 'wives,' but only uses to bear children. He really doesn't care about the two women, and his girls only earn, usually with great effort and danger, the tidbits of praise he rations out to them. She thinks of him as a feudal hot-blooded bastard who brags about his prized possession and the tightness of his skinny jeans.

She knows she should have left what was called home long ago, and disappeared, but she also knew he would find her, especially now that he has a use for her. Is this how prostitutes feel, she wondered? Doing day after day horrible acts that they hate, just to satisfy their pimp? But she knows the real reason; she is terrified of him. She's just a piece of living meat, he will chew up and spit out on a whim.

She had been busy as all these thoughts went bouncing through her mind. The daybed has vertical metal spindles all along the side and the two ends. She attached one side of the wood clamp to a spindle on the end with double duct tape running it back and forth as she wrapped it securely.

She grabbed a handful of Katrina's hair and pulled her head up into position so she could slide her head between the two ends of the clamp. She wrapped duct tape around that end and pulled it tight around the spindle on the back side of the bed. She tested it by jerking it back and forth rapidly. She laughed with childlike glee as Katrina's head was whipped back and forth. It was secure.

She sighed, sat again in the chair that is so out of place in this stark, almost empty little room.

Katrina's body is lying straight down the long side of the bed, but her head is turned at almost a right angle as it fits into the corner where the end meets the side. She must be extremely uncomfortable, Lori smiles.

Katrina starts stirring but doesn't open her eyes.

Couldn't she feel the wooden clamp fastened to her head? Why didn't it wake her up?

Lori was getting impatient and would wake the brat in a minute if she didn't wake up, she decided.

What a crazy idea, she thought, as wanting to see her mother raced through her mind. Why would she want to go back down there? Hibiscus Island sometimes haunted her. There had been the bragging and taunting from across the fence that their house was the biggest, but she and Launie and Diana had spit right back that theirs had more beachfront on Biscayne Bay.

She had learned that the proudest day in her father's life was when she and Launie had been born twins, but not identical ones.

Rumor always flew about that her father hit her mother when she brought them home to the big mansion. Hit her because they were not identical.

If only she had the nerve to do away with him.

She hated the man with every thought she had. She hated that she and the others never went to school but had the same teacher in the same classroom. That hadn't worked out so well, had it, Dear Father, for that silly lecherous old man didn't have the balls to keep things in order. She had done some of her best jokes to the other side as they all were put in the 'cell' for the entire morning.

And here she had the other side in a cell again.

A thought flashed through her head that the others were just as trapped as she, for they were only allowed to do whatever he wanted done. That's what got Launie in trouble, she knew, but why had he chosen Katrina to be the one to kill Launie? She felt tears entering her eyes as she thought of Launie, her twin. Then it hit her squarely, he was just egging on the rivalry that he had created ever since they were born.

Katrina twisted in the bed, opened her eyes, and looked with hatred at Lori, "What the hell is this contraption on my head. Get this silly piece of wood off me."

"Oh, Baby Katrina, you are in for such a surprise. It's so simple that I can hardly imagine my genius of coming up with it."

"What the hell are you babbling about? Get me out of this thing. The doctor said my father sent his love when he was here to set my leg and wrap my ankle."

"That was weeks ago, and our father always sends his love.

Haven't you figured out that's not what it means many times?" "Take this silly thing off me. I'm not going to hurt myself by trying to get up and escaping."

"No, my little Baby Katrina, you are not."

Lori laughed with that taunting laugh that signaled she was about to perform one of her sadistic pranks.

"You can't scare me. I don't believe you have permission to hurt me, and you'll get in trouble if you do."

"Oh, Baby Katrina…. little spoiled Baby Katrina who always got her way. You shouldn't have made a spectacle of yourself in the courtroom witnessed by all those people. You shouldn't have proved you could seduce that son-of-a-bitch Diana picked for a husband. I hope he satisfied you every way so you can remember how it was."

Katrina was struggling now, but quickly saw that it was hope- less as Lori had tied her securely to the metal spindles. She looked at Lori and fear entered her mind for the first time.

"Okay, my little one, are you ready? I feel that what you did to the others is what you deserved to happen to you."

She moved to the bed and took the sides of the wood clamp she had secured around Katrina's head in both her hands.

She bent down and her face was almost touching Katrina's as she looked into her eyes and said, "You feel how the clamp presses in on your ears, so you won't hear what happens when it does? It's not as good as your silencer, but it will have to do."

Terror filled Katrina's face as she spit at Lori.

"Just like always…Little Baby Katrina spitting when she knows she is in trouble. You should have died in the explosion. None of us can understand why that didn't kill you, But I am so thankful for duct tape. You know why? Because it keeps this clamp tight around your head. Good old duct tape! And now, dear little brat, do you see the space between the ends of the clamp right in front of your face? Sure, you do because that is probably all that you can see. Only one more thing is needed…oh, no, I'm wrong. Two more things are needed. Do you know what?"

Katrina struggled, kicked, and started to scream for help.

"That's not going to help you this time No one can hear you. But listen to me, if you struggle as you are now, you will not last long…."

"Why are you doing this? Please, please, let me loose."

"Now, that's exactly what I want to hear. I might think about it. Okay, I thought about it. It's NO, NO, NO. You killed Launie like she was a rat caught in a trap, and now I have snared you in a better trap—thanks to good old Duct Tape."

She took the revolver from the chair where she had been sitting. It was an exact model as the gun Katrina had used so many times on so many people. She walked back to the bed.

"And now my pieza de Resistencia!" A gun just like the one you used. Can you guess where I got it? I will tell you… Our father sent it up to me…."

She slid the gun into the space between the two sides of the wood clamp, "And now more, good old duct tape. Thanks be to duct tape!" She taped the two sides securely to the gun handle having to struggle with

Katrina who was twisting and trying to turn with all her might. "Please let me go. I will go away, and he will never know," she whimpered.

"No, my deary. That is not what our father ordered. Oh, look, I must tell you how this works. You see, this is the second thing I need—this little piece of fishing line that I am tying securely around the back of your ear after I tie it to the trigger."

"And now, I must explain the bullet to you. Oh, I know you already know about bullets… Right?"

She smirked as she held the bullet up in front of Katrina's face, "You see, this is not just a bullet. I forget what you call it, but upon impact, it explodes into bits. Pow!" She clapped her hands together and swung them wide apart with her fingers spread out.

"Shards of this little piece of destruction are going to rip through your whole head and blow the back off. Just don't move and it won't happen—just try to not move…."

"Just listen to yourself… You've lost your mind. You sound like a blithering idiot."

Lori stepped back, sat down in the fancy chair, and rapid little gasps escaped from her mouth.

"You may be correct about that."

She took the bullet, opened the cylinder of the gun and inserted it, and twirled the cylinder until the bullet was in the firing chamber. She put it in front of Katrina's face to show her where the bullet was. "Now, if you don't move, nothing will happen. But if you do move, if you barely move, it will shoot you right between the eyes because the trigger has been filed so thin that a tiny movement will fire it. Father had that done. But there is only one bullet, so maybe you'll miss!"

Lori laughed an almost insane laugh as she left the room. She enjoyed the complete stillness.

She shouted back, "You know deary, the sweetest revenge of all is when you set it up, and the victim does it to herself. You're going to do it for me, baby Katrina. Remember, just don't move. You hear?"

She pushed the law book back even with the other ones on the shelf. As the door slid shut to close the secret room, she jumped involuntarily, startled, and gave out a little shriek at the sound of the bullet exploding.

She felt exhausted, decided to hurry back to the Rental Office at the La Mancha to sit in front of her aquarium.

After all, she is one of the few people who has a foot long Great White shark in their aquarium. It was growing too big, she thought. She would just turn it loose in the Sound as she had several others and call her father to send her a new one.

33

The Pride

Pride cometh before the fall....

The Gulf is upset today like an old-maid spinster grumbling and scolding anyone who might want to change her plans.

The waves are fighting each other in a chaos of breakers that slap each other on the sand bar on the other side of the gulley that separates our beach from the deep water of the Gulf. Rain is expected before midmorning and the television stations have prognosticated heavy winds.

The Security guard let Dolf into the La Mancha property saying, "The Prof isn't here if you're looking for him Mr. Gaines. He left a few minutes ago to go over to Destin. He will be sorry he missed you as he said a couple of days ago that he hadn't seen you for weeks."

Dolf smiled at his good luck, told the guard he would leave a note on the Prof's door and then leave.

He had spent the morning carrying supplies down to the *Choctaw Pride* and loading the refrigerator in the gally with food to last a couple of days. He made sure he had everything for White Russians and that plenty of ice was in his big Igloo cooler until the onboard refrigerator froze ice.

Crab Island appeared in front of the *Pride* as he guided the big sailboat across Choctawhatchee Bay, and even at noon, he saw several boats bobbing in the shallow waters. The Island itself had long ago been swallowed by the tides, but the water was shallow enough to stand in, and since several permanently moored their concessions there, the place was always popular with locals and tourists.

As he steered around the three big catamarans, he smiled as he had piloted each of the three kinds in his earlier days and that the trophies were stashed down below in a box to prove it.

He carefully skirted the Island to the left keeping away from the Coast Guard Station that is on the shore of Okaloosa Island to the west. The *Pride* passed under the Destin bridge, past Noriega Point that creates the entrance to the harbor to the east, and on out into the Gulf.

Twenty minutes later, Daniel Sheraton, standing on the beach in front of the gazebo at the La Mancha, saw the *Pride* go by and then quickly veer out into the Gulf.

"You see how it suddenly veered to the left?" Cam laughed. "Dolf would have made a smooth curve to port and the *Pride* would have skimmed over the water like it was sitting on top. Certainly isn't Dolf steering it today."

In the distance, Dolf saw that silly Pirate boat that looks like a Spanish galleon of long ago. It anchors at Destin Harbor, he knew, and would be full of tourists that got a half-day cruise taking them back to sailing days.

"Hey, Dolf, remember me? It's Max who used to work the beach at the La Mancha. How you doin? Freakin crazy meeting you out in the middle of the Gulf!"

He relaxed and waved as the big boat passed behind the *Pride* and waved at Max again as it appeared on the other side of him. The whole world is too damn small he thought as he remembered Max was the one who found that very first body that washed up on the La Mancha's beach.

He set the course and walked down below to fix a pitcher of White Russians. He was proud of the *Pride* and had spent too much money on it when his parents had bought it for him. His dad had thrown a fit about the ultra-modern kitchen that was better than the one at their home. The bedroom had a round king-sized bed which became very popular with the ladies. The ice maker tup was full of fresh ice, and he mixed a big frosty pitcher full.

The bright yellow and green flag he had made for the 2021 Billy Bow Legs carnival lay on a table. He thought, "Hell, I'm out so far now that no one that knows me will be out here."

He took the flag up on deck with him, and out of the corner of his eye as he climbed the steps to the deck, he saw the bright neon green workout ball he had left from the celebration as it rolled across the floor. That had been a fun weekend as the Pride was full of big- bosomed scantily dressed 'pirate' ladies who partied late into the night.

He sat the pitcher of his favorite drink on the pilot's table, hoisted the flag up the pole, and sat down to admire the late afternoon skies. On the distant horizon to the northwest, a long line of dark storm clouds had formed.

The flag suddenly pops in a strong breeze, and he understand he is in for a good squall. Looking up, he laughs out loud at the flag. "What a piece of genius," he says a loud as he looks at the bright banner shaped like a race victory flag. The yellow and green pieces were sewn diagonally and almost covering them was a tall black bicycle. It had taken weeks for him to hand-sew it, and his Choctaw High buddies, who came to watch the Super Bowl in his condo, must never know he had made it himself. Its large square border was alternate black and white squares and inside that, was the pennant of green and white. No one could doubt who is the captain of the *Pride.*

He was headed to one of the most fantastic places Dolf had ever encountered on the Gulf even though he had been to almost every dock along the coast from Mobile to Port St Joe way over to the east. During the summers of 2001 and 2003, he had tied-up to a deep-sea exploration survey barge that some government agency had financed with Vanderbilt to survey the bottom of the Gulf along the Panhandle of Florida and the few miles of shoreline that Alabama claimed.

He had been totally fascinated by the 3-D seismic imaging to map the area around the Desoto Canyon as high-powered underwater air guns were towed behind a boat larger than the *Pride* and when the guns were fired, they created waves that traveled down and reflected up what the floor looked like.

The most amazing thing of all to Dolf was the huge slide of what appeared to be pure white sand that is so famous along the shorelines of Florida. It covered a large part of the bottom and tilted down to the edge where the shelf fell off into over 4,500 feet of water. As he thought about it, he thought about sledding down the Matterhorn as a teenager, but its steep-sided underwater mountain of sand and silt would make the Matterhorn look like a crab's tiny disturbance in the sand on the beach.

He lowered the anchor, got his fishing gear from the wall, mixed a bucket of chum from what he had thawed out earlier and decided to spend the afternoon and maybe the night, fishing. He was out far enough he was sure no one he knew would be coming this way, so he was in no hurry to get to his final destination.

The next morning, he awoke stiff and disoriented as he had slept in his fishing chair all night. The *Pride* chugged along till midmorning as he was down below several minutes fixing three eggs and several thick slices of bacon. He didn't give a rat's ass if the *Pride* hit something or not, or if it went around in circles. He went back on deck, took a bearing reading, and decided he was in no rush to get out to the Canyon as he had a few things he wanted to do before he got there.

He anchored the *Pride* again, this time about ten miles off the coast from the beach at the La Mancha and was soon visited by a school of dolphins that swam around and around the *Pride*; soon several of them were leaping in and out of the water and sticking their heads up and 'chattering' as they seemed to be asking for food.

He got his rod and reel and took some more chum from the refrigerator. He fished for nearly an hour, but the dolphins had apparently chased all the fish away. He dumped all the chum over the side, but as some of them swam up to it, they turned quickly away and seemed to turn up their noses at it. Soon they were nowhere to be seen.

Suddenly a good-sized bull shark was circling the *Pride* as it obviously smelled the chum. It dove under the boat, and he saw it surface a few yards away on the other side. It came at the *Pride* again, he saw its mouth open wide, and it scooped up much of the chum and a lot of water. It didn't stay around long, and he relaxed in the pilot's chair and wanted a drink bad.

By midafternoon, he finished the third one he had in the last hour, but they did nothing of erasing the fear he felt since finding an envelope wrapped around the steel reinforcing rod next to where the *Pride* was docked. As he pulled it off the rod, the fear had begun, and he looked around, too quickly he thought later, to see if someone was watching him. If someone was, they knew he was scared.

He took time to open the envelope after he had turned away from the beach at the La Mancha this morning and when he reread it, he was really scared. Inside was a copy of Steinbeck's little novel about two bums who traveled around; one of them was obsessed with mice. It was the only novel he had read in school that he really liked, and he saw that the copy he held in his hand was his own and someone had taken it from the shelf in his condo. The usual 'Damn it to Hell' filled his mind. There was a torn piece of paper marking a page and a speech underlined on the page. George was saying after he had killed Lennie why he had to do it, 'He couldn't stand to be put in no cage and locked up like some animal. It would have killed him. I had to do it. I had to set him free.'

The message sank in quickly. Someone knew what he had done and was ready to turn him in to J C Blevins, or some policeman, or Marvin who was a DEA agent. It was clear that someone knew he was involved with Launie Sanderson's real business and probably that he was still involved with whoever was running it now.

Whoever wrote the note was right. He wasn't about to be locked up in a cage for the rest of his life. He would go nuts, he knew.

He drained the glass and poured another and drained it.

He must have dozed off because the sound of an airplane startled him; it was coming straight at him and not very far above the surface of the water. It pulled up a little several hundred yards from the boat, and the big C130 trainer from Eglin roared overhead as it passed. It had scared the pee-waddin out of a bunch of people on the beach recently as it flew straight down the water line just a few feet off the sand.

He had been in the gazebo and had laughed so hard he had tears running down his cheeks as all the people down on the beach had fallen flat on their faces or had tried to run away as the huge plane had rumbled over them. Now it was not so funny because he had nowhere to run and couldn't duck down.

He hurriedly raised the anchor line and headed toward his destination as the C130 roared over his head. It went straight on out to the horizon, and he didn't see it turn back. The sun was low and would soon be setting. Like it happens lots of time, the dark storm clouds had disappeared and now the sky was filled with large puffy clouds, and he knew the sunset would be one of the famous Florida ones.

He stopped the engines and once again anchored the *Pride* as he decided this would be as good a place as any to spend the night. He went below and came back up with his little gas grill, sat it on the piece of marble he had placed on the deck to prevent a fire, went back down and came back with a new pitcher of White Russians and a plate with a thick rib steak that was seasoned heavy with salt and pepper like he liked it.

He brought the bottle of Absolut vodka with him in case he needed to add a little to each glass he poured. He read the label as he sat waiting as the steak began sizzling on the grill. Absolut: distilled till pure, no need for anything to be added—the final absolute quality. He thought of the Prof a few minutes later, "Damn if he isn't right. Rib steaks are a hell-of-a-lot better than sirloins." The steak wasn't on the grill more than two or three minutes because he liked it very rare, "Here's to you Prof. The best to you." As usual, it took him little time to devour the big steak, and something leaped out of the water to snatch the bone he threw overboard.

The sun set and he caught that moment as those strange green light flashes as it sinks down below the water on the horizon. A cool breeze started, and he wondered if there was a storm out to the west of him, but it must be far away if there was, because it was clear out that way. Soon it began to get dark, and he was amazed as usual as the sky was magically full of stars that were bright and looked to be so close, he could reach out and touch them. There were no lights anywhere around him and he looked out into space—a never ending space filled with more swirls of stars than he could imagine. He thought how small he was and how little he mattered in the big scheme of things; if only he could get that feeling when he was dealing with others or caring about what they thought of him. He felt he could see forever to the start of the beginning.

He pulled his sleeping bag out of a hold beneath the platform of his pilot's chair and shook it out like he was throwing a sheet on his bed. He would sleep on deck tonight even though the outrageous king-sized bed was down below.

Even though his hip hurt him as always, he rested flat on his back and stared up into the sky. He was thinking of all the things that had gone so wrong in the last year, until he thought about the gigantic barges that travel across this part of the Gulf. He had no idea if they traveled at night, but he thought he shouldn't take a chance. He struggled to get to his feet and turned on the gas-powered lamps he had installed as he fished so often at night. He turned on the high- powered lights he had installed beneath the hull of the boat and, soon the water, he could see, was filled with many kinds of fish and some sharks. He sat for what must have been a couple of hours watching. He was filled with peace and the guilt and regret left his mind.

He had been right as a tugboat, bigger than the ones out on the Sound he watched from his balcony at the Sea Shell building, loomed into his view. It was too close, and he reached for the *Pride's* horn. It went past him just a few yards away and he heard someone yell, "You crazy jackass! You're right in the barge lane."

He saw the tight cable that was attached to the tremendous barge that glided past so close he thought it was going to broadside the *Pride.* It took minutes for it to pass, and when it disappeared into the black of the night, he let out the lung full of air he had been holding.

Soon he was wet all over for a sudden storm came from the southwest and poured squall after squall of rain on him. He felt dirty, physically dirty, so he stripped his wet clothes off and danced in the rain—as much as his weak hip would allow. He didn't care if he was naked, but he laughed his signature loud laugh as he thought someone might be watching him.

Lightning flashed all around him and for a minute or two he feared being the tallest thing in the storm for he remembered that was how a beach boy had been killed last summer. No 4th of July display he had ever seen compared to the display that filled the sky for the next half-hour. When the thunder boomed a fraction of a second after the flashes, he knew he was in the middle of the torrent. Heavy downpours raced past him in almost a continuous heavy pounding. Then the rains and the storm stopped as quickly as it had started.

The croaking and racket of the palm tree frogs at the La Mancha whirled through his mind. He distinctly heard their vibrating grumbles that went back and forth between the buildings. They always sing their songs after the storm passes. "I hope to hell they sound good to each other, because they sure make a lot of noise," he growled out loud. But it's always after the storm passes, he thought, like they were rejoicing they made it through. Would they be singing after his storm passed, he wondered?

He sat in his chair, with the metal cold and damp on his bare butt cheeks, thinking how little his neighbors at the La Mancha knew him. He knew he was almost an expert at covering up his feelings with his show of bravado and boisterous laughing.

Most people didn't know how smart he was and the education he had searched out; he was a master at trivia. The Prof knew, for he beat the Prof with several tests of stuff that made no difference in the world of what really mattered.

Lately he had been looking at different beliefs around the world, and some from civilizations that had long ago vanished from the human society.

He liked the idea that all humans look straight into eternity at some point in their life—that was Chinese he thought, but it should relate to any religion. The idea from the Navahos that a rock thrown into a body of water will sink and if someone follows it, that person will go on to the next level of existence, but if for some reason the rock comes back to the top of the water, that person is not ready, nor acceptable for the next life. He had been preached his Dad's Catholicism and hoped his Purgatory would be short, but he knew better. He wondered if his Absolution would be quick, or painful as he suspected it would. He had read that little book the Prof liked so much about the seagull that flew for the joy of flying and not like the rest of the flock which just flew from place to place for scraps of garbage. He liked that idea, and as all of mankind from the beginning of time, wondered what it would be like to fly.

Well, it was time he thought.

He opened a drawer in his captain's desk and there lay the luger his dad had given him when he was eighteen, the only gift he could remember his dad had made a point to say was his. He took it out and saw that it was fully loaded. He had oiled and cleaned it just two days ago. He hurled it over the rail of the *Pride* and heard the splash as it slapped into the water.

Next to where it had been in the drawer, was the set of handcuffs he purchased a week ago at a pawn shop on Beal Parkway. He lifted them up and didn't remember that they were so heavy. He clasped one end around his right wrist and reached down to jerk the three ropes that were laying on the deck boards. As he did, he snapped the other end of the cuffs around the metal railing that ran along the side of the boat.

It had taken him nearly all day, four days ago, to lift the *Pride* up to a drydock position, and then drill holes into the hull. He had stuffed them with canvas rags and had tacked the rags around the holes just deep enough that he knew he could pull them out.

He thought why the Prof or others had not come to search for him in the little house that sits next to a water filled ditch that runs next to a channel that opens out into Choctawhatchee Bay.

He wondered how long it would take for the *Pride* to sink. From his time spent on the water, he knew a hold as small as three inches would let in over a hundred and fifty gallons a minute if it was below the water line, and he had drilled three holes on each side of the Pride.

He wondered if it would slide into the water, or if it would sink suddenly like a rock. He hoped that if it slid into the water, it would go down so that it would slide on that huge sand dune before it tumbled over into the bottom of the Canyon. A brief memory of the fun of sliding down the Matterhorn flashed though his mind.

He waited and waited. He thought he heard someone laughing and heard his father's cruel laugh, "You'll never amount to anything as long as you just mess around with football, dope, and girls." He cried out loud that "Damn it to Hell, you never cared anyway."

Suddenly the *Pride* tilted toward one side, and he recalled that part of the hold was lower than the other and that it had filled up with water, and the boat was now listing toward that side because of the weight.

Minutes went by, he sat up straight so that he could see down into the hold, and he could see the water now. Would it come clear up on the deck before the *Pride* sank? He didn't know and tried to calm his mind about what was going to happen.

Pride... Had he subconsciously named his boat after the biggest fault he had. He remembered reading that crime doesn't happen unless the instigator has the idea that he will get away with it. He knew he felt that way about helping Launie Sanderson and taking all that money he had made from her. He wondered who would find the new box on his doorstep, the box for his part of blowing up the *Lollipop*, the shoebox sized box full of $50 bills. If he had stayed the 'good old boy' Dolf Gaines, and not got caught up in the contest of who had the bigger 'pick-up truck' with Judge Bickel, he wouldn't be doing what was happening now.

He felt his feet getting wet and look down to see that the water was about to cover them. Damn it was cold. It seemed to be filling the deck faster now, but he couldn't understand why that would be happening as just so much could get through those six holes. Hell, he thought—what a Dumb Ass I am. It's because of the weight.

As it reached his stomach, he ran his left hand through it raking it back and forth, and then began to slap it so that splashes arose to hit his face.

He laughed like a little boy remembering his mother's shout as he had splashed through puddles of water on Brooks Street after one of the winter's storms.

"Dolf Gaines, get out of that water," his mother yelled. "You hear me, Dolf? You'll catch your death of cold."

"I can't Mom, I can't. But the water is cold, Mom. It's so damn cold."

Just then there was a groan, a low dull guttural sound, from down below.

As the *Pride* plummeted into the water, an eerie strange emotion filled his mind as he vanished below the surface. He gazed up through the water; overhead his flag spread out flat in the water outlined with the bright sun glistening through it. The last thing he saw was the bright colors of his bicycle. It wrinkled into a twisting rag as it descended with him.

34

Where it first began

Pizza and a Visit to Ollie

She turned over in the bed and as usual the other side was empty. On his nightstand, he had propped an envelope against the lamp base. She reached for it, but just at that moment Little Mitch burst into the room.

"I know J C is gone and I thought you needed someone to keep you warm," he shouted.

"It is not cold this September morning, but you can get in bed with me for fifteen minutes and then I have to get up. But before you get in here with me, go pee-pee. If you were to pee on J C's side, he wouldn't be your best buddy for long."

"You mean, go take a piss?" He asked as he started from the room with the exaggerated swagger he had recently developed.

"What did you say, young man? Where did you hear that word?" "That's what J C said once when he was going to take a leak." "Well, you can just add that word to the other three words on your list of words not to say." "You mean…"

She hurriedly cut him off, "If you say them, you know the consequence. No dessert for a week."

"Oh, gee, Mom." He said as he headed for the bathroom.

When he came back into the room, Ester said, "Did you wash your hands?"

He held his two wet hands in the air saying, "Yes, Ma'am, I knew better than not too."

"Good, but you could have dried them too. Now, you have ten minutes left."

"Hooray! And then I want grits, scrambled eggs, two sausage patties, and chocolate milk," he said with exaggeration repeating what he heard J C say one morning he was lucky enough to have breakfast at home—except for the chocolate milk, that was his own addition.

"Good luck. You might get the chocolate milk. Clearly this morning, I don't have time to do the rest."

"Gee, I bet if J C asked for them, you would have time."

"J C is different, Little Mitch. He is so busy and so stressed about what is going on, that I just might do as you say."

Little Mitch jumped up on the bed dragging his killer shark stuffed animal that had parts of its 'guts' sticking out, but that he wouldn't let his mother repair because the needle would hurt. The college student who used to drive the John Deere tractor that pulled the sand rake on the La Mancha beach, Kelsey, had given it to him one day over a year ago when he saw it hanging from the mirror in the tractor's cab. Ester thought she had to remember to talk to J C about how Little Mitch was picking up everything he said or did, and that they were living with a very precocious three-year-old.

She reached over Little Mitch who had snuggled deep into J C's pillow and took the envelope from J C's nightstand. Curiously, it was sealed, and she knew he had done that just out of habit not thinking about what he was doing. She smiled and tore it open.

My Dear Mrs. Haynes

I request the presence of you and that brat of yours to join me at 6:30 this evening for a time of feasting and merriment. Even if I am in a gun battle with 25 drug runners or fighting a fire-breathing dragon, I will call a stop to the action and pick the two of you up in my

chariot which blinks blue lights at criminals and causes
the brat to squeal with laughter.

Sincerely,

Your Semi-Gallant Knight

She laughed aloud.

"What's so funny? J C isn't funny. He's the best buddy a guy could ever have, but he's not funny," Little Mitch proclaimed.

She hugged the little boy to her, and tears were running down her cheeks.

He wasn't late and took only fifteen minutes to shower and get into shorts, his Gator T, and flip-flops.

"And now young man, where do we eat tonight?" "Fokkers!" "Pizza again?"

"Yep, and only cheese. Not one of those nasty big ones."

J C looked at Ester and they smiled. It sure wasn't time for Little Mitch to get the double entendre of Fokker's big Mother.

They ate wings, too much pizza, and sat for a long time at one of those three tables Fokkers has outside. Finally, J C indicated it was time to go.

"This was so much fun. Just like a normal family night," Ester looked at him and he felt good.

"Yes, without the worry of what might happen in court tomor- row. What the heck Judge Bickel might call a recess about, and why in the Sam-hell I can't figure out who is behind all this."

"Watch your ABC's, Mister, we have a little genius listening." "Oh, I'm sorry." He said as he looked at Little Mitch who was climbing into his patrol car.

"He didn't hear you," she said. "Too much fun waiting to ride with the siren blasting."

Instead of going east on 98 when they pulled out, J C turned west. Ester looked at him questioning where he was going, but he kept the patrol car moving through the heavy tourist traffic without saying a word until he turned north of Memorial Drive.

"Ollie!," Little Mitch blurted out.

They turned into Memorial Cemetery and J C drove slowly to the corner where the sign says 'Slumberland' where he pulled to the edge of the roadway. Ester looked at him as he got out of the car, came around and opened her door, and took her arm as he headed them toward Ollie's grave. Little Mitch was far ahead of them already picking up the beer can discs and lining them up on the three concrete benches that ring one of the big cedar trees.

"Why did you bring me here?" Eater asked trembling.

"This is where I saw you first. You wanted no part of talking to me. You thought I was going to arrest you or something. It took me thirty minutes to convince you that I only wanted you to help me and Porter convict Launie Sanderson of his murder.

She was shaking uncontrollably by now.

"Oh, Ester forgive me. I'm so sorry. I'm a damn fool for starting out this way," he said as he put his arms around her.

He turned her loose and walked over to Ollie's headstone and laid his hands on it. It was the first time he had ever done that, even though he had stood in front of it hundreds of times trying to work out in his mind just what the hell was going on in Fort Walton and the surrounding area. Someone was pulling strings somewhere that was causing so many drugs being brought in. Everyone knew now that Launie's place had been a front, but he couldn't figure who else was involved.

"I've understood what you are going through and how much you have been hurt. I think I have been patient and kind to you and Little Mitch. He is a joy to me. I know I will have to live with Ollie's presence in your life, maybe forever."

He took the box from his shorts, knelt on one knee, and said, "I promise to love you and Little Mitch with all my heart. I promise to take care of both of you if it costs me my life. I'm asking if you will share your lives with me? Will you and Little Mitch marry me?"

She had to laugh at the way the words had come out. She smiled at him, "Yes! Yes! But J C, you must know I still have all those mem- ories and I can't just erase them. I will be faithful and love you with all that I can, but you have to know I will never forget him."

It was her time to walk over and touch Ollie's stone.

J C stood, took a silver chain from his pocket, and said, "Here, take this and put his ring on it and wear it around your neck as long as you want."

She took the chain, removed Ollie's ring from her finger, slid it onto the chain and clasped the chain together.

She walked to J C, "Put your ring on my finger."

He looked at her with love and affection that she had never seen in him. He slid the ring on her finger.

She leaned into him and raised her lips to kiss him.

"Oh, puke! That's so gross," Little Mitch hollered as he ran toward them and wrapped his little arms around his mother's leg. Ester and J C were laughing so hard they could hardly stand.

She turned and hung the chain with the ring over the carved arrow that is on the top of Ollie's headstone.

J C looked at her, but she took his hand and led him toward the patrol car.

"Can we blow the siren? Can we? Can we?" Little Mitch yelled as he ran ahead of them.

35

Just Need Some
Advice, Ma'am

A Message from New Orleans

He had been following Judge Boyd for several days, and undoubtedly, she knew he was, but he couldn't get up the courage to face her and ask for her help.

The little Mini Cooper turned off 98 and disappeared down the lane toward her house. He knew she lived down there because he had followed her home several times and had seen her turn there, but he had never worked up the courage to follow her down her lane. He wished he had more nerve and bit his bottom lip and made a quick left turn after her.

He went past her house—at least, it must be her house for the Mini Cooper was sitting in the drive. He didn't slow down or look toward the house but went on down the lane to where a heavy barricade stopped him from driving into the Sound.

He turned around and headed back up the lane, and there stood Judge Boyd blocking the lane with her stout solid body. Coxy, her Australian Sheep Dog, stood by her with his ears pointed forward like he was ready to attack.

"Young man, why are you following me? The last two days I have ignored you as you have kept your distance, but when you come down my lane, you and I need to talk. Stop your engine right there, get out, and come over here."

He had no way to get past her and besides, he didn't dare. He knew she was a retired Supreme Court Judge for the State of Florida, and also the influence she had with the Okaloosa County Police Department—that, and the fact, he better see her, or he was in trouble with his boss.

Sheepishly, he did as she told him and walked toward her with a little grin on his face, "I didn't mean you any harm ma'am, and I know I have gone about this in the wrong way, but I need your help." "Aren't you the young man that wanted red and green chili on your breakfast at Tides Inn the other day?" I was sitting at the table next to you.

"Yes, I am. I didn't tell the truth that morning, not the whole truth, and I ask you to excuse me. I'm in Fort Walton Beach on an errand for the most important man in my life who lives in New Orleans, so on the spur of the moment, I said I was from New Orleans. I'm beginning to think that Mister Mitch picked me from all the men he has helped over the years because I'm from Santa Fe and I believe he knew you were down here also.

"Whatever are you blabbering about? I have no idea what you are saying but I will ask you to come and sit with me on my bench. Remember, Coxy here, will lick you to death if you attack me."

They both laughed and walked toward her bench.

"Now, you have me at a loss because you know my name and who I am, but I have no idea who you are."

"Yes, ma'am, I did that all wrong. I'm Eric Jacob from Santa Fe, and I've been sent here by Mister Mitch Haynes, Retired Judge of the Federal Court in New Orleans.

"Good Lord! Sneaky old Mitch who fought me hard and long about the border of Florida and Alabama. How is the old 'coon ass' doing? Excuse my cussing."

"He would get a kick out of that. He lives over in Buras, Louisiana and has a fleet of shrimp boats. But his main thing in life is to find some young person who needs help. He's sent me over here to find a young man he helped one summer just as Katrina hit New Orleans. I've found out what happened to Ollie, but...."

"Ollie? You mean… Oh my Good Lord. Ollie Haynes…sure, and Ester Haynes and their little kid…"

"Yes, ma'am, and the little kid is named Mitch too."

"I didn't know that. Never heard anything about that. How do you know about that?"

"I've been over to the cemetery and have seen the little boy with his mother. I heard her call him by name. My problem is… well, I have a…. Heck, I have a record like most of the guys Mister Mitch helps, and I know that Ester Haynes has a boyfriend who is a Sergeant with the State Police. And I am afraid to approach them because he might think I'm a weirdo who wants to hurt her and little Mitch. I found out from the trial that she worked for that woman who was killed in the courtroom, and that Ollie did too, and I just don't know how to handle this."

"I've always thought the easiest way to do something is to face it straight on, so that's what I suggest you do."

"I'm not trying to change the subject, but what are those spar- rows pecking at over in front of your door?"

"Maize."

"Yes, ma'am, I knew. You are Navaho, right?" "Yes, but what does that have to do with anything?" "You follow the Blessing Way?"

"What would you know about that? But, yes, I do. I spread maize in front of my door every morning so the day will be a happy, safe, and blessed one. But what would you know about that?"

"I am engaged to a beautiful woman who believes as you do, and I think I am right that if I ask you for your help, you will help me…"

"Yes, I will. But I'm telling you that you don't need my help. J C Blevins, Ester Haynes' future husband—I'm guessing that, will listen to you. What is it that Mitch Haynes wants you to do?"

"He wanted me to find Ollie. Then I talked to him and now he wants me to give Ester Haynes a deed to five of his shrimp boats."

"Good Lord. What? Is he out of his mind? Why?"

"I thought you knew him, ma'am. When Mister Mitch decides to do something, even Miss Alice can't stop him."

"Yes, I know. How is Miss Alice? She's been putting up with that old geezer for over fifty years. I'm surprised she puts up with him and hasn't shot him. She surely runs his house for him. Well, Eric Jacob, we have a little fun ahead of us. Come back over here at ten in the morning and I will try to have a meeting set up for you with Ester and J C."

"Thank you, ma'am. May the Great spirit shine and bless you and yours."

She looked at him closely, but Eric Jacob got into his car, drove up the unpaved lane, turned onto 98, and headed back to the La Mancha.

36

Twice the Trouble

J C and Ester get Important Information

"**Y**ou know what a mess I have right now, Judge Boyd. I don't see how I can meet you in the morning." J C told her that afternoon. "And getting Ester and Little Mitch and me all together is like chasing a dozen crabs on the beach. But I'll try."

The next morning at ten J C, Ester, and Little Mitch who was in a very angry mood because he had his heart set on playing with Dylan and Zathan, arrived at Judge Boyd's little house near the Sound. It didn't take long to get Little Mitch into his usual good-natured way for he and Coxy instantly became best buddies.

"We'll have to wait until Eric Jacob gets here," she said, "Oh, there he is now."

Eric pulled up in his little Corolla and sat for a minute as he was nervous.

"Hurry up, young man! No one here is going to hurt you or scare you."

Eric walked up the front path that Judge Boyd had carefully packed down and swept this morning, careful not to step on the maize she had sprinkled along the way.

She held the door open and went in ahead of him holding the door open behind herself.

"Eric Jacob, this is Sergeant J C Blevins of the State of Florida Police

Department, and this is Mrs. Ester Haynes, and that is Mister Mitch Haynes over there tormenting my dog, Coxy."

Eric walked over and held his hand out to J C, and they shook hands. "That's an unusual name you have, I mean two first names," J C said as they stood facing each other.

Eric turned to Judge Boyd and she smiled like she already knew what he was going to say. He grinned, "My people have unusual names, sir."

Judge Boyd said, "Good Lord, you do have the right to ask the Great Spirit to bless me. I thought so."

"Well, not really, ma'am…er, Judge Boyd. I'm from the Nambe Pueblo north of Santa Fe, so I certainly know who the Great Spirit is even though we have a different name for it."

J C looked at Eric, "You have. I remember names and I've seen yours before. You in trouble?"

"No, sir, I ran away from Nambe about five years ago and headed for New Orleans because, like, for a lot of young people, that place sounds exciting and easy."

They all laughed at his unintended pun, and he continued, "And as I wondered around the city looking for a job to make some money, or looking for something to eat, I met this old man in Louie Armstrong Park one day who has changed my life."

Ester jerked to attention as this was the first thing she had heard that interested her. She almost let out a little squeak.

"That's what Mister Mitch does," Eric said as he looked at Ester,

"He finds us that need help and tries to make us better."

Ester looked at J C in a rather guilty way, but said, "He found Ollie, didn't he?"

"Yes, and he tried to find him again after Katrina slammed into us, but he couldn't. Then he got lucky and found a man he knew that had rented Launie Sanderson the two vans that brought you all over here. Yes, I know you were one of the women that came with her because Mister Mitch has done some investigating."

J C spoke up, "She hasn't done anything she's ashamed of, or anything that's illegal."

"That's what I've heard too."

Judge Boyd butted in, "When Mitch Haynes investigates something, he finds out everything about it."

Ester was shocked again, "Mitch Haynes? His name is Mitch Haynes?"

"Yes, and he was the toughest lawyer I ever met in the court- room. We never were friends until we became judges."

There was absolute silence in the room for a long minute, except the growling and giggling from Coxy and Little Mitch.

J C broke it, "Okay, you've found Ester and you know about Ollie because I saw you in the courtroom at Launie's trial. Now what?" Eric took his brief case from the floor where he had placed it when he came in and opened it out on his lap. He took a binder from it and handed it to Judge Boyd, "Here, you will understand this better that I do, and I think you can explain it better than me too."

"You started this, young man. Now, you finish it, or I will tell Mitch you didn't do your job," as she pushed it right back at him. "Yes, ma'am," he looked at her and grinned. "Well, I'm only an accountant, but I believe it says here that Mister Mitch is giving Ollie five of his shrimp boats after Mister Mitch passes away. And he told me on the phone night before last that the five boats now belong to a young Mister Mitch Haynes."

Ester sat very still and then she began to shake. J C touched her shoulder with his hand, and she looked up with tears in her eyes.

"I understand," J C said. He turned to Judge Boyd and said, "You know, it's hard to compete with a memory, but I'm trying."

Ester took his hand and squeezed it.

"And he sent this to me in overnight mail since he found out about you, and said to give this to you," Eric said as he handed Ester an old, tattered envelope.

As she opened it, it fell into her lap, and she was crying now. There were three pictures in the envelope, and when she had regained some composure, she whispered, "How did he get these? I mean how did he get this one of Ollie standing in front of the Prytania movie house? Ollie told me about going there and seeing *The Green Arrow* and naming himself Ollie because of the main character in the movie, and here he is standing there, and the marquee says, *The Green Arrow*. Look at him...."

She pushed the picture, which was torn and aged looking, toward J C who took it, "Looks like he's about twelve or thirteen just like you said—running around anywhere in New Orleans on his own. Little Mitch looks just like him, you know...."

"Yes, I saw that, but I already knew that. And this other one? Is that Mister Mitch, as you call him?"

Eric smiled, "Yes, that's the old man who says he spent two summers in Armstrong Park teaching a kid to read and write and learning a great deal about life from that kid. Mister Mitch has kept these for nearly seventeen years and shown them to hundreds of peo- ple still in New Orleans after Katrina hit. He even went over to the Prytania movie house because Ollie had told him about it. The old man there had that first picture, and after that Mister Mitch sat on the bench for weeks after the hurricane tore up the city, waiting to see if Ollie might show up again.

He says it broke his heart that he didn't' take Ollie to Galveston when his shrimp boats made the trip over there to escape Katrina's path.

Ester breathed deep, "Thank goodness he didn't...." And then she realized Ollie might still be alive, and she continued, "I would never have known him, but he still might be running around New Orleans... and look at this last one with Ollie strutting around those statues of the marching band...Little Mitch struts around like that when we go to Memorial Cemetery to visit Ollie's grave.

She started crying again.

J C sat down next to her and held on to her hand as she put the last picture in his hand. He looked down at it, and there was Ollie with a cheap looking baton, one from a Mardi Gras Parade proba- bly, marching around the big bronze statues of the funeral dirge in Armstrong Park.

Eric's cell phone rang, and he said, "That's Mister Mitch now and he has some information for you Mr. Blevins. I won't be allowed to stay and hear what he is going to tell you, and he said last night that Ester and Little Mitch should not stay either. It is about the trial. That's all he told me last night."

"Why don't the three of you walk down to the Sound and let Little Mitch toss rocks in the water. Coxy can go with you, but you must be careful he doesn't 'fall' in because he loves to do that. It's a job to pull him out."

As they closed the door behind themselves, Judge Boyd who had Eric's phone said, "I'm turning on the speaker now, Mitch, only J C and I are here.

"Hello, Bonita, I do hope you are well and happy and have won some cases since I whipped your butt." He laughed the belly laugh she recognized from their past meetings.

"Get on with it, you old reprobate. You always did talk too much." He laughed, "Well, Mr. Blevins, your Prosecuting Attorney, Mr. Curtis Porter, was kind enough to send me a transcript of Launie Sanderson's trial. I must say that ended in a violent climax. I bet you are sorry you weren't in the courtroom when it erupted into gun fire and deceit."

"Yes sir, I was outside the door trying to break the two-by-four Schaberg slid through the handles of the door. Too many people on the other side were pushing against it trying to get out, so I couldn't slide it out of the handles. I had the two witnesses that would have convicted Launie of Ollie's murder."

"Yes, I know. But you can't whip up on yourself and continue to blame yourself for what happened. But that's not what Mr. Porter's trial was about, and I believe you know that too. I have informa- tion for you that may help you catch those bastards once and for all. Bonita, you must excuse my foul language. Now, Mr. Blevins.... May I call you J C like all your friends do?"

"Yes sir."

"Well, you already know that things are controlled down in Miami but you're not going to believe how. The family is headed by a man who has two wives, and they live in houses side-by-side and they have daughters, bunches of daughters, and those daugh- ters from opposite wives had been taught to hate each other since they were born. One wife is legal in Mexico and the other in Florida. Launie was one of the daughters. The other sisters were never in New Orleans, so I don't know who they are or which side of the family they belong on. I'm sorry but that is all I have for you."

"That's a real help. We're tailing one of them right now, but we didn't know that there were several of them. That makes a lot of sense now because when Launie was caught, the drug running didn't stop. We haven't solved that yet. I guess you have told Mr. Porter what you just told me?"

"No, I am telling you this right now and it is the first I have told it and if it hadn't been for the trial and Ollie, I might never have told anyone. What the sisters call themselves could be anything under the blue sky. The strange thing is they don't resemble each other—at least that's what I was told. I'm finished now and am going to hang up, but I wish you the best."

"Thank you and I wish you the best too."

"Good day, Bonita, I do hope you will come over and see me soon."

"Good day, Mitch, and I hope that Miss Alice torments you till you run away from home."

He was laughing wildly as he slammed down the receiver of the ancient desk phone in his library.

A little later, there was a knock on the door and as Judge Boyd opened it, she said, "He's off the phone and probably planning more devilment for Miss Alice. Here's your phone."

When they were all inside, a strange silence fell over the room— even Little Mitch sense he should be quiet—and it was Judge Boyd who broke it, "Well, you see that went really well. That was quick, and now I want you all to have huevos rancheros with me, and Eric, I have 'Christmas chili' for you."

"You might get hugged. I haven't had a decent meal since I started out on this trip weeks ago.

"Keep your hugs for that young lady at Nambe. What's her name, Neisha? By the way, do you know what happens to the other shrimp boats when he finally kicks the bucket?"

"He says that two of them are mine, and the rest are Miss Alice's"
"Good Lord, she is older than he is."

"Yes, but he says she is not about to die before he does, just out of spite."

There was laughter, real laughter, in Judge Boyd's bright little kitchen.

Ester looked at J C but turned to speak with Eric, "How in the world is Little Mitch going to take care of five shrimp boats."

"Mister Mitch says not to worry that the Cambodian who runs his shrimping business will take care of everything. There are thirty-nine boats. One of them is deeded to the Cambodian. I'm sorry, I don't know his name…that's why I have to keep saying 'the Cambodian'." The huevos rancheros with tablespoons full of Christmas chili on Eric's, and little side dishes of both red and green chili for the rest of them, the pinto beans, the chorizo, and the diced sauteed papas rajas were a hit with everyone except Little Mitch. The bites he fed to Coxy didn't go unnoticed by Judge Boyd.

As he was leaving her house, Judge Boyd handed Eric a sack, "Here, Eric Jacob, is a large jar of Hatch green chili sauce I made about two weeks ago. I hope it keeps you alive until you get back to New Mexico."

He leaned over to the beautiful little woman and kissed her on the cheek as he left them with a smile on his face that reached from ear to ear.

37

Shrimp Boats A Coming

Why is my name on that boat?

It took several hard weeks of work to prepare the two boats after Judge Boyd told him about the wedding.

"Now, she doesn't want a big ta-doo, but I know you. Just keep it as low key as you can."

"I'll work on it," he answered, "but she is a New Orleans girl, you know, and it's really for me to resolve what happened to Ollie, and what's going to happen to my namesake.

"He certainly is your namesake. He acts more like you every day. He doesn't know a stranger, gets into all kinds of predicaments when he's at my house with my Coxy, but then is just as polite as a Southern Gentleman sipping bourbon, when he's sitting at my table. Yes, he's just like you.

The two boats had to be dry-docked, sanded to the woodgrain so the grain of the Live Oak they were made of would be rough to take the new paint, then varnished, and renamed. They were decked out with new furnishing from the keel to the high-test steel masts which are strong enough to hold thousands of pounds of shrimp. Below the pilot house, the captain's quarters were remodeled with slick new furnishings that Mister Mitch said he was going to move into to get away from Miss Alice's constant pestering.

He and his fleet Captain, Dith, the trusted Cambodian who has worked for him since the middle of the Vietnam War, looked with pride at what they saw before them-the seventy-five-foot-wide hull crafts sat low in the water with their towing booms pulled almost straight up with new nets blowing in the breeze.

"You want to make the trip with me?" Mister Mitch asked the diminutive man who stood before him.

"It would be a great honor," Dith answered, whose English was better than his boss's Mister Mitch admitted.

"That would please me very much, and who will captain the other one?"

"My son?"

The old man looked at him, realized Dith's a most trusted and good friend. The little man had about as much grey hair around the bald spot on top of his head as Mister Mitch saw when he looked in his mirror as he shaved each morning. He was pleased to know that the little man's son would be taking more responsibility for the fleet because Dith probably wouldn't be around much longer than he would.

"And Miss Alice? Will she be going with us?"

"Yes, and she will be on your boat, and I will be on the other." The little captain laughed his high-pitched giggle and said, "Chicken."

"You are right! How long will it take us to get there?"

"It's about 250 nautical miles, and if the water is good, we will be there in 6,7, or 8 hours."

"Wise ass…. I dislike your time for our trip but value your common sense. You are right for we never know what the Gulf will surprise us with."

"Yes, if we get a southerly along Mississippi, you will be throw- ing up your guts over the side," Dith loudly laughed this time.

They both turned to look at the gleaming newly remodeled boats that were being loaded with way too much stuff, Dith thought.

****

We sat on my balcony after having a supper of grouper grilled on my little grill, smashed potatoes, and a green salad. Little Mitch didn't eat much, and I saw that Skipper was munching away on lots that had 'fallen' on the floor.

We were enjoying a glass of my favorite wine and I was laughed- at when I poured my usual four ounces.

"Hope that little mouth-rinse sized cup doesn't get you drunk!" J C laughed.

Ester suddenly stood up, "Why are we wasting this beautiful sunset from up here? Let's go down to the gazebo where there is nothing to obstruct our view.

I couldn't have planned it better as I was getting ready to sug- gest the same thing, for I knew what was on the way to our beach.

As we walked along the walk toward the intersection where the sidewalk to the gazebo meets the sidewalk that runs along my build- ing, Little Mitch ran over and climbed on the wall where I have sat thousands of times looking out at the tremendous, sometimes tumul- tuous Gulf, and thinking just how small man really is.

"You better be careful, or you'll fall over into the sand dune and skin your knee again," Ester warned him.

"Oh, Mom, you are such a weenie!" He looked to see if he would get away with that word because it is on the list of 'do not say words.

Because Judge Boyd giggled, Ester did not correct him.

As that moment, Ester pointed at the western horizon and exclaimed, "I've never seen boats like that over here."

"I think they might be going to a party," I smiled as Judge Boyd poked me in my side.

"Look! Look! That's my name," shouted Little Mitch, as they got near enough for him to read the newly painted names on the sides of the boats.

"And look at the other one, Mom, that's your name."

He shouted as he ran down the ramp, across the sand, and stood where the waves were lapping at his feet.

The two boats stopped about a hundred yards off the beach, and I heard the anchor chains as they spun down out of their wheels.

A little boat was hoisted down into the water from each boat. A tiny woman sat upright and stiff in one of them as she was lifted down into the water. She looked very much out of place as she was dressed like a classic Southern Lady going to a Sunday picnic, but no one was about to tell her that, I learned later.

A man as old as I am, or at least he looked to be, tried his level best to be dignified as he climbed down the net ladder into the other boat that was now bobbing in the almost calm water.

We heard a loud shout from one of the boats as it went over the sand bank into the trough that is out about fifty yards from the shore, "Bonita, you're looking good! That must be the Prof. Little Mitch, come help me pull this boat up on the sand.

Mister Mitch laughed a genuine greeting as he saw the look on Little Mitch's face that this strange old man knew his name.

Mister Mitch jumped into the water that was waist deep and started pulling the boat to shore. The man steering the boat didn't have time to stop him, and I saw a look of amazement on his face.

"Why is my name on that boat?" Little Mitch pointed to the one decorated with all the paraphernalia of Mardi Gras, "and why does that one have my Mom's name on it?"

Mister Mitch tried to look half-way like a gentleman as he said, "Because I want it that way."

"Why?"

Ester hollered from the shore where we were all standing now in the sand, "That's his favorite word, sir, and I advise you to stop the conversation."

Mister Mitch smiled and did a grand bow getting his shirt wet in the water, "You must be the beautiful Ester that Bonita has been talking about."

Ester looked at Bonita and said, "Oh, you did know about this." "Yes, I did. I promised to furnish shrimp, scallops, and oyster for the wedding. I just didn't know until yesterday that they were being delivered by this old scallywag.

As the other small boat grounded onto the beach, the man steering it stood and picked up the little woman still sitting stiffly upright and sat her on the beach. J C hurried out to help her where she now stood in the sand. She objected at first and then realized that her shoes were not make for walking on the beach. The little housekeeper straight- ened her skirt as J C picked her up and carried her up to the gazebo. As they approached us a stab of recollection shot through my mind as I saw the little twist in her mouth and the concern in her eyes; I had seen it many times on the face of the lady much the same size as her—the one who took care of me and my siblings when there was no one else to do it.

We stayed up way into the night as my balcony was full of new friends and lots of laughs. Little Mitch gave up about ten o'clock and Ester put him to sleep on my bed as he insisted. Skipper snuggled in against him.

Miss Alice went home with Judge Boyd, and Mister Mitch returned to the *Little Mitch* where he said he would have some peace and quiet.

Ester and J C decided to spend the night in my guest bedroom and not drive back to Destin. As she picked up Little Mitch, he said, "I have a boat named after me…."

Ester carried him into my guestroom where we had made a pal- let for him. Skipper spent the night guarding the closed door.

I sat on my balcony far too long that night after everyone was asleep and felt joy of what was about to happen. A vision of Ollie came to me. He was smiling.

38

There's Going to
be a Wedding!

Hardly a weekend goes by during the busy tourist months when we don't have a wedding on our beach. I suppose brides like that there are one more condo complexes west of us so the beach will be free from people—makes it good for pictures. And we have a lovely ballroom on the second level of the Sand Dollar Building with a complete kitchen where a simple, or very elaborate, dinner can be prepared.

But the La Mancha residents seldom were excited about a wed- ding on the beach until this one. J C and Ester had become one of us in a lot of ways. J C had spent so much time on the grounds, as so many horrible things had happened since the first body was discov- ered down on the sand below the gazebo.

Ester had spent many afternoons on our beach with Little Mitch, who never met a stranger, and who was now loved and spoiled by a lot of the La Mancha residents. He could call fifty, or more, of us by our names, and made a point of asking how our days were going and if he could do anything to help. He's surely going to be a politician.

Labor Day was two weekends ago, and the biggest part of the tourists are gone home for most of them had children who had to start school. Things are noticeably quiet, maybe too quiet I think.

Ester didn't want a big wedding, but Sally Smyth, our social chairperson, said that was not going to happen. I walked through the kitchen about two days ago, and some most delicious looking entrees were going into the refrigerators to be cooked later.

Ester had asked me to walk her across the sand to Paster Greg Stone and J C, but I had begged off saying that I didn't walk too well on the sand. She looked at me as if 'What do you do when you walk every morning?'

After several of us talked to them around the pool on evening, she and J C agreed that Little Mitch should escort his mom.

Besides, I knew something that only Judge Boyd and I were privy too, as the precocious Little Mitch had asked us what we thought. Ester was in for a big surprise.

39

Do You Take These Two?

Mister Mitch keeps his word

Sally Smyth was about to lose her mind. Judge Boyd had been so helpful to her when they planned the wedding reception, but when Mister Mitch arrived, all things began to change. Ester had explained to Sally that they were not going to spend a bunch of money on one night when they could use their money to buy a house and start their life as a family. Judge Boyd had slipped an envelope to Sally that had $1500 in it, and Sally was shrewdly using it to make the wedding memorable for the couple she had grown to admire.

But when Mister Mitch burst into the Fiesta Room and started talking about things he envisioned, Sally had gone home that night and told Lewis that she probably should let someone else do the reception.

"He's talking about ice sculptures and a band and a champagne fountain and a chocolate fountain, and I just don't have the money." "I bet he's planning on paying for those things. Did you ask him?"

"He didn't say anything about paying for them and I certainly wasn't going to ask him."

The next day as she arrived at the kitchen, Mister Mitch stood waiting for her. Her first impression was from that popular Broadway musical, as all he needed was half his face covered with a mask.

He dominated the room and she fully expected to hear discor- dant chords from an organ.

229

"Miss Sally, I was not kind to you yesterday. I realized it last night as I recounted the events of the day. I always do that, a habit I've had since my first loss of a trial. I thought of the many things I suggested to you and recalled the look on your face, so here is money to take care of all of them. It this is not enough, please do not hesitate to tell me."

He handed her a big manila envelope full of money, "How do I explain this to Ester? It's her wedding, you know. She will know I could not do all those things with the money she and Judge Boyd gave me."

"Good Gracious, if Bonita gave you money, then Ester cannot deny me the same opportunity, and I will tell her so. You just leave it to me. Let's make this a night Fort Walton Beach won't forget."

"Well, it's going to be difficult to get a band this late. I only know one in the area that could play music for a wedding, but I will try. I don't know anyone at all that does ice sculptors except there is a big resort east of here, but they certainly won't be able to come here as they have their own banquets to do."

"May I assist you with those two things? I have good friends in New Orleans that I can get over here in time. What kind of ice carvings do you want?"

"How can I answer that? You just threw that at me. I haven't had time to let this sink in."

"I suggest, just suggest I am saying, that we have a giant sea scallop piece of ice and fill it with some of that wonderful shrimp I brought over on the *Little Mitch*. Then we can have another one shaped like a dolphin that has a bowl beneath it filled with oysters. What do you think?"

"Sounds remarkable to me, but who's going to carve them?"

"I have two men on one of the boats right now that will get started on them right away. We can keep them in the freezer hold of the *Ester Haynes* until we bring them here."

"So, you had no intention of asking me about these things?" "You are as smart as Bonita, Mrs. Smyth! Forgive this old man for butting his nose into your business."

"Oh, just get on with it! But no changes unless we discuss it. Okay?"

All that afternoon and the morning of the next day, vast quan- tities of food arrived. At first, Sally and the women who were pre- paring things were delighted when a new box would arrive, for they hurriedly opened it to find out what epicurean delight Mister Mitch's people were delivering, but as time passed and they ran out of room, Sally wanted to scream.

When Mister Mitch appeared in the kitchen about noon the next day, she was waiting for him, "I thought you promised to talk with me if any changes were going to be made?"

"Yes, ma'am, I did. I haven't made any changes since I loaded the boats when we left New Orleans."

"Out, out of my kitchen. And stay out! Judge Boyd is right, Little Mitch is just like you," Sally shouted as he retreated out the door, "But thank you also."

Mister Mitch retreated to the Destin-Fort Walton Beach Airport where he picked up a jazz band famous in New Orleans where they play in an abandoned garage that has dirt floors, and with them on his private jet was a string quartet that plays with the New Orleans Symphony.

He took them to the La Mancha where he had rented several condos from Lori Cherry the day before. "I'll have to just take ten as a beginning because I don't know how many my crew will need to spend the nights in, for we are going to party on those boats."

Everyone seems to have forgotten that Ester grew up in New Orleans, and when I talked to J C, he thought it was a wonderful idea, Mister Mitch told himself.

Daniel Sheraton and a dozen of his beach crew spent the after- noon rotating from whatever condo complex they were assigned to, to sitting up 130 beach chairs on the La Mancha beach as that was the number Ester had finally invited.

Cam Piper was in charge and when they were finished, the chairs were in a wide semi-circle with the rows staggered, so that everyone could see the platform in front of them that had been built of beach equipment boxes. They dug down into the sand, turned the boxes on their sides, and they became a low platform for Paster Stone and the wedding party.

One of the small boats appeared on the shore and the beach guys unloaded a heavy tarp creating a square in front of the platform. Soon it was surrounded with Tiki torches and large pots of wisteria from the boat. Two of the crew carried a trellis and attached it to the ends of the platform, and minutes later wisteria vines with clusters of bright purple flowers were climbing it.

When they finished, Mister Mitch handed Daniel an envelope, and Cam, a wad of money.The afternoon couldn't have been better. The beach looked like some guys had come up from Orlando and decorated it.

The Fiesta Room was filled with tropical flowers of all colors in pots that stood side by side almost against each other all around the room.

The string quartet was practicing in the corner.

J C and Little Mitch spent the afternoon together and around four o'clock, J C said, "You know it's time to get ready and go."

"So, you are going to be my daddy, now?"

"Nothing is changing. We will still live together as we have for months. I love your mom and so do you, but I'm not taking her away from you. It's all just a matter of having a piece of paper saying we're married."

"Yeah, I know. I'm going to surprise you tonight!" "What do you mean," he asked with suspicion.

"Oh, no, you don't. I'm not telling until it happens."

J C was even more nervous now than he was before. He dressed in a new pair of board shorts, a T without any advertising or design, and a new pair of flip-flops. Little Mitch looked very much like him when he was dressed.

"I thought I was on the other side. How come I look like you?" "Things just worked out that way. I'm waiting to see your mom."

"Bet you cry. Bet you cry! You're going to cry." "You might be right.

They rode to the gazebo in one of the La Mancha's golf carts. J C told Little Mitch to wait for his mom, then walked down the ramp, and stood in front of the platform where Pastor Greg awaited them.

He shook hands with Daniel who was standing up with him and smiled down at Dylan, Little Mitch's buddy, who had the ring, he hoped. Daniel whispered under his breath, "It's safe. It's in my pocket." They both laughed but got serious as Pastor Greg cleared his throat.

J C looked out at more people than he thought he knew and saw familiar faces that he smiled at and was proud to see.

Another golf cart came down the walk and Ester stepped out.

Little Mitch ran to her shouting, "Oh, my you are so beautiful!"

Ester wore a simple short white dress that had a corsage pinned to one shoulder, and a pair of flip-flops that showed her bright red toenails.

Dylan's mom, Lyn, walked across the beach, and stood oppo- site Daniel.

As Ester and Little Mitch walked down the ramp together some- one on one of the boats started playing a Cajun version of the wed- ding march. The crowd stood and everyone was laughing with sin- cere happy laughter.

Little Mitch started walking faster and faster urging his mom across the sand and when they arrived at the tarp, the music suddenly changed in "When the Saints…" Everyone started swaying and sing- ing and Little Mitch look up at J C when they got to him, and said, "I told you so! Surprise!"

The ceremony was short. Little Mitch took his mother's hand and held it out to J C, and she leaned over and kissed the top of his head. He retreated over to stand by Dylan and mouthed, "Gross" which many of the crowd saw, and another round of laughter filled the beach.

It took Paster Greg about three minutes to marry the two of them, but he said, "J C Blevins, do you take these two to cherish the rest of your days?"

"I do."

"And Ester Haynes, do you take this man to cherish as well?" "We do."

Little Mitch poked Dylan in the ribs.

Ester and J C exchanged rings and kissed.

"You are married in the eyes of the State of Florida, and more important, in the eyes of God."

I was sitting next to Mister Mitch. As it was over, he leaned to me and said, "You think I 'm going to have to change the name on her boat?"

I doubt it, I said. I don't think J C minds.

The feast was more than it should have been. I was reminded of Forrest Gump's buddy, Bubba, and knew he could not have named the many ways the shrimp was fixed.

Little Mitch, Dylan, Zathan, and their new friend, Pol, Captain Dith's grandson, ate more chocolate covered marshmallows than anything else. Sally was afraid the chocolate fountain would go dry. Huge loins of prime rib were carved at two stations across from each other in the Fiesta Room. Vegetables of so many kinds I quit counting filled serving dishes on three tables. Scallops in their shells were fixed in at least four ways, and oysters challenged them with every imaginable way of serving them I had ever heard about—and they were Apalachicola oysters too.

There was no wedding cake, but none of the guests had ever seen what one of the little Cambodian women, who came with Mister Mitch, created in the semi-circular alcove at the end of the main room. A wisteria vine as big around as her waist seem to grow out of a huge pot sitting at the side of the area. It wasn't real, of course, but one she had made of silver covered wire that she twisted and turned all the way to the ceiling of the room, and then branched it out into many long-curled tendrils until it formed a canopy tall enough for us to stand under.

Real clusters of the same grape-colored flowers as those down on the beach were wrapped around the many branches, and they hung dripping down a foot long.

Many silver platters hung on chains from the branches in various places under the canopy at different heights. Lewis Smyth, Sally's husband, and a very fine baker made hundreds of small cupcakes of many flavors that sat on the platters. It was a dazzling array like none of us had ever seen.

Ester and J C had their picture taken there as they fed each other a cupcake. Little Mitch was disappointed they didn't smash their cupcakes into each other's faces.

Sally Smyth checked on the area, as she did everything in the Fiesta Room, and found a crudely written note taped to the trunk of the tree; 'Cupcakes $1' was written in a scrawl.

The four little guys sat straight as soldiers at attention in their chairs nearby. They couldn't control their giggles as Sally saw the sign, and they scampered out of the room.

She saw the pile of $1 bills, shook her head, took the sign and money, and went back into the kitchen.

We ate and ate and ate. Toast after toast was made to the happy couple. Three hours later as Miss Alice finished her toast, she said, "Now, you all are invited to the *Ester Haynes* where you can dance till you see the sun come up if you want.

There was a loud announcement from the other end of the room by a very familiar voice, "The *Little Mitch* is off limits to you unless you are invited."

Many trips were made out to the *Ester Haynes* and the *Little Mitch*, as the guests were met with just as much food and drink as they had left behind. The air was filled, far into the night, with Cajan and Jazz music and happy laughter.

Miss Alice, Judge Boyd, Mister Mitch, and I took one of the little boats to shore long before others left the merriment. We sat by the big Y shaped pool at the La Mancha way into the night hoping that the happiness and good times would not be over.

40

Cam

Suspicion at the Gazebo

Cam Piper had been to Fort Walton Beach long before he rented that wave runner, sped through the explosions of Launie Sanderson's big blue yacht, *The Lollipop*, rescued Katrina Hart from the destruction that was happening around him, and had taken her to the house over on Yacht Club Drive. He knew the code to the gate of the property when he took the unconscious Katrina over there because he used to live there.

He was amazed when Aunt Lori gave him instructions to pull out the only law book in his father's library that didn't have anything on its spine. When the door slid open and he carried Katrina into the secret room, he wondered why Lori told him to make sure she was tied up to the daybed in the room. He guessed he was supposed to do it, so she wouldn't wander away and maybe hurt herself because Lori had told him his grandfather was sending up a doctor to take care of Katrina.

Now, of course, he knew that had all been a pack of lies, and he was worried—no, he was scared.

He had been a quiet, pleasant little boy with a clever, but mischievous sense of humor at Edwin Elementary over near Fort Walton Beach High School. Now that he was a grown man, slim and muscular, he doubted if anyone would recognize him as being that little boy who went back down to Miami with his mother and brothers and sisters.

Besides that, he realized that his was a lonely life, and if it weren't for his girlfriend, Hailey, he probably would have gone back down South as he had told the Prof last fall.

"Why didn't you sleep?" Hailey asked as he turned over in the bed to face her.

"You know the reason. I could never tell anyone else," he said, as he leaned in to kiss her good morning. "I keep thinking that J C Blevins, or some other law enforcement, will appear on the beach or stop the Jeep somewhere and arrest me. No one is going to believe that I didn't know what was going on when I picked her out of the water and took her over there. I know I've told you a hundred times that I didn't know what they were going to do to her, but the odds of anyone else believing me are zip to none."

"I know I've said this before too, but don't you think it's time to talk to Daniel about it?"

"Daniel thinks a lot of me, I think, but he doesn't get into personal stuff with us. I like it that way too because he probably would give me good advice, but I can't let him down by telling him that I'm an accessory to a murder. I know they killed her because that house didn't just explode by itself. Lori probably did it, or someone was sent up here to get revenge."

He reached for her and soon they were wrapped in each other's arms. They clung to each other several minutes after their passion passed, and he knew things were getting serious; a few minutes later he was lying by her side. They lay that way until he realized he was late. He jumped up, took a military shower, pulled on his shorts, leaned over, and gave her one last kiss, and rushed out the door. He pulled up at the La Mancha Security Gate a few minutes later, said hello to Lyndell, and headed his Jeep around the Sea Turtle Building on his way to a hot, muggy day on the beach.

He was late, and if Daniel were to show up unexpectedly, he might have a hard time explaining why the thirty sets of chairs and umbrellas were not lined up like soldiers on the beach

The gazebo where the Prof holds court with Them Three as they discover the wonders of the Gulf and torment Cam who becomes so important to them. The crenulated wall around the La Mancha becomes their hiding place from Cam—it hardly ever works.

41

Expedition Force

Them Three invade the La Mancha

Daniel gave me word yesterday that Little Mitch had told Miss Camelia Ledbetter that the three of them would be spending the day with me today. I wonder if I'll ever get to meet this lady, Miss Camelia?

I was on my balcony having my second cup of Folgers, fortifying myself for the onslaught, maybe, when I heard the elevator start up. Skipper bounded down from his 'high-rise' seat I built for him on top of the high bar chair that I pushed up against the balcony railing, so he could guard his domain by barking at every other dog that passed and was at the front door of my condo by the time there was a loud knock.

I knew immediately that it was Little Mitch who knocked, for he was the only one of the three who was not intimidated by me. I opened the door and said, "Good morning J C! Good morning crew!" Skipper was having fits wagging from one end of his little Corgi body to the other, and like rocks, the three fell to the floor and started scratching his body—he loved it, naturally, and turned from one angle to another to let them scratch in different spots. Little Mitch raised his hand to Skipper's ragged ear, cupped it in his hand, and gently started rubbing it. "Prof, why did Ollie, my biological dad, shoot arrows at your balcony?"

I looked at J C, and he looked back and nodded his head, "He was scared of dogs, Little Mitch. When he was a kid in New Orleans, about thirteen, I think, and he was trying to escape the wall of water coming down the street because of Katrina, that super hurricane, a pack of dogs chased him through the streets because he had food and they were starving. One of them clamped down on his leg as he jumped to grab hold of a fire-escape, and he never overcame his fear of dogs. Years later one day when he was on the beach looking for a package of drugs for Launie Sanderson, he got scared and angry because Skipper was furiously barking at him from my balcony. Ollie came back to get even with Skipper."

I looked at J C, and he nodded agreement that I should have told them the truth. Kids have this thing about them. If you dodge around something and not tell them how it really is, they somehow figure it out—sometimes before you even evade the issue.

Dylan came to stand by me and reached out and touched my right arm, "Why did he shoot you, Prof?"

"He didn't mean to. I just got in the way. That's enough now. Let's get ready for the day."

J C filled a cup of Folgers for himself and headed for the balcony. I pointed to the kitchen counter and said, "Go for it!"

"We'll need at least three apiece," Zathan announced, "for we are going to do a lot of exploring, and we have to sit on the wall with the Prof too."

I had a loaf of bread, which I now doubted had enough slices, two kinds of peanut butter, for I never knew which they would want, crunchy or smooth, some grape and some strawberry jelly, a bunch of bananas, and about a dozen oranges laid out on the counter.

"Don't be skimpy," Dylan said as Zathan started making the sandwiches. "Cut the bananas thick," he said to Little Mitch as the peeled bananas became slices to put on the sandwiches.

I saw that Dylan was so much like his dad, straight as an arrow, but with a little too much pride, maybe. He looked like his mother but walked and talked just like his dad. His best trait is he always tells the truth, no matter what.

I had gone over to the Army Surplus Store on Beal Parkway a few weeks ago and bought three cargo belts and three canteens that attached to them. I took the belts to my little lady at the cleaners who alters my clothes, and she took a section out of the backs of each, and now they fit snug enough around the thin, little waists of those three explorers.

Ester spent one whole morning with them as they had spent hours identifying their own, so it was different than the other two. She was either brave, or not so smart that morning, as she let them use big sewing needles and different colored threads to make their IDs. Dylan had stitched a long board squarely in the middle of the back of his, Little Mitch stitched a big shrimp that looked like it was still alive, and Zathan had made a red and black sea turtle that looked very stylized like it was a symbol for something.

Dylan had asked, "What's that turtle?"

"Great grandma Camelia has a jug on the floor in her kitchen with that on it."

"Now, all we need are Pith helmets," Little Mitch announced as they were finally ready to go outside.

Good Lord, I thought as Brantley raced through my mind. Weird little Brantley who was lost in this world, for he never belonged anywhere—no, I thought, he belonged in his helicopter where he was an ace. Has it been almost five years since he wondered around the lawns of the La Mancha picking up trash wearing that silly Pith helmet and Speedos? Poor Brantley who, for some reason killed that hooker who worked for Launie Sanderson, then killed his own mother, which I believe was an accident, and who evaded the law by flying his copter from one oil rig to another out there in the Gulf, and finally insanely crashed it into our gazebo and pool and did all the damage here at the La Mancha.

"I don't want to be Group Leader today. Trade with me," Little Mitch said.

"Yeah, I know, you want to be Point man, so you can scout ahead and make sure we stop to talk with everyone," Zathan said.

"Oh, Okay, I'll be Leader again."

"Well, I am an Indian, you know?" Zathan beamed with pride. "As if we hadn't heard that before," chimed in Dylan.

"Judge Bonita Boyd is an Indian too," Little Mitch interrupted.

"But she is a different kind than you. We do need to visit her over there on her little lane that leads down to the Sound. She has a real neat dog named Coxy."

I almost laughed out loud as I pictured them racing down to Judge Bonita's house and her look of horror as they tromped up on her front porch.

"Dylan, you are Quartermaster as usual. Be sure and keep a close account on our provisions and water," Little Mitch announced in his best Master Sergeant voice.

"Yes sir, Sir!" Dylan answered. "The canteens are full, and the PB&Js are secure in the belt pockets. We'll have to carry the oranges in our board pants, though."

"Then, move out, Scout Zathan! We are ready to Recon this facility!"

J C surprised me, "Remember to stay inside the perimeter fence, and the gazebo is off limits."

Little Mitch objected, "But the gazebo is our outpost. Sometimes it's the only place where we can get Cam's attention."

"You all leave Cam alone. Daniel said he's real busy today and that he didn't want you all to bother him."

"Phooey! He gets as big a kick out of playing our game as we do," Dylan declared.

"Might be so, young man, but I bet you don't want your dad to find out you didn't follow instructions?"

The three of them were subdued to silence until Little Mitch broke it with, "We can still sneak around running bent over and hide behind the pillars of the fortifications and make all our noises until we get Cam's attention."

J C looked at me, grinned, and shook his head, as I said, "Okay, you three, I'm going to take Skipper outside the fence, so he can do his business, bring him back up here, and go sit on top the wall where I usually do. When you can, please come and check on me to make sure I'm still okay?"

"Skipper to the Poopland!" Little Mitch almost hollered. They giggled uproariously.

They were beaming again, and as they attached their now heavy belts, grabbed the oranges and canteens, the noise level was almost too much. They were out the door, and I heard the elevator ping as it went down the three floors.

J C and I sat on the balcony for a few minutes until we saw them come around the end of the Pelican Building running bent down low, so they couldn't be seen above the wall, and sneak to the next pillar where they could stand up and peak over without being seen from the other side.

The expedition came to an abrupt halt as Little Mitch stopped to say hello to Lewis and Sally Smyth who were walking their two almost identical red-brown retrievers up the walk toward the gazebo. All three of them became busy greeting the dogs—Missy and Sam Two—as Little Mitch inquired about how Sally was?

"He's going to get into trouble one of these days, stopping and talking to everyone he meets. Ester and I don't know how to stop him as we have threatened and explained a hundred times that he shouldn't just stop and talk to strangers. I bet he knows more people here at the La Mancha than you do, Prof."

"All that might just be a good thing, for they all know him too and know where he belongs when he is on the property."

"I'm not worried about the people who live here all the time; it's those visitors that neither of us know anything about."

"I think they'll be okay. I'm going to go down and sit in the gazebo and wait."

"If it's okay with you, I'll sit here with Skipper and make some calls I need to make."

"You don't need to ask, and you know it."

By that time, Zathan had opened the gate to the big Y pool enclosure, and the three of them scampered across the pool deck to exit the gate on the other side. They attracted quite a bit of attention as they crossed the deck, and several people lounging around the pool turned to watch them cross—three straight little troopers running single-file across the deck. Their full stuffed cargo belts stuck out in front and back. The Quartermaster didn't seem to care about how much noise they made as he let the gate clang shut behind him.

They spread out, and crawling through the thick grass, they popped up behind three of the pillars that are spaced about twenty feet apart along the wall. They started making all kinds of bird noises repeating them back and forth to each other. Their caws sound very much like the crows that pillage at the La Mancha and tear up dove nests. Zathan started a shrieking that sounded just like a seagull and Little Mitch joined in, but they were too much in sync, and Dylan laughed out loud when he saw Cam perk up and turn in his beach chair, but quickly hushed himself as the other two shushed him. They increased the bird calls that grew louder and louder. Dylan hissed at the other two, "If we get too loud, we sound fake, but we have to be loud enough for Cam to hear us."

Suddenly, Little Mitch let out a "Hoot Hoot," which caused the other two to stop to look at him in wonder.

Cam stood up on the sand, "Really? What was that? A Snow Owl on our sugar-white sandy beach? I didn't know we had owls around here especially in the daytime. Or is it three sneaky scally- wags out being mockingbirds behind the fence?"

"Run Away! Run Away! He's on to us," Zathan yelled as he started running as fast as he could for the corner of the Dolphin Building. The other two were right behind him and almost collided with him as they went around the corner.

He had abruptly stopped, "Men, we have to make a run for it from here."

They were on the extreme southwest side of the La Mancha property where it juts up against the Air Command from Eglin Air Base. The only division is a tall ugly chain-link fence that has strings of barbed wire running across the top. There was no place to duck and hide, just wide-open space for several hundred yards, but they took off zigging and zagging as if they were running from one hiding place to the next.

Craig saw them speed by the entrance to his maintenance office and laughed, "Guess the Prof has important company today."

When they came to the edge of the tennis courts, Zathan slowed to a walk and then stopped, "Sir, do you think we need to take some nourishment?"

"Good idea, Scout Zathan. At ease, men, and eat them if you have them."

They were soon sitting in the usual triangle they always formed, eating PB&J sandwiches and talking about how they had fooled Cam until Little Mitch had messed up. The other two looked at him and shook their heads.

A basketball was laying on the basketball court nearby, and they spent a great deal of time trying to make goals, but the basket was way too high for them. They hiked the boundary wall that runs along Santa Rosa Blvd daring each other to climb on top of it, for it was forbidden.

Almost two hours later, they worked their way back by tak- ing the sidewalk between the Green Turtle Building and the Seagull Building. Zathan stopped them, holding up his hand for them to obey as they stood at the crosswalk to the big parking lot. He looked both ways, instructed them to stay within the crossing lines, and they marched across.

They ran free and easy down the walk past the pool fence, almost to the boardwalk to the gazebo but stopped because they had been told not to go on the gazebo, but Dylan saw me sitting on one of the benches in the gazebo.

"Permission to come aboard, Sir?" Little Mitch shouted. "Come aboard."

They scampered down the boardwalk, and a minute later all three were standing on the bench leaning on the railing looking out at the Gulf. "At ease, men! We're safe."

A loud laugh came from down below as Cam walked up the ramp from the sand, "When you three ever get 'at ease,' the sand will turn green."

"Hey, Cam," Dylan greeted him with a big smile. "My dad said to leave you alone today for you were going to be busy."

"Yeah, lots of chairs and umbrellas out today, but I got dis- tracted by an owl this morning. Weirdest thing I have heard on the beach, but I never could see it."

They all giggled, and Cam was smiling as I said, "Well, we better go to the fortifications and see if there are any pirates or Spaniards attacking."

They said good-bye to Cam and followed me to that place on the wall where they had sat with me so many times.

They climbed up on top of the wall and swung their legs over the other side. I noticed that Little Mitch was really going to be the shortest of the three as his legs were clearly shorter.

"There's no seagull on the volleyball goal post," Dylan said, looking up at me.

"No, there isn't, Dylan. Last fall, I found a dead seagull near that post, scooped it up, and Cam and I put it into the trash can." A little stab of pain went through me as I suddenly knew it was really Jonathan L, and that I would never see him again either.

"You think it was Jonathan L?" Little Mitch asked.

I looked at him and smiled a wry little smile, "We all have to die, young man. All of us. It's just the nature of things."

They were silent for a long time, a really long time for those three. "I do believe it's time for R&R for you three."

"Oh, come on!"

"Really, I slept late this morning." "Phooey, naps are for little kids."

But they swiveled around and scooted off the wall, as I did, and followed me around the end of the Pelican Building to go up to my condo.

Five minutes later, the three were on their pallets on one corner of my balcony with three pairs of identical flip-flops lined up on the floor beside them. I had seen that before and knew when they awoke, they just grabbed a right one and a left one not paying attention if they were the ones they just took off.

Just before they went to sleep, I heard Dylan whispering, "You guys, wish we could use Paul Bishop's longboard up there," as he looked almost straight up to the board leaning against the wall. "He was one of the Prof's very best friends. Killed out there on 98 in a horrible accident."

The other two diverted their eyes from the board, and I felt them looking at me as I intentionally stared over the balcony.

Skipper was in his padded seat atop his lookout but was fac- ing inward so he could see everything the boys were doing. As they dozed off, he gave up and soon he was snoring that familiar sound I know so well.

J C, who hadn't said a word since we returned, broke the silence with a question, "Prof, are you getting too old for these rambunctious little boys?"

"Never, I've had rambunctious older boys in class before, but these three are fun and funny."

We visited for almost a half-hour, and the three awoke almost as one. Of course, it was Little Mitch who said, "Prof, there wouldn't be some Klondike Bars in your freezer for us, would there?"

J C and I both laughed, but he said, "You shouldn't ask for things." "If I can't ask him, who can I ask? He's family."

Out of the mouths of babes, I thought, "Yes, there are three chocolate-chip cookie ones just like you three like."

They made a beeline for my little kitchen and were soon back sitting on the floor of the balcony unwrapping the ice-cream bars. Minutes passed, noisy minutes for how do you keep little boys quiet? Above the smacking of lips and crunching of the crispy chocolate covering the bars, the giggles and secrets whispered among them three filled my balcony with a happiness I hadn't heard for some time.

J C once again broke the silence he and I had as we sat watching and listening to them, "I need to get three varmints out of your hair, but I'd like to come back after a while and talk with you, if you have time?"

"Sure thing, I'll hunt us up something to eat. Okay?"

"That would be nice as Ester is taking them to the *Suds and Cinema* to see *Peter Rabbit*. They love that place where they can sit and eat pizza and drink root beer from frosted glasses and watch a movie. Sure glad she's going and not me."

"Yes," I said, "and she can have a glass of wine as she watches with those three."

"Usually she could, but not now. We're going to have a baby!"

I raised what was left of my four ounces of wine, "Congrats! I expected it."

He grinned sheepishly and said, "I couldn't be happier."

The sun was setting through a layer of dark storm clouds when J C returned. I was on my balcony, and when he let himself in my front door, I was startled. He had keys to my place since the horrible day when Bette went off the sixth-floor porch of the Green Turtle building landing face-up impaled on a sago palm spike, and Shirley and Don Herd had died the same day—Shirley, with a horrible broken neck sprawled out on the floor in the open door of the elevator where we found her after hearing her frightened yell as we stood down in the lobby waiting for her, and Don in his sleep knowing, I think, that he couldn't go on without Shirley.

"You startled me," I said.

"Sorry, but I thought you would be out here and not hear me." "You are just about right. There's a beer in the fridge."

"You want one? Nope, I see you have the famous four ounces of red wine."

"Good for the blood and good for the mind. Second round today. By the way, there are some steamed shrimp and sauce in there too if you want some."

He came back with a frosted glass that I always keep for him in the freezer compartment; the beer was making it shed streams of condensation down its sides. He had the bowl of shrimp in the other, and even though I had planned to have them for my own supper, he sat there and ate them all. He sat on the tall bar stool across the little table from me, looked out over the Gulf and smiled. It was one of the few smiles I had seen on J C's face in months.

"Prof, the happiest afternoon of my life was right down there on the beach. I first thought it was just stupid that I fell for Ester in that courtroom during Launie Sanderson's trial, then I knew it was stupid that I could believe that Ester would forget Ollie and have me, and then I just couldn't believe it when she took my ring and put it on her own finger out there in Memorial Cemetery and put Ollie's on a chain around the top of his headstone."

"Well, you were persistent," I said, and we both laughed. "I watched you in the courtroom and guessed that she meant more than what everyone else seemed to be seeing."

"You will never know the fear, and then the anger, when I was barricaded on the outside of the courtroom door and could hear the gunshots inside and then the screaming and yelling right after that. It was hell. Someone slid a mop handle into the handles of the door, and the crowd inside were pushing up against it trying to get out, so I couldn't jerk the thing out of there. Finally, it broke, and I was nearly trampled as people poured out."

"I remember you standing there looking round and round trying to see Ester...."

"The first thing I saw was Launie Sanderson slumped up against the end of that table with a hole in the middle of her forehead." "Yes, I will never forget that either. And DA Porter was sitting at his table staring at her in disbelief—I won't forget his face either." "Then the explosion happened, and glass was flying all over the place, great big shards of glass, and people who were still in there were screaming, and I saw several get hit and fall with blood all over them.

And I couldn't see Ester, and then I saw you looking out what was left of that window, and you were shielding Ester with your body. That's when you became family, good friend."

"Anyone would have done that, I believe. Besides, by that time, I really liked her—not like you did—but...."

He laughed, "You know the best thing that ever happened to me happened right down there in front of the gazebo. But do you believe that two shrimp boats were anchored out there when it happened? Little Mitch escorted his mom across the sand, and someone on one of the boats changed the music to 'The Saints go marching in,' and he didn't miss a beat because he had planned the whole thing. What a night it was too, with all the friends and music and food and my happiness.... But you too, saw it all....

"She's a good lady for certain. I really don't know what she sees in you, but..."

We both laughed, and he suddenly got serious, "You know I came back to sit with you because I need to pick your brain about so many things."

"Well?"

"I have a good idea why Dolf Gaines went down with his boat knowing that he couldn't face the shame of the whole town knowing he had been a part of Launie's business from the very beginning. I also know that someone must have had the goods on him, or he never would have ended things like he did. That is what I don't know. Who do you think it was?"

"You seem to be pointing at Debbie Locke. I remembered one thing last night that I don't believe I told you before. That morning when Bette was impaled on the Sago palm, I saw Debbie go over and raise up the quilt that Pam Dowell had put over Bette, and she broke into what I would call uncontrollable crying. Her shoulders were shaking, and she was crying out loud. I saw her look up at the top floor of the Sea Turtle Building, and a look of rage went across her face. As we entered the elevator and the door was closing, she seemed to be saying she would get even."

"I agree with you. I think she knows what happened, but for some reason, I don't think she had anything to do with Bette's death or anything that happened in the courtroom of Launie's trial. I sus- pect she had evidence on Bob that would have shone the whole town who and what he was, but I don't know."

J C let out a long breath of air, "Yep, that was a rotten time for me. I thought about just walking away from the whole mess, but I would never be able to face Ester or myself again, much less facing Little Mitch."

"He's got you around that precocious little finger of his, you know...."

J C grinned this time, a little wry grin that he knew better than the Prof how much Little Mitch outfoxed him a lot of the time, "I'm sure glad Ester decided that I should adopt him, but he still calls him- self, Little Mitch Haynes."

"Seems like you might have wiped the ghost of Ollie out of one in your house, but the other one is hanging on to him."

"Seems that way, and Little Mitch never met his father...."

"I imagine it has more to do with Mister Mitch Haynes than it has to do with Ollie."

"You could be right. Who would ever have thought that out of the clear blue-sky Mister Mitch, way over there south of New Orleans, would have become such a big part in our lives? Little Mitch talks all the time about how he wants to go visit and see his boats. Guess I will have to take three lively little boys when I go."

"Talking about going, do you know what time it is?"

J C almost jumped to his feet, "Why didn't you say something earlier. I'm in trouble because Ester has been home for quite a while by now. But she knows that I sometimes spend a lot of time sitting in Judge Bickel's old office trying to figure out in my mind the answer to too many questions. Thanks for the beer, and most of all, your time."

"You seem to have someone else in your sights that's tied up in all this drug business; someone involved in Katrina Hart's death?"

"We're working on it, and for once, I'm not telling you who 'we' are. Just wait and see."

"I enjoy your visits and those three rowdy boys."

"They want me to bring them sand crab hunting some night, but I'm trying to pawn that off on Zathan's dad."

"Do the boys have flashlights?" "I don't think so."

"I'll get each of them one of those little slim pen lights that can hook onto their cargo belts."

"Not that they have you wrapped around their little fingers too…"

He was laughing at me as he closed the door behind him.

42

The Second Foray

On the Beach – The La Mancha

I've known Justin Ledbetter, Zathan's dad, for nearly three years now, ever since I finally figured out what the postcards with the red Buick on them meant. They always have a series of letters and numbers on them, and one day it hit me that they might be a bank account number. I had gone over to my bank on Beal Parkway just past Hollywood Blvd and had been shown into Justin's office. He quickly punched the number on the most recent card into his com- puter, and the account with that outrageous balance became a part of my life. It would be over a year before we knew that Chuck Kroeger, Launie Sanderson's son, who escaped her domain, put the money into it, and then had opened an account for Ester.

I immediately liked Justin and later would understand where Zathan gets his happy personality. Justin is tall and lanky, has intense dark brown eyes that are almost black, and bronze skin, so there is little doubt where Zathan gets his looks. There is little doubt too that both have Native American ancestry.

Justin won the 1500-meter event at track meets all four years of his high school life. He had his pick when college time arrived and had chosen Vanderbilt. Of course, I had asked him one time when I was visiting his office at the bank, and he had laughed that free innocent laugh that Zathan has inherited, "I knew I could run anytime anywhere

I was, but it was Vandy's research library that I wanted to be able to be in whenever I wanted."

I also asked him once when he had called me about a big deposit made into Ester's account and I had gone over to his office, why he had returned to Fort Walton Beach. His reply surprised me a little, "Where else would I go? My ancestors were here, but most of all, my Grandma Camelia is here.

She has no one else now, and she won't be with me much longer. You know she claims to be one-hundred-and-two? I don't know about that, but she's had a hard life, and even though she walks up to church every Sunday and all around her little street without a cane, or even a stick, she is getting frail. The only things that haven't changed are her hearing and sight—oh, and yes, her mind. She's sharp as a tack." Justin was on his way to the La Mancha with the three boys and had called me. He drives a stretch-cab Chevy pick-up that the boys love to ride in. It's a necessity, for Camelia insists that she has one of her rockers in the bed whenever she goes riding with him.

Dylan and Zathan are envious of Little Mitch this late afternoon because Ester had filled the cartilage holders on Little Mitch's cargo belt with 3A flashlight batteries and had attached a pen-light flash- light that snapped onto his belt.

Each of them carried a sand crab net that had a pole longer than he was tall, and a little plastic bucket. Dylan and Zathan carried their now despised flashlights but were glad when Justin had said before they left me, "Little Mitch, the salt will ruin those batteries on your belt, so you need to leave it up here in the Prof's condo." It was Little Mitch's turn to be upset, but soon they were all buddies again and laughing and bragging to each other about who would catch the most crabs.

Throwing their poles aside, they started scampering across the sand attacking the crabs bare-handed as soon as they reached the beach. They had pretty good success, and soon several crabs were scurrying around in each bucket. All three of them were licking their hands as drops of blood was oozing out as all of them had been pinched by the crabs' razor-sharp claws.

"Men, we have conquered the foe—what's a little blood? Just shows we are three tough crabbers! Now let us show mercy to them," shouted Little Mitch. They ran into the waves and heaved the crabs out as far into the water as they could.

Of course, Little Mitch 'fell' into the Gulf, and the other two had to jump in to 'save' him, so they had a great time.

They trudged up the ramp to the boardwalk where they stopped at the hose to wash off the sand and to squirt water on each other, for they knew they would soon have to go home, and it would be bedtime. After many pleadings and objections, they followed Justin, soaking wet with streams of water running down their legs, when he told them it was time to go.

I headed them off at my front door telling them they could not bring in their sandy poles and buckets. They sat them on the porch at my front door. Zathan's bucket tipped over, and a crab scampered across the porch.

They laughed in unison as they made their way out to the bal- cony, and Little Mitch said, "Told you it wouldn't work! Besides if a crab got loose on the Prof's balcony, Skipper would make quick work of it, or it would escape over the edge to crash to its death on the jagged rocks below."

Dylan said, "Sometimes, you are so weird. There are no rocks down there, and it would probably bounce on the thick grass, and besides it's only a thirty-foot fall."

Rolling his eyes at the other two, Zathan said to me, "I suppose there is a Klondike bar in your freezer for us?"

It caught Justin off guard, and he started to reprimand, but Zathan butted in, "That's just normal, Dad. He expects it."

I laughed, which caused Justin to laugh, and I said, "As usual." For now, their worlds were good. They were safe, and the only worry each one had was how soon he would have to nestle down in his bed, say his prayers with his mom, and go to sleep.

43

The Fourth of July

Fireworks on the Beach

Down below at the pool, a tremendously serious race was in progress, it appeared. The three were creating a lot of attention as they stood with their toes hooked over the edge of the pool and Justin yelled 'Get Set' and then 'Go!'

They dove into the water, and within ten yards, Zathan was ahead by almost a body-length. Dylan was gaining on him though with every stroke, but Little Mitch was losing ground to both of them.

They are so different, I thought, even though most people call them 'three peas in a pod.'

Zathan is as slim as one of the three bean poles his Great Grandma tied together to form a teepee for her pole-beans to grow on. He has no hips at all it seems and has trouble keeping his pants up at times. He complains bitterly when he must have a haircut, so usually it hangs down even with his ears in the back and surrounds his face—he brushes it out of his eyes constantly. His hair is already turning the straight, almost black that Camelia recognizes. He has high cheek bones and piercing dark blue eyes. He doesn't look like either of his parents, so he must be a throw-back to one of his ancestors. I imagine Camelia Ledbetter knows which one, too.

Dylan is almost as tall as Zathan, and though he looks much like his mother, Lyn, he stands and walks just like his dad with his shoul- ders squared back, with a little strut, and hint of pride. His slender almost seven-year-old thighs already show the outlines of muscles as he runs daily with his boxer, Rocky. He has an infectious laugh, and his long slender fingers invariably crisscross his face when he is embarrassed, pulling a joke, or when he laughs. He has a devilish look in his eyes when he knows he is pulling a joke on his buddies or especially when he is teasing with his dad, Daniel. There is little doubt he will become a good athlete—maybe become a catcher like Daniel.

And the other one, the one who will probably become President someday, never shuts down. He doesn't know a stranger, talks with adults better than most adults do, seems truly interested in how people are and how their day is going. He talks nonstop, plans elaborate schemes, convinces his mom of too many things, and has a vocabulary that's better than a lot of seniors I taught in school. I smile and wonder what J C and Ester will have on their hands when Little Mitch is a teenager.

We are 246 years old today, and the La Mancha is totally filled with owners, long-term renters, and hundreds of families from all over the country.

Justin and the three boys are surrounded with at least fifty people at the big pool. The lawns are full of kids kicking soccer balls, throw- ing footballs, or just running and joyfully—and loudly—playing.

There are three games of corn hole going on among a group of adults on the lawn at the side of the Dolphin Building across the way, and I hear sounds of 'that just cost you $5' so I imagine betting is going on.

Three almost teenage girls have set-up a lemonade stand and are doing a brisk business. More adult drinks are being passed around at the corn hole tourney.

Looking down toward the beach, I see where much of the noise is coming from; a hotly contested game of volleyball is happening. I feel a tinge of regret that the top of the beach net side pole is empty; Jonathan L is flying high and fast somewhere, I imagine. Further down the beach three of those new-fangled kites are high in the air where yet another contest is happening, I imagine.

The Gulf is calm this afternoon, but filled with swimmers, long boarders, and kayakers. A large bank of dark clouds is forming out to the south. We might have thunderstorms that could ruin the fireworks the Association has planned.

The boys to get out and dry off. Claire and I grin for we know that the troops are coming, and our quiet visiting is about to end.

There is a knock on the door, and then it opens as J C and Ester enter. I tell Ester that she is to have the big wicker chair in the corner of my balcony where she can relax but still see the fireworks. She is carrying the baby real low these days, and I bet it's a girl. Little Mitch will be disappointed because he has asked for a boy. I grin to myself.

There is another tap on the door, and Daniel and Lyn come in.

We're going to have a balcony full I think as I have my little electric grill set up to grill hot dogs. This time the door flies open, and the three little rascals burst in with Justin lagging.

"We are starved," Little Mitch announced, "Aren't we, men?"

The other two nodded agreement, and they headed for the three stools at the bar that faces the kitchen.

"Well, you will just have to wait," Daniel said. "We're going to grill hotdogs, and we haven't started yet."

"Are we having the ones that rhyme with Zathan's name?" Dylan asked.

I laughed thinking the wrong one asked that, for it was definitely a Little Mitch question, "Yes, we're having Nathans."

Claire said she had to get biscuits in the oven if we were having strawberry shortcake. "I'm making Great Grandma's recipe with all the butter and sugar."

"Where is Miss Camelia today," I asked. "Why didn't she come with you?"

Justin broke in, "Oh, Grandma will never come over to Okaloosa Island. She has some real fear about this place. She's fine today as Mylee is with her, and they are making Pho. When Mylee first came to Fort Walton Beach, Grandma Camelia wouldn't have anything to do with her 'foreign' foods, but now they make Pho about once a week using all the fresh things from the garden and the seafood Mylee catches."

Daniel broke the silence as we all sat there, "I'll be back in time for strawberry shortcake, and three someones will get double knuckle sandwiches if I come back and it's all gone."

Dylan whispered to the other two, "He's kidding. He never follows through. We'll save him some though."

I carried the platter of hotdogs to the kitchen where Lyn had taken charge. She loaded their hotdogs, potato salad, and chips in their metal canteen trays, and they headed to their regular spot on the balcony beneath Paul Bishop's longboard. Skipper was right on their heels expecting to get handouts no doubt.

"I'm going to want another hotdog," Little Mitch announced as he came back to the bar looking into the kitchen.

"Skipper cannot have hotdogs, or he will get a stomachache," I said.

"Then, I won't need another one," he said as he headed back to the balcony.

We heard him say, "Men, the mascot can't have hotdogs. He has dysentery."

Where in the world had he come up with that word?

We carry our food out to the balcony, and I saw the La Mancha pickup coming down the beach and stop in front of the gazebo. Lyn said, "Daniel and Cam are down there pulling out the big wooden boxes that hold the beach chairs and umbrellas, so I guess they are going to light the fireworks on top of them."

Time passed. The three troops dozed off on their mats, and Skipper gave up and I could picture him crawling under the covers on my bed. The women insisted on cleaning up the dishes and the kitchen, so J C and I sit in peace and see the beginnings of the storm. High out over the Gulf, a 'dry' storm was forming—there would be no rain, but the display of lightning and the booming of the thunder would be spectacular I thought.

Daniel reappeared, and Claire said the shortcake was ready. I'm not sure how they heard her, but they did, and they made a mad dash for the bar.

"I want the top half of the biscuit," Little Mitch almost shouted. "Me too!"

"I do too!"

"And why, may I ask?" Claire said.

"Because it is crisp and flaky." Little Mitch responded. "And I want a whole lot of strawberries and lots of juice on it."

"That will just make it soggy, and then it won't be crisp."

"That's the way we like it though," he said as he turned to the other two for their approval.

Ester called from the balcony, "Little Mitch, you better behave."

We ate the most wonderful strawberry shortcake. There wasn't anything special about the strawberries, but the biscuits, Miss Camelia's recipe were just like my own grandma used to make.

I was right about the storm, for when it was dark enough for Daniel and Cam to sit off the fireworks, at times it made the fireworks look puny. It was high in the sky, so the lightning and thunder didn't really bother us, but the continuous streaks of lightning flashing through the gigantic black clouds to be followed with the deafening claps of thunder got my attention more than our fireworks.

Once or twice, the lightning seemed much closer than it had been, and the boys ducked under their mats on the balcony floor. Streaks of it crackled across in every direction, and little curls of it crackled and popped in crisscrossed patterns that looked like splintered mirrors. I heard the boys squealing in fear and saw them clutching each other as they huddled together.

I could see streak after streak of heavy rain race across the horizon way out to the south. In one of the big flashes of lightning, I saw tall thick black clouds that looked like old pirate ships.

Of course, it was Zathan who saw the same vision as I did, and I heard him say to the other two, "See those looming ships out there on the horizon? They're getting closer to us every minute."

"You're not scaring me," Little Mitch said back at him.

I heard Dylan laughed, "You're right Zathan, looks just like old galleons with skeletons on board."

Zathan laughed.

Skipper must be whimpering and shivering under my comforter, and undoubtedly has scooted down farther in the bed.

At other times, we were amazed when the storm and all fire- works synchronized as a beautiful display of fireworks and a long flashing streak of lightning would fill the sky at the same time.

Once, I glanced over at Ester and saw her wince as a stab of pain had obviously caught her off guard as the baby must be kicking. I, of course, had no idea then how much danger she and her unborn baby would have in just a few days.

44

Foray Caught in a Tempest

Attack Cam, Reconnoiter to the Outpost, and HIDE!

I sit on my balcony most afternoons after four o'clock with exactly four ounces of wine in my big red plastic tumbler that advertises Fort Walton Beach and which probably holds at least a pint, but I measure four ounces carefully and savor it as I sit and watch the visitors, the people who work here, and my neighbors, and I learn a lot.

Visitors leave usually on Sunday mornings and by that evening, the La Mancha is full of new vacationers who come to our beautiful beach—with its fine white salt-like sand.

As I remember the hundreds of students I had in class over the years and how each of them was unique, the same is true for our vis- itors. I guess I just like to watch people.

As I sit on my tall bar stool, I think how J C always teases me about drinking exactly four ounces of wine, but I remind him that Brother Paul in the Good Book tells me that a little wine is good for my stomach.

Ester called last night to plead that I have the boys today as she was to have them but would so much like so J C and she could have a day together alone without them three.

I said that they had not been with me this week, so they were welcome I told her they were really a pleasure to me, and that I meant it. I said they go out in their gear and torment Cam for a while, and then go off on a bivouac to unknown parts, till they come back hungry.

They arrived after noon and when they had had a romp with Skipper and snarfed down Klondike Bars, they loaded their belts with bottles of water and string cheese and announced that the bat- tlements surely were being attacked and they had to go do their duty. I gave them the usual warning that they were to leave Cam alone because he was busy this late July afternoon. I reminded them that Daniel would not be happy if they caused Cam to have trouble with any guests.

They promised, of course, that they would not bother him. I noticed that all three exaggerated crossing their legs, like that meant crossing their fingers and fibbing.

I was happy about having nothing to do as I sat on my balcony in the afternoon sun. I thought they would be returning in a little while, hungry as bears, so I should get up and find snacks for them, but then I saw one of those sudden summer storms forming on the western horizon of the barren sands of Eglin Air Command.

Suddenly the weather horns at Navarre, about ten miles to the west started blaring their distinctive blast. A few seconds later the horns at Mary Ester joined in only to be followed quickly by the ones at Fort Walton Beach. The big horns at Eglin Air Base joined in and in a couple of minutes the ones at Destin followed. We obviously had some bad weather headed toward us.

I stood up and leaned out over the railing to see if I could see the boys, but they were nowhere in sight.

The La Mancha is the last condo complex on Santa Rosa Blvd and bumps up against an ugly, old unkempt chain link fence that is about twenty feet high that is ripped, in many places, with jagged edges that would cut through almost anything in this coming wind.

On the other side of the treacherous old fence are the new fence the county has just finished over twenty feet high with barbed wire in coils on its top and the barren sand mounds which were stripped of their pine groves by a series of storms over several years ago. Scrub bushes and new pines are trying to regain footholds with sporadic bunches of sea oats and bitter switch grass struggling just as hard to hold the sand in place—but mainly the area is barren for at least five miles to our west.

I see the fast-moving ominous black clouds hurrying toward us and could see the line where the heavy rain was moving with them. Thunder blasted through the air and echoed off the Gulf and Sound. The sky was a spider web of lightning which snapped and sputtered in one place to suddenly jump to another place. I grew apprehensive as I sat there out in the open on my balcony, but I kept thinking what can I do about them three?

I could see Cam down on the beach, but I didn't have any way to contact him, so I decided to go down and find out when he saw them last.

Suddenly a waterspout appeared out from the shore in the Gulf; it was growing larger and larger as it sped toward the shore. People from the Midwest know what tornados are, and that is just what a waterspout is—a swirling mass of extremely fast wind except it is filled with water and debris it picks up as it goes along.

I see Cam run across the sand warning people to get off the beach and start lowering umbrellas and throwing them flat on the sand. He grabbed a chair, collapsed it flat, threw it on some umbrel- las to hold them down, I guess, and hurried to get another one. There were too many umbrellas and too many of those heavy lounge chairs, I thought.

As I had been looking at him, I turned back toward the spout and see that it is much closer and much, much larger now and was completely over the sand of the Air Command. Getting bigger and bigger around, it looked to me to be way over two hundred feet into the air. I am filled with wonder as I comprehend that it is strong enough to pull thousands of gallons of water that high in the air.

Frantically, I looked in every direction for the boys, but they were not in sight. They know enough about our bad July storms as Daniel had spent one afternoon with all of us explaining how serious they are. Surely Zathan would be the usual leader and get the other two back to my condo. Unless they were already caught. But I had my bets of Zathan that he would get them inside somewhere.

When Ivan went through the Island all the growth—the pine grove of trees thirty to forty feet tall, the half dozen Live Oak trees which had survived previous hurricanes, the undergrowth of azaleas, saw palmetto, and wiregrass—were ripped from the ground and sent tumbling across the Sound into Fort Walton Beach.

New growth sprang miraculously from the barren sand and was making a strong come back, but I now I see the little pines and shrubs ripped up into the spout.

It swirled and wobbled from side-to-side like a drunken sailor and finally crossed over the Island and went whirling into the water of the Sound.

I saw the dark water of the Sound start swirling and spewing high in the air; a vortex formed and I saw a small fishing boat caught and thrown at least ten feet into the air to come crashing back down, upside-down. Whoever was in it fell into the water yards away.

I have no idea what the effect of that water had on the spout, but it erratically jumped back on the barren sand and zigzagging back and forth, cut a wide swath as it headed straight for the La Mancha.

A flight of pelicans, usually my majestic 'air patrol,' frantically flapped their wings trying to get out of the way, but they were losing, and I knew they would be sucked up into the spout in a few minutes. Cam saw it and ran as fast as he could in the heavy downpour which the spout had pushed in on us, toward the gazebo that sits close to the beach immediately in front of the big Y shaped pool. I must have looked like a fool as I found myself jumping and shouting for him and all the beach goers to run faster.

Out of the corner of my eye I see Daniel pull up in the Sun- Setter pickup. Daniel is about thirty-two-or-three but built like all the guys he hires, strong and fast. He dashed down the sidewalk by the pool, down the boardwalk and on down the ramp from the gazebo and shouted for Cam to help him. They began frantically dragging chairs and umbrellas up close to the gazebo, but like I already knew, there were too many of them.

As the waterspout hit our beach it was full of sand, along with driftwood and the flight of pelicans. I saw a bright red beach towel whirling around and around within it and wondered if the red was pelican blood. The towel and what was left of pelicans whirled up and up until they were flipped out of the top way above our heads—a bloody mass of skin, bones, and feathers.

It really looked extremely dangerous up this close to us, so I got down on the floor of my balcony and watch it approach through the ornate railing. I knew Skipper was deep under the covers of my bed, and I kept hoping my front door would burst open and them three would dash across my living room and out onto my balcony.

The waterspout smashed into the low crenulated stout rock wall—the boy's battlements—that surrounds the perimeter of the La Mancha as the whirling saw-like ring of sand was ripping through the little wooden fences strung along the beach to keep the sand from blowing away.

As the whirring ring bounced along the rock wall, I heard a gnawing like a power saw ripping through a two-by-four.

I watch in amazement as Daniel and Cam run away from it and go hurdling over the railing into the ditch where the beach sunflowers and sea oats flourish from the shower water where the beach goers wash the sand off when they come up from the beach.

I watch in weird fascination as the spout starts tearing off planks from the west steps to the beach and from the west boardwalk.

Hitting the perimeter wall had caused the spout to roll errat- ically again, and for what seemed two or three minutes it sat still in one place spinning out a deep hole in our beach and spitting out whirling rings of sand. Then, just as quickly as it started, it jerked to the right and spewed out over the Gulf.

Beach chairs and umbrellas whirl around and around into the center of the spout as they were caught up in it as it left the beach.

Suddenly one umbrella snapped open and spun to the top of the spout where it looked like one of those little paper umbrellas stuck into a drink. It rotated slower and slower and looked like a spinning top on the floor as it slows down ready to fall. It was spit out of the top and went sailing way off into the water.

What was left of the perhaps twenty to thirty pelicans dropped from the sky and hit the waves below.

The spout was full of many fish and lots of seaweed along with gallons and gallons of water. I looked in amazement as a small sand shark fell out of the swirl and went flopping down followed by what looked like many, many Red Fish.

One of the shrieking sea gulls got too close to the spout and was sucked in. I saw it swirl around and around as it was thrown to the top just like the umbrella had been and then spit out to fall toward the water. I knew it was dead because it fell like a rock.

It didn't take more than five minutes from when I had first seen the spout form until it disappeared toward the horizon.

Daniel was the first one to appear in my sight as he crawled out from under the mass of sticks and brush. One of the kayaks they rent to guests flipped over and Cam sat up. He began to smile and gave a little wave at Daniel.

I guess I must have been hollering a lot louder than I thought for they turned and waved in my direction giving me a thumbs up.

Umbrellas and chairs were scattered all around and probably thirty or so were smashing about in the angry waves, some way out in the Gulf. The rain was coming down harder than ever as Daniel and Cam rushed up to get inside the gazebo.

As I picked up my chair which I had overturned and stood back from the railing so I wouldn't get soaked, there was a loud pounding on my door. It burst open and there they stood with Israel standing behind them.

"They came by the shop to watch me work on one of the mow- ers as that thing started. I wouldn't let them leave, Prof, because I was afraid for them. It's probably my fault they didn't get here before it hit us."

"It's probably your fault, Israel, that they are still alive. I don't know how I'll ever thank you."

He ruffled Little Mitch's hair, smiled big, and closed the door behind himself.

"I said, you three don't know how much you owe that man. Now, Dylan, get out there on the balcony and let your dad see that you are all right. We'll have to try and call Ester and Jason to let them know you other two are safe."

The waterspout tore the roofs off several houses on the Island, bounced across the Sound hitting and destroying two docked boats, and went up the street by the LotABurger where it knocked over electric poles and set five houses on fire.

45

Remembering John
F Kennedy

Camelia's Backyard

"**G**reat Grandma, what's that box up on the shelf in your kitchen that has a sticker on it? It's always been there since I can remember, but you never move it," Zathan asked.

They were sitting with her in her backyard as they did many afternoons when Dylan and Little Mitch were allowed to be there. She was in her usual place—the big rocker underneath the parallel branch of the Live Oak, and they were scrunched together on the wooden crate that was usually Zathan's seat.

She smiled the closest thing she allowed herself to show pride, and said, "You go git it if you want, and I'll tell you about it."

Zathan jumped down and raced through the back screen-door and was back in a minute. He carried the box to his Great Grandma and returned into his seat on the box, giving the other two a little push to make space.

They are getting too big to be scrunched-up like that Camelia thought.

"You three probably don't know and haven't heard about President Kennedy…"

"He got shot in Dallas one day," Little Mitch said. "I saw it on PBS one day."

"Yes, that's right. That happened about ten years after he was here at Eglin to watch some F102s do some air-to-air shooting and drop some fake napalm bombs way out in the edges of the airfield.

I declare I haven't ever seen that many people in Fort Walton.

They came from all over the Panhandle to see him.

He was a real handsome man who many were concerned about when he was elected President because he was a Catholic. It didn't bother me about his religion, but I sure had a hard time understanding him when he talked. Sounded so funny to us Southerners."

"Why did they want to bomb Eglin?" Dylan asked. "My dad grew up out there when his dad was a Ranger."

"They didn't want to destroy Eglin, didn't even do any damage.

They wanted to show the firepower of our weapons."

Zathan had been quiet until now, "I don't understand war at all.

People just get killed, and then it happens again later…"

She looked at him with a pain in her chest that she would never be able to explain to him. "It's always been that way. Some tough guy somewhere wants to be the rooster in the chicken house, and so he starts a fight with the other roosters."

They all understood what she meant, for they had seen that before, and they all went into fits of elbowing and laughing.

"But that's not about the box," Little Mitch said.

She could always depend on him cutting right to the chase if he wasn't messing around with people, "No, that happened later on that night."

"That was over fifty years ago, and I was an old woman then," She paused as she saw them nod agreement. "Now, you three be nice, or I will just stop the story right now."

"Yes, Ma'am, we will," Little Mitch said. "You're a lot older now."

She laughed now, and continued, "Well, I was invited to a din- ner that night with President Kennedy, Vice President Johnson, and some Generals that I can't remember their names. A bunch of local people were there too. Mose went; now he was really old, I tell you. We had to wheel Mose in a wheelchair."

"The was after Grandpa Elmer left us, right?" Zathan asked. "Yes, Grandpa Elmer had passed on to what he hoped would be a better place, I'm thinkin."

"Well, the dinner was something else with about seven courses from some appetizer that I had never heard of and didn't like—some French thing, I think, to a strawberry shortcake that your mom, Claire, could've cooked better.

After about two hours, the tables were cleared, and the President stood up and started to speak.

"'I don't think anyone could have watched the flying that we have seen today and the commitment to this country demonstrated by those who manned these airplanes and serviced them without going back home a great deal happier. But there are those who manned some other planes twenty years ago—Big B-17s—that started out right here at Eglin and who have never returned home. That's what I wish to honor tonight, and there is one lady among you that lost her love on one of those planes."

I wanted to git up and leave, but Mose held my arm, and I assumed he knew all along what was going to happen at the dinner.

The President went on, "Jeremiah Elmer Ledbetter was a gunner in the bottom turret of one of those monstrous planes that was shot down over France. No parachute was seen floating down before the plane hit the Atlantic and burst into flames. Tonight, I want to honor his service to our country, so will Mrs. Camelia Ledbetter come up and stand with me?"

I don't know how I made it up to the front as I was shaking with nerves and crying inside, but I did.

"Miss Camelia, it is with extreme great honor that I present to you in Jere's honor, the Presidential Medal of Freedom."

"President Kennedy asked me to say something. I couldn't. I just couldn't. Finally, I said, 'Jere wanted to go and serve. I am proud of him. I miss him more than I could ever explain, but I am proud of him.'

The three of them sat, and for once had nothing to say. "You want to see it, don't you?"

They jumped down as one and with two on one side and the other on the other side, she opened the box. Inside was another box; a simple flat box with a gold leaf double zig-zag border.

"Plain, huh? Well, look at this," She opened the box, and the inside was lined in gold.

The boys became very quiet and serious as they stared at the golden star with white enamel around its edges and a red enamel pentagon behind it. It had thirteen gold stars on a blue background with a golden ring. Two Golden Bald Eagles with spread wings stood between the points of the stars.

"Wow, Zathan said, "That's beautiful."

Everyone turn to look at him as it was unusual for him to express that much excitement.

Then, once again they were silent. Little Mitch broke the silence this time, "I bet President Kennedy gave it to you really for all the years you haven't known what happened."

Camelia looked at him and her face looked so tired and haggard, "Now, go away, and let me be. There's fruit bars in the freezer. Sit on the front porch and eat them and leave me alone."

Dylan and Little Mitch didn't understand, but Zathan said, "It's alright. She just needs to feel her sorrow by herself."

46

Salt Cellars

The Abbey — Guerande

"How much longer you going to polish that one?" Father Jean asked.

"Until I get it just the way I want it. The finish must be just right. It must stay in the jar when I push it in."

Alain was polishing an irregular piece of Beech wood, and he frequently placed it in the mouth of one of the jar-shaped pieces of pottery he and Father Jean had fired in the kiln over the last few weeks. There were dozens of the little jars and a pile of the wood pieces before him on the stone table in an ancient part of the Abbey where they sat together so many times—Father Jean talking of many things and Alain soaking it all in.

"Now, to make it ours," Alain said as he took a red-hot pick from the brazier that sat on one of the rock ledges that circled the room. He carefully burnt 'enjoy' into the wooden top in a distinctive cursive handwriting.

"Clever idea to advertise our salt," and I hope the members of the Guild repay you for it.

The fired pottery jars had been Alain's idea, and his stubborn attitude that each must be perfect and have a perfectly fitting lid pleased the old priest. Alain had helped him pick people who worked in the salt marshes to take them around the country, even into Paris and across the Channel to London, to get fine dining places to buy their salt. Father Jean wondered how long they would be able to hand-make these little treasures Alain was so proud of, for they were way behind on their deliveries. Guerande had a new business: not just the finest sea-salt in the world, but fine salt cellars to serve it.

"You have come a long way, my friend," the old man said.

"Yes, and I have had the best of help," Alain answered. "There is still that mystery which I will never have answered, but my life here has been a joy with the likes of you and the rest of the village."

47

Puddles, The Last Foray

Last Foray to Pester Cam

As the Prof carried his cup of Folgers through the sliding door out to the balcony, Zathan whispered to the other two as they started fixing their food for the day, "Be quiet, he mustn't hear us. Great Grandma said last night that we are eating too much sugar with PB&J sandwiches when we come over here, so she cut radishes, carrots, and cucumbers, and put in some string cheese for us, and put them in zip bags. Let's just put them in our belts and make sandwiches like we always do except not as many, so he won't feel bad."

"Miss Camelia is sure old, isn't she?" Little Mitch asked. "Yeah, my dad says she claims to be older than she really is, but she's old," Zathan replied. "She has a driver's license to use for identification, and it just says centenarian instead of giving her real age. She doesn't have a birth certificate."

"Why would she be called a Centurion? She's not Roman," Little Mitch asked.

"God, you are so dumb sometimes. Centenarian is someone over a hundred years old. I asked my dad when she told me that one day," Dylan butted in.

"You don't have to be a bully, you know?" Little Mitch growled at him.

They stuffed a sandwich and a half in each of their cargo belt pockets and headed toward the balcony.

"We're off," Dylan announced.

"You have plenty of provisions?" I asked. "Dylan, remember what your dad said, and leave Cam alone because he will be busy today."

"Oh, we will. I guess Cam is just busy all the time because that is what we always hear." Dylan answered as the three elaborately crossed their fingers behind their backs.

I had to smile a little for that was so Little Mitch talking.

"Yes, sir. We are prepared to explore that sandy beachhead and the frontier," Little Mitch answered.

"It rained nearly all night so you three better take extra water today as it is very humid, and you three will get hot and thirsty."

They went out the door carrying extra bottles of water—little bottles dangling from loops on their belts.

Back in the kitchen, I noticed that extra bread was in the pack- age I bought for them last night but didn't say anything. If they get hungry, they will be back faster than usual. "Well, where are you off to?" I asked as I stood in the doorway as they waited for the elevator. "We will scout the fortifications along the beach and then travel west and north along the fence till we get to our rendezvous." Zathan proudly announced.

"Yeah, and since we don't have a ferry to take us across the mighty expanse of the pools we will encounter, we will have to swim for our lives," Little Mitch interjected.

"Well, just don't get your clothes all messed-up because I don't want trouble with your mothers."

As always, I returned to my balcony, so I would see them as they opened the pool gate and hurried across to open the opposite gate.

Zathan appeared down below me on the sidewalk running as fast as he could until he came to the first palm tree down by the barbeque grill. He peered around the tree, then raised his arm and motioned to the other two that they could follow him, and they appeared striding in step with each other toward the junction of the sidewalks.

Little Mitch shouted, "Fall out," as Sally Smyth was coming down the walk that runs along the fence by the big pool. I smiled as I thought those little rascals know she will be coming along, and they have it planned out. The three of them waited until Sally came up and then dropped to their knees to pet Missy and Sam 2.

Missy, the slightly smaller of the two dogs, seemed to revel in their attention more than Sam 2. She seemed to especially like Dylan as I saw her edge her way around until she had his full attention. He rubbed behind her ears and scratched her nose, and she nudged him when he stopped to get him to do it again.

I imagined the conversation that Little Mitch was having with Sally and that Zathan would stand silent unless Sally addressed him directly. That's just the way the three of them are.

"Miss Sally, we would be honored to walk Missy and Sam 2 in the dog run on the outside of the perimeter fence any time you need us. We wouldn't be allowed to take them down on the grassy space next to the Blvd. because we aren't supposed to go down there, but we could walk them along our fence," Little Mitch offered.

"Well, thank you very much, and I'm sure the dogs would love you to walk them, but Lewis and I need the exercise every day, so I guess we will keep walking them."

They said goodbye to Sally, and of course, Little Mitch, ever the 'politician,' said "I hope you have a wonderful day, Miss Sally. And I'm sure we will meet here again soon."

I heard Sally's laugh and her goodbye to them as they scurried through the gate and across the pool deck with Zathan in the lead.

They dropped, as usual, to the ground after the far pool gate clanged shut behind them, and I heard Zathan say very clearly to Little Mitch, "Your ass-end is sticking up too far. He will see your butt." Little Mitch dropped and started inching his way toward one of the posts. None of them appeared to think about Cam hearing the same conversation, for they were in their own fantasy until someone interfered.

Three little quixotic adventurers on a safari, I laughed.

I saw that telling Dylan to leave Cam alone was just wasting my breath, as I saw each of them pop up behind one of the perimeter posts—their rampart, their protection from Cam and the beach.

Cam played his usual part with them as I could hear him moaning and groaning like he was in pain.

They all stood up and I could see the concern on their faces. Then, Cam jumped up, scrambled up on top of the perimeter post, and began screeching and clawing at them with his arms outstretched. One of them said a dirty word, they all screamed, and ran for the corner of the Dolphin Building. I saw two bottles of water go sailing through the air, saw Dylan bend over and grab his crotch as one of his bottles had wacked him, and in a flash Little Mitch and Zathan reappeared as they had already gone around the corner, grabbed the bottles that were on the ground, raised their fists in the air in defiance at Cam and run back out of sight.

Zathan brought them to a screeching halt just as soon as they were around the corner of the Dolphin, "Men, he was ready for us and it was our fault. We have to reconnoiter a lot quieter next time. And look ahead of us now, there are puddles of water all the way to the Green Turtle Building. Group Leader, I ask permission that we take off our flip-flops and wade through this mighty flood?"

"Great idea, Scout Zathan. Permission granted. Fall-out and take off footwear."

"We only have to step out of them and then pick them up and carry them," Dylan said.

Little Mitch looked at him with a hint of anger. The three of them were soon wading through every puddle they could, zigzagging to make sure they didn't miss any.

They stopped under the portico at the Green Turtle Building to put their flip-flops back on.

"Let's stop at the Rental Office and see if Miss Lori will let us go around the counter and watch the fish in her big aquarium. I heard she has a new fish." Little Mitch suggested.

"Good command, sir," answered Dylan, "and maybe she has some peppermints."

They looked like three pudgy little elves as they marched up to the Rental Office door. Their fat belts stuck out in front, and the bottles hit against their thighs.

"Well, what do we have here? Need some rooms? Or are you just here to get peppermints from my dish?" Lori Cherry asked.

"No, ma'am, we were wondering if we could stand in front of the aquarium and watch the fish for a while?" Little Mitch asked.

"Yes, you may, but don't peck on the glass as it bothers them, and don't get in the way if we have customers checking into their condos. I have a new fish I think you will be interested in. I'm getting ready to leave for a week, and I don't have time to stay in here and watch you," Lori said as she disappeared into her office. "Oh, by the way, there will be three peppermints on the edge of my desk as you leave." They giggled their usual success, gouged each other in the ribs, and marched to the aquarium. The new fish did indeed get their attention, and they would talk about it the rest of the afternoon. Fifteen minutes later they had the peppermints and were walking out the door. Lori Cherry was already outside loading her luggage into her Soul. It was new, and they were very interested, so they walked around and around it.

"Guess you want to see inside?" she asked. They were inside it in a flash and from the back seat, Dylan exclaimed, "Bet we look just like those hamsters in the commercial." They were in fits of laughter and did their best to imitate the music of the commercial. Zathan went, "Ding, ding, ding," like a train crossing the road, Dylan and Little Mitch were swaying and shaking, and the three broke out into "Hold on to the Moment!" They were almost beyond themselves, bowing and dancing, as they left Lori Cherry.

Steve, the La Mancha maintenance men they all know, had seen them in the car as he went by and waved at them.

48

Revenge, the Sweetest

Hibiscus Island - Miami

Lori Cherry loved the car with its coat of dark cherry red with black stripes running almost vertically just behind the front wheels, and the large spokes on the wheel coverings.

Realizing her foot was getting heavy, she lifted it and felt the little car slow down. She couldn't afford getting a ticket as she made this trip.

She had contacted her mother that she was on the way down to the compound but knew that her father would also know she was coming, for nothing, it seemed, got past him.

His two wives lived in their own mansion with an area between them that now looked like a jungle as he had spent millions creating a space between them. His South American blood almost exploded within him with pride as he casually laughed whenever one of them complained about the other.

Each of the wives had given him a string of daughters, and he had used all of them, to hate each other by the time each of the girls could walk. He knew that they obeyed out of fear of him and what he would do to them as he had shown the ones who were still alive just how cruel he could be.

He met Shelby Knowland when he was doing some renovations on his part of Hibiscus, was impressed with her quiet knowledge of real estate, and when Bette was getting out of hand at the La Mancha with her inability to stop drinking—she didn't hide it from the staff when they came into her office, had convinced Shelby and her husband, Pat, to go up there and purchase several condos. In a few months he had established Shelby as the manager. His real business at the La Mancha was on hiatus until he had figured out a new way to distribute the deliveries.

He had let out a string of cursing when Launie had become hooked on the very stuff they were selling and had lost her mind and killed Ollie. Her trial and the explosion in the Sound after the violent shooting within the courtroom, had nearly exposed his whole opera- tion to that State policemen, J C Blevins.

Shelby had no idea what he did or who he was, but that was about to change, for he had figured out a way to restart his very profitable business.

As she drove South down Interstate 75, Lori's mind was filled with the horror she and her sisters and half-sisters had lived through the last four years. Why she didn't have the courage to get out of the mess tormented her. Her father would have walked away if he were caught up in mess he didn't like, and everyone said she was more like him that any of the others.

She knew why Launie, one of her sisters, had been brought to Fort Walton Beach from New Orleans to set-up the strip joint—to pull in the thousands of tourists from all over the South where it was actually a front to buy drugs. She knew the drugs were coming up from Miami and that her father oversaw everything. Launie made a spectacle of herself as she bought a powerful yacht and had her henchman to pilot it out into the Gulf to snag the bundles of drugs.

Lori was jealous of that henchman because he escaped one day— just had the guts to drive away from the mess. She found out later that he was really Launie's son who couldn't live in Launie's world and had escaped to some city up North where he is running a soup kitchen for those down on their luck.

She slapped her hand on the steering wheel of the little Soul as she remembered how Launie had destroyed herself with the very drugs she was supposed to be selling for her father.

Lori knew Launie was skimming money off the top, and that their father would soon send someone to end it. Launie would just disappear and never be seen again.

Launie had become a frail, sick druggie who looked like a homeless person as she went about in public like nothing was wrong. Her grotesque figure became known around Fort Walton, and when she killed Ollie that dark night on the Sound, her usefulness to her father ended.

She had solved the situation herself. Her drug infested mind began to believe that Ollie was calling attention to her illegal activi- ties. Ollie was a strange young man who had helped Launie and her girls escape from Hurricane Katrina as it roared down on them in New Orleans.

So, at almost sunset one afternoon, she took Ollie down the Sound in her big Yacht, and over a deep black pool of the Sound, shot Ollie in the back of his head and then dragged his body, weighted with two heavy buckets of paint, off the back of the yacht into that cold water.

But that had also ended her value to their father.

She needed gas, so she stopped, filled the tank, and bought a Mr. Goodbar—her favorite. She was on her way to end things, and if need be, she would end it the same way her father would have done it. He would disappear and never be seen again if her plan worked.

She didn't pay any attention to the black SUV that pulled out behind her as she left the gas station.

She thought of that morning she and Bette fought on the sixth floor of the Green Turtle building at the La Mancha. Bette had been after that old woman who lived up there since she had been ask- ing too many questions, but she didn't have to kill her. That's what started the end of everything. It was no accident that J C Blevins appeared on the scene right after it happened.

She had been lucky to get away unseen as there had been so much confusion and outright fright as all those people saw Bette's body impaled on that Sago Palm.

She hadn't meant to kill Bette. She had wanted to warn Bette that they all were going to be in trouble unless Bette sobered up. When she saw the body of that old woman sticking out of the elevator door and she had turned to find Bette standing there smiling, she had lost control.

She slapped Bette as hard as she could and they began to struggle. Even though Bette was a much bigger woman than she was, Bette was almost drunk. Lori had shoved and pushed as hard as she could and Bette went flying over the railing to her bloody death on the Sago Palm.

That was just the beginning of the end though, she knew. Launie was shot by that bitch, Katrina, in front of the whole town. Lori had just found out that Katrina and Jeffery Bickel were shacking up almost every day during that long drawn out trial. Bickel was an idiot if he thought he could return to Miami and not pay for what he had done. Even as evil and immoral man as her father was, he would make Bickel pay for embarrassing his family for Bickel was mar- ried to the only sister—only child—their father had allowed to not be a part of his business on the Panhandle. Lori wished she had not involved Cam, her nephew, in the mess but she had been told to have him near the *Lollipop*, that huge yacht that Lounie had flaunted in front of Fort Walton Beach. Lori wonder how her father had known the yacht would explode in the Sound, but she thought, "He knows everything." She wonder if he had any notion what she had planned?

She drove across the causeway onto Hibiscus Island a few hours later: his domain, and pulled up in front of the huge ornate gate.

A guard, or more likely a bodyguard, approached and said, "Your father is not on the compound tonight and says he will see you tomorrow night at his apartment where you will have dinner with him."

Her mother was waiting for her. While her mother did her nails, they talked until it was early morning about things that Lori knew nothing about, for it had been nearly four years since she had seen her mother.

She saw that her mother had 'several things done to her body' since she had seen her, and it hit her that she was just playing his game also. Of course, she always had done his every whim. Why else would she live almost next door to his other wife? Lori thought she was going to be sick at her stomach as she remembered the many fights and arguments she and her real sisters had with the other girls. "Hold your hand still. It's just like you're a little kid again and I'm doing your nails, and you have either done something bad or getting ready to. Now, just hold still." her mother scolded.

She looked at her mother, and their eyes locked on each other for a second until Lori lowered her head to look at her hand and said, "That's really nice. You can still paint a scene that makes me happy!" Her nails were polished with beach scenes with one thumb showing a large orange sun setting much as it did at the La Mancha. A thought flashed through her mind as she thought if she would ever see that again.

Since his crazy plan for getting rid of Judge Bickel at Launie's trial— the Judge was her brother-in-law, and Katrina, one of her half- sisters, had been carried out by her, she had grown to hate her father more than ever. She was still afraid of the overpowering sixty- five- year-old, well-built man who still made women stop and turn to see his trim body as he would pass them.

"You be very careful how you act and what you say around him because he will do away with you just like he has with all the others." Her room was on the second floor overlooking one of the six pools that surrounded her mother's house and, looking out to the east, she saw the skyline of Miami about three miles away. A large box from an awfully expensive designer lay on the bed. She tossed it onto one of the leather chairs grouped in the window's alcove. She knew what was in it and wondered if she would have guts enough to not wear it when she went down to his wing of the house when he summoned her to dinner. Of course, she would wear the dress for hadn't her mother warned her to make everything seem like he was in control as usual. At eight o'clock the next evening, a knock sounded on her door.

She opened it to find a man very similar to the guard who let her into the compound. He stood almost at attention as he said, "Your father is expecting you, and I'm to walk you down to his apartment." She almost laughed in his face but closed the door behind herself and followed him down the hall toward the stairway.

He was seated at a table which had been placed a few feet from the long pool that ran along that side of the house. She had to walk fifty feet, or so, to reach the table and felt herself trembling as she slowly walked toward him.

A woman dressed in a maid's uniform appeared from nowhere, she thought, and pulled her chair back from the table.

"You look very nice," he said. She was surprised at his comple- ment but realized he was talking about the dress, not her.

"The dress is expensive. I will have little use for it when I return to the La Mancha," She replied.

"Ah, but if you just wear it once, it has accomplished its purpose." "Thank you."

He stood and turned to walk over to a little table that was set with glasses, some mixes, and a bucket of ice that had beers in it. She almost laughed aloud as he walked away from her for his slim matador-like pants were so tight she could see his body as if nothing covered it. He returned with two bottles of Mexican beer and two frosted glasses, "I believe the dinner will be to your liking."

A waiter appeared and started sitting dishes on the circular table and soon it was filled with little plates of crocodile guacamole, cotel de camorones estilo mexicano, and grilled oysters with chorizo but- ter. Lori recognized all the things she had loved as a child, and she looked at her father who sat looking at her with pride.

"I have made certain that there is no cilantro in any of the dishes just as you like."

"Thank you, again. I don't know where to begin…"

"Just follow my lead." He reached for a dish, sat it on his Fiesta dinner plate, and reached for another little plate from the table. Soon he had one of each of the dishes at his place at the table.

"The shrimp were swimming around alive and free down at the Keys this morning. It's wonderful how fast we can get the best of food so quickly. Just like the oysters that were flown down from Apalachicola last night. They were alive and secure in their beds, and now we are about to eat them."

She felt nervous for some reason, and the thought that something was not quite right crossed her mind, however, she began selecting dishes and placing them before herself.

"I see your mother has been doing your nails. Just like when you were a kid; not with butterflies and unicorns, but with seashells and a sunset."

"Yes, she seemed to get a lot of pleasure doing them for me," she said as she held out her hands with the nails up, so he could see." "That sunset is nice—it looks like it is raised up above the surface of your nail."

"It is. That's a little paste-on so that the sun is perfectly round." "Interesting."

"Yes, but I like the seashells best, I think."

They ate a few of the appetizers and sat back from the table. A woman appeared and cleared away all the plates until the table was bare. The waiter appeared with his cart and started serving spiny lobster tails with papas rellenos and a bed of watercress with radish and mango salad.

She looked at her father as he stood and walked to the table across the way to return with glasses of ice water. His long sleeve white shirt with ruffles on the chest shone in sharp contrast to his still dark, almost black hair which hung in a ponytail half-way down his back. She knew something was up when he turned to come back to the table because he had that look in his eyes, she had seen so many times—that look that said he was deceitful and treacherous. She thought, I must be careful when I say anything and be cautious about what he is doing.

When they had finished, and the table was cleared once again, he said, "Carlos, you and Leona may leave now. I appreciated your service. There will be a little something extra in your pay this week." The waiter bowed a sharp little bow, and said, "Thank you, sir."

Lori wonder if everyone except her father and her were really gone. She suspected the burly man who had brought her down to dinner was lurking nearby.

Her father said, "I think your new little car is cute. And will the cost of it be hidden somewhere in your rental sales?"

She knew she was turning red, but said, "No, it will not. When have I ever cheated you?"

"Shelby Knowland was wondering the same thing I just asked when I talked to her last night."

"Who is that woman? And why are you taking her word for anything? You haven't known her that long. The only thing she has ever done is buy some condos up at the La Mancha."

"I have plans for her. No, I believe you about the car. I just wanted your reaction about Shelby."

"Well, she's alright, but I don't know just what she is doing now except the everyday running of the La Mancha. She hasn't asked me about rental sales nor anything else about what I'm doing."

"Oh, she will. She just has to get things running the way she wants; I mean the way I want." He laughed. "We've had to close down all operations up there, and we're losing a bundle of money every day. We have all those customers that are clamoring for our product, and they can't get it. But we have them hooked, and as soon as I get this plan started, we'll furnish them with what they want again."

Lori didn't like the way things were going, so she said as she stood up, "May I make us some margaritas? You know, like I used to make them for us when I was too young to have one, but you let me anyway?"

"Yes, that might be amusing."

"You will have to rim the glasses," she said, as she carried two glasses and a saucer of Tajin from the table across the way, "as I don't want to ruin my nails." A thought raced through her mind, 'why aren't my hands shaking?'

She returned to the side table and making sure she was facing him, so he could see everything she was doing, poured three ounces of Patron, two ounces of the Citrange Pineapple, and the pineapple and lime juice into the sterling silver shaker that was filled with ice. She closed the lid on the shaker and held it as he had shown her many years ago, up even with her right shoulder. She shook it vigorously and sat it down. She walked to him, took the two glasses he held out to her and returned to the side table. On the way, she flicked some grains of sand from one of her nails onto one of the glasses and popped the 'sun chip' from the sunset into another.

She steadied her nerves, turned, walked back to the table, and reached out to hand him the glass that had the 'sun chip' in it.

He immediately noticed it and said, "Did you do that on pur- pose? Is that more than it appears to be? Do you want to leave here alive and become a part of my new plan, or do you want to have an accident that no one will ever solve?"

She started shaking uncontrollably, and she was not acting, she knew. She had to regain control of herself, she thought. Then she started crying, lowered her head toward the table and sat sobbing. She raised her head, "No, no… That is not what happened. It fell into the glass. I'm sorry. Forgive me. Here, you take the other glass, and I will take the one with the chip in it."

"Maybe I was too fast to accuse you, but someone is forever after me," he said as he took the other glass. She raised the glass that he had accused her of doctoring to her lips and took a big sip. He raised the other glass and did the same.

"Okay, I apologize," he said.

She knew better, for he never apologized, but she nodded her head. "That's okay. I am just sorry that it has ruined this beautiful meal we just shared." Then she laughed out loud as she saw him licking the rim of his glass. "You are doing just what you always did when I was little, lick the rim all the way around."

He smiled, stuck his tongue out again, and she involuntarily giggled as the thought it should be forked raced through her mind. He turned and wiggled his tongue back and forth. She laughed again.

You sinister evil bastard I am about to settle things with you.

He swirled the glass's rim around and around on the tip of his tongue, "It's my favorite part. The flavors are…"

She saw the glass in his hand begin to slide from his grip, and she caught it in midair, but his head smacked onto the table with a hard knock. The Rohypnol, she and her mother had taken from his stash in his nightstand and sprinkled onto the sandy scene on her nails, worked quickly.

Her mother appeared at the top of the stairs carrying the little cooler that she had prepared a few hours ago, "I'll clean up and git rid of anything you might have touched. I told everyone to git out of the house, and I believe they did. What are you going to do with him now?"

"You don't want to know. No, I don't want you to know, for then you won't get caught in a story about what happened to him."

She wondered if he had done to someone else what she planned to do to him now?

She had secretly watched him open the enclosure he had built between his two wives' houses. It had taken her several times to watch his fingers push the buttons in a certain order for the two big sliding gates to open and make the area that included the pool into one big area.

It had taken several months for the divided area to become a big, covered dome. It looked like a lanai, not a regular lanai, but one that was covered with heavy metal bars connected with stout steel wiring. During the next few years after he finished the enclosure which covered over an acre, they were allowed to walk around the outside of it on the fancy paver path. Lori had wondered how much had been spent on thousands of tropical plants and hundreds of birds that flew around in there.

But what bothered her most about the place, was the underlying putrid smell of something that was somewhat familiar, but out of place.

The pool has a diving platform in the middle of it that raises and lowers by a hydraulic lift. The water at that end of the pool was not really 'lap' deep, as the depth marker indicates eight feet.

She took double flex cuffs out of the cooler and cuffed his wrists together. She started to cuff his ankles but laughed to herself that if he kicked and struggled, her scheme would work quicker.

She hurried to the pool house with the little cooler. She slipped out of the expensive designer dress and made a mental note she had to text her mother to be sure and get it, as she put on the swimsuit from the cooler. When she got back to the table, he still sat with his head on the table, dead to the world.

She pulled him to the tile floor and toward the pool. He was trim and lightweight, so she had an easy time sliding him into the pool.

It was easy to guide his body over to where the diving platform was even with the surface of the water.

She struggled to get his body situated on the platform, but when she was satisfied, she pulled his arms around the end of the platform and pulled them back until they were tight against the board. That caused his head to hang over the end of the board and his ponytail dangled down and floated in the water.

She pulled the foul-smelling necklace of chicken necks from over her head that she had taken from the cooler and hung it over his. It hung down just about as low as his ponytail.

She swam to the edge of the pool, got out, and went to the panel and pushed the button that raised the platform. She was satisfied when it rose out of the water about six feet in the air, and his body was somewhat balanced on it. His ponytail hung limp toward the water below.

Then, she sat down and waited. It seemed way too long to her, and she was afraid that someone would come and discover what she was doing. Finally, she saw him stir and then open his eyes.

"What the hell is this?" he shouted as he grasped where he was. "I'll have you shredded into strips if you don't take me down from here."

"Oh, I don't think so," she raised her voice. "You have destroyed everything around you, made us all do horrible things we never would have thought of doing, and it's just for the money you wallow around in. Oh, I've seen the piles of money in your private room where you and your whores play."

"You are funny, little girl. I'll have you wishing you never started this. What are you going to do, drown me? You lower the platform, and I'll slip off into the water and swim over and get you."

"Better check how you are fastened up there."

He struggled pulling his arms as far toward the end of the board as he could, but they would not slide forward. He started hollering for someone to come and help him, calling names that Lori knew were his henchmen, but nobody appeared.

He screamed at her, "You crazy bitch! You always were the insane one. Let me down right now, and we'll forget this all happened."

"Sure, you will. Just like you always forgave us… Just like you promised all the others you would forgive them, so the odds of me letting you down are about the same as your forgiving me."

"Someone will come and stop this, you just wait," he bellowed. "What the hell is this stinky thing around my neck?"

"Just chicken necks…. The cheapest part of the chicken…. The part that's best for you, and that works the best too." "What the hell you talking about, you crazy bitch?"

"Watch and listen carefully. It is about to begin. I will get to hear you beg me to stop it. Oh, I know you will, but I won't stop, not this time. I finally have the guts to end this whole mess. Listen!"

She wished she could erase that terrible night she had disobeyed and followed him. He was throwing chicken parts over the fence, and she heard the grunts of something she didn't want to see. She had nightmares for weeks after that.

Now, she was ready to pay back all the humiliation, deceit, and torment that he had put in her life and the lives of those she cared about. She walked to the panel to push the button in the sequence she had memorized. He hadn't changed the code, for he raised his head, and a look of terror crossed his face as he saw what she was doing.

She pushed the code into the panel and let out a sigh of relief as she heard the clicking sound at the gate of the other side of the pool. He had not changed the code.

It seemed forever to her before the gate completely slid back opening the full enclosure.

It seemed longer than that until she finally heard a sound.

It was a scraping sound as the monster pulled itself up the stacked rocks from the dingy pool that was filled with aquatic plants. Streams of dirty water slid off its leathery body creating black swirling puddles as they both saw the thick undergrowth separate as something huge was moving toward the grassy lawn along the edge of the pool. It didn't look in either direction but stood high on its legs like it knew it was the alpha in the drama to come. When it came into the light, she saw it was monstrous. It rambled across the little strip of grass and slid into the pool.

He was now screaming and yelling for help, but suddenly became quiet.

"Yes, you idiot, be quiet. Be incredibly quiet and maybe it won't smell the chicken necks. You know what's going to happen, and I bet you have done similar things to others who crossed you in a deal or someone who didn't bow down and kiss your ass."

She was amazed at the size of the gator when she turned on the underwater lights. It jerked a little when the lights came on and started down the narrow pool toward the deep end. It had to be twelve to fourteen feet long and was very thick. She shuddered.

He screamed again, and this time he was begging her. "Get me down from here somehow, and I will give you half of all I have. I will forget this ever happened."

You think I would believe that?" she shouted back at him. "No, I'm too much like you. I'm ashamed of it, but if I were up there about to have my head chomped off, I would make any promise and then go back on my word in a second if you turned me loose. You created this mess, you rotten bastard. When I was hiding one time and listening to you and some men talking, you said that the sweetest revenge of all is when you set it up, and the victim does it to himself. No, you filthy scumbag, I'm just going to stand up here and watch—watch the whole thing, if I can.

The monster glided along underwater headed straight to the diving platform. She saw her father shaking now uncontrollably but trying to lie quietly, she thought. The gator veered to its left and slowly circle around the platform. As it came around, it raised its head out of the water, and she thought if sniffed the air.

Suddenly it submerged, raced through the water, and she saw its tail twisting and turning as it leaped. Its gaping jaws opened wide, and it clamped down on the chicken necklace around her father's neck. It broke loose, and the huge creature hit the water with a loud splat, and water sprayed high into the air.

Her father was laughing now; she couldn't make out if it was real laughter because he thought he had escaped, or if it was a hideous, cringing laughter because he knew it would leap up again. Then, he started whimpering like a baby, crying little fits, and Lori smiled, and then he was shouting and screaming and kicking his feet onto the board struggling with all his might to free himself, or to scare away the gator, she thought.

This time, the gator didn't hesitate. It lunged toward the plat- form, flicked its tail, and rose out of the water. Up, up it went till it was almost even with the diving board. She saw its jaws snap out and swallow her father's head. Its thrust caused it to clamp down way past his head to his shoulders. Somehow, it started slashing back and forth, and little by little it dragged his body off the board.

When it hit the water, it started what she had read was the death roll. It rolled over and over in the water making sure its prey was dead. Strings of blood ran through the pool, and a new gush came out of the gator's mouth.

It appeared above the surface of the water again, climbed up out of the pool, and she saw it was dragging his body toward the strip of grass on the other side. It stood up as tall as its legs allowed and walked away through the opening in the enclosure with his body dangling on either side of its powerful jaws. It slid down the embank- ment of stones into its murky pond.

She was shaking uncontrollably. She pushed the buttons on the control panel and the opening in the enclosure closed.

She couldn't believe that she now had an opportunity to leave a mystery that might never get solved. She pushed the first set of buttons, and three large drains opened in the bottom of the pool. The water started swirling around and around as it sped through the drains. She saw a tattered shred of his fancy ruffled shirt as it was sucked through one of the drains follow by those strings of blood.

She punched the buttons for the next commands; the power tubes that blasted the sides and bottom to thoroughly clean them and the command to refill the pool.

She had to leave this place, for she had been here way too long. She turned and gripped the railing around the balcony where she stood and looked down where the nightmarish events had just taken place. She felt no grief nor regret. She was sorry she hadn't had nerve enough many years before to end the destruction and deaths of her so-called families.

She had planned evil to destroy a bigger evil, but she wondered if she had been right in doing it. Can evil destroy evil?

She looked at her nails and saw that they were entirely ruined—scraped and chipped—and she wished she had time with her mother to redo them, but she must get away from this place.

She burst into little fits of nervous laughter as she realized that silliness of thinking about her nails as a time like this.

She drove the little square car across the sound that separated Hibiscus Island from Miami and merged onto I-95 heading north toward Orlando not knowing really where she intended to go, for she didn't really know who or what she would see whenever she looked over her shoulder.

49

Ambush

Disaster Spying on the Air Command

When they left Lori Cherry and her cool car, they didn't stop until they were in front of Craig's maintenance shop where they found him working on a lawn mower with Israel, one of his men. First, they stood way back as the two men kept trying to keep the mower running. Little by little, they got closer until Craig looked up, "Better run along and keep away from here. This thing might explode and blow you all to kingdom come."

They scattered like someone had thrown a firecracker into their usual triangle and kept running until they came to where the ugly chained-linked fence that the county has recently put up was only a foot or a little more from the backstop fence around the La Mancha's tennis court. The two fences ran like that, parallel to each other, for several feet, so they pretended they had to fight their way through the narrow space hacking the air with imaginary machetes. Finally, they made their way to the hard surface of the court and collapsed as one.

"Quartermaster, shall we eat?" Little Mitch asked.

Dylan stood straight and announced, "No, Group Leader, we need to recon the enemy before we eat."

"Very well, then. Scout Zathan lead us to the lookout."

They jumped to their feet and instantly hunkered into their stalking positions. As they came toward the far northwest corner of the La

Mancha property, Zathan dropped to the ground and the other two followed him. Zathan reminded the Group Leader to keep his butt close to the ground, and Dylan laughed too loud till the other two admonished him to be quiet. They pulled themselves with their knees and elbows until they were able to peek down at the Air Command's guard shack. Zathan start inching his way backward and the others got out of his way.

"They're down there. Four of them. Two have guns. Two look like they are getting their jackhammers ready."

"Well done, Scout Zathan. Now, can we eat?"

Dylan was ready to reply, but two mockingbirds flew out of the big Oleander bush nearby and started diving at them. Again, and again, the birds fluttered, shot straight at the boys, and flew back up to dive toward them again. A long, white tail feather floated down to the ground. The boys screamed with genuine fear and made a dive under the Oleander bush.

"What the heck are they doing this time of year?" Zathan asked. "They should be finished with their nest and their babies should be gone by now. That's strange."

In the sandy soil of Florida, Oleander bushes secure themselves in the soil with a crisscross webbing of roots—looks like a piecrust. The roots are sometimes no larger around than pencils with shoots that bore down into the sand. The roots might cross the area three or four times above the ground creating a 'trampoline' of roots.

As they slid under the bush, Little Mitch knocked a bird's nest to the ground.

"Look, Sir!" Dylan said, "It's empty."

Zathan, who was the last one under the huge old shrub, said, "That's last year's nest. In last year's nest, there are no birds this year." "Where did you hear that? You sure didn't make that up by yourself," Dylan said.

"Great Grandma read it to me. It's about a strange old man who fights windmills and says all kinds of silly things."

"You're kiddin me? Who would fight a windmill?" Little Mitch said.

"I don't know, that's what she read to me. He's on a quest—that means he is trying to find something. He sees everything in a good way. Everything is beautiful."

Dylan said, "I bet he would enjoy sitting with Prof on the fence and watching the Gulf. That's beautiful."

They had landed in a heap as they scooted under the Oleander and soon found that the roots made a springy pad.

Zathan said. "Let's start shaking everything and maybe they'll fly away long enough for us to escape."

They began bouncing and wiggling around so much that the roots snapped and gave way—maybe because of all the recent rains, or maybe because of the vibrations of the jackhammering.

Little Mitch was the first to go tumbling down into the gaping hole slamming onto wet mounds of sand as he went. He caught Zathan's leg as he fell, and Zathan soon bounced along behind him. Dylan clung to the roots for several seconds trying to pull himself back up and do a 'monkey bar' like Daniel had taught him, but finally gave out and fell headlong on top of the other two.

The two mockingbirds that had been attacking them fluttered out of the Oleander bush, circled it twice, and flew up to sit on a power line. The opening the boys fell through collapsed back on the sandy soil and filled in almost as quickly as it had opened.

From the lawn by the tennis court nothing appeared different about the Oleander bush.

50

Closure for J C

Cam confesses

Daniel was walking around the end of the Pelican Building to get into the Sunsetter Beach Service truck as Cam returned down the ramp of the gazebo to sit in one of the chairs, he had positioned near the bottom of the ramp under an umbrella to keep off the sun, so he could talk with potential customers as they arrived at the beach.

He looked up at the gazebo to see a very attractive older woman sit down on one of the benches that are around the railing. She had a book with her, and he guessed she was going to sit up there and read.

J C Blevins walked down the boardwalk and leaned on the gazebo railing, "Want to come up here and talk with me for a while?" Cam's insides churned a little, but he answered, "Been expecting I might have to talk with you."

He walked up the ramp and sat down on the nearest bench. J C stood across the gazebo floor from him, then crossed over, and sat next to him. They both looked in the direction of the lady who sat reading, but J C turned to Cam. Cam turned his face toward J C and stared straight into his eyes.

"Why'd you sign for the wave runner under a false name?"

Cam smiled a slight smile and let out his breath, "I didn't. That is my real name. I am Cameron Bickel, Judge Bickel's son."

"No kiddin? You're being dishonest, one way or the other, because when you applied for work with Daniel, you had a driver's license that said, 'Cameron Piper,' so which is it?"

"My Grandfather took care of that when he sent me up here." "That's the other thing, who is your grandfather?"

"I can't tell you."

"Okay, we'll come back to that. Who sent you to pick up Katrina Hart's body out of the Sound when the explosion blew-up Launie's yacht with Judge Bickel, Katrina Hart, and that lawyer, Schaberg on board? How did that person know there was going to be an explosion?"

"Once again, I can't tell you. All I can tell you is that I was supposed to get her out of the water if I did find her and get her over to where we used to live and put her into a secret room that I never knew about. I didn't know what they were going to do and actually got sick and threw up when the house burned down, and we started hearing rumors that you found something horrible in there. Mr. Blevins, don't you think we better talk about this where it is more private?" Cam glanced at the woman reading the book.

J C looked at the woman, didn't answer Cam, but said, "Now, what made 'them' think Katrina Hart might still be alive?"

"I really don't know. I mean it, sir, I don't know. I never thought about that. I was just doing what they told me to do."

"Why?"

"Because if I didn't, they would hurt my Mom. And then me...." "Then, don't you think you should be telling me, so I can help you?" "Oh, you don't know how simple that sounds. If he makes up his mind that he doesn't need someone anymore, he has no feelings or qualms about anything. He has us all scared to death of him and doesn't care if we all hate him—everything in me hates him.... He's almost seventy but acts like he's thirty—and some days like he's a teenager who doesn't care about anything but himself and money and women. He's done away with so many of our family, that it is just too sick to think about."

"Okay, Cam," J C said in a calm quiet voice, "I know all this. Have since last night. Daniel knows I'm here, as I guess you have already guessed. That lady over there is a retired judge who has listened to everything we have said. Curtis Porter, the Prosecuting Attorney for

Okaloosa County knows we are talking here right now, and Judge Boyd, over there, will be a witness to what you have already told me."

"I think I had better leave now. This has all been unfair and sneaky. Tell Daniel I'm sorry I misled him. I think he is a good and honest man who would never do to me what I did to him."

"Hold on a minute, there is more you need to hear."

"I can outrun you, and you don't have your gun on. I can make it to my Jeep and be gone before you can stop me."

"And where would you be going? Listen, I'm sorry I had to fool you, but we had to hear you say how afraid you were and that you didn't know what was going on, so sit down and listen now to the real reason I'm here.

Your Aunt Lori is dead. She went down to Hibiscus Isle, to kill your grandfather in a very gruesome way, but something caused her to back off at the last minute—something good that she probably didn't know was inside of her.

At least, I hope she had those feelings as she headed back up this way when she veered into the path of a garbage truck. The mech- anism on the front of the truck broke loose somehow and crushed her little car, and it pushed it out into Biscayne Bay."

"How do you know this?"

"Because Marvin has been down there all this time, and he was following her and saw the accident."

"I don't know who Marvin is."

"Yes, I guess you wouldn't. He is a DEA agent who has been working on this case almost since it started. He was here at the La Mancha when another of your aunts, Launie Sanderson, was pushing drugs all over the Panhandle. He went back down South during the trial and watched what was happening on your grandfather's enclave. He followed Lori when she headed up here, watched them pull her and her car out of the water, and then watched the Jaws of Life as it took them over four hours to get her out of the tangled mess."

"He was that man we called Craig… Gee…What about the other?"

"You mean the insane way she planned to kill your granddad? She didn't do it."

"How do you know?"

"Because your grandmother told us. She wasn't going to watch as it happened, but she did. You ever see what was in that enclosure in the middle of the property?"

"I saw its tail once and had enough sense to keep my mouth shut. I had nightmares for over a month after I saw it."

"Well, your Aunt Lori wasn't the only one who knew the but- tons to push to open the enclosure, and her mother pushed the but- tons, and then stood up on the second level as that gator snatched your grandfather off that diving board. We found the prints where it pulled his body back into the enclosure. The pool had been drained and flushed, but there was blood all over the place—up on the walls and through the grass where it dragged the body."

Cam was visibly shaking now, "My God, it's over. Is my mother okay? I'll tell you everything I know now."

"I think you already have, but you have names and relationships of all the people who have caused this horrible mess for me. You'll have to come to my office and write out what you know. I'm not going to take you in because Daniel and the Prof think you will come on your own, and I do too, now. So, I'll see you tomorrow?"

"I'll have to check with Daniel…. That sounds funny…. I mean…."

"I think I know what you're saying. That's why I'm not arrest- ing you right now. Now, Cam Piper, or Bickel, this is Judge Bonita Boyd."

The beautiful woman who had sat near them all this time stood up and walked to stand in front of Cam, "Young man, you're going to be okay." She held out her hand but had to backed up a step as Cam stood to reach out his hand to her.

The only thing J C was wrong about is what Lori Cherry's mother had lied about. Mothers are like that when they think they are protecting their children, for, she did not know that Lori was already dead when she told the lie.

51

Jurassic Park Underwear and Terror

Wet Skivvies

"Zathan? Little Mitch?"

"Here, I am," Zathan said as he touched Dylan on the arm. Dylan jumped at the touch, for it was pitch-black wherever they were.

"Little Mitch?" Dylan said again.

Suddenly, Zathan turned on his flashlight, and the tiny beam lit on Little Mitch's face. His eyes were closed, and a large red spot covered most of his forehead.

"He's out cold. We need something wet to put on his head to try to wake him up," Zathan said. "I saw it on TV. You put a wet rag on his head, and it wakes him up."

"We don't have anything to do it with," Dylan said. "None of us has a top on cause that's sissy stuff when you go on an outing like we do."

"What are we going to do? We can't just throw water in his face." Zathan asked.

Dylan stood up and looked around at where they were, using the beam from his pen light. He couldn't see his hand in front of his face.

Daniel took him in a cave once, and they went in so far that it was just black all around. It was like that now.

He sensed they were in trouble and thought of his dad. He unbuckled his cargo belt and gently laid it down at his feet. He unbut- toned his shorts and let them fall, and then he took off his underwear. "My Mom made me put on clean underwear this morning, so we'll use them," he said.

"He'll hate you when he wakes up and finds out," Zathan laughed.

"Heck, they're my brand-new Jurassic Park ones. Dad's going to take us all to see the new movie as soon as he has time," Dylan laughed.

Dylan saw Zathan's hand reach out with an open bottle of water, and he held his underwear out so Zathan could see where to pour it. He felt the water running down his arm, so he told Zathan to stop. He reached down and placed the wet cloth on Little Mitch's forehead.

The two of them waited a long time; at least it seemed a long time for two frightened little boys. Finally, Little Mitch shuffled a little, and his hands went straight to his forehead.

He mumbled, "Where are we? Crap, my head hurts."

"That's one of your don't say words, and you know it. But I guess it means you're okay. We fell down into this place when the roots on that stupid bush broke," Zathan answered.

"Yeah, and we needed a rag to wet to put on your head to wake you up. We used my underwear. I've only farted in them about twenty times today," Dylan almost shouted.

Little Mitch flung the wet cloth away from him as far as he could, "I'll get even you know?"

But then, maybe it was because he was embarrassed about having Dylan's underwear wiped across his face, or maybe it was the swelling red bump on his head, or maybe it's just that it takes a long time for kids to understand they're in trouble, but Little Mitch became the leader of the troops again as he said, "Listen, men, we've got to recon and figure out where we are.

"What if we don't have air coming in?" Zathan asked.

"Let's not think about that cause we'll all just get scared of smothering, and one of us might start crying," Dylan answered. "Let's start by seeing what provisions we have. Shine your lights here so they will all be together."

The three pen lights didn't light up much of the dark, "Okay, let's take inventory. We all have our belts, and they have batteries.

What luck is that? And we have Miss Camelia's zip bags of veggies, and the PB&Js we made. Only, we just have one and a half of them. Too bad we didn't make more."

"We didn't have room," Little Mitch announced.

"That's right, Captain Mitch," Dylan replied. "And I'm going Commando because my underwear is wet and has been on your face too."

At that, all three of them broke into their usual fits of laughter. Little Mitch spoke again, "Scout Zathan, you need to find out where we are."

Again, they paused.

"What if our flashlights don't work?" Little Mitch asked.

"They've been on our belts for a long time."

"I don't think batteries wear out if they haven't been used," Zathan said, "and mine worked when we needed it to see where to pour the water on Dylan's undies."

"The only way we can find out is to try them," Dylan laughed. "Yeah, but if we do that and they don't work, then we only have two flashlights," Little Mitch argued.

"You are not making sense. What difference does it make if we have two if they don't work anyway? Well, we'll never know unless we do, or if we wait until the batteries in the flashlights do go out, and then we'll be in a fix." Zathan argued right back.

"You two are like two of Miss Camelia's old hens arguing about whose nest is whose," Dylan said.

He picked up his belt that was still on the floor, took two batter- ies out of the loops on one side, and unscrewed the top of his flash- light, and put two in and re-screwed the top and turned it on.

Zathan looked at Little Mitch and said, "See, I told you it would work. Now, we've got to see if we can find a way to get out of here. Shine your lights over this way." They all pointed their lights to the end of the room where they had bounced down the slick mud. "I don't think we can climb that. Looks very slick. Besides, it might cave in on us too," Dylan said.

He turned the beam up toward the ceiling and they could see the skinny roots of the oleander bush hanging down. Big balls of mud clung to the roots and it looked like they could break lose any second and clobber them.

Zathan said, "We sure can't get out that way. We'd never make it up that slide of mud and even if we did, we couldn't break through and get out.

Dylan answered, "We have to keep our heads. That's what my Dad always says. Just keep our minds on what is going on around us, and then we won't get scared."

Zathan aimed his light away from them, and all three broke out in screams of real terror. They clutched at each other and fell to their knees on the ground hiding their faces against each other as they huddled.

Dylan dropped his pen light and was covering his face with his long slender fingers. All at once, he reached out and started shaking the other two, "Quit it right now, or I'll give you a knuckle sandwich. Quit it!"

The other two backed away a little and looked in his direction, Zathan said, "You're not hitting me, buddy."

"Nah, that's just what my Dad says when I'm crying or upset.
And he's never hit me either."

They grabbed their lights and aimed all three at the other end of the chamber they were in. A skeleton sat facing them way up above their heads on a pile of bags.

Zathan said, "Look it's dead, men, and dead men can't hurt you.

Dylan butted in, "That's what my Dad says too. Dead men can't hurt you as long as you don't touch them."

"Look, one of its arms is missing," Zathan went on, "I bet it got hacked off cause you see the torn shirt all ripped up there at his shoulder? Gee, he got closed up in here and died from bleeding."

"Sure looks like it. I've never seen clothes like those. He sure looks old," Little Mitch said.

"There's an arrow sticking through that big rip in his pants, and it looks like it's stuck in his backbone," Dylan said. "I saw a deer that someone had shot that had the same thing one time when I was with my Dad up at the cabin."

"It can't be in his backbone, or he wouldn't have been able to move at all," Little Mitch exclaimed. "Gee, you are dumb sometimes," he added getting a dig in at Dylan probably about the underwear.

Zathan became very quiet, but he walked toward the skeleton, and the other two were amazed and scared for him as he sat down looking up at it.

"What are you doing? You're crazy," they said.

"I know who this is. Great Grandma told me about him and what he did. This was my grandpa way back there many years ago, and I'm named after him."

Soon, Dylan and Little Mitch were standing next to where Zathan sat. "You're foolin us, right?" Little Mitch asked. They hesitated, then sat on the ground by him.

"No. She told me how he tried to saved Walton Landing's treasures and how the stinkin Creeks attacked them as they were coming back from the Island and how Zathan B... I can't remember his last name, Zathan Bor...something, never came back. She said some of the folks blamed him and thought he took the treasure and ran away, but we know different now. He must have been a real dude if he made it all the way up here from the Sound with fighting going on all around him. Great grandma said a big tropical storm blew in as the fighting was going on and scattered those heathen Creeks all over the place. A lot of people were killed that day, and she said the settlement was almost destroyed too."

"Gee, she's going to be happy when we tell her." "We have to find a way out of here first."

They flashed their lights around the room together and soon knew they were in a room about thirty feet long, and they couldn't agree on how wide.

Zathan said, "Look, the rocks are in order like someone placed them there. And look at those posts that are driven in all the same height, almost. You know what he's sitting on? The treasure! The stuff that belonged to Great Grandma's folks. Zathan Bordelon's treasure. That's his name, Bordelon."

"We've found lost treasure! We'll be famous and rich!" Little Mitch bragged.

"Heck, you are already rich with those shrimp boats Mister Mitch gave you," Dylan interrupted.

"Let's cut out the fighting," Zathan said. "We're in trouble, men."

All three of them became very quiet thinking about what little boys think when they are in danger.

Another Treasure

That's Not a Spider You're Peeing On

"I've got to pee. I'm gonna go over here and turn my back to you guys and don't you sneak around and watch me."

"Why? We go swimming naked all the time," Dylan 0asked.

"Yeah, but I can't go if someone is watching," Little Mitch almost growled.

"Oh, come on, let's see who can pee the farthest!" Zathan chimed in. "That way all of us will be doing it, and you won't be scared." "Who said I was scared. I just said it makes me not want to go."

The three of them lined up, side by side, and Dylan turned on his pen light. In a minute, all three of them were aiming at the far wall and Zathan's stream was going way up the wall.

"Man, you really needed to go, didn't you?" Little Mitch asked. Suddenly, Dylan let out a little scream, "What's that crawling on the floor over there. I hate spiders, that better not be a spider. Pee on it…. Hurry pee on it."

They all turned and aimed at a fuzzy thing laying on the floor a few feet in front of the skeleton. As they drenched it, something metal was uncovered that glinted in the light of Dylan's pen light.

"Stop! I know what that is. Stop!" Zathan hollered. "Can we wash it off with a little water?"

"Why don't you just pick it up?" Little Mitch couldn't help himself. "You and Dylan got a big kick out of washing my face with his underwear."

Dylan reached down in his pack and pulled out a bottle of water, "We've got to be careful with this cause we don't know how much longer we'll be down here." He poured a little water on the metal thing on the floor.

Zathan reached down and picked it up and wiped both sides of it on his shorts.

"What the heck is that?" Dylan asked. "That's a guimbarde." "A what?" Little Mitch demanded.

"A guimbarde. Great Grandma Camelia has another one hang- ing on a nail in her kitchen. She said most people call it a 'juice harp,' and many people say 'Jew's harp,' and that he had two of them when he road into Waltons Landing a long time ago."

"What's it do?"

"If it isn't broke, I'll show you." Zathan said. He wiped the metal flange clean and said, "I can't believe this flange hasn't broken off. It probably will when I play it."

"What do you mean, when you play it."

"Listen," he said as he put the juice harp to his mouth and began carefully flicking the flange with his finger. The other two started laughing at him as the weird sounds filled their underground room.

"That's neat! Can I do it?" Little Mitch asked.

"I don't think so. I think it will break if you don't know how to use it. Great Grandma showed me how."

"You are probably right," Dylan said. He looked at Little Mitch and said, "I'm not pickin on you now. But you know that thing belongs to Zathan cause the man he was named for is right over there."

Little Mitch turned toward the skeleton and said, "You think he played on that until he died? I bet he did. I bet it kept him from hurting so much."

Zathan held the juice harp in front of the beam of light from Dylan's pen light and stared at it with a new respect, "I bet he did too."

Dylan said, "Wonder how loud you can play on that thing? You think someone might hear it?"

"It's not loud, but when I play it in Great Grandma's back yard, the chickens all perk up and that rooster hates it when I get real low and the thing vibrates a lot."

The Lost Boys

The Prof's Worse Fears…

I made my way down to the gazebo knowing they would be returning soon and would want to stand at the railing of the gazebo gazing out at the Gulf and shouting remarks at Cam. The beach is covered today with hundreds of gulls complaining and bat tling each other for scraps of food. I sit down on the bench and look out at the vast water stretching to the horizon.

We are lucky, I think.

Huge, fluffy clouds fill the sky from horizon to horizon, so we probably won't have rain today unless it's in the late afternoon. The clouds are tinted with the oranges of the sun, and occasionally rays burst through holes and send streaks of light clear to the water. No artist could paint what I'm staring up and marveling about. I think it is silly to believe that all this happens as happenstance and am thankful to the creator of it all.

Then I think of other days when I couldn't possibly sit here in the gazebo or on the wall because of the mighty storms that hit us.

Most people know that hurricanes come across the Atlantic in late September, but mostly in October and almost the whole Nation knows what damage one of those can do.

But few people know that July is just as dangerous to us for that is when we get our heavy downpours that might dump over ten to twelve inches of rain on us in a single day. That's when the Gulf turns the dirty grey, and we don't dare step into it.

We couldn't step in it if we wanted for the waves hitting the beach would knock us for a loop. We have too many tourists who didn't respect the might of the swirling waters and huge waves or are ignorant of how dangerous it is. We have someone caught and drug out into the Gulf almost every summer.

But today is a beautiful day in the Gulf is calm. Three kayakers are way out past the trench that runs close to our shore, and like I saw over a year ago, one of them is trying to keep up with a pod of dolphins. Those dolphins are very smart so he's not going to catch them, and unlike what some people believe, dolphins can be contrary things too. It is not unusual to hear about a swimmer getting butted by one of them, or a boarder getting flipped way up in the air off his board.

I don't think this will happen today as this kayaker looks like a rookie. He's not going to catch them.

I don't think I have seen the sea-oats any taller than they are this year, and there are thick patches and rows of them. If you stop to think, it's special how those spindly wobbling thin stalks can hold the dunes in place; of course, it is their grasping roots that hold them in place. Nature takes care of herself if we just leave her alone. The boys must have stopped, and Little Mitch is probably visiting with a resident he hasn't seen for a while—like since this morning, if I know him. They didn't take as much food as usual, and they're going to want more than a Klondike Bar when they get back.

I must have dozed off—I find myself doing that a lot lately. Getting old is not nearly as much fun as we thought it might be when we were teenagers.

I jerk upright on the bench as Cam said, "Hey Prof! You take a snooze?"

I grinned sheepishly and said, "Guess I needed it. Had those three this morning, and they have too many questions to answer. Have you seen them since you scared the dickens out of them?"

"Nope," he grinned.

I pull my cell phone out of my shorts and see it is almost noon. I decide to call Craig to see if he had seen them.

In a few minutes, Craig came motoring down the sidewalk toward the gazebo in one of La Mancha's golf-carts.

"Come on, let's try to track them down," he said. "Where did they say they were going?"

"The usual. Little Mitch said they were 'prepared to scout the beachhead and go on to the frontier,' which means they were going to hide behind the fence and torment Cam and then go on down and see what was happening in the Air Command."

"They came by my shop and got in the way as Israel and I were fixing a lawn mower and they headed toward the tennis courts."

Craig drove around the pool house and down the sidewalk on the other side, so we would go by the perimeter wall. As we went around the corner of the Dolphin Building, I decided that I should call J C and tell him I was concerned about the boys.

"I just wanted to tell you that I'm concerned about the boys. They have been gone at least two hours longer than ever before, and Craig and I are out looking for them," I said in the calmest voice I could muster.

"You don't sound so sure about this, Prof. I'll be right over there," J C answered just a little too quickly, I thought.

It wasn't two minutes until we heard the siren blaring from his Patrol Car as it screeched out of the driveway at the new jail almost straight across the Sound from us on 98 and made its way through Fort Walton Beach. We heard its loud siren as it crossed Brooks Bridge and the change in the sound as we sensed it had turned onto Santa Rosa Blvd and was speeding toward us.

Diana Page walked out of the lobby door of the Green Turtle Building leading Emma, her cute little Labradoodle, the newest of the lovable dogs at the La Mancha. As they came towards us, Emma pulled ahead on her leash as far as she could to lick my hand and get rubbed on her head.

"Have you seen them three?" I asked.

"Yes, they went by here earlier." Diana laughed not even both- ering to ask who I meant, "Emma loves to see them, and they all got down on their knees and petted her for a good five minutes. One of them, and I know you will know who I mean, told me they were off to see the fish in the aquarium in the Rental Office. He assured me that we would see them again, and then they marched off with Zathan leading the way. Why? Is something wrong?"

"We don't know yet because we haven't been around to the tennis courts and the yard back there," Craig answered.

We heard the siren turn into the Security Gate, and it seemed to not even slow down as the cruiser rounded the corner and headed toward us.

"Have you found them?" J C asked as he was out of the car almost before it stopped.

"No, but we haven't been around to the tennis courts, and this all might be a lot of hoopla for no reason," I answered.

J C took off running toward the tennis courts, and Craig and I followed in the golf cart. We passed by Craig's workshop and whizzed around the corner. J C was standing on the edge of one of the courts looking out at the lawn as it stretched out toward the corner of the property. No one was on the courts, and no one was out in the yard. J C walked slowly over and sat down on one of the benches people use to watch the tennis games.

I got out of the cart and went and sat beside him, "Listen to me, don't get rattled. We've got to check this all out. We'll find them."

We got into the golf cart with J C sitting on the back rack and headed back to the Rental Office. We found out that they were there, and that Lori Cherry had let them sit in the back seat of her new Soul, and that they did that silly commercial music for the car. When we came out of the office, we encountered Steve who also said they were in Lori's car. We went to see Lyndell at the Security entrance to the La Mancha, and she told us that she hadn't seen Lori leave the prop- erty but that maybe Lori went out the back gate, or maybe she had been out on the property when Lori left. As we stood there, Daniel drove up to the gate, and J C quickly told him what we knew.

We walked back to the Rental Office building and gathered in the Coffee Lounge.

"What are so many people with such long faces doing in here?" Shelby Knowland asked as she came into the room.

I don't think I have ever seen Daniel so shaken before—even more than that morning the rattlesnake bit his ankle, "The boys are not where they should be. We have looked all over the property and can't find them."

"Steve saw them get into Lori Cherry's new car, and that's the last we know," J C broke in as he looked Shelby straight in the eyes. "I think you had better put out an all-points bulletin about this,"

she said. She quickly left the room.

It didn't take J C long to call in the information about the boys, and an hour later, someone turned on a tv set, and a loud buzzed sounded as the Amber Alert was broadcasted.

Someone had called Justin, and he was now sitting with the rest of us in the Coffee Lounge. His face told all of us how hard it was to believe this had happened.

"What am I going to tell Grandma Camelia? She won't come over here, I bet—no, she just might. I'm going to go after her and Claire."

Camelia said no about ten times that she wasn't about to go over to that evil place. She sat stiffly in the front porch rocker and defiantly said, "Mose told me long ago about that place and the awful things that have come upon us from over there."

"Great Grandma, Zathan might need you, you know?"

"Now, don't you start that with me mister, and I'm not your Great Grandma."

"But you're his. Claire and I are going back over there, and you are welcome to go with us. I'll even put one of your rockers in the back of the pick-up, so you'll have that assurance while we are over there. Shoot, they might find them before we ever get there, but you'll always regret not going…."

"Don't you go trying to make me feel bad…." She sat just as defiantly as she was a few minutes ago, but you could see the uneas- iness in her face and the dread and worry.

Five minutes later, she said, "Okay, load my rocker, I'll go. What if something happens to me over there, I ain't got much time on this earth anyhow."

"You shouldn't talk like that, you know," Justin laughed as he headed to the back yard to get her favorite rocker.

"You just mind your own business, mister."

Thirty minutes later, Camelia sat in the gazebo in her rocker. She kept humming something, and every once and a while, we heard her mumble something.

"What are you humming, Grandma?" Claire, who was sitting with her, ask.

"Just a few songs I know and some words I say once in a while. Can you imagine the mighty power of those waves out there? Oh, I have seen the Gulf when I went with Justin at times when we cross the Destin bridge, but I have never sat and seen it like this. I understand why the Prof and them three can just sit and wonder at the beauty."

Along about sundown, Justin borrowed the golf cart and took Camelia over to the Sea Shell Building that faces the Sound and Fort Walton Beach from Okaloosa Island, where he had rented a condo for them on the ground floor.

He went back to get her rocker, and now she was firmly planted in it on the porch facing the perimeter fence and the Sound. He and Claire asked her several times to come in and go to bed, but she declared that she was going to sit out on the porch—maybe all night.

54

Fever Dream

Dylan takes Command

They were worn out—like little boys who play as long as they can, and then deny that they are tired, but fall asleep denying later that they did fall asleep.

Their sleep came in little fits of twisting, crying out—one of them kept calling for his mom. Two of them swung arms into the air like they were fighting those mockingbirds, but the other one—the stoic one made little movements with his legs tensing up and occasionally stomping the floor of their prison.

Maybe they all had dreams, but Little Mitch's head hurt so much he wanted to cry in his dream, but his usual swaggering set in— he wasn't about to let Dylan see him cry, and he gritted his teeth. He screamed as the pain shot through his head, and Zathan fumbled around in the dark until he found him. He squeezed Little Mitch's hand and Little Mitch calmed down.

The calm wouldn't last very long because the Prof and his step- dad came into his dream. They were sitting on the Prof's balcony and J C was talking about the time Launie Sanderson took Little Mitch's real dad, Ollie, down the Sound and killed him.

He and the other two had been napping under the long board that stands on the Prof's balcony. Little Mitch had been faking sleep for he wanted to hear J C and the Prof. J C's voice was quiet and calming and the real world left his mind, and he sank back into rest- less sleep…

"It would never stand up in court, and I'm forever thankful that young couple was up there on the dune to hear and see the whole thing, or we would never have a case against her. We had known for a long time she was dealing drugs and thought about bugging that yacht of hers, but we didn't.

We always had someone on the Sound near her little dock, and the afternoon she took Ollie out in the yacht, we had what looked like an old man fishing in a small boat. He could only hear part of what they were saying. He heard Ollie shout some cuss words at a dog that was barking at them, and he saw Launie slow down and look at the new jail across the Sound from here like she was afraid someone was going to get her.

"She was for certain out of her mind on drugs, and if anyone doubts that they should have seen her when she came into the Tides Inn to buy lunch one day. Her eyes were empty holes—you couldn't see anything behind them," the Prof had said.

"Ester told me about how Ollie was terrified of dogs as one had ripped open his leg as he tried to leap out of its way on a fire escape as they were trying to flee New Orleans and Hurricane Katrina.

That's why Ollie was running around at night scaring the wits out of you because Skipper had barked and snarled at him when Ollie had come back to the beach to get that package of dope for Launie. That's when she turned on him because she thought he was the one calling attention to her drug-running, and that's when her crazy mind set-up how to get rid of him."

Ollie's shooting rampage down the Blvd made the top headline in the Daily the day after it happened and was on the front page the rest of the week.

"Ester told me that Launie threw the paper in the floor in anger and fear. She started yelling out loud, "What if that State Trooper started snooping around my place?"

Little Mitch squirmed and turned over as his dream continued. He heard J C, the only man he had ever known as his father… *"She worked a plan over in her head. Ester said the next morning, Launie bought Ollie a classic* More Fun *Comic which introduces Oliver Queen as the Green Arrow, from the comic store in Mary Ester. It cost her six hundred dollars.*

She also inquired if her purchase could be returned and was told that it could, if unopened from the plastic wrapper it was in.

"I think Launie was caught in her emotions of caring for Ollie as she felt some responsibility for him because Ollie was the only one who had food as he and Launie and her girls had waited on top of a high rise in New Orleans to be rescued by a helicopter, as Katrina flooded the streets below, but now her fury at what he had done so close to her business on the Blvd, filled her diseased mind. She had hidden him, she thought, but now he had made a spectacle of himself. She wondered how long it would be before someone came asking about him. Surely someone had recognized Ollie on the beach that day, or on the Blvd when he acted like a maniac.

Launie blamed herself, Ester had told me that night. She told me the whole story as we lay in bed together, for what had happened because she was so concerned about finding the lost drug package and had exposed Ollie to the outside world. Launie seldom went inside the Library these days as she realized her appearance was not the sort of thing the johns would want to see. Besides, she had much more important business to take care of, but she had no doubt that locals were in the place every night—someone knew Ollie and would contact the police sooner or later.

She knew she could not have anything like that happen again. All she needed was that State Trooper who was spending so much time in Fort Walton, to come around asking questions.

Little Mitch was kicking and throwing punches into the air now as his dream turned into the nightmare, he had slept through many times during the last three years. He had heard his mom tell J C the story before and he knew what was coming next.

It was still J C's voice that Little Mitch heard in his tossing and turning.

"I found out later after a lot of investigation that Launie ordered two five-gallon buckets of paint from Lowe's and had them delivered to the Dorm. When the salesman asked what color she wanted, she had replied she wanted sea foam green. There was much talk in the paint department at Lowe's about who in the world still used that color, but they had mixed it in the big plastic buckets and delivered it to her."

"Ester told me she heard Launie knock on Ollie's door the night of the murder.

Ollie seemed embarrassed and started straightening things up that were thrown around the room, and it sounded like Launie had never been in his rooms since he had moved in.

Ollie had stammered, "I'm sorry about the mess Launie. No one ever comes to visit me."

"Don't worry about it, Ollie," she had assured him. "I should be the sorry one for bothering you. I need you to help me carry some buckets of paint to the yacht, and then go with me to Pensacola to help me there. Okay?"

Ollie had never been on the Lollipop, Launie's big blue yacht, but he admired it from his window as he could see it down at the little pier back of the Dorm.

The report I received from my plant—the seemingly old man fishing in the Sound, who was a romantic, J C laughed. "He said Ollie looked like he was fantasizing that it was the boat Oliver Queen, his hero, had fallen off before getting stranded on the island where he had to shoot his food with his arrows.

"That would be the trip of a lifetime, Launie! I would like that!"

He grabbed one of the buckets and ran down the gravel path to the dock and ran back for the other one. Launie showed him where to place them.

He stepped onto the loading ramp and climbed the three steps up to the back deck. He looked around the expensive yacht and knew his billionaire hero, Oliver Queen, would have been at home here. Ollie was smiling with a pride and happiness he had never experienced. Then, Launie gave him his real surprise.

He sat down at the little table at the back of the deck and turned the plastic package over and over.

"Is it really mine?"

"Yes, Ollie, you have earned it. I wanted you to have it."

"May I open it?"

"Why don't you wait until we get there?

At least we had a witness that heard that conversation. I reasoned that Launie knew that if someone were watching the Lollipop and she headed down the Sound they would not likely be followed. They would think she was taking the yacht to the slip at Pensacola.

I found out right away that I was wrong on how Launie was thinking that night.

Little did she know she was being taped by my man in the boat. She started the big boat and Ollie laughed aloud. He nearly danced as it pulled away from the pier.

A dog, on a chain behind one of the houses, barked savagely at them as they passed, but Ollie laughed at it for he knew he was safe on the boat. But it brought back to his mind, the yapping dog on the balcony, which we know was Skipper, that had scared him as he ran up across the lawn with the bundle of drugs, he had found on the beach that Launie had sent him after.

He yelled, "Shut up! Shut up, or I'll shoot you like I did that barking bitch on the balcony."

Launie eased the Lollipop through the channel slowly as they passed the new jail directly across the Sound from the La Mancha. She could see people standing on the porch of the first floor above the dock for the patrol boats. She always had the fear that those boats would suddenly rush out and surround the yacht.

About a mile west of Fort Walton Beach, the Black Drainage Ditch deposits silt, debris, and sand into the black waters of the Sound every time we have our heavy downpours, as you know, Prof. Once every five years or so, the Sound has to be dredged to keep the barge lane deep enough to navigate. Launie had seen the huge piles that had been scooped out on the bank from the dredging. She thought the water would be deep there.

When they arrived, she maneuvered the boat out of the barge lane and to one side of the big deep hole. She stopped the Lollipop and turned on the lever that automatically dropped the anchor. She got the bottle of wine she had brought and two glasses and carried them to the table where Ollie now sat with the plastic bag in front of him.

"I thought we would stop here. Look, I brought the wine you like best!"
"Launie, you are so good to me."

That's when the couple up on the dune was watching all that was happening, but they were being very quiet because each of them was almost nude.

She poured the wine, and sat his on the little table as she stepped around behind him, "Why don't you open it now? I'll watch you turn the pages from here over your shoulder. No, wait, let's drink the wine first."

He was so excited that his hand trembled as he picked up the glass and started to turn to her.

"No, don't turn around Ollie, look at your comic book. I want you to see it and I want to feel your happiness."

As he lifted his glass to drink, she pulled the little plated revolver from her skirt pocket.

He took a big drink of the wine and put the glass back on the table as he reached for the comic.

Her hand trembled for just a second and she shot him at the base of his skull.

He shrugged, collapsed on the table, and a little blood started running across the plastic package.

She snatched the package and as she pulled it away, his hand smeared the blood across it leaving the imprint of his fingers.

She had the handcuffs she had used in her raunchiest days. She put one around each of his wrists, dragged the buckets of paint one by one up to him, and put a cuff around each handle.

Foul smelling sweat ran down her bare sides inside her blouse by the time she pushed him over the back of the boat. She stood, took a deep breath, walked over to the table where her glass of wine still sat undisturbed. She collapsed into a chair breathing in quick little gasps. She was entirely out of breath, and her gulps of air were loud and raspy. She grabbed what had been Ollie's glass and raised it to her mouth and drank it in one gulp.

Launie's luck had been all bad that night for she hadn't seen that young couple lying on a blanket on the high north bank of the Sound. Sam Ripley, a military Med Corpsman at Eglin, had taken his fiancée, Alice, there many times since he had been stationed at Eglin. They had hurried to conceal themselves when they heard the Lollipop approaching because they were nearly naked.

They peeked over the edge of the bank where they were lying, and in the light from the deck lamp of the yacht, had seen the murder as it happened. Alice had cried out just as the shot went off, but Launie had not heard her.

Sam held his hand over her mouth as they watched her pull Ollie's body to the back of the yacht and heard the splash as it hit the dark water. They saw her collapse in a chair at the little table and drain Ollie's glass in one gulp, and then take a paper from her pocket, raise it to her nose and sniff at it violently. Sam knew what that meant.

Launie lurched her way to the captain's seat of the Lollipop, twisted the key in the ignition, and slammed her foot on the gas pedal. The powerful boat jumped forward sending the water in a surge against the bank behind it. The water smashed into the muddy bank causing a whirlpool that swirled around and around from bank to bank. Launie tossed Ollie's wine glass into the water, and it was suck down into the whirling pool.

Launie would have seen the glow from Sam's cell phone if she had looked back, as he was alerting the Security Office on base about the murder before the lights of the Lollipop disappeared into the darkness.

Twenty or so minutes later as Launie steered the yacht slowly past the jail and toward the dock behind the Dorm, she heard the wail of sirens on our police cars as we raced east through Fort Walton and over Brooks Bridge. She had just anchored the yacht and headed up toward the Dorm when she realized all the cars had turned down the street toward her.

We piled out of the cars and headed toward her. She whirled around and stumbled back toward the Lollipop and saw the flashing lights of two Okaloosa County Patrol Boats blocking the dock as they had sped across the Sound from the new jail. Launie's fear about that had happened.

She stood there on the gravel path shaking uncontrollably. Then she plopped down on the gravel as I walked over, pulled her arms behind her back, and put the cuffs on her.

Finally, Little Mitch's noises had awakened Dylan. He called out, and Little Mitch woke up.

"Man, you have been having one scary dream," he said.

"It was just like I was there. I was napping with you and Zathan under Paul Bishop's long board that the Prof has hanging on the wall of his balcony, and J C was telling the Prof all about the night Ollie was killed."

"I remember my dad telling me about the night he rescued those two teenagers that someone had locked up in a tool shed way up there in the National Forest where our cabin is," Dylan said.

"My dad is so smart for seeing that the weeds into that place were all bent in, and no weeds bent back out in that dark little lane. Whatever made him turn around and go back to save them, he says he will never know, but he did. As it turned out, they weren't even needed as witnesses at Launie's trial. The shooting in the courtroom took care of that. But my dad saved those young peoples' lives."

"It's a good thing Daniel got his butt back to Fort Walton after taking so much time finding those teenagers."

"Yep, cause my mom would have been very upset, for he walked into the delivery room just as I was born."

Zathan was awake now from their noise, and he said, "You guys have any idea how long we've been down here?"

Dylan and Little Mitch jumped and let out little yells of surprise.

The three of them laughed, and as they reached out, they found they could all touch each other.

"No, but I'm scared. I know we ate part of a PB&J and then went to sleep, but how long did we sleep?" Little Mitch said with a quiver in his voice.

Zathan looked toward him, "Maybe we just napped… Or maybe we slept all night, but someone will find us. Just you wait and see…"

"You don't know that. And my mom is expecting a new baby boy, and this will really hurt her… She might even lose the baby cause J C says things are not looking good for her anyway…."

"Your mom is tough. She went through that horrible trial, didn't she?" Dylan said.

"Yes, Ester was the hero in our town during all that time," Zathan tried to console Little Mitch, and Great-Grandma Camelia thinks it is a great love story how J C and Ester fell in love during the trial.

"They had plenty of time as that trial lasted a long, long time."

"Listen, we've got to be brave. We've got to play our game of military discipline." Dylan said. "My grandpa was a Ranger out at Ruder on the Base, and he is still tough."

He thought that what he was saying was hurting Zathan because the sorrow and pain Miss Camelia was still living after eighty years. "We play it every time we go on our forays around the La Mancha. Every time we try to pester Cam. We've got to do it now."

"I'm scared, Dylan."

"I am too."

"Me too."

And then as little boys are apt to do, they once again became the inventive little boys they are.

"Let's inspect Zathan Bordelon and see if there is more treasure," Little Mitch said.

"I'm not sure we should," Zathan answered. "After all, he tried so hard to save what the people had trusted him with."

"Aw, that was a thousand years ago. What do you think they will do with all this treasure?" Little Mitch asked.

"Probably take it for taxes," Dylan butted in. "That's what my dad says the government always does."

"Bet some archeologist comes out here and conducts a dig, just like they do on the PBS channel," Little Mitch said. "We might be on TV!"

"And I bet we don't get any of it," Zathan said. "Wish there was some way to have part of what he tried to save."

Suddenly, the ground began to shake, and their cave was filled with a rumbling sound.

"What is that?" Little Mitch shouted.

"Turn your flashlights up toward the ceiling," Zathan shouted back.

Dylan hollered, "Look, the ground is shaking all around the roots of that big old bush we fell through."

They stood amazed as the ground around the roots of the Oleander bush shook, and sand and rocks started showering down on them.

They ran to the other end of the room and stood alongside Zathan Bordelon as the rumbling and shaking grew louder and stronger. Great chunks of earth fell and slid down the slide where they had tumbled into the cave.

And then it stopped—just suddenly went away; the rumbling passed over them, and the sand and gravel quit falling. They saw the roots of the Oleander bush as it fell into the hole above them and once again plugged the hole in the ceiling of the cave.

"Gee, that wasn't those guys jackhammering that concrete over the fence in the Air Command," Dylan said.

"Nope, that was some kind of wind, and look, there's water seeping in up there now," Zathan pointed at the ceiling.

"Damn, I'm going to puke," Little Mitch whispered.

"Quit saying one of your no-can-use words, or I'll give you a knuckle sandwich," Dylan threatened.

And then they were all laughing, and once it hit them that they were so close to Zathan Bordelon's skeleton, they hurried toward the other end of the cave.

Little Mitch stepped in the mud that had slid down the ramp, "Yuck! that stuff feels like puke!"

"Group Leader, you are wrong again, Sir! It's just mud." Zathan whispered.

Laughter filled the room again for a minute, but soon all three had moved to a dry place on the floor and sat down. There was an unnerving silence now. None of them made a sound. Dylan tried to look at the other two, but one by one, they turned off their flashlights and sat in the darkness.

The rumbling and shaking started again, and this time it was worse as it kept pounding and pounding in blast after blast. They huddled together and wrapped their arms around each other as they shivered in the cold. They were in their shorts when they started out on what was to be their happy excursion, but now their shorts were caked with mud and wet sand from the floor of the cave.

Once the shaking was so severe that one of them let out a shriek of fear. The other two did not laugh but squeezed harder to keep them all together.

"I don't pay much attention when my dad is listening to the news," Zathan said, "but I think I remember something about a Hurricane named Michael was headed toward Panama City and then to us."

They had no idea how long the pounding and shaking lasted, but when it subsided, they were very hungry. Zathan and Little Mitch turned to Dylan as he turned on his flashlight and opened their pro- visions. There was little left, but he held out a small piece of a PB&J sandwich, that had teeth marks in it where they had eaten some of it earlier.

"Better just take one bite, if you can," Dylan said. "And don't cram it in to get a big bite either cause that's all there is unless some- one wants a piece of this limp celery. The carrots are all gone."

The other two took a small bite and handed it back to him, and he returned it to the pouch.

Water was running down the slope into the cave in a steady stream now, but luckily for them, it was draining out one corner at the end of the room where Zathan Bordelon's remains sat.

Zathan realized it was running down into the Sound which was less than a hundred yards away.

Their silence was broken and as usual it was broken by the one you would expect, "I think we are in big trouble. How in Hell will anyone know where we are?"

"Group Leader, permission to play my juice-harp?" Zathan asked. "Permission granted, Scout Zathan."

Great-Grandma Camelia's beloved rocking chair in the corner of her backyard where she remembers her life story, and visits with her own Grandfather Mose who has left this earth long ago.

55

Camelia

In her Rocking Chair, the La Mancha, Okaloosa Island

I know You know who this is and I'm havin trouble holdin my tongue, cause I jest don't understand. I've walked up that old sidewalk every Sunday morning to get to Your house, and I have never stepped in a mud puddle in all these years. But now I want to talk to You about two times—jest two—when I don't think I been treated like I'd treat You. I've lived with the first time now for over seventy years and I've cried in my sleep until I wake up with eyes that are caked dry—dry as sandpaper. I have done the best I can and never said a word to You about it til now. I can't ask You why and I don't aim to blame You, but I don't understand. I hear Jere saying, "Milly, I've got to go fight the war, but I'll be right back," but he never did…. He called me Milly when he wanted something or when he wanted to show how much he loved me. Those sapphire eyes would twinkle, and he would grin, and he always scuff his big left foot across the dirt or the floor or where he was standing. He said he would be right back… But he never returned. Oh, I can hear Mose saying, "You jest better watch out Missy, the way you talkin to the Lord. You goin to be seeing Him right away and you better watch your step." Mose is right. He was almost always right. He saved me so many times I can't even start to count them all. He led me just like his namesake, Moses, led Your children out of Egypt, and he never did ever complain, at least to me he didn't. I don't spect I'll ever know what happened to Jere and the stab in my heart *right now is jest as much pain as it was when they came to tell me his plane went down. I took it all in stride then. I had the boys and failed so awful bad with Dwayne and then Albert was took from me too, but now I've got to complain. Zathan is a good kid and he's almost all I have left. Take me before you take him home to You. Take me so I won't have to go through another death. He's strong. He's young and with them other two, he will forget before long—but I can't. So, I'm asking. No, I'm beseechin You to let them be found and safe.*

This awful storm, that some little person sitting somewhere, named Michael, hit so hard, and maybe them three got caught in it. What a mighty wind it was today, scared us all, and here I am in the very place I said I would never go to lookin back across the Sound toward home instead of always lookin over this way and havin a little dread goin through me. I could see the Mound where Jere and I would go on Sunday afternoons and sit and watch the Sound and have a pic- nic and cuddle, if all of them businesses along 98 were not in my way. I could see my street almost too if it wasn't for them. I'm thankful that Michael almost missed us, even though it caused a lot of shakin and blowing around here today, and I am asking special help for them that was in its main path…. Prayin about their suffering and their loss….

Oh, I know a thing or two about who that huge disastrous storm was named for and I'm wondering if that Michael jest might be able to come and guide us to the boys, if You want him too. You know that song we sing about Michael and his boat washin us to shore. I need it now Lord, cause them three are good little boys. Usually,…. I'm asking. I know you don't barter, so I won't mention it.

"Miss Ledbetter! Miss Ledbetter!"

Camelia jerked her head up to find that Sally and Lewis Smyth with their two Labrador Retrievers were standing on the other side of the perimeter fence. Missy, the smaller of the two Labs, had her front feet up on top of the fence and was whimpering and looking around with her ears perked forward. Sam 2, the other one, was on the other side of the fence but barking loudly which was very unusual for the two dogs. Lewis scolded them and pulled them back from the fence. "Miss Ledbetter, we were wondering if you shouldn't be in the condo as it is really chilly this afternoon as that always happens when a storm has passed by?" Lewis said.

"I'm alright, and I thank you for your concern," she answered. "If it's okay with you, we will come around and visit for a while," Sally said as she intended to rouse Justin and Claire from inside the condo as she was concerned about Miss Camelia.

As Lewis and Sally and the two dogs came around the end of the building, we were close behind them in the golf cart. J C had picked me up at my building, and we were going around to take some food to the others. Daniel hung onto the back of the golf cart holding the big bag of chicken strips, red beans and rice, and biscuits.

Soon all of us were sitting around on the little porch or in chairs out on the lawn. Claire had given Miss Camelia a cup of hot tea, and the rest of them had glasses of sweet tea that Claire made last night. I declined mine because I don't like that stuff. I had water. We were about to eat.

J C's phone rang, "What? When? Are they okay?"

We all thought he meant the boys, but he said, "Ester just had a healthy boy and Lyn says they are doing fine."

It took us a minute to let it sink in, but then we were all congratulating him, and J C said, "I'm glad Dylan's mom was with her as I couldn't be there."

Just then, Missy strained at her leash stretching toward Miss Camelia. Lewis took the end of the leash loose from where he had put his chair leg through it, and casually handed it to Miss Camelia. It caught her off guard, and Missy sensed she was free.

Lewis and Sally's two Labs are never off-leash when on the property at the La Mancha. They never bark, and they follow the Smyths closely wherever they go.

But now, Missy started running toward the big Oleander bush barking fiercely. Sam 2 struggled and he, too, somehow broke free, and was close behind Missy. The two stopped, turned toward us, and then turned again toward the bush and started their fierce barking once again.

Lewis was after them in a flash and caught up as they stood facing the bush. They began pawing the ground and digging up close to the bush and then stopped and looked up at him.

"Here! Come here! All of you, over here," Lewis shouted at us. All of us except Miss Camelia hurried toward Lewis and the dogs. "Listen," Lewis exclaimed.

A strange twanging sound seemed to be coming from the Oleander bush.

"That's a juice harp!" Justin shouted. "Great Grandma has one in her kitchen that she lets Zathan play with."

All of us rushed toward the bush, but Daniel stopped us, "Wait! Wait! We might cave it in if we aren't careful."

We stopped and agreed. He took his phone and punched in a number, "Get the sand auger and get up here at the tennis courts as quick as you can. Hurry!"

Some time ago, I had thought that Cam was different than most of the beach attendants Daniel hired, for he was long and lanky and thin. It wasn't three minutes until he came running toward us carrying the sand auger.

J C had gone back and brought Miss Camelia over in the golf cart. She sat upright and stiff as she watched what was happening.

"You do it because you are lighter them me," Daniel said as he told Cam to stretch out by the Oleander bush and carefully drill down into the soil. "Be careful, cause your buddies are down there."

Cam looked confused at first, and then he heard the noise of the juice harp, and he fell on his stomach and crawled across the grass to the base of the bush. He held the auger up and turned it on and pushed it slowly into the ground.

It broke through, and we heard squeals of laughter and yells of 'hurry, hurry, hurry' coming up toward us, and then we heard, "It's about time." No one doubted who said that.

Cam put his face down by the hole the auger had made, drew his head back and hollered, "Man oh man, it smells like poop down there." The tension was broken, and everyone laughed, but a voice came up from the cave, "We'll get even with you, you know?" None of us doubted who had said that either.

"Careful now," Daniel said. He shouted down in the little hole the auger had made, "You three get back as far as you can from under the hole. You hear me?"

A tiny voice answered, "Yes sir! And if we don't, I get another knuckle sandwich, right?"

We knew they were all right as the stoic one was the only one we hadn't heard. Daniel had a look of relief in his eyes as he and the rest of us were laughing again.

It took twenty minutes or more, to enlarge the hole as we were afraid it would collapse on them. Finally, Daniel thought we could pull them out if we could reach them.

"Okay, you three! Gather together under the hole. Stand real close together."

We looked down and they stood there, caked with mud and stinking to high heaven. Their mouths were open, and they had their arms stretched up toward the light.

"Now, listen carefully. Cam is going to lower a rope down to you. Tie it around you under your arms, and we'll pull you out one at a time. Do you understand? Help each other tie the rope."

"I can do it Dad. I will be last."

He almost choked as he said, "Okay, let's give this a try." He and Justin held onto Cam's feet as Cam hung down into the hole to pull them up. Several times the side of the cave would start falling in as gravel and sand would sprinkle down on them, but finally they were all out.

All three started crying as they understood they were safe, and Little Mitch bellowed, "I want my mom."

J C grabbed him and held him tight, "Your mom had to go to get the new baby."

"Well, let's go see him, now."

"Hold your horses, we have to get all three of you to the ER to check you out."

Zathan ran to Claire, and she held him close.

Then he turned and went to Miss Camelia who gathered him in....

Guess I owe You a big apology...You sure answered real fast... Thank You....

Dylan had been the last one out. He stood up straight, and when Daniel was also standing, he walked to him. Daniel knelt beside him, and Dylan said, "You were down there with me the whole time. I remembered things you had told me, and they worked." They hugged each other.

"You did really good for a seven-year-old." "Seven? I'm only six, Dad."

"Nope. You had your birthday down there. No cake…no party. Zilch, this year!"

Dylan raised his hands over his eyes and peeked out, "You're the one who wants a knuckle sandwich?"

Daniel grabbed him and hugged him close.

Then all three turned almost at the exact time and raced toward Cam and tried to wrap their mud-caked arms around his waist.

"Get away! Get away from me! You all look like worms. Yuck!" he laughed as he backed away from them. "You all scare me, and you smell like dead fish!"

They got his joke and turned toward the chicken strips that J C had brought from the condo porch. They had to be told several times to slow down and chew their food.

Dylan stopped suddenly and walked over to me, "Prof, I want you to know we had plenty to eat while were down there." He pulled a small piece of PB&J from his shorts and held it out toward me. "See?"

It was smaller than a quarter of a sandwich and had teeth marks around two sides of it.

"Why are there only two sets of teeth marks?" I asked. "I thought we might need some for later," He said.

I leaned down and hugged his head. He seemed taller than the last time I hugged him. I looked over his head and saw that Daniel's eyes looked wet.

Then the three of them ran to Missy and Sam 2 and there was much fussing and barking and tail-wagging and squirming and rubbing of ears, and I saw that little piece of sandwich disappear down Missy's throat.

J C had called the ER station up at the end of the Blvd and we heard the sirens coming toward us. There were two vehicles, but the three demanded they all go together.

Someone pulled the golf cart as close to the hole as they thought was safe, and Camelia stretched up as far as she could to looked down at Zathan Bordelon sitting on the treasure that had been there for nearly three hundred years.

My.. my.. my Zathan Bordelon, you sure do look like I thought you would. You didn't run away with the folk's treasure jest like I knew you didn't. You sure been sittin there a long time. That's a mighty big mound of leather bags you are sittin on. Mose told me that there are bags of pearls and Spanish coins and crosses with valuable jewels on them and what I want to see most, the old folks oyster shell jewelry. I hope you don't get mad that we have found your hiding place. Guess you ought to know that a whole bunch of people are goin to be comin to aggravate you and steal your treasure away from here. I don't know what they will do with it, but I sure would like to have jest one little piece of it. I sure hope it ends up over in the museum by the Mound. We'll see....

The stress and fright of not knowing where the boys were for the last four days melted on the faces of those who stood there.

Camelia declared to herself though that she wanted away from this place. *My, my. my how things work out....*

"Justin, will you please take me home?"

56

Going Home

Remy takes Melisandre to the airport

"**G**ood Morning, my foxy sister!" I said as I opened the back door of my car and put the single little bag in the back seat.

"You are about as blind as a fruit bat in a cave, Remy, if you think this old woman is foxy," she laughed.

"I worry about you making these trips all the time because you are 'this old woman,' I said.

"I'll be just fine. This may be the last trip though. I don't like the airport at Brest as it still shows the destruction of the war after all these years. I hope I don't have to wait long to get the plane to London."

Two hours later as they drove through Brest, Remy and Melisandre looked with curious dread as they passed through the outskirts of that once beautiful seaport. There were so many apparent scars left from the war that ended eighty years ago. Like many places in France, there would be a new street with houses and shops built after the war; their construction clearly showed how quickly and carelessly they have been thrown up. Then, for blocks, nothing had been done and rubble still filled alleys.

"We are a strange and proud people," Remy said. "We have our big show places in Paris and our mighty Chunnel running under the Channel to London and our smooth paved freeways running in all directions, but we live in the disaster of the past close by our houses."

"But we don't, Remy." She spoke. "We have been so lucky in Guerande. Momma told me once that our walls had not been overrun by an enemy since the Thirteenth Century. Even the Nazis found out they couldn't dent the walls much with their machine guns."

"You are right. We have been lucky. No, that is wrong…we have had leaders throughout who were smart and planned for the worse. You, my foxy sister, are the last of them."

"You and Eli have the name, too…."

"I know, and I am so grateful to Papa and Momma," he looked at her. "I could never call them anything but that."

Remy guided the car into an unloading slot, got out, and went around to help her will the little piece of luggage, "I hope you are successful on this trip, and you don't encounter anything that will upset you," he said as he kissed her on both cheeks.

"I do too, my big brother who worries too much. Just like our mother," she laughed as she kissed him back, grabbed the suitcase and disappeared into the terminal.

The trip back to Guerande was a memory trip for Remy. As he left Brest, he tried his best to get a glimpse of anything that would remind him of the time a woman struggled to keep two little boys from getting lost along the way. His chest hurt as he did remember a woman in a green coat walking away from him and Eli, but he couldn't put a face on that woman now.

As he approached Guerande, he came to the wide point in the Marsh Road—the place where Father Jean, Marcel, and Alain, with most of the village, had built the platform to load wagons with salt. He knew what was buried under the platform for Alain had told him once. He had a sudden gruesome picture in his mind of the Nazi skeletons that were under there.

He didn't know why, but a few hundred yards past that wide section, he turned on what was now a smooth paved road and drove toward the Atlantic. Less than the length of a soccer field brought him to the high hill above the ocean.

He stopped, sat in the car a long time, but finally got out and walked to the granite bench. For several minutes, he looked out at the Atlantic before he sat down.

Father Jean was the first to come into his mind. Eli had always been Father Jean's favorite, but Remy was glad for that. Eli needed a strong honest man to lead him, and Father Jean was there for him.

It was no mystery to Remy that Eli would become the success he is. He was so sharp with numbers and organization. Father Jean found that out quicker than the rest of us, Remy thought. He had Eli figuring sales and plantings for the vineyard even before Momma knew about it.

Now, Eli is married to one of Henri's granddaughters, Ambre, and they have a house full of children. Father Jean, as always, was true to his word, and saw to it that no one blamed Inez or her children for the betrayal Henri had pulled off.

When Father Jean died in his sleep one night, the monks at the Abbey found a long letter he had left. It recommended that Eli be put in charge of the vineyard, and that happened.

Our wines have won many more medals of excellence around France and Italy, to go with the ones Father Jean had been awarded. Eli, that little Jewish boy sucking his thumb by the sign that his mother had lied to Remy and him about, had become a big success.

Guerande had mourned for two weeks when Father Jean died. It was during Lent, and the thought that he had gone to his Heaven during that holy time on earth, drew many to St. Aubin cathedral to worship—many who had not been there very much during the war and afterward.

It seemed like Momma would never stop her trips to anywhere she thought she could sell Guerande's salt. She came home from one of her trips exhausted and weak. We watched as Papa put her to bed, and then he did something I found hard to understand at the time. He ordered—not told but ordered, us to go to where I live now— Marcel's house, and not come back until he called for us.

After it was over, Eli was very bitter he wasn't there when Momma died, but we finally convinced him that Pappa was trying to defend us from the virus she had caught on that last trip. We were invaded with that virus, just like America was, and none of us knew how to battle it. The Americans were smarter than those in control in France, and when Dr. Salk came up with his vaccine, America got the shots, but the French didn't. We were told about another cure… and it didn't work. Momma was the unusual adult that the virus killed…. Most adults were crippled or spent their lives in iron lungs, but Momma had been that uncommon fatal victim.

Pappa the same as died when Momma died. He lost all interest in living. He would go to the church, which we now called 'Father Jean' in our everyday conversations, and just sit in a pew and stare at the stained-glass windows or the quire with its fancy wood carvings in the front of the sanctuary. I once thought the crucifix must be embossed on his eyes as he sat and stared at it so much.

Many nights, one of us would go there to bring him home. He cared little about eating nor with what was going on at the salt lagoons.

It wasn't long before we decided that I would start overseeing the salt ponds. It was a hard job at first for the paludiers did not trust me or believe that I had sense enough to know what to do. I proved them wrong—perhaps too quickly, for that is still my job. No one over eighty-years-old should have my job, but we have become so famous, someone must do it.

I live in Marcel's house as we have always called it. Jacque's stall and manger have been empty since he kicked his last kick.

Guerande hasn't changed much. The women in our village are proud of their yards and baskets of flowers hang on many window- sills.

The high wall gleams after a heavy July rain and the water in the moat area is full of feisty white and black swans. Of course, every spring the mother swan leads her trailing line of cygnets across the water holding her head proudly high.

Those mysterious birds return twice a year in the marshes where Poppa would stop and turned to where they were and listen carefully. The Breton cattle graze the pastures out past the vineyard, and we don't talk about what is buried in the peat bog out past those pastures.

When a storm hits us, especially one of those cold ones from the North Sea, we stay in for the day and the salt lagoons take care of themselves.

57

The Prince Albert Can

Justin Gets a Call

About three weeks after Zathan, Dylan, and Little Mitch were rescued from Zathan Bordelon's final resting place, Justin Ledbetter answered a call his secretary put through to him in his office at the bank over on Beal Parkway.

A woman's voice said, "Mr. Ledbetter, I will be coming to your town in about two weeks, and I am wondering if I can meet with you?"

The transatlantic call didn't erase the woman's accent which Justin recognized as French. He was curious, "Certainly, but can I ask why?"

"I know this will sound rude, and you may say no to me, but I would rather wait to tell you until we can meet face to face."

"Then, sure. I'm always here at the bank. Oh, wait, I'll even pick you up at the airport if you will give me the time."

"That would be very considerate of you. One other favor, will you reserve a room for me somewhere on your island there, so I can be close to the water?

"I will."

"Then I will text you my arrival time and I am anxious to meet you."

Justin told Claire about the unusual call, and they sat on their porch late into the night wondering what a sudden call from France could have to do with their lives.

"She's French, I will bet, and I suggest we don't mention this to

Great-Grandma Camelia, as it must have something to do with Jere after all these years."

"She would tell you that she is not your Great-Grandma if she heard you, but I agree let's find out what this is about. She doesn't need any more stress than what she went through with the boys."

He decided to send a taxi to pick her up at the Destin-Fort Walton Beach Airport and decided she might as well stay at the La Mancha for she was certain to hear about it later.

The next day, he looked up from some papers he was working on as his secretary looked in and told him the woman was waiting to see him.

"Sure, ask her to come in."

The woman, an attractive lady who would be about the same age as his parents if they were still alive, dressed in clothes that didn't fit the beach attire that most people wore in Fort Walton Beach, walked through his office door.

He stood and held his hand out to her and said, "Please have a chair. Would you like something to drink?"

"Water would be fine," she replied.

"Mr. Ledbetter, I am Melisandre DesMarais—most people call me Milly—and I live in a little village in Brittany, France. I've brought you a little present from our town, a salt cellar handmade by one of our citizens you might have known," she said as she handed him the cellar. "But more important than the little gift, we've found a long-lost item that maybe has ties to you and your family."

Justin sat down in his chair.

"It's an old tobacco can that has some pictures, a letter, a wed- ding ring, and some GI dog tags in it."

"My God, that happened years ago long before I was born."

"Yes, I know. It was before I was alive too." She pulled the rusty old Prince Albert can from her purse. "I had quite a time explaining this to the Security Forces as I left the Brest Airport as I was getting on the plane."

Justin stared at the can, "My Grandma told me about this long ago."

"That's how I came to be here. I read the letter she had written and saw the pictures. I wish I could have given it to her myself."

"But you can. We'll go over to her house."

"Mon Dieu, she's still alive? But that's almost impossible. She would be so old."

"She ain't going to die till she wants to, and she'll tell you that just in those words too," he laughed.

"She is well over a hundred years old?"

"She claims to be a hundred and two, but no one knows for certain."

"This will be quite a shock to her, I would suppose. It was to all of us when it was found," she said.

Justin noticed the sadness in her eyes and said, "You are right. We've got to prepare her for this someway. Where did you get all this?"

The can and its contents were laid out on his desk now, but he couldn't take his eyes off the dog tags—Jeremiah Ledbetter.

"He was my Grandad that I never knew. My own dad was only about two years old when Jeremiah flew out of Eglin."

"He was my father."

Justin jerked his head up and looked at the woman closely for the first time, "What?"

"Yes, Momma told me just before she passed away how he came to our little town and some of the things that happened to him during his life. It was war time, the Nazis were everywhere, and he must have been in one of the American planes that was shot down.

Momma was always ashamed in a way that she didn't send him down to be taken across the Pyrenees into Spain to escape with that brave young woman who became known as the Nightingale, but as it turned out, he was very lucky she didn't send him.

And she was ashamed too that they didn't go somewhere and have him fingerprinted. She fell in love with him, and he professed his love for her. She was a very hard-headed woman at times, and she lived with her love and her shame.

She loved him so much and he loved her too, so she lived with knowing he had a life somewhere else. It was all a question then as nothing was known about who he had been until when he was dying."

"Why didn't he tell your mom and the others?"

"Because something shocked him badly, and then he hit his head as he went over the spillway in the river that runs next to our town. He never knew who he was or what had happened to him."

"How did you find all this?"

"Momma died—polio—when I was very young. It was one of the scourges that hit Europe just as hard as it hit America. It was the Black Plague of our time. After she died, Papa would get glimpses of things that had happened.

Father Jean, our beloved priest, died some years after he married Papa and Mama, and the people of our village started calling the Nave of St Aubin, 'Father Jean.' That might sound silly to outsiders, but that's what we called it. Papa would say he was going to visit 'Father Jean' and I would find him there after I finished my lessons, or later on when I was old enough to be in charge of our house. Or one of the two boys Papa and Momma took in would go sit with him for a while and then bring him back home. He would sit there for hours. I have no idea what was going on in his head.

The other place he would go was to 'their' rock, a granite slab that is on the high hill overlooking the ocean where he and Momma always sat. Someone in our little town built a park bench out of rocks next to the piece of granite, and he would go there and sit until I was afraid, he would get a cold or sunburn depending on the time of year. Then Remy or Eli or I would go after him. He probably told Remy more than he did to Eli or me, for Remy is so much like him.

Remy and Eli are two Jewish men who Papa and Momma took in—they found them by the sign on our Marsh Road after their own mother had walked away from them.

Please do not condemn her for she was wondering the road being chased by Nazis and she had no other choice. Besides, they became my brothers, and Papa and Momma loved them as much as they loved me.

When I flew to London to get a plane to the US, Remy took me to the Brest Airport. He is now in charge of the Salt Business that Guerande is famous for, and Eli is in charge of the vineyard that Father Jean had built into a prize-winning one.

Two little Jewish boys in Nazi occupied territory saved by two brave loving people."

She paused, but went on, "Many times Papa would insist that someone drive him up the road that runs by the river and he would always want to stop and look at the river in a certain place as if it was familiar to him.

Finally, we started searching around the area where he always wanted to stop. One of the girls spotted a faint scar way up on a tree that looked just like a chevron on a soldier's sleeve."

"That's how they used to mark the pine trees around here if they were going to peg them to get the sap to make turpentine. A sharp pointed shovel makes almost a perfect chevron."

"We didn't know that, of course, but the girl who saw it also saw a speck of red up in the fork of that tree. We had to cut it out as the tree had grown around it during all those years.

When Papa saw the can and what was in it, tears ran down his cheeks, and he sat for many minutes looking at the pictures and the wedding ring.

He put the dog tags around his neck, got his walking cane, and I watched him struggle as he made his way through the salt pans until he made it to the bench by their rock. He sat out there all day until I went and brought him back to the house.

The next morning, he got up early and dress in his best clothes and went to sit in Father Jean. He was there most of the day. I looked in on him several times.

He didn't have anything to say to us, nothing. He passed away a few days later. He was an old man then. He took Mama's last name for he didn't know his own. You must realize he didn't remember anything that happened to him before he came to Guerande. He fell in love with my mother, and she adored him. Her last word was his name, 'Alain.'"

"How will we ever know what went through his mind after you discovered the tobacco can?"

"I have often wondered that. It's the reason I'm here to let you know what we learned."

"Whatever we tell Camelia, will surely destroy her."

58

Them Eyes

Camelia's Backyard

"**Z**athan, you come and help me walk down this path. It's slick from the sprinklers and I need you to steady me."

Zathan hurried from the corner of the house where he stood with his dad and mom and that woman who had come from far away to bring Great Grandpa Jere's tobacco can.

He caught up with her and flinched a little as she dug into his shoulder with her hand. He wanted to say it hurt, but somehow it raced through his mind that he shouldn't.

They reached the rocking chair under the Live Oak, and she reached out with her free hand and took ahold of the arm of the chair. Zathan looked at her old hand that had heavy veins running in many directions under her thin skin, and then up at her face. He had never seen her look so haggard, so old. He looked at her glistening eyes. She's been crying all this time, he thought.

"Here, I want you to have this," she said as she poked around in her apron pocket and pulled out the guimbarde, Zathan Bordelon's juice harp, that usually hung on the nail on the kitchen wall.

"They won't let you have the one that was down there with your namesake cause them State people who are scouring over that place say it belongs to Florida. So, here take this one and know that it was his too. You don't have to tell nobody that I gave you this."

Justin, Claire, and Milly DesMarais had decided to not tell Camelia how Jere had spent over eighty years living another life never realizing who he was. They had decided that Milly would tell her story of how the Prince Albert can was found by a bunch of kids out exploring in the woods by the river.

Camelia leaned back in her chair, "Zathan, you go on with the others. Your Mom will have supper ready by now, and you do have company. Be a good boy...."

She took her hand off his shoulder and as he looked up at her, she knew that he knew she had just said more than what the words implied.

He smiled at her, reached out, and touched her hand, and said,

"I'll be right back, Great Grandma, and bring you some sweet tea."

His words were like a dagger piercing her very soul for they were so much like what Jere had said so long ago.

Her eyes followed him as he scooted around the corner of the house, and she heard him bound up onto the front porch of his house next door. She heard the screen door slam shut behind him and knew that he would get scolded for that.

She had a glimpse of her street and laughed to herself as she thought of the silly name, she had called it many years ago— Chanticleer Lane. What a silly thing she thought.

The hole in the honeysuckle vine was nearly closed because she hadn't had it cut—there were no mockingbirds to come through it this late in the year.

But the last rays of a brilliant sunset fell through the hole on the other side of the back yard, through the hole in the camellia bush, and filled her eyes and made her face shine with a golden tint. She squinted, looked directly into the sun beams which blinded her, and muttered, "Why?"

Yesterday, Zathan brought her the empty nest that blew from the almost horizonal limb of the Live Oak a week ago. He brought her the nest proudly and repeated the words she had said to him nearly a year ago, "In last year's nest, there are no birds this year."

"You know why there are no birds in it this year, don't you?"

"Sure, Great Grandma, they get feathers and fly away, but they're going to have a nest of their own later on."

She looked over at the empty nest where she had place it on the garden table beside her rocker. He had been right—it was empty, as empty as her heart was right now.

No, that's not right, she thought, *its burstin with a hurt that I jest can't stand. All them memories....*

She pulled the salt cellar that Justin had brought home to her from her apron pocket, strained to lift herself from the rocker and carefully walked to the corner of the fort Jere had built so many years ago. It took her a long time to bend over and peer under the corner, but she saw, as she had a long time ago, the clear distinctive writing he had made with a thick carpenter's pencil— 'enjoy.'

It was exactly like the writing on the salt cellar in her hand. She ran her finger along all the letters in the word, and then she slowly did it again. She realized Jere had carved them into the clay. Her finger tingled and she saw his face as clear as it had been the day, he had said good-bye.

Her hand shook violently, and she dropped the cellar. It hit one of the steps that led up to the fort and ricocheted off into a tall patch of rosemary. She didn't have energy enough to bend and pick it up.

She made her way back to the rocker and settled down into the chair and pulled the lap blanket over her knees. *Justin ain't lied to me since he was a kid and then it was only fibs. He never lied about anything that was important, but now he has.... Didn't they think I had the good sense to know her eyes were Jere's eyes? Didn't they know how many times I laid awake at night—not jest back then when I couldn't stand to not be able to turn over in bed and touch him—but now when I know the other side of the bed is empty. I see his eyes. Nobody who ever knew him would ever forget those eyes. I feel the rage inside because I've been cheated, I think, but I guess I better shut-up about that. How can I blame anyone, especially God? Look at all the blessings I've had all these years. It's jest like making that trip up to God's house—I had to walk around those mud puddles where the way wasn't solid and paved.*

Mose, what you doin here? I ain't thought of you for ages.

She heard the clanking of a bell and saw a cloud of dust coming down the road toward them.

She heard a rapid squeak, squeak, squeak. Yeah, you smarty pants, you got sand in the axel grease., didn't you?

"Here comes Elmer Ledbetter hauling some logs over to Cracker's Neck to the sawmill."

"I'll have to pump some water for the oxen."

"I see Jeremiah is with him today. You jest be nice to him, you hear?"

"He thinks he's so dang smart being two years older than me"

"He's just fourteen…. Boys are like that at fourteen. Maybe, he's lookin at you different than he did before."

"Phooey! He's skinny, his nose is too dang stuck-up, and his feet are way too big."

"You noticed that? You noticed his eyes? They is the strangest blue I ever saw. Hazel, I guess you would call them."

"Have I seen those eyes…jest every time he races through my mind. How could anyone miss those eyes…those outrageous sapphire eyes…yep, Mose, they're sapphire—nobody I ever saw had eyes like him…."

The wagon pulled away after I rubbed Minnie's ears and made a fool out of myself when I put my feet in the water tank and you, and Elmer had a good laugh at me.

"We was laughing at him jest as much as we was at you."

And the wagon wasn't gone a hundred yards till I had to look up at his back. I saw him take that floppy felt hat off his head and wipe his forehead on his sleeve jest like he is right now…

Yes, I'm watching….

She saw him turn around toward her on the wagon seat. He was alone now. He grinned at her and jerked his head two or three quick times toward himself for her to come on and go with him.

She pushed as hard as her old arms could, on the arms of her rocker, but she couldn't raise herself.

She stared at his back, and the rays of the setting sun almost blinded her.

She reached out to him, struggled to get up into the wagon seat, and he bent down and lifted her up off the ground into the wagon, and smiled, "Come on Milly"

59

Respect

For three weeks after those three were rescued from Zathan Bordelon's burial place, I spent almost every day with Miss Camelia. She wasn't about to come back over to Okaloosa Island, so I sat with her in her backyard where Justin would carry the rocker off the front porch so we both had a chair to sit on, or if it was raining, he carried the rocker from the front room out onto the porch and we listened to the pounding of the rain on the tin roof of the porch as we talked.

We spent so much time talking with me taking as many notes as I could, and some days, her head would fall onto her chin, and I knew to stop talking. I would just sit until she would jerk awake and apologize.

Then, we both laughed, and she would tell me to go home, or that a special treat was waiting on her kitchen table, or that I was not too keen between the ears sitting and watching an old woman asleep in her chair.

Justin had taken a picture of her sitting in the golf cart looking down into that muddy cave where Zathan Bordelon's skeleton sat on the fortune he had saved from the Spanish and the Creeks. I had written an article about the almost tragedy them three had escaped, and the picture had appeared in the *Northwest Daily* with the story. Because of the rescue of Them Three and the discovery of Zathan Bordelon's treasure, National News outlets set teams of paparazzi to Okaloosa Island, the hole where the boys had been buried and where the treasure had been, and our town was invaded by more curious gawkers than we have tourists in the summer.

Miss Camelia had become a sensation overnight, because before that, few people in town except her church people and her friends, knew about this old lady. She wasn't too happy about the publicity and told Justin so, but I saw her sit in her backyard as strangers now came to purchase some of her many herbs, produce, or eggs and there was a twinkle of pride in her eyes. Mylee told me that was not unusual for Miss Camelia surely had her dose of pride. I had laughed when Mylee told me that because she sounded more like Miss Camelia talking than herself.

Them three had an awful hard time getting over Miss Camelia's death. Zathan covered-up his feelings, at least on the outside, as he always does. Dylan had a hard time it seemed to me as I found him several times sitting on the front porch with his legs dangling off the edge not talking or being with anyone, or I found him sitting on the fort's steps staring off into space. Little Mitch might have been hurting worse than the other two, but we would never know because he would cover it up with some wisecrack or by wheeling and dealing with the other two about some new thing to do.

People who had no idea she had lived in Fort Walton for over a hundred years—even before it was Fort Walton—wanted to pay homage to the old lady. I'm not sure whose idea it was, but just like in the old days, she was laid out at her home for people to come by and pay their respects. I guess Justin, and maybe J C and Daniel, had set-up her front porch where her casket stayed one afternoon.

It was just like a wake I remember being horrified by when I was a kid. The casket was on two big two-by-sixes that rested on two wooden chairs. The line reached all the way down past the Monkey- Ward house and the shattered Live Oak which was struck by light- ning a few weeks before she died. I looked around to see if 'them three' were anywhere to be seen, but I guess their mothers had them safely off somewhere else.

The procession that happened the next day went all the way through town to the Landing down on the Sound—down where Buck's store had been—down where Elmer and Jere had parked their wagon so many times.

It took nearly two hours for the line of cars to wind down past the Indian Mound and the Fort Walton School where she and Jere had been married, and then J C and his patrolmen stopped traffic on Highway 98 as the hearse led the hundred or so cars down to the Landing.

I saw the three boys squirm in their seats as they had to sit up on the platform and try to behave. The little Vietnamese lady, Mylee, was close by and I don't think she ever raised her head during the almost hour of the celebration of Miss Camelia's life—for it was a celebration.

Sunday, I arrived at Chanticleer Lane to find it almost vacant. It was so different than two days before. I parked down the street from Miss Camelia's house and walked up Chanticleer Lane to her flagstone walk.

How many times had that old woman made the same trip up the lane, I wondered? I saw the Monkey-Ward house that she had told me about once, the Montgomery Ward house that her father had ordered for $810, and he and Jere and Jere's dad, Elmer, had built.

She told me about the silly thing she did that embarrassed her so much she wouldn't go back down to watch them build the house.

She had said, "I laid up there on that limb of the Live Oak—not the one struck by lightning—but the one by the walk that leads up to that house—where I had my hiding place when I was a kid. There was a hollowed-out place that I could stretch out in, and nobody could see me. I was hiding that day so I could see Jere as he carried lumber in. We weren't married then. We weren't even seeing each other, but I was already struck on him. I guess I wasn't hid much for along about quitting time, he stopped under the tree and said, 'Somebody's been painting her toenails.' I didn't move an inch and stayed up there until after dark—long after he had gone on home. I never went back down there until the house was finished, and him and his dad, Elmer, quit coming down my lane."

"Poor, poor, Elmer," she said. "His life and his family's life were torn to shreds because of that horrible war Jere never came home from…"

And what about yourself, Miss Camelia, I thought. What about all it did to your life.

I sensed it was going to be a sorrowful day for them all, but especially them three, but I was wrong.

60

The Celebration

It started raining about midnight and it poured. The trip was a familiar one now, so I turned into Chanticleer Lane in a few minutes.

It was barely daylight, but Zathan had called me after I got home last night and asked if I could come meet him at the house, and as I approached, I saw him sitting in her rocker on the front porch.

"How long you been out here?" I asked him.

"Long enough to be in trouble with my mom. I had to hear the rain of the tin roof just like she always did, so I came about two or something."

"She would have said, 'You're not too swift between the ears,' to that young man."

"Don't make me cry before we get to church," he said with tears already in his eyes. "I want you to help me do something."

"I would be happy to, if I can."

"I need to tell her something today, and I want you to help me with the right words."

"Your own words would be the ones she wants to hear, and besides, she will know what's in your heart if that's possible."

"What do you mean, Prof, if that's possible."

"Well, we don't know how that works, do we? We don't know if those who have gone on know anything about what we who are still here are doing or thinking… The greatest minds have forever wondered and written about that, and they have never come up with a definite answer."

"I still want you to help me with it."

"I would be proud to."

"We will have to hurry because I don't want the others to know that I'm even going to get up and say something."

That was the first time I had heard one of them three saying they wanted to do something alone from the other two. I looked at Zathan and visualized a grown man who just might become famous because he knew how to think and sure didn't hesitate when it came to work. Wonder where he might have gotten those traits?

"I think you ought to talk to her just like you have a thousand—no ten thousand times—right around there in the back yard."

"You're right! I know what will help me and I want you to take it up to the church and put it right up front by her. Someone might tell you to not do it but tell them I need it."

I wondered what he was talking about, and when he led me around back and showed me, I understood.

"Now, only you can say what you feel, and you remember that she is the one you're talking to. Not the other two and what they might be feeling, nor your dad or mom, nor the people sitting in the pews paying their respects. Just what you want to say…"

"I feel better now, and I want you to have this, Prof, because it meant so much to her."

He handed me a little book that she had written in for many years. It had all the common things she had done, like baking cookies for them three, to crying herself to sleep when her two boys were little because she didn't know how she could manage, and especially missing Jere after he didn't return from France. But each page always ended on a note of encouragement or happiness or hope.

"Zathan, I can't take this. This is the story of her life as she lived it each day. You will want this, or your dad will, so I can't take it."

"I knew you would say that, so why don't you just keep it for me for a few years and maybe you will want to do something with it in the meantime."

I looked at him and realized what he was saying, "Oh, no you don't. I am not going to write this into a story. You're worse than she ever was."

We were both laughing as the sun peaked through the honey-Suckle vines that draped the back-yard fence.

That night we all sat out here on the top step of Great-Grandpa Jere's fort: all three of us because I begged that Dylan and Little Mitch could be with me. I knew you would have been pleased we were together.

Even Little Mitch didn't try to pull his usual shenanigans and teasing as we sat on the step and cried until our cheeks were dirty streaks and each of us kept wiping his runny nose on his sleeves. We didn't care who saw us.

61

Later on Jere's Steps

Them Three in Camelia's Backyard

"MY, *my, my,*" she would have said, if she had time, after she found out what happened to Great Grandpa Jere and that he had been alive all those many years.

But it wouldn't have been one of her common 'my, my, my' that she so often said. It might have been filled with rage; rage so fierce she would question why God had done it to her—and then, she would have apologized and say her life had been so full of blessings; or it might have been an awful pain that was really piercing her heart now; or the deepest sorrow, I bet.

I found her in the very chair I'm in now when I came back with a glass of sweet tea for her. She looked like she had a smile on her face, not slumped over like you usually saw people after they had passed away, but with her face straight up and I was sure a smile curled her thin wrinkled lips. I first thought she was just smiling, or praying, but when she didn't reply when I said that I had her tea, and still didn't move when I tugged at her arm, I knew she was gone. I guess I dropped the glass of sweet tea and let out a yell and ran to tell dad and mom.

That night we all sat out here; all three of us because I begged that Dylan and Little Mitch could be with me. I knew she would have been pleased we were together.

Even Little Mitch didn't try to pull his usual shenanigans and teasing as we sat on the steps and cried until our cheeks were dirty streaks and each of us kept wiping his runny nose on his sleeves. We didn't care who saw us.

I thought I could almost hear you saying, 'them three,' as I sat between my best buddies.

We huddled there as we had when the oleander bush had given away over at the La Mancha and we went tumbling into the darkness of the cave where Zathan Bordelon's skeleton, sat on the treasure you had told us about so many times.

You didn't know that what you said that day didn't come true for we shared some of the money from all those things they found down in that hole. I asked for some pieces of that shell jewelry and will put one in your casket tomorrow because I know how much you wanted it. Miss you so much, Great Grandma…. Miss you running your old slender gnarled fingers through my hair and then telling me to go home now and be a good boy…. Just miss you something awful…

The hearse had taken you away to the funeral home, and Daniel and J C and Dad had removed the boards and chairs that had held your casket during the wake when so many people came down your Chanticleer Lane to pay their last respects, and we sat in the gathering dark. We all needed to be together, like you always saw us.

Then us three came back here where you were comfortable and nearest to us. Dylan sat on one of the fort's steps and Little Mitch started marching up and down between your flower and herb beds. I just sat down in this rocker.

"Little Mitch said, 'What if it doesn't rain?'"

"Oh, it will rain. She told me so last night."

Dylan almost mocked me as he said, "What do you mean? She told you?"

"Well, she did. I had these thoughts as I went to sleep. She was sitting right here, I told her our idea, and she said that it would rain."

"I believe you," Little Mitch chimed in. "All of us know how she seemed to talk with somebody, usually Mose, a lot, as she sat here with her eyes almost closed. Then she always had a story to tell us about… just like someone had just told her."

Dylan gave in, "You two just might be right, but I don't believe in ghosts and I'm not going to go talking to someone who has left us."

I challenged him, "She said you were to cut the rosemary and that I was to cut the camellias. She said to ask you if you remember what 'rosemary' stands for?"

"I remember she was talking about it one day, but I don't remember that."

Little Mitch jumped in, "I looked it up last night. It said, 'a symbol of friendship, loyalty, and remembrance' and that… 'it is traditionally carried by mourners at funerals' and you two know that something has to be going on because, Zathan, you thought about us making corsages to wear to her funeral."

"Why did you look it up last night? You memorized all that last night, didn't you?"

"Took me three minutes. I looked it up because something told me to."

"Yeah, but no one could have thought up your idea but you," Dylan said as he looked at Little Mitch.

"I do think it was a flash of genius if you do say so. You got to admit it is a pretty neat thing to do. How many times has she told us about her walking up to her church?"

I was quiet for a long time before I said, "Yeah, talking about her high-top shoes and long dress to hide them, and the cracks in the walk, and the place where there is no walk, and it has mud puddles in it from a rain. Then she would say 'Just like life.'"

"Like we were old enough to know what she had been through," Little Mitch said.

Dylan climbed down from the fort's step and walked over to the huge rosemary bush that they all had seen Miss Camelia cut stems from as she had handed each of them one to sniff. At first, they hadn't liked the scent because it was so strong, but soon they all waited with an open hand as it became a smell they associated with her and her love for them.

"We can't cut them until we get ready to go home and we all must ask our moms to tie them up with a ribbon. I don't want a sad ribbon on mine, so I'm going to ask my mom to use a bright orange one."

"Me too, just like the sun that shines through that hole over there when the sun's going down and hits clear across the yard on her chair."

"I will take them all home because I know my mom has orange ribbon in her craft box," Little Mitch said.

There was another long pause as Dylan looked at Little Mitch and their usual competition dissolved.

"You get along with your little brother?" Dylan asked.

"Sure, all he does is sleep and poop," Little Mitch laughed. "Nah, he's okay but what can you do with a brother who is less than a year old? He does say 'Mitch' though because that's what I repeated to him over and over."

"Yeah, you would," I said. "What did they name him?"

"Cam," Little Mitch almost shouted.

"Bet that was your idea," I said.

"Cam's the man…and we'll never have a better friend…and I wanted my little bro to remind me of him every day," Little Mitch smiled as he embarrassed himself with his emotion.

All three of us laughed and there was a lot of talk of going over to visit the Prof and Skipper and attacking the beach wall to challenge our buddy Cam who we didn't tease much anymore for he had saved our lives.

I picked up the shears from the table next to her rocker and walked across the back yard to the other fence.

The other two watched me as I cut three of the biggest and most perfect camellias from the bush that hung heavy with her namesake flowers.

I handed the shears to Dylan who carefully cut three long twigs of rosemary from the bush that was nearly as tall as him. One of the twigs slipped from his hand and he reached to cut another.

"No, pick up the one you dropped. It was supposed to be the one," Little Mitch whispered.

Dylan leaned down and his eye caught something on the ground hidden in the bush. He leaned further in and picked it up and held it out for the others to see.

Dylan and Little Mitch looked quickly at me as I knew I was standing with my eyes filling up with tears. They walked to stand by me but were careful not to touch me.

"Here," Dylan said as he held the salt cellar that everyone had look for since the night Miss Camelia was found in her rocker.

I said, through tears that were streaming down my cheeks, "Now, everything is complete. My Great Grandpa Jere's salt cellar makes everything complete. Let's not tell anyone and tomorrow I will put it in Great Grandma's casket for all to see. We'll get it in the morning as we leave to go to church."

Dylan climbed the steps and put the salt cellar inside the fort that Jere had built so many years ago.

All three of us walked to the corner of the fort, bent over to peek under and read the word 'enjoy' that Jere had put there nearly a hundred years ago.

I reached out and rubbed my hand over the word. "Careful, you might rub it off," Dylan said.

"No, I've touched it hundreds of times and it won't rub off. He put varnish or something on it."

Then, maybe to cover our tears or to get past the tension in the air, I led us single file around the outlines of all Great Grandma's Garden beds and finally around the corner of the house ready to go home and wondering what would happen tomorrow.

62

"My, my, my, Stop That, Right Now!"

We sat on her porch, like we have a thousand times, with our legs dangling over the edge as I saw the hearse pull into the Lane and slowly make its way toward us. I was surprised to see that only members of my family, Dylan's, and Little Mitch's folks, and Mylee were waiting at Great-Grandma's house.

It was almost time to leave for the church when a big car pulled into the lane and stopped down in front of the Monkey-Ward house. Mister Mitch, Miss Sally, and Judge Boyd got out and stood by the curb, nearly at attention.

It had rained most of the night, as she had said it would, and we were ready. We walked ahead of the hearse back down Chanticleer Lane and turned onto the street that led up to her God's house.

Mister Mitch, Miss Alice, and Judge Boyd got in with Mylee as we started.

I suspect no one will believe it, but her current resident rooster crowed suddenly.

We stopped and took off our flip-flops and started slowly up the street. We all matched that morning with the same color shorts and tops. Little Mitch's mom had pinned the camellia and rosemary boutonnieres to our tops.

Little Mitch whispered just loud enough for Dylan and me to hear,

"Imagine you are following a dirge band over in New Orleans. Keep in step and stand proud cause you're leading the band."

He wasn't trying to be funny, and Dylan and I knew it. Both of us had heard the story so many times of his real father, Ollie, and how he had wondered the streets of New Orleans. We knew about Louie Armstrong Park where Ollie had met Mister Mitch. We knew about the bronze statue of the funeral dirge and how Ollie had marched around and around it with his imaginary baton striking the air.

We had heard this so many times while we sat on the steps of the Fort in Great-Grandma's back yard. Suddenly we were in step and marching proudly along. This time I was in front and Dylan and Little Mitch were marching along side-by-side behind me.

We stepped in every mud puddle, I think—not splashing in them, but we made a deliberate step into each one of them. Our music skipped a beat as we paused at the cracks in the sidewalk.

I was so intent on what we were doing that when I looked up and saw that the street was lined with people standing shoulder to shoulder, I almost lost my step and my legs felt weak.

I looked over my shoulder and saw that the adults were walking along behind us. I saw Dylan's dad grin as he put his foot solidly into a mud puddle.

We washed our feet at the water spicket on the side of the Church building, put our flip-flops back on, and entered the church. Someone guided us to the front pew, and as we sat down, I looked up on the dais in front of us and there was Great Grandma in her casket. The lid was open, and I shuddered. I knew she would be so embarrassed that everyone would be looking at her. I wondered if someone had put those high-top shoes on her that she hated so much.

I was glad that no one could see her from the waist down.

I wonder what Dylan and Little Mitch would do, but right then I couldn't turn to see if they saw what I was seeing.

My mom and dad were on one side of me, Dylan was on my other side, then his folks, and then Little Mitch. J C and Ester were next, and I wondered who was on the other side of them. I leaned forward, and Cam leaned forward at the same time looking my way. I looked him in the eyes and wanted to whistle like a mockingbird, but I didn't dare. She would have scolded me something awful for that.

I had been here at church before with her many times, and when the Minister stood up to speak, I knew it would be a long-winded drawn-out story about Great Grandma with verses of Scripture mixed in all the way.

He motioned to me when he was finally finished, and somehow, I got to my feet and walked up the three steps to the platform. I turned and motioned for the other two to come up with me.

The only flowers on the platform were on Great Grandma's hats that hung on a folding screen behind the casket. They were all covered with camellias, of course, which I knew my mom had spent hours gluing them on, and that they would make Great Grandma happy.

I led Dylan and Little Mitch around behind the folding screen, and saw I was not the only one who had put something back there.

We lifted the tomato crate together and struggled to get it across the carpet—it was much easier to scoot across the dirt in her garden, but I guess that's because we had done it so many times. We finally had it out in front of her casket, but to one side of it. We sat down on the crate all scrunched together like we always were when we sat in front of her listening to what she told us that day. I whispered to Little Mitch that he go first.

He went behind the screen and came out carrying her broom, went to the center of the platform, turned his back on the congregation and stood in front of her casket. In a loud clear voice that had no nonsense to it, he said, "Miss Camelia, you don't know how much we miss you— how much I miss you…. You know here in the South, we call ladies we respect and honor with the title 'Miss,' so 'Miss' Camelia I want to tell you I have this broom, the one you sent me for that day when you told me to get it from behind the kitchen door—that day when we three were pulling weeds out of your garden. They were picking up the 'pullings' as you called them, and I was to sweep the path clean.

I guess I was being cute as I walked up to you and said, "Miss Camelia, I jest got to git this off my mind. I jest ain't able to live with it."

Then you said, "Are you trying to imitate me, young Mister?

You quit talking like that or I'll tell your mom or spank you myself."

I said, "Sometimes, you talk that way, Ma'am...."

Then you said, "Maybe I do, but I'm a whole lot older than you and didn't have the schooling you're getting. Anyway, you just stop talking that way."

I said, "I have to tell you that I hit that rooster of yours with the flat side of the broom one day when you were in the house, and I believe that's why he leaves Dylan and me alone. He never did bother Zathan cause ...because...Zathan is always here.

You laughed out loud and said, "My, my, my... So, that's why he doesn't bother you two. It's okay cause you didn't slow him down at all. He still jumps the fence, pecks around in my beds, and thinks he rules the back yard."

"I blew out a sigh of relief and started sweeping the paths between the many beds. This broom has been in my bedroom since you left us, and I plan to keep it with me wherever I am. You taught me a lesson that day, and I haven't even been saying those 'do not say words' much either, just ask my mom."

He sat down, and Dylan stood up. He faced the people in the pews, "I can't pick anything of Miss Camelia's because I wouldn't know where to begin, but I did ask for this." He held up the Prince Albert can that Jere had carried when he left for France.

"I am putting a twig of rosemary in it because you told us it's for remembering," he said as he turned to her casket. "I also pressed a camellia flat in a book, and it goes in. I also wrote something to you, and it goes in—it's just between you and me. I'm going to shut the lid and not open it again until I graduate from college, but you better believe it will always be with me."

His face started to pucker-up and he couldn't hold back the tears anymore. The other two hurried to him and they stood in their usual triangle hugging each other.

Suddenly they jerked apart like they had been hit with some- thing. Later each of them would swear that he heard, "My, my, my... Stop that, right now!"

The congregation saw it happened and a whispering went among them.

Zathan led them back to the tomato crate. They looked at each with wet eyes, and he started, "That rooster crowed this morning, Great Grandma, but it sounded awful sad to me…"

Dylan and Little Mitch scooted up against him.

"What am I going to say? Where would I ever begin? You were my run-to when I was in trouble at home. You met me hundreds of times very early in the morning, come rain, storm, or pretty day, when you would find me on the front porch, or in your rocker in the back yard. You treated us all the same. You just loved us…. there were no strings attached. I have that dollar you gave us that day for pulling weeds. We all joked about what we were going to buy, but I didn't spend mine."

He pulled the neatly folded dollar bill from his pocket. Dylan reached into his pocket and pulled out his. Little Mitch turned toward them with a guilty smile covering his face.

Zathan turned a little toward the congregation, but looked straight at his mom and dad, "I have so many things that were hers or that ended up in her back yard, but I would give up all of them to have her back. She would scold me and say I shouldn't say that and remind me that the bird's nest always becomes empty finally, and I must start my own."

He pulled the juice-harp from his other pocket and placed it against his lips. It took a while for the congregation and Dylan and Little Mitch to recognize what he was playing, but finally someone started to softly sing the words,

"Precious Memories, how they linger. How they ever flood my soul…."

He stood up and picked up the precious piece of cut-shell jewelry she had admired so much, and gently laid it on her chest where it appeared to be a brooch. He looked at her face for the first time and thought, *she looks like she might open her eyes and say, 'Good Morning' Zathan.*

Dylan came and stood beside him and the people in the pews saw him take something from his pocket and lay it in beside her.

Little Mitch came and stood on the other side of Zathan, and then them three took off their boutonnieres of rosemary and camellias, and they carefully laid them on her gnarled vein-covered old hands that were at last at rest.